Praise for Heather Cumiskey's *I Like You Like This*

"Hannah's story is primo, and the surprise twist of the epilogue will have readers stoked with anticipation for a sequel. Overall, a tubular story for readers looking for their next great melodramatic love story."

—*Kirkus Reviews*

"A poignant coming-of-age read full of heart-pounding drama and a swoon-worthy romance, *I Like You Like This* is guaranteed to captivate readers from beginning to end. Think *Riverdale*, but set in the 80s."

—BuzzFeed

"For fans of *13 Reasons Why*, Heather Cumiskey's new novel takes a spin on a classic."

—POPSUGAR

"This teen narrative will pull at your heartstrings. *I Like You Like This* is a book you'll definitely like!"

—*RT Book Reviews*

The Sooner I Go

Published in 2026 by
She Writes Press, an imprint of The Stable Book Group

32 Court Street, Suite 2109
Brooklyn, NY 11201
https://shewritespress.com
The Library of Congress Control Number is available upon request.
ISBN: 979-8-89636-090-2
eISBN: 979-8-89636-091-9

Interior Designer: Tabitha Lahr

Printed in the United States

The Sooner I Go

A NOVEL

HEATHER CUMISKEY

SHE WRITES PRESS

Also by Heather Cumiskey

I Like You Like This

I Love You Like That

For all those who hide, this one's for you.

Chapter 1

BRYNN

Elmsford, New York

If Debbie Harry could create magic in the '70s at CBGB, a dingy punk rock club in the East Village, so can we out here in the sticks of Westchester. I fold my arms over my chest and slide my teeth under my thumbnail. My shins ache balancing on these stupid kitten-heel boots. This itchy lace camisole. Another bad idea of Cody's.

I pull up "the girls" again, staring down the steakhouse-pub patrons while breathing through my mouth. Tonight's special: wild boar burgers. Not exactly Radio City, is it?

Someone hooks a sweaty arm around me.

I jump back.

Cody extends his phone in his other hand. "You good?" Without waiting for my response, he grips my shoulder and starts filming. "Hello, CB Drunken Waters fans and future Rock and Roll Hall of Fame nominating committee."

I cringe. He sounds like a game show host.

"Really?" I swat his well-shaped pecs, pumped up from all of his pre-performance pushups. "Next one, be serious."

"I *am*." He bugs out his eyes and the corners of his mouth curl up. "This evening . . ." He raises his voice, surveying the room.

A few heads turn.

"We embark on the first night of our North American . . . uh, *East Coast* tour . . . wait, I messed up." He sweeps his sandy-blond tresses from his face, ready for his closeup.

I can see the movie playing in his head. Tonight, he's Mark Wahlberg in *Rock Star*.

He lengthens his neck, gooselike, buzzes his lips like the over-the-top thespians at our performing arts high school, winks a mischievous eye at me, and repositions his phone. "I'm here with my girl Brynn, kicking off the first night of our tour in Elmsford, New York, at the infamous Pete's Saloon, where many unknown artists have gone on to achieve greatness. CB Drunken Waters will be no different, no doubt. Care to add anything, gorgeous?"

I check his screen. The beachy waves I worked so hard to perfect in my long Lake Placid hair have fallen, much like my boobs have in this old bra.

I press back my shoulders with a sigh. "Tonight . . . they won't know what hit them."

The skin between his brows pinches.

"Hey, no time for nerves now." I smile big enough for the two of us. "We're going to blow this showcase away. One more thing." I give him a soft hip check. "I love you."

He puffs out his chest. A rogue tendril falls over his bottle-green eyes, giving me a glimpse of what he must have looked like as a little boy.

My insides melt.

"You heard her. Tonight, great music and love are in the air." He bends down and reaches around my thighs.

I fly off the ground, the room becomes a brown blur. I slide down the front of him. The tips of my pointy boots touch down.

His lips part mine, flavoring my mouth with his cinnamon Ice Breakers tongue. He cracks open an eye and readjusts his phone.

"Lovebirds, let's go." Adrian, the band's drummer, throws an imaginary football toward the stage. "We need to be ready to impress tonight's VIP guests." He winks at me.

Cody winces, his fingertips drum his forehead. "I may have . . . um . . . mentioned your parents coming to the show."

I grit my teeth. I'm already freaking out about them coming tonight without the band making a big deal about it. My parents aren't exactly fans of Cody's—or mine, at the moment. I didn't invite them, Cody did. They have a way of ruining everything. "So much for keeping a secret. Don't worry, I'll drill Adrian later to learn all of *yours*." I bite the inside of my cheek, throw him a look, and step away.

He reels me back in by my hand and plants a kiss on my head.

I close my eyes for a second. The sound of clacking dishes and conversations fades.

The high-back stools at the long wooden bar near the entrance sit vacant; half of the wagon-wheel tables in the rear are still filled with families finishing their meals. Cody said he invited everyone in town he knows, but besides those diners and us, all I see are a couple guys with sunken cheeks and pocket chains tuning their guitars by a speaker and their bored-looking girlfriends, all of whom seem to be glaring at me.

I turn to comment about the weak turnout and catch Cody frowning over his phone.

Our eyes meet.

He slips his cell into his pocket.

I nibble on my half-chewed thumbnail. "What's up?"

He squeezes my hand and signals to Adrian.

I sigh and head in the opposite direction of the stage.

⁂

The ladies' room muffles the din of Pete's. I yank the zipper on my bag a few times, unable to budge it. I try again.

Cody says he's got this. *Trust*, he said. I do trust him. He'll come through and we'll have an amazing opening night . . . with no *distractions*.

I take a beat, blow out a long breath. The zipper opens. I blend some kohl liner into my upper and lower lashes to make my deep-set eyes pop. I dab on more blush and lip gloss and lift my lashes to the shiny-eyed girl staring back, the one who snagged the talented and oh-so-handsome singer-guitar player before those little groupies got to him. I see the way they gape.

I head back out into the main room to find that more bands have arrived, including an all-girl trio in cropped leather jackets and short skirts, their hair slicked back.

I stop by the side of the stage—a rectangular riser with brass railings, very 1980s.

Cody fiddles with a snapped guitar string. "Guys, I need a sec." He exits the platform. His brows pull together when he sees me. "I'm an idiot. I didn't bring any extras."

"What about the other guitarists or another band?" I tilt my head, unable to snag his gaze.

"I got this. I'll have someone run me down to the music store in Dobbs Ferry. Twenty minutes, tops."

"Cody . . ." I bite my lip.

His head jerks up, mouth sprung open.

My pulse thuds in my ears. I lower my gaze and stuff my hands into the back pockets of my jeans. A feeling wells up inside me, like I'm waiting for the floor to drop.

We're so close now. *Trust*. Cody's got this.

I kick the scuffed wood floor. "Never mind."

He lifts my chin and cocks his head until I muster a smile. When I do, his lips graze the side of my head.

I close my eyes, lean into his warmth, and breathe in the sweet musk of his sweat.

Our foreheads rest on one another's like the first night we kissed. The night his fluttering flock of admirers at school fell away because he'd chosen *me*.

I exhale.

"The sooner I go . . ." His voice is low, soothing.

My throat goes dry as I swallow. "The sooner you'll be back."

My chin drops to my chest; something tugs at me inside.

Wait.

My breath gets stuck in my throat when I see him already halfway across the restaurant. "Cody!" I call, but the soundcheck onstage drowns me out.

I rush after him. My right heel slips, kicking my leg up like it belongs to a Rockette. The wood beams on the ceiling slide into view. Somehow, my butt doesn't hit the floor. I twist around in time to catch a glimpse of his blond hair flowing over the back of his hoodie before the door to the street clanks shut.

My feet don't move.

He'll be back. He said he will.

Twenty minutes, tops.

Chapter 2

BRYNN

New York City

June, Present Day

One would have to step inside this human-shaped box I climb out of every day to understand why even vampires wouldn't live here.

I call it *the coffin*.

Its sixty-eight sprawling square feet boast narrow, tobacco-stained walls, paint chips falling off the ceiling, and buckling wood floors. On rainy days, the suffocating stench of mildew clings to my hair and clothes.

No bedroom or private bath here. Unpacked boxes double as furniture, a rolling rack for a closet. At the moment, my leftover udon and a bag of baby carrots share sole residency of the temperamental half fridge that stands beside one of two working gas burners.

My mattress—my nocturnal raft—lies in the center of the floor, cockeyed from another restless night. I laze upon it now, searching for beats in the staccato drips produced by the dollhouse-size sink.

One dish and one cup sit inside, adjoined by an orange countertop the size of printer paper.

Not a microwave or an Easy-Bake Oven in sight.

I sound like an ingrate. I know I'm fortunate to have shelter when too many people in this city don't. But this wasn't supposed to be my life.

I inherited the coffin from my late parents, Katia and Basilio Gallardo. Both seduced by some form of real estate spin:

QUAINT STUDIO APARTMENT [read: closet-size]
IN HISTORIC WEST GREENWICH VILLAGE
[rundown old building]. MINIMALIST LIVING
[zero amenities]. AFFORDABLE [not so much].
HURRY, BEFORE IT GOES [suckers welcome].

Look at me, singer songwriter turned rookie copywriter. What a joke.

I can hear Cody now: *You gave up your music for this?*

If only I could summon my parents' voices. They've gone quiet. My memories muddle like a swirling blender. The pain builds so intensely, it takes all my strength to contain my screams.

I'm so tired.

Seven months since that night. I want to hear my mom call me her *baby girl*, hear my dad's throaty laughter traveling from our large sunlit kitchen in our two-bedroom Bushwick apartment as he cooks up one of his infamous supper surprises. I'd do anything to relive one more day with them . . . when things were good.

I squeeze my eyes shut, picturing the three of us around that pedestal table with the folded newspaper underneath so it wouldn't wobble, spilling stories about our day. Laughing until it hurt. So long ago. Was it real or a dream?

I sit up and pull my knees to my chest, the sheets twisted around my legs.

"Do you even know I graduated yesterday, Mom . . . Dad?" I lift my face to the peeling paint overhead. "I went for you . . . so you could see me."

I stood in a daze in that line-up of black caps and gowns. Greta Hardin had to shove me when they announced my name. The rest of it is a fog. Except. Cody should have been there.

I slap the mattress in unison, kicking my legs free. My hands fly up to my face, rubbing so hard I could swear I'm about to tear off my skin. I'd do it willingly, if only to feel again. Something. Anything. I'm cried out, sinking through the floor of this dank apartment. Reminded every day that I'm the only one left.

I don't want to die. I don't want to live, either.

"What do I do now? Tell me and I'll do it. Bring all three of you back."

The sink's drips switch to a half-time rhythm.

I dig my fingernails into the sides of my arm, rocking forward and back, imagining being in my mother's arms.

I hate this. I'm not good at being alone. Never have been.

Why did you have to leave? Why didn't I stop you?

This stabbing blade in my chest never leaves. It travels with me in my sleep, sleepwalks with me through my day. It's there when I drag myself off the floor, when I summon the energy to dress, perhaps brush my teeth . . . in every thought, every breath.

No one deserved to die that night. No one. So how is it possible that they're all gone?

Two cars. Two accidents. Three deaths.

Who am I if I'm no one's daughter?

No one's girlfriend?

No one's best friend?

No one to anyone?

Just an echo of the person I used to be, haunted by the words I didn't say—

"Stay, Cody. Stay."

Chapter 3

MICAH

I find it highly improbable that Mercury reversed course overnight. But it might as well have. The subway stalling between stops this morning. My favorite coffee vendor deported, forcing me to bear the serpentine line at Starbucks. The first couple of elevators at work immobile, refusing to work.

Me climbing fifty-four flights is not happening. Luckily, security has assured me this third one's working.

I go to tap my floor and spill my coffee in the process. Instant scalding. My hand jerks back. Colorful words exit my mouth. I flick my wrist, splattering my Grande Doubleshot Espresso on the confetti tiled floor. I tug on my shoulder strap. My leather bag knocks against my back. Come on, close already.

The elevator gods fail me.

My thumb tap dances on the lit button. I scan the metal threshold for obstructions.

Why, Mr. Otis Elevator, why?

More expletives fly out. I clench my jaw and lean back on the chrome handrail, crossing my legs, trying to be the relaxed guy I am most certainly not.

At least I have the elevator to myself.

Voices sound.

Come on, doors, close, dammit.

A pair of heels clicks along the black-and-white marble floor, echoing up through the vaulted ceiling of the Empire State Building's tenant lobby. They grow louder.

Get the next one, I'm begging you.

A bell rings and the doors start to move.

A girl clutching a portfolio and wearing a small backpack purse slips inside, sidestepping my spilled coffee.

The doors bounce back open.

I exhale through my nose like a dragon.

She turns her back to me and stands off to the side.

Behold, another gnat in my day. I take a fast sip of my half-filled cup and scorch the inside of my mouth.

The doors converge again.

The girl karate chops the air between them.

What the hell?

We could have embarked on a full roundtrip to and from the eightieth floor in the time that it takes for a white-haired woman with wrinkled, puckered skin, dressed in a rain jacket and white canvas sneakers, to join the party. With great care, she steps inside the elevator.

Then hovers, doing nothing.

"What floor?" The girl's cheeriness hurts my ears.

The old woman's Darth Vader breathing consumes me. Her highly likely sudden collapse, followed by the onslaught of paramedics, will mean waiting for another elevator. In that time, the lobby will swell with more sweaty bodies, equating to even less oxygen in this steel box hoisted by mere cables and ropes.

The girl remains chill, her eyes steady on our latecomer, waiting.

My chest constricts. I swig a gulp of air, then seal my lips closed. I check the time on my phone. *Let's go, let's go*. I move into the corner, creating a bigger space between me and the newly formed crowd.

"What floor, ma'am?" The girl's eyes remain kind.

My mind sets the side of her head aflame.

The elderly woman glances around. Her flowery perfume makes my nose twitch.

I shift my weight, breathing out more fire. I fill my lungs to capacity this time and count the tin ceiling tiles.

The girl points to the elevator panel. One floor is lit.

I cup the back of my neck to suspend my dress shirt from scraping. A conga line of sweat glides down my vertebrae. Enough of this. I open my mouth to speak. What's about to come out will not be pleasant.

But the girl beats me to it. "Are you okay?" Her forehead crinkles with concern. "Do you need to sit down?"

The lady freezes.

"Here." The girl switches her portfolio to her other hand. She takes the woman's elbow, motioning her head toward the doors, and waits for the woman to respond.

Like a bride milking her entrance, they step-together-step out of the elevator.

On her last step, the elderly woman drags her Keds through my spilled coffee. She slips and stumbles forward, pulling her escort with her.

The girl's portfolio slams to the lobby floor. "Help!"

Their gripped hands pull in a counter-tension, their respective balances dependent on that of the other, both sets of eyes unblinking.

Witnessing this unanticipated match of tug-of-war, my bet is on the girl.

I punch my lit floor with the side of my fist. A rush of air shoots between my gritted teeth as the doors close, sealing me in.

I step onto my floor before the others, passengers only I can see, can follow suit. In long strides, I start across the cream tiled floor with the broken black line down the middle like a road. A scrolling Art

Deco design in different-colored pastels outlines each of the five sets of facing elevators. I can almost smell the hospital antiseptic.

No sooner do I exit than I get stuck behind a woman in a silver coatdress, her red hair tied up like a Cinnabon.

She meanders down the narrow hallway, stopping at each office's placard.

The scent of fresh-brewed coffee hits my face while I chew my tongue, waiting for her to finish.

Her head perks up when she arrives at the double glass doors to my agency.

Must be a client.

Like a doorman working hard for that holiday bonus, I reach around her, pull open one of the doors, and hold it for her. One good act erases another, right?

Her eyes stall on my face, her heavy red lips part. "Are you that singer?"

I shake my head, breaking eye contact. She could be my mother. I imagine letting the door hit her in the back. Of course I wouldn't. But even thinking it proves I'm an a-hole.

I blow past Ms. Cinnabon in the lobby and head straight for the one friend I have around here—only to realize a blond-ponytailed delivery person with a hand truck stacked with pink boxes is monopolizing Eunice's tall, horseshoe-shaped reception desk.

Grumbling to myself, I veer down between the two metal screens that comprise the central hallway, through to an open space with exposed ceiling beams and rows of long, rectangular, honey-colored wood tables. I lay my bag on the last one near the exposed brick wall.

I fall into my chair, my humming laptop the only sound in the room. Another drawn-out yawn. I rub my eyes, emptying myself onto the pages of my notebook. My breathing steadies. My shoulders release their grip.

I look up. The streaming sun's turned the room a golden yellow.

People from other teams shuffle in.

I tuck away my notebook and wander back out to the lobby in search of my nine o'clock.

Eunice's eyes follow me. I walk over and she hands me my messages.

"No sleep?" She crosses her arms over her crisp white oxford.

"Took the red-eye."

"Bring lunch?"

I laugh. "Never."

"I brought something you like," she says knowingly.

I perk up. "Hope it's your pho."

I lean on the raised glass counter above her tan laminate desk, my head in my phone, listening to her work.

Staffers filter in through the glass doors, a few bestow an obligatory wave to me.

All ignore Eunice fussing about the IT guy leaving greasy fingermarks on her screen again.

She fiddles with her oversize pearls, her dark, silken hair tied low with an Hermès scarf. A present from me last Christmas.

Jamie from media stands beside me, her pointed red fingernails drumming Eunice's desk. "Nielsen leave something for me?"

"Nope." Eunice raises her metal stapler midair.

Jamie snatches her hand away with less than a second to spare. She sends me a look, her eyes wide, mouth flung open. She storms off with clenched fists.

"Lots of drama, that one." Eunice returns her stapler to the white masking tape outline on her desk.

Bobby, one of the production managers, steps up. "Hey, did you guys see anyone deliver—"

"Nope." Eunice wields her shiny letter opener like a samurai.

I shake my head.

She frowns and lowers it.

He waits a couple more seconds before turning on his heel.

"Don't... get me... started." She sticks her tongue out at her screen.

Eunice has known me since I was eight years old, gripping my granddad's finger and getting paraded around the agency. She's endured everything from my misguided prepubescent years to my slutty teens to . . . well. Now that I'm twenty, she continues to look out for me, and not because of my last name.

People in the industry consider the Kershaw family advertising royalty. My granddad's father formed the agency in the early 1940s before Ogilvy met Mather and when the Camel Cigarettes billboard in Times Square featured a man blowing smoke rings using actual steam. These days, my granddad's retired. Just Aunt Max and I work here now.

Eunice has put up with the Kershaw family for years, never once treating me like the spoiled kid that I am. She understands this weight I carry. More importantly, she treats me like I'm normal.

I love her for that. I'd do anything for her.

A sudden thud stops my thoughts. My head swings toward the entrance.

The girl from the elevator just ambushed the entrance doors with her face. Not the first time someone's tried it. The lobby's suspended steampunk lighting, Edison lightbulbs strung from plumbing fixtures, casts a deceptive shadow that throws new people off—they're like baby birds flying into a window.

She steps back, blinking.

I don't move.

After a few attempts, she finds where to push on the door and then barrels toward the reception desk, where Eunice is busy pulling out drawers and speaking to someone on her headset.

A red mark blooms on the girl's forehead.

I suck in my lips, suppressing a smile, and slide over to her. "How's the old lady?"

Her eyes squint as if I'm speaking a foreign tongue.

I tilt my head. "In the elevator . . ." *I'm the coward who couldn't be bothered to lend you a hand. Remember me?*

Her eyes zero in on my tie, a throwback to the '80s skinny tie bands. I detect a small wrinkling of her nose. She brushes up against Eunice's desk. "I'm here for an interview. I'm late."

Eunice side-eyes her, rifling through another file drawer.

I bite. "Who are you here to see?"

Her eyes search to either side of me, her shoulders up by her ears.

I'm struck by the girl's ocean of hair, a brilliant black with ripples of midnight blue, the ends damp.

I extend my hand. "I'm Mic—"

She spins back to Eunice, turning me into wallpaper.

Eunice slams her palm on her desk, killing an invisible mosquito. She juts out her elbow and conjures up her best *are you an idiot?* face.

The girl exhales and drags her gaze back to me. "Brynn." She grips my hand like we're opponents at the US Open.

Ow, you can let go now.

She peers at what looks like one of those lined notecards they used to put inside of library books to record borrower information. "I'm here to meet . . . um . . . Micah Kershaw."

"It's pronounced with a long *I*." I gesture across the desk. "And this is Eunice, if you were wondering."

One could write poetry about this girl's bow lips, clamped together and changing from a rose color to frost. I sniff back another smile. Her crimson cheeks have caught up to her forehead.

Eunice's eyes bounce between us as we size one another up across the net. My old friend gives me a funny look.

I've got this, Eunice. I screen new interns all the time. Come on, don't act like I've lost the match before I get a chance to play.

Chapter 4

BRYNN

The shower pelts my back as I rake a wide-tooth comb through my hair, trying not to think about the dark mildew between the tiles inches from my face or the two-inch rust ring around the tub drain. Yuck. Who would ever take a bath in here?

I squint at the digital wall clock before the conditioner comes for my eye. Less than two minutes. Soon, a stranger will knock and start jiggling the handle.

The water cuts off from the white-encrusted showerhead without warning, leaving me to pat my soapy skin dry. Why does this keep happening? And today, of all mornings. My showers aren't getting longer—the building manager's a tightwad.

I avoid looking through the mirror's black-rotted spots at the cringy dark circles underneath my eyes. No amount of makeup magic can fix that. Cody said makeup accentuated my features, so I wore it for him. Never was me anyway.

Wrapped in a robe, my hair in a towel, swinging my all-purpose cleaner in one hand (a must before every shower) and a toiletry basket in the other, I hold my breath while my flip-flops squish along the gray tile to my door. I sigh, grateful not to have an audience like the other day when the beer-belly guy from 4D kept poking out his head at me.

At the first crack of sunlight bending around my blinds this morning, I wanted to roll over and sleep the day away like I did yesterday and the day before. Moving hurts; the downward pull on my body is like being drawn into a vortex. Not the oceanic whirlpool kind, more like an ear-splitting airplane lavatory.

I can't get sucked in now, though—I need to nail this interview. The funds from the sale of our Bushwick apartment barely covered my family's bucket o' debt. It was the best Rhonda, my parents' accountant, could do. Not her fault Mom and Dad were better musicians than businesspeople.

Tears spring to my eyes when I think about how much they kept from me.

My parents pooled everything, including my college fund, into a dumpy single-stage venue—and look where it got them. Rhonda has had to liquidate just about every last asset they had just to keep me off the street.

This place on Bleecker Street was their first apartment. Mom found it in the *Village Voice* after they graduated Berklee. They pinched themselves at the prospect of living in the heart of the Village. Their googly eyes for one another glossed over its many shortcomings—the biggest one being, no private bathroom.

They used Mom's graduate school money to help buy the place, which infuriated her mami, my abuela. What my grandmother didn't know was that a month after graduation, my parents found themselves pregnant. Sadly, at twenty-three weeks along, after they'd moved into their new studio apartment, Mom awoke to sharp lower back pain and feeling like she'd wet the bed. She said something about an incompetent cervix taking away their first baby girl. A year later, I came along. She always called me their miracle baby.

I wished they'd listened to my abuela. The communal bathroom is where they'll find my body.

I see it all unfold. Act One: 3:00 a.m. I need to pee. A stranger comes around the corner as I unlock the bathroom door and pushes me inside, a sweaty hand stifling my screams.

Day or night, I listen outside my door for any movement coming from the bathroom before I dare venture out. Once I've assured myself it's unoccupied, I bolt down the hall and secure the door behind me. I need to make haste before another tenant pulls on the handle—which always seems to happen when I'm going number two, changing a tampon, or standing naked in the shower. Sometimes I call out, "In use!"—but then all I can think is, *Great, now they know a female's in here.*

Act Two: 7:00 a.m. Someone is waiting for me on the other side of the door or behind the shower curtain. From there, the same horrid scene plays out in my head. My eager imagination never delivers a happy ending, which only adds to my constipation.

After moving to Brooklyn, my parents rented out this place to broke "promising" musicians. This resulted in my parents being frequently behind in mortgage payments. With rising taxes and interest rates, Rhonda says it's no wonder they hadn't paid it off yet. When she couldn't sell this place, she suggested I live here. Now I need a real job so I can stop waking up with heart palpitations over the monthly mortgage.

Speaking of which. Focus, Brynn. You have an interview to get to.

I head toward the subway at West Fourth. My feet pinch big-time in my mom's best shoes as I dodge commuters like I'm in a video game. Her suit restricts my diaphragm, robbing me from getting a full breath. When I raise my arms, it pulls across my back. Leaving it unbuttoned will have to do.

I think she wore it back when *Sex and the City* was popular, as evidenced by the Carrie-esque flower on the shoulder. My petite mother was more compact than I am, from her boobs to her butt.

I favor my dad's side and the curvy, Rubenesque women in his family.

Mom said I should be grateful for my figure. Today, I can't quite get there.

I swear, once I get hired, no more heels, no more suits. I hope I can wear jeans. Don't ad agencies dress like super casual? They're creative types, right?

I'm banking on it, since it's the whole reason I applied. If I can't live my dream as a singer, I might as well work at a creative place. Beats flipping burgers, especially considering I've been vegan for years.

I trot up the stairs, escaping the sticky, humid subway, and emerge onto the streets of midtown's fashion district. I swivel my body around to get my bearings. Seventh Avenue heads downtown . . . great, this way is east.

It lifted my spirits to see the agency's address. As a kid, I loved skipping across the Empire State Building's marble floors and being mesmerized by its gold ceiling and metallic sunburst on the wall. Waiting in line to take the elevator to the observation deck, my parents would distract me by taking my hands and swinging me between them . . . *One-two-three jump . . . come on, Brynnie-girl.*

I sniffle, blinking watery eyes. I need to get a grip and wow this agency, the only one that looked past my obvious lack of experience and responded to my application. Dining dollars have hit an all-time low this month, and I refuse to apply for state assistance. Call it pride, call it stubbornness. I already grapple with enough guilt from that night, I couldn't live with myself taking aid from families who have no other way. I must do this on my own.

I enter the building on the Fifth Avenue side and scramble through the lobby used by the building's office tenants. After passing through security, I approach a long bank of facing elevators. The doors of the elevator at the far end are still open. I make a dash for it.

It's empty except for a tall, olive-skinned guy in a skinny black tie with his head in his phone. I rush in before the doors close.

I turn and see someone's grandmother waddling toward us. My heart squeezes. She reminds me of my late abuela. I hold the elevator, which sets skinny tie guy off into a symphony of sighs behind me.

He slings his black bag to his other shoulder and glowers at his phone, seemingly pissed at the world. What a prick. He's the least of my problems. With his untamed, dark prep school hair, fitted white dress shirt, and tapered black pants, he looks like an intern as well. Or a waiter. Take those athletic quads and chill, dude.

The woman smiles at me.

My mom's mother had thick white hair and dark, deep-set eyes similar to this woman, who's wearing a rain slicker though it's sunny and threatening to reach ninety today.

She rotates around, hovering her hand near the wall.

I envy her pink stretch pants and sensible white sneakers. No purse, either. She travels light. Maybe she has an appointment in the building or she's a tourist looking to go up to one of the observation decks on the eighty-sixth or hundred-and-second floor and doesn't know she's on the wrong side. How did she get through security?

Waiting for her to announce her floor, I look into her eyes. My heart sinks. Vacant, like my abuela's when she succumbed to dementia. I get it. I'm lost, too. *Come stand next to me and we'll be lost together*, I will silently. Her perfume reminds me of those tea rose sachets, the ones my abuela used to place between her folded underwear and sweaters. When I was little, I'd stand on my toes and peer into her dresser drawers, fascinated by the long silky slips that became sexy evening gowns for my many Miss America acceptance speeches. A short-lived girlie-glam phase of mine.

I love how women from a certain era keep their clothing perfumed. Why doesn't my generation do that? Healthier than using fabric softener filled with toxins. If I owned a proper dresser, I'd use sachets with herbs and essential oils. Yep, I love this woman already.

More attitude ambushes me from behind.

My skin bristles. What is up with this a-hole? Huffing like he's a CEO. Wait your turn, buddy. Better yet, take another elevator. This is about my abuela and me.

I lift my chin. "What floor?"

She smiles like she understands.

My gut tells me I can't leave her alone. Maybe she needs to rest a moment on a bench in the lobby to figure out where she's going or whom she's meeting. I can at least do that and get her some water from the vendor on the corner. Maybe she's dehydrated. My abuela would forgo water when she was away from home to avoid public restrooms. Getting her some shouldn't make me late for my interview.

"What floor, ma'am?"

She looks away, her eyes unfocused. I point to the panel, hoping to help her understand, but she doesn't respond.

"Are you okay? Do you need to sit down?" Not expecting her to answer, I motion my head toward the lobby—and away from the a-hole in the back. "Here." I tuck my portfolio under my left arm and offer her my right. She takes it, and I help her shuffle out of the elevator.

Just before we get clear, she slips. Her body pitches forward.

I gasp. My portfolio goes flying.

We teeter like we're on a log, grasping hands. She'll break a hip if we both go down. My racing heart slides into my throat. My dad always handled my abuela when she had difficulty keeping her balance. I may look sturdy, but I'm not strong. These dumb heels don't help.

I hold on to my new lost friend and call out, "Help!"

The a-hole ignores me.

Chapter 5

MICAH

The girl hesitates before joining me in the side office. I leave the door open. Her knees won't quit bouncing once she sits down.

"Do all of the interns have their own office?" She looks around, examining the gray room's stark contents: a black Parsons table with a swivel chair on either side of it and a dusty bookcase with agency manuals.

Her eyes, an unusual shade of amber, rest on my face.

I blank for a moment. "I'm the head of the interns." I meant, I hire them. "I'm an associate creative director." I leave out the fact I've been working summers here since I was sixteen and know the intern position better than anyone. The whole agency skews young. Scott McKenzie, our creative director and one of the partners, just celebrated his thirtieth birthday last week.

Still, I bet she's thinking I'm too young to possess such a title. She's right. Nepotism, baby. But titles mean squat anyway.

"I sit out there with my team." I point to the tables outside. "We use this office for interviews."

She crosses her arms over her navy suit jacket, squinting to read her resume and application before me as if I'm about to quiz her.

"So, what kind of name is *Brynn*?"

"Welsh."

"You're Welsh?" I have no idea why I've started down this path.

"Ah—no. My mom got my name from one of her favorite books. My family's Peruvian."

My brain stalls again. "What kind of accent do they have?" What? Why did I just say that?

"Brooklyn." She stomps her foot and recrosses her legs. "Who else am I meeting with?"

Shit. "No one." My head hangs heavy off my neck. Should have grabbed more coffee.

"What kind of accounts would I be working on if you hire me? I have a lot of experience—"

"Says here you graduated from LaGuardia, a performing arts high school?"

Her cheeks redden. "I can write. I've written ad copy for school events, concert and music reviews for my school's paper. Um, lyrics too. Oh, I was also on the yearbook staff—"

"We get a number of applicants every week." *Though not quite like you. Not even close.* Stay on track, Micah. "The hiring process is very competitive. We only consider candidates with previous marketing or brand management experience. Have you interned anywhere else?" I already know the answer. She's as green as they come.

"I'm looking to—"

"Even if you came with some marketing experience, you should know that summer interns at Kershaw McKenzie start at the bottom." Saliva inexplicably floods my mouth, causing me to cough. What is my deal today? "Excuse me . . . um, they fetch coffee and lunch for their team. Clean up after client meetings, pick up client samples, office supplies, dry cleaning, and so on. They record the minutes at team meetings. The smart ones take advantage of their time with us, absorbing all they can."

Her lips twist. She sinks lower in her chair.

I try hard not to smile. "I'm not going to sugarcoat it. We work long hours. I reviewed your writing samples. Come back when you have a few years of college behind you. We don't hire high school graduates." Except for me, of course.

"I can do this. I *need* to do this." She straightens up. Her eyes drill into me.

"I appreciate your enthusiasm, but like many who apply—"

"I'll work for free." She winces.

Typical. "We don't need to fill this place with aimless bodies."

"I'm ambitious, smart, and catch on fast. Coffee, dry cleaning—I'll grind the beans and find the best eco-friendly, cost-effective dry cleaner in Manhattan. I also specialize in tidying up conference rooms. Clients love me, coworkers request me because I get things done. I'm no-nonsense and direct. You'll only ever have to tell me something once. Um, I also write jingles. Really . . . I can sing. People say I sound like Halsey."

I lean back in my chair. "Halsey? That's your pitch?"

"I thought it hit the mark."

I pull a face like she's smoking something.

She gazes down at her lap, her fingers curl around the edge of her skirt. Her eyes slowly rise to meet mine. "More like Annie Clark."

"St. Vincent's cool." I rest my elbow on the arm of the chair, pressing the top of my pen to my lip. Meredith complained the other day about needing more support. This could get her off my back. "The senior account supervisor on my team could use some help over the next couple of weeks."

"I'm in."

"Before you accept: We can't put you on the payroll. Due to your inexperience, it doesn't make sense. You will, however, get to work with the best creative team in the business. Maybe score some samples for your book. You can say you wrote them even if you only helped brainstorm. We won't tell."

Her eyes tighten. "I would never *lie* about work I didn't create."

I bite back my response. Her indignation stems from her naiveté. Everyone lies in advertising. We lie to sell products. We lie more to sell ourselves or no sooner get replaced by the next bright kid walking through the door.

I gather her paperwork and rise. "Can you follow direction?" I snicker at my joke.

"Wait, what about my book?" She shifts her portfolio onto her lap, eyeing it.

"Like I said, I already looked at your writing samples." I'm halfway through the door before she realizes I'm leaving. She should be kissing my ass for allowing her to hang out for two weeks and shadow one of the most respected agencies in the country without any real experience. I acted like a jerk earlier. Call us even, sweet cheeks.

I wait outside just past the doorway. *Okay, new intern, when I asked if you could follow direction I meant can you follow* me.

At last, she appears. Her jaw rigid.

Hot eyeballs track us across the open-floor workspace as I show her to one of the long tables and drag an extra black-mesh chair next to the printer. The usual clamor of conversations and clacking keys comes to a halt. People in the adjoining glass conference rooms crane their necks. Outside, the window washer's squeegee pauses.

"We'll find you a laptop." I point to the bottom drawer of a nearby filing cabinet. "You can put your bag in here." May or may not be stuffed with client folders.

She doesn't look at me. She might not last the two weeks.

I toss her an *Adweek*. "Team meeting in thirty." I wheel back around.

The eyeballs drop back to their laptops. Feels like I'm serving up a baby lamb to a pride of hungry lions. Her new coworkers will want to know where she came from, the agencies on her resume, her previous accounts, and most of all—if she's a threat. Won't they be surprised she's only eighteen.

They'll test her and be mean to her at first. Some will try to get in her pants. Others will make up stories that they have. She's rough around the edges, which may serve her. But if her Girl Scout act in the elevator is any indication, she may not be hungry enough to make it in advertising.

I don't recall her writing samples and can't fathom why we even brought her in for an interview in the first place. I wouldn't have greenlighted her resume. Someone dumped her on me and now I'm passing her off. Good luck, Meredith. This should be interesting.

My phone vibrates. Not again. I shake my head and dismiss it. I look to see if my latest hire is still cozying up to the printer where I left her. I attempt to turn away again before she sees me looking.

Too late.

Chapter 6

BRYNN

If I'd known I'd be starting today, I would have worn flats. Everyone here is dressed on trend and I look like an accountant—one with a crushed silk purple flower growing out of her shoulder.

My stomach rumbles, distracting me from being the go-getter I need to be in order to last here.

A jock-looking guy pops up from behind a large monitor at the only other long table facing mine, which isn't a workspace at all. At least Micah didn't put me in a closet.

"First day?"

I nod, scanning the floor for the communal coffee pot, hoping one exists.

"I'm Donovan." He offers up a robotic wave before picking up some folders from his desk. "Senior copywriter. I guess you'll be joining our team."

He flips his dirty-blond hair out of his eyes like a young Justin Bieber. The guy's sockless and wearing salmon-colored khakis, a blue button-down, and a T-shirt underneath that reads, THE FUTURE IS FEMALE.

I extend my hand. "Brynn. Coffee?"

He grins. "Well, Brynn Coffee, walk with me. I'll show you the Starbucks."

"Um, anything like . . . complimentary, for the employees?"

"I gotcha." He clamps the folders under his arm, his hands in his pockets, and flips his hair in the direction I'm to follow.

I hurry after him. Show me the free food, new favorite person. "Have you worked here long?"

"I joined Kershaw McKenzie last spring. You'll like it. We work killer hours, sometimes weekends. But we play hard too." He winks at me. "Have they assigned you to anyone?"

"I'm helping out one of the account supervisors."

"Probably Meredith. She's . . . um, cool most days. Don't get on her bad side."

"I haven't met her yet. I only interviewed with that guy Micah. He wasn't going to hire me. Then said I could shadow his team for a couple of weeks. Is that typical?"

"Who knows, things change fast around here. We refer to him as *For*-mica, like the countertop. Shiny on the surface and out for himself. He's a punk. Around your age, I'm guessing. No offense. He got his career handed to him. His great-grandfather started the agency back in the Stone Age. He's smart, I'll give him that. He doesn't hang much. Thinks he's better than us. The ladies call him a 'specimen.'"

"Oh, like Captain America?" Posters of Chris Evans once plastered my bedroom walls in middle school; I may have practiced my kissing on one in particular.

"I guess. I don't think he's so great looks-wise, personally. But you know, whatever side you're on—or both." His eyebrows rise.

Let me guess, Donovan. You're straight.

He leads me to a freestanding vertical garden, a massive partition in the center of the floor covered in lush green vines that climb the agency's two stories.

My feet trip over each other. "Geez, who waters that?"

"They call it a 'living wall.' Supposed to reduce stress."

"Kind of *Little Shop of Horrors*, but without the mouth."

He gives me a funny look.

Why did I say that aloud?

I spot the free coffee and continental breakfast behind it. Free food? I'm less stressed already. "Thanks, I'll take it from here."

"Let me know if you need anything else." His eyes wander over my suit, camping out on my chest. "Nice . . . flower."

"Yeah. It is." My voice quivers. I turn away, cutting off his view.

This is my dead mother's suit, you creep.

The guy looks to be in his late twenties too. Ew. My eyes sting, but I draw in a deep breath. Not here. Not now. I'll never have to work with him, only this Meredith person. And I don't need to make friends here. Relying on myself is the only way to get out of this financial hole. I'll impress them so much, they'll pay me to stay.

Ooh, sesame bagels . . . and peanut butter. I spread some on my bagel. My stomach churns with happiness, albeit not the extra crunchy kind.

Alas, you can't have everything.

Chapter 7

BRYNN

I shift around, sitting on my clammy hands at my printer desk, my knees locked and feet lifted like the wood floor is lava. Rows of tables, four workstations across, lie empty. Their computers hum with large monitors scrolling the agency's logo.

That last coffee sent my bladder over the edge. It's got to be close to thirty minutes since Micah left me here, though, and I don't see a restroom sign anywhere. I can't miss my first team meeting.

At last, Micah motions for me to join him in one of the glass-walled conference rooms, where a glossy gathering of twenty-somethings has assembled.

My stomach sinks.

"Everyone, meet Brynn Gallardo."

My team, I presume.

"Meredith, senior account supervisor." Micah's up-facing palm slices the air toward each of them. "Josie, art director, Priya, media, Lucius, design, and Donovan, senior copywriter. Scott McKenzie, one of the partners and the agency's creative director, arrives back from our San Diego office later today."

Their eyes fasten on my face.

I've clearly walked onto the set of *Gossip Girl*. Each member of this team gives off an I'm-not-trying-to-be-chic-because-I-already-am air sitting behind their designer coffees and shiny electronic devices. Compared to them, I look like a kid playing dress-up.

Micah takes a seat at the other end of the oblong white table and opens a notebook.

I lower myself into the nearest vacant chair across from Meredith, whose long auburn hair flows in soft waves around her freckled white shoulders. Her tortoise Warby Parker–esque glasses, with their oversize frames, give her that nerdy-pretty vibe. I bet they're just for show.

Micah's eyes stop on mine then peel away. "Brynn will be assisting Meredith over the next two weeks while we prepare some new client pitches."

Meredith's head bounces up from her rose gold laptop. Her eyes expand, lips pursed. "Would have been nice, Micah, if you'd told me this was happening and given me a chance to interview a few candidates."

"Surprise." His tone comes off matter-of-fact. "Brynn appeared today and though we've filled our summer intern slots, I thought you could use the help. Consider it a gift. Use it wisely."

It? What a dick.

Meredith rolls her eyes and turns to me.

Her mouth moves but I miss what she says, too overwhelmed to pay attention.

"Where . . . are . . . you . . . *from*?" As if I don't speak English.

Everyone stares.

My cheeks burn. "Heeere . . ."

Snickers spread around me.

I tug on the hem of my skirt.

"Where do you go to school?"

"Um." I clear my throat. "I graduated from LaGuardia."

"High school? What the hell, Micah." She sniffs.

His head stays buried in his writing.

Meredith sighs like a prom princess. Her shoulders slump as if I'm adding to her workload. "I have you for two weeks, and then what, you're off to college with a stop in Europe first—Lynn, was it?"

"Brynn. With a B." *For bitch, Bitch.* I squint hard at this girl for being nosy. I don't share that I bought my MetroCard with loose change this morning. Forget college, let alone travel outside the Tri-State area. I'm stuck here. And, Miss Nerdy Pretty, my personal life doesn't concern you.

Except. I do need her to like me.

I soften my stink-eye into a smile.

She arches her brow.

Micah closes his notebook and rests an elbow on the back of his chair, his other arm on the table. "What do we have this week, Meredith?"

She adjusts her glasses and peers at her screen. "Quotagian Inc. launches its new dating app this year, aimed at twenty- and thirty-year-old fans of historical romance—e.g., Shakespeare, Austen, Brontë, James, Hemingway, etc."

She reads her notes like they're a soliloquy from *Macbeth*. Her delivery reminds me of the theater kids at my high school, including her distracting facial expressions.

Cody's impersonation, one of many private jokes we shared, floats into my head. My throat squeezes.

"It generates love letters for unattached literary romancers wanting to find like-minded classic prose enthusiasts and poets for a possible rendezvous. They call the app Couplet Couplings."

Told you—*Macbeth*.

The team groans.

"No, not really. I made that part up." She grins.

"Nerds." Donovan makes eye contact like he and I rank above them.

"How does it work?" Priya, wearing a baby pink, puffy short-sleeve top and the only other Brown girl besides me, raises a tentative finger. "Do people use inspirational quotes or lines from their favorite authors in place of their bios, like, 'Austen girl seeking

Dickens boy'?" Her large doe eyes flicker underneath a silky fringe of bangs, her wide smile dazzling.

I suck in my lips, concealing my Scooby-Doo canines.

"Dickens? Speaking in code or you looking for *action*, Priya?" Donovan cracks a lopsided grin and high-fives Lucius, another male model type.

This place boasts more runway castoffs than reality TV.

Priya's face reddens; her scowl is almost as pretty as her smile.

"Sort of." Meredith looks at Priya. "'Within our cold texting world lies a desire to bring back the art of love letter writing to woo your next true match,' says here." She makes a small popping sound with her lips. "People can swipe on your profile and contact you through a digital love letter created by the app. Users fill out a questionnaire about themselves and the kind of person they're looking for. They're encouraged to be as detailed and honest as possible, and PG in their execution."

Donovan murmurs something under his breath.

Lucius's jaw drops, eyes pop wide.

The two of them suppress a laugh as their shoulders shake.

Micah's eyes narrow. "Mature, Donovan."

Donovan lowers his face into his iPad.

I peek over at Micah without turning my head, taking him in fully for the first time. The guy's striking when he's not acting all jumpy, with his inquisitive khaki-brown eyes and that messy, dark, Ivy League hair. He exudes an artsy vibe—which I used to fall for—with an edge. His skinny tie is growing on me.

He catches me staring.

I look away.

"What do they need from us?" Josie sighs, acting unfazed by this group. In fact, she looks positively comfortable in her long-sleeve graphic tee and jeans. Wish I could switch clothes with her. Not sure my suit would go with those facial piercings and edgy haircut, though.

Meredith slides her pink-manicured fingers over her touchpad. "They need help with brand positioning, logo ideas, tagline, website, and a social media campaign to start. I'll send you guys my notes and a preliminary wireframe of the app. We're competing with Day & Foster."

"Of course, they do all the big dating apps." Micah sighs.

Lucius crosses his arms over his pecs, pushing up his vein-popping biceps under his white polo. "I think this app needs some hot celebrity from one of those period films. How about the actress who came in last time?"

I'm not sure who this one's trying to impress. Maybe himself. I can't place his accent. He sure works hard to keep up with Donovan.

Lucius shifts his unreturned grin to the other faces around the table. Our eyes meet, and his lips bend even farther up. He likes attention. With his caterpillar eyebrows and light beard scruff, he reminds me of Zayn from One Direction. Another of my middle school crushes.

"I got this." Donovan arches his back and stretches overhead.

Micah turns to him. "Decide how you're going to split it up with Meredith and Brynn. The three of you should brainstorm together."

Oh no.

"Sure." Donovan's upbeat tone sounds forced. "Three minds work better than one." He throws me a blank stare.

I roll my fingers into fists under the table.

No one says anything for several seconds.

"What about bookstores and poetry slams?" I wince.

All eyes cut to me.

I should explain that I once helped my parents organize an open mic night at their club for new artists and got the actress/rapper Awkwafina, a LaGuardia HS alum, to host. And how I used to help them brainstorm on promotional ideas to attract new audiences and bands through TikTok and other social media. But the lump mounting in my throat stops me.

The team waits, unrelenting.

"I-I mean, maybe we focus on the right media platforms where people with similar interests discuss using the app and what they like about it." Like what influencers do, I guess? I don't even know what I'm saying.

Donovan side-eyes Lucius.

"You mean publicity?" Meredith blinks.

"We create marketing campaigns. We don't *do* publicity. Do you even know the difference?" Donovan whistles through his teeth.

Ouch. "O-of course." I haven't a clue. Aren't they sort of the same? "I can write a press release." With Google's help, of course.

No one responds.

My face grows hot. I need to shut up.

Meredith clears her throat and turns back to the group. "I've asked them to send over research from test groups to give us some parameters. Lucius, that reminds me. See if you can get that same photographer, the one with the reasonable fees."

"Yeah, make sure he shoots some fine-looking ladies." Donovan snickers.

"Inspire, not intimidate," I blurt, my voice low. Why am I still talking?

"What was that?" Micah's khaki-brown eyes throw me off.

Focus, Brynn.

"Um, I think we should inspire people to have fun with the app, not intimidate them."

Donovan pulls a face. "Wrong. A dating app is only good if hot people use it. Otherwise, why bother? Look at Hinge or Tinder. Hell, maybe you already have a profile."

Meredith's brows lower over her eyes. "She's a bit young."

I grip the seat of my chair. Dating apps? High school was a free-for-all when it came to hookups. I never heard of anyone using one. I couldn't tell you what went down senior year anyway. I'm shutting up for real this time.

"Let's meet again and see what you guys come up with." Micah rises. His eyes drop on me, then pull away.

Meredith closes her laptop and stands. "I agree, L—Brynn, was it? I think those flawless models *are* intimidating."

"Maybe you should hit the gym, then." Donovan wheels back his chair as if to block her passage.

Meredith's eyes become slits, but she just sidesteps him and strides away.

How does he get away with these comments? This place is so high school.

The IT guy delivers a silver MacBook Air to my desk and mumbles something about creating a passcode. He rushes off before I have a chance to ask his name or for a tutorial.

I open it and three default avatars with a gray floating head appear across the middle, one labeled *Maia*, another *Celeste*. I tap on *Brynn* and a chat window pops up from Meredith to me and Donovan: *New client samples arrived.*

I retrace my steps through the metal screens and find the lobby.

Eunice, seated at her curved desk, looks up from her monitor. Her dark, overplucked eyebrows wiggle together in the center of her forehead. She clutches her phone tighter to her ear.

I hold my elbows behind my back and wait.

Her eyes grow icy.

I gaze at the white exposed ceiling in the center of the lobby. A cluster of vintage lightbulbs dangle from black cords wrapped around pipes. Two camel-colored tufted leather benches fill the corner of the sitting area, a royal blue cylinder table between them. An abstract painting of a rocket blasting off hangs behind Eunice's head. Its conehead and fiery dog bone shaped base give me pause.

Eunice ends her call.

I press on a smile. "I'm looking for some customer samples that got delivered?"

"Receiving."

My feet don't move.

She points her boney elbow back toward the metal room dividers I just came through, then reaches for a flowered Kate Spade lunch tote. Her narrow shoulders twitch as she unzips it and pulls out a bowl full of what looks like bean sprouts, bok choy, and jalapenos over rice noodles.

The aroma of the medley of spices reaches my nose and hunger pangs stab my stomach, despite the peanut-butter bagel I consumed a mere hour ago.

The agency reminds me of a modern factory with its tall, black-paned windows, open layout with rows of workstations, primary-colored upholstered seating areas, and quirky meeting nooks.

My head whips back to a mural of graffiti pop art that connects a couple of unisex restrooms. Aha!

Coming out of the bathroom, I continue my hunt for the samples. I pass the same floating staircase twice. Finally, out of desperation, I approach a skinny White girl with blue spiky hair, her makeshift desk similar to mine. Her 1960s-inspired dress looks like it was lifted from the set of *Mad Men*.

She perks up when she sees me.

I offer her a tentative smile. "Um, which way is Receiving?"

"Head left and down the long hallway." She tilts her head, examining my flower.

I cross my hand over my chest, covering the crushed bloom. "Um . . . are you new as well?"

"Been here about a month. I work on Benji's team. I'm Zoe."

"Brynn." Her long limp fingers are like cold asparagus in my hand as we shake. "Thanks," I say, already backing away. "Appreciate the help!"

Without waiting for a response, I speed walk down the hall and through a double set of doors. I find Meredith just inside, standing by a tower of pink boxes.

"Is Donovan coming?" I spy the wall of packing supplies next to her.

"He didn't think he needed to be here." She gives me a side-eye and hands me a box cutter.

I slice open a box stamped with a scroll monogram: *BPC*. I stop short from asking what's inside.

"New client pitch—Bradley Products Complete. Scott McKenzie brought them in."

Inside lies rows of baby-size dumbbells no bigger than my hand.

"They're pink." I hold one up. "I can curl it with my pinky."

She puckers her lips, thinking. "Open all the boxes for other sizes and colors."

"Purple, green, orange . . . are they marketing them to kids? What makes them *complete*?"

She considers me for a moment. "You ask a lot of questions. That's good."

"What did they tell you about the product?" I smile, feeding off her praise.

"I haven't met the client yet. Scott forwarded me a photo. He said they are trying something new aimed at sixteen- to twenty-five-year-olds."

"They weigh nothing."

She pushes the bridge of her glasses. "High reps, I guess."

"You're not going to get strong lifting one of these." I twirl it between my fingers. "Maybe they're part of a weight vest, like the ones runners wear in Central Park."

"Hmm, I like that idea."

I play with it some more. "Look, this end unscrews. Weird."

She purses her lips again. "Maybe you fill them with water or sand?"

I twist the bottom and a waxy, hot pink tip emerges. "Nope, it's a lipstick." I grin.

"Come." She claps her hands together. "We have a call to make."

Chapter 8

MICAH

I glance around my monitor at the new intern, who is scurrying by for the umpteenth time, her eyes and mouth pulled tight. Sure I could help her, but where's the fun in that? Sooner she goes back to Brooklyn, the better. She probably has a Mama Leone or two back home ready with a big bowl of spaghetti—or the Peruvian equivalent—to congratulate her on finishing her first day.

She scampers by again, flitting around in that tight suit. Her first test at resourcefulness. She better make friends fast before she wears out the floors.

Scott asked me to take a stab at writing some new client proposals before passing them on to Meredith. But all I can see is my notebook poking out from the mess on my desk, waiting.

I scan the sea of workspaces. Everyone appears busy. I sit with my back to the wall so I can keep an eye on any oncoming visitors. Safer that way.

I grab my notebook and jot down a few lines. Like a light switch, the knots roped across my shoulders release. Inside these white blank pages, I call the shots instead of others dictating my story. I'm careful never to leave it out in the open. Its contents wouldn't make sense to most. I don't understand my own brain half the time.

I stayed up well into the evening working on something last night. A letter. I was on a mad tear, as evidenced by my erratic penmanship. My sentences become less jagged once I began to settle and be myself again. Sometimes I can almost get back to what I felt like when I was a typical teenager—before I woke up in someone else's body.

I was sixteen, a sophomore in high school, when I experienced my first psychotic episode. I'd been cramming for a precalculus test the night before. I remember stressing over it, unable to fall asleep. Eventually, I did.

When I woke up, these grayish human forms were standing at the foot of my bed.

The dark sky outside my window convinced me I was dreaming. I rolled over and fell back asleep.

But when my alarm sounded, not only were the Shadow People still there, they began speaking. They said terrible things. Things I believed to be true. How I'd become a burden to my family—mainly Granddad and Aunt Max, who got stuck raising me while my father lived on the road, forgetting his own son.

That day, those demons personified all my insecurities. Their presence unhinged every cell in my body, imprisoning me in my bed for hours.

I peed myself and cried for my mother.

Aunt Max found me later that evening.

The doc who examined me called it *schizophrenia*.

I hear voices and see people who don't exist. I also experience bouts of paranoia and other stress-induced adventures.

I responded well to treatment at first. I could manage it. No one needed to know. But my body soon became resistant to the antipsychotic meds and the Shadow People moved back in.

That summer after my diagnosis, Granddad thought it'd be a fine idea for me to start interning at the agency. He alleged a job would fix me.

I didn't fight it, though I knew I wasn't ready. I had already disgraced my family enough.

Four years later, and my cocktail of meds keeps changing. Some leave me listless and bloated and insatiably thirsty, others bouncing off the walls and sleep-deprived. I've lost my friends and I had to finish high school online. I went from being a regular teenager to a recluse. I couldn't even hack my first college class.

The Shadow People occupy my world now. Ignoring them is near impossible. I never know when they'll show up. Take the guy who keeps pounding my desk. I'm certain he's not real. I would have remembered hiring his ugly mug.

An alert for my weekly financial meeting with Aunt Max pops up on my screen.

My gut knots up. Talk of cutting staff makes me want to pull out my eyelashes. Thankfully, I don't do that anymore.

The number one person on Scott's chopping block is Eunice. He wants to eliminate her position.

Her last merit increase, unbeknownst to her, came from my paycheck. I don't know what I'd do if I lost her. I won't let that happen.

When Granddad presses me about the agency acquiring new clients, I redirect. Been a bleak few months, but things will turn around. These next campaigns just need to hit their mark.

I don't have to look up to know Scott has landed. His cologne gives him away. "You're back," I say.

"Short trip this time." Scott points a manila folder at me, then rests a corner on the top edge of my screen. He's dressed in one of his carefully stylized ensembles: a suit and tie with a violet blue pocket square that brings out his indigo eyes and brown skin. Whenever he needs to dazzle a client, out comes the blue. I've seen men and women lose their train of thought after a mere glance from those eyes.

"Congrats on getting Bradley Products. My team's working on the creative now."

His bottom teeth dig into his lip. "Skip your meeting with Max. I need you in the one for Quotagian."

I nod and wait for more.

Scott's been careful around me as of late, treating me like one of Granddad's spies. Aunt Max, insulated upstairs in her corner office, doesn't ruffle him in the way I do sitting among the creatives and seeing all the drama unfold. I'm not sure why he worries. Granddad can't get his socks to match these days, let alone interfere with how his agency is being run.

Scott got hired to be the new creative director the first summer I interned. At twenty-six, he became the youngest CD in the industry. The guy's talented, the way he manages the designers, copywriters, and art directors impressive. He's taught me everything I know. When he discovered I could write, he promoted me to associate creative director, bypassing my lack of a college degree. Most say he's kissing up to my granddad. Probably true. He also likes to pass off work that he doesn't want to do. Like these proposals.

I've learned a lot in my four years observing him. We're not buds. But I can sense when something's up. Something big.

He pivots and strides through the open room, his fingers already inside his necktie, tugging it to either side. He gives it a hard jerk before removing it over his head. He marches up the open black staircase.

Heads turn in his direction.

The slam of his office door travels all the way back down to me.

A moment later, Meredith breezes past my desk. She's trailed by her new intern, who is pulling a hand truck filled with pink boxes—and who, right as she passes me, trips and narrowly avoids a face-plant.

I squint to hold back from laughing. I swivel around in my chair, letting my smile grow. At least she's entertaining.

My thumb slides across my phone. Time to check in with the psycho.

Chapter 9

BRYNN

These stupid heels. Donovan should be the one pulling the BPC boxes. I ride my chair over to Meredith's table and open another pink box.

She found the client's phone number in Scott's email; now, she's leaning back in her seat exchanging pleasantries with whoever's on the other end of the line. She shifts forward, her face full of questions. "So, a complete makeup line?" She looks in my direction. "Some are filled with cream blush *and* eye shadows?"

I unscrew each dumbbell, showing her the shade inside.

A few of these reveals make her eyes expand in approval, others twist her perky little nose as if it's smelled something offensive.

She ends the call. "We may be able to target a younger demo with these."

"Yeah, grown women aren't going to pull a mini dumbbell out of their bag. But maybe preteens will. I can see them stacked or lined up on a tween's dresser. Do they make a lip gloss?"

"There you are." She waves Donovan over. "You and Brynn can start brainstorming ideas for this new Bradley Products line."

He shrugs. "How's now?"

I steel my jaw, closing my eyes. This can't be happening.

Holding my newly acquired laptop, I ride my chair to the other end of the table, where he sits.

He stares at his monitor. "Um, conference room. Bring one of the boxes with you."

I replace all the ends, repack the dumbbells in the box, and lift the wobbly cardboard, stabilizing it with one knee underneath. I balance my laptop on top, then head to the conference room.

"They're not what you think," I say between gasps for air as I place the large pink box between us on the table.

His eyes narrow. "It's makeup."

"How did you know?"

"Scott said he scored a new cosmetics client."

I smirk like we're in this together. "So, why the dumbbell design?"

"Why worry about *why*?" His face hardens.

My cheeks warm. What's this guy's deal?

His thumbs tap a text on his phone.

I study the Chrysler Building's sunburst pattern out the window. My gaze drops to the back of his phone, then to the people at their desks on the other side of the glass from us.

He picks at the skin on the side of his face and swipes at his screen a few times. "I'm not coming up with anything right now." He stands and leaves.

What the hell?

I trudge back to my desk and fall into my chair. Tears threaten. I tighten my jaw, digging my fingernails into the armrests. I eye the way I walked in here. No one would notice if I ran back to the coffin, curled up on my mattress on the floor, and pretended today never happened. What am I doing here? I can't do this. It's not like they taught us advertising in high school. Where do I even start? Donovan's no help.

The printer comes to life, rattling my desk.

I jump out of my chair. That constant occurrence won't become *too* annoying, I'm sure. I sigh and open up a new Word doc. I type, BRADLEY PRODUCTS COMPLETE. I change the font to one I like better. I bold it, underline it, and save it to my desktop. I stare at the sea of whiteness, thinking any other color would be better than white.

Okay, enough.

I thumb through the copy of *Adweek* Micah gave me. Shouldn't be this hard . . . and . . . where did my team go? I look around and see Zoe and another girl walking toward me. After they pass, I stroll between my team's two tables and pick up some magazines—an *Advertising Age* from Meredith's desk, a few issues of *Communication Arts* off Priya's, and a *Wired* and *Direct Marketing News* from Lucius's.

I memorize agency names and accounts awarded. I check out the campaigns getting attention and those attracting controversy. I learn about something called an ADDY and the agencies who won one this year. I find everything I'm looking at to be a big snooze—except for the *Communication Arts* magazines, which contain one advertising campaign after another. Many I've never seen before.

Like writing songs, maybe ads follow a formula? These all have an image, a headline, and a logo with a closing—I mean, a *tagline*. It's surprising how entertaining they are. Some make me smile, while others stir up a whole different set of emotions. I'm in awe of how talented these copywriters and ad designers are. What would *they* do with a line of dumbbell makeup?

"Where are all my *CA*s?" Priya stands by her computer, second one down from mine, a hand on her hip.

"I borrowed them." I cringe a little. "Is that okay?"

Her face softens. "Be sure to return them."

"I will. Thanks." I watch her in profile, contemplating something on her screen. Her legs turn out, reminding me of the ballerinas at my high school. "Um, Priya? Do you know what Meredith means by brainstorming campaign ideas? Do I have to come up with entire ads like this?" I lift a page from one of the *CA*s toward her.

"Scott will want to see ad concepts, including headlines and a few taglines. Donovan usually does those. You should shadow him."

"Thanks." I force a smile, pressing my lips together.

She reads my face. "Is Donovan here?"

I shrug. "We were supposed to brainstorm ideas for the new Bradley Products line. He left before we got started."

Her brown doe eyes grow tall. She scans the open room, then the hallway that leads to the lobby. "Alright." She reaches for her bag, flipping her bangs to the side. "I can look at your ideas when I get back."

"Really? That would be great."

She exits like the agency's on fire.

I sit up straighter, moving my hair off my face, and type: SPORTY TEEN MAKEUP. I wrinkle my nose. I reexamine the sneaker ad I showed Priya, the one that promises a better bod and a more fulfilling life—all from a shoe. Maybe I can come up with something along those lines.

Makeup in general helps one feel more attractive . . . it can help to erase the undereye circles I'm sporting these days, for example.

Meredith circles back to her desk at the other table across from me.

Micah materializes next to her a moment later. "Scott's back. You coming to the meeting?"

"Be right there. Brynn too?"

"I haven't told him about her yet." He glances over at me for a millisecond.

Once they leave, I blow out the air I've been holding. I'll be lucky to stay the two weeks Micah promised.

I check to see if Priya's returned before lifting a blank notepad off her desk.

Dumbbells and makeup. Dumbbells and makeup? *Why* is right.

1. *Both can enhance your appearance*
2. *Dumbbells help you stay fit and feel more attractive like makeup*

3. *Both can make you feel better about yourself, improve self-esteem*
4. *Help you transform into a new and improved version of yourself*
5. *Someone that you're not but strive to be . . .*

Hmm.

Chapter 10

MICAH

I seize the last seat on the F train before the doors close. The lack of air-conditioning in the first two cars has packed this one with weary-eyed commuters. I check for expectant mothers and old people. Not because I care. I just detest the pressure to give up my seat when I'm writing.

Sitting here on the train, the weight of the day lifts from my shoulders at last. Unlike at the agency, it doesn't matter if someone here sees me making faces or arguing with the Shadow People. The subway's a rolling circus of poets, entertainers, and crazies like me.

I run my hand down a fresh page. My pen scratches along, free and unbound.

A ripple of outcries travels from the far end of the car.

Here we go. Some guy in a green shirt shouts the *f* slur and something else. The receiver of the taunts: a slender, young, androgynous-looking person with bright, red-dyed hair, glittery makeup, and a beard.

Faces tense around me. My fellow passengers sit riveted.

I sigh, forgetting what I was about to write. My pen hovers.

Nothing happens for several minutes. A calm permeates the car. The train travels on, screaming through the tunnel. Commuters return to their books and phones. I resume writing.

Someone shrieks.

I reluctantly watch round two unfold.

Green shirt guy points at the young man. Yells something about God and damnation. He steps toward him and spits.

His victim recoils, his face stretched in horror.

The adjacent onlookers freeze—including that girl Brynn, who's leaning on a center pole.

The train drags into the terminal. "The next stop is Twenty-Third Street," a robotic voice announces.

Green shirt guy lights a cigarette.

"You can't smoke here," a woman calls out.

The schmuck blows a white cloud in her direction, then aims his lit cigarette at the young man's face.

A collective gasp sounds.

The doors open.

Brynn stomps on green shirt guy's foot and pushes the young red-haired man farther into the car.

A few commuters spring to their feet. Forming a sort of scrum, they propel green shirt guy out through the doors and onto the train platform.

More obscenities get thrown.

"Please clear the closing doors."

Green shirt guy breaks free, attempts reentry.

The doors shut.

His balled-up fist meets the glass, accompanied by a string of expletives.

Brynn rights the young man, whom she knocked down with her initial shove, onto his feet.

I lower my head into my notebook. Someone give that Girl Scout a merit badge.

The theme song from *Psycho* plays in my pocket.

I decline the call for the umpteenth time today.

Chapter 11

BRYNN

I walk in the opposite direction of where Micah gets on the subway. I can't lose this guy. What a day.

Of course, no seats are left. I wrap my arm around a pole and close my eyes for a minute.

The train jerks forward.

My body goes with it.

Bright purple shoes paired with a teal pencil skirt catch my attention. The dark beard and bright red lips startle me at first. They smile.

Rikki and I became friends in seventh grade when we were assigned to the same group project on ancient Macedonia in our world history class. Our small team of researchers met for weeks after school at my family's apartment, one block from the Dekalb Ave L train.

Rikki always came hungry and requesting jelly-only sandwiches.

I preferred only peanut butter on mine.

My dad would shake his head, claiming if only our tastebuds could agree, we'd have a winner of a sandwich.

We stayed tight even after our project received a measly B+, which I disputed to no avail, pulling Rikki along to plead our case. The rest of our group didn't seem to care. Our friendship worked;

being so different, we never competed. At twelve, they loved tight, trendy clothes, where I found comfort in a baggy T-shirt and athletic shorts. They obsessed over the movie *Twilight*, especially polar bear–white Edward, and I fantasized under the covers about the entire wolfpack from *New Moon*. We did share similar musical tastes, singing at the top of our lungs in my bedroom to Carly Rae Jepsen and begging our parents to let us see One Direction at the Beacon. We remained close until we ended up at different high schools and lost touch.

What a body they have now. Unlike me, Rikki's narrow hips can rock a slim look; I'd look like a stuffed sausage in that outfit.

I open my mouth to say something.

Their earlier smile falls and they glance away.

Guess they changed their mind.

Ugly words stream from the guy behind me. He sounds like a character from a bad '80s coming-of-age movie with his less-than-creative homophobic slurs.

For a few minutes, he lets up. I sigh with relief.

Then the a-hole spouts off something about God, closes in, and spits.

Not everyone's a fan of Rikki's.

My old friend's eyes widen. They back away.

My palms slip around the pole.

Wrapping their arms around their waist, Rikki stares at the ground, eyes swimming.

The train enters the station.

One of the passengers, a man in a utility uniform, leans into my line of sight and winks.

I follow his eyes and connect with the other faces around us. A silent agreement is passed.

I catch a whiff of a cigarette and hear Rikki's cry before the lit end enters my peripheral. I spin around, slam my full weight on that a-hole's foot, and then rush my tall, skinny friend before they know what's happening.

They fall backward, onto the train floor.

A lump clogs my throat and I dive forward to help them up.

For a brief moment, we're touching, and I try to come up with something to say. But then we reach the next stop and Rikki bolts out the train doors without a word or second glance.

A nameless sadness spreads through me. We used to be so close.

Dragging myself up the four flights to my apartment, I'm hit first with the tangy aroma of barbecue and then, on the next floor, red sauce and garlic bread. Climbing higher, my mouth waters. I picture my mom and dad taking these same stairs and my heart squeezes. I want them to be there to hug me when I walk through the door. Want to tell them about my bizarre first day.

"God, what I wouldn't do for a beer." I thrust my key in the lock.

"What's that?"

An unfamiliar face exits the communal bathroom.

"Oh, um . . . I wish I had some beer in my fridge."

"I've got some. Want one?"

"Oh, no . . . thanks, though."

She extends her hand. "Debra."

"Brynn."

Her fingers wrap around mine, all warm and soft.

I smile a little at her orange and pink floral caftan, half expecting an officer of a cruise ship to be nearby. Her long, blue-silver hair drapes in a loose braid down her back with a few rogue strands framing her face; a simple gold cross hangs from her neck.

"I haven't seen you before and I've lived here for nearly thirty years." She grins, revealing teeth that are ultra-white for someone her age. "Did you just move in?" Her smokey blue eyes study me.

"A couple of weeks ago. My parents used to rent it out."

The skin crinkles around her eyes. Her mouth falls open. "Basilio and Katia?"

My breath catches.

"You're their baby girl! Of course—you favor your mom. We met when she was a little older than you are now, I suspect. Your dad would crack us up with his jokes. They didn't live here long. I think you have the smallest unit in the building."

"Yes, and the cheapest." I blow out a heavy sigh.

"All sorts of recording artists have stood right where you are. I used to jam with a couple of them." She presses her shoulders back.

"You're a musician?"

"I sing and play guitar. You may recognize me from a long-running children's television show."

"*Sesame Street*?"

"The same." She flashes her teeth again.

"I grew up watching it. My parents never mentioned they knew a cast member."

"Well, well, come here, baby girl, and give your Aunt Debra a hug!"

"Aunt?" I pronounce it like she just did—rhymed with *font*.

"Nah, not really." She chuckles. "I did babysit you a few times, though. Such a pretty little thing."

Knowing she knew my parents somehow soothes the upset belly I've had all day. "Thanks. I think I will take that beer, if the offer still stands. Been a long, strange day. The air-conditioning broke on the subway. We all jammed into one car. Then this a-hole on the train . . ."

"That's Man-hat-tan." She sounds like Cody doing his booming announcer voice.

Cody. My stomach feels sickish one again.

She stops. "What's wrong?"

"Nothing." I rearrange my face.

She cocks her head. "Have you eaten?"

Debra's apartment could swallow mine three times. It reminds me of an antique shop, one that smells like soup that's been cooking all day. Everywhere I look, another thing draws my eye. Decades of concert and theater memorabilia from the '70s layer the tables and walls.

"Did you paint this?" I motion to a canvas of a man shaking a pair of maracas, his chest glistening beneath his open shirt. "Wait, is this Mick Jagger?"

Deb laughs. "Yep. 1977. When I attended Skidmore. I'm not much of a painter, but it captures his sensuality, don't you think? I met him once."

"The energy coming off his body is electric," I agree. "God, I wish I could move like that."

I peruse her place like it's a museum, stopping to study every charcoal drawing and dusty oil. I spot an old pop art poster with the logo of my parents' club, the Flaming Flamingo, and memories flood back of waiting at the club after school to take the train back to Brooklyn with my dad so he could cook dinner.

My nose stings. I wipe it, sniffling. I work up an excuse to leave.

She strolls back into the room carrying two beers in one hand, the necks laced between her fingers. Her eyes flit over to the poster and then back to me. She frowns a little, then pops off the caps and passes me one. "Here, sit."

I follow her to a pink-upholstered sofa with an S-curve back. I step around the vintage trunk covered in band logos and album stickers and half-drunk cups of tea that serves as her coffee table, and plop down.

She lowers herself onto a blue vinyl bench that looks like it was pulled from an automobile. "I read about your parents' car accident in the *Voice*." Her expressive face drips with motherly sympathy.

My eyes fill.

"I used to love how your mom and dad jammed with the bands onstage at the end of every show. The room would erupt. Their passion invigorated the downtown music scene. Many artists owe their careers to that tiny club."

I nod, my lips on lockdown. *Do not cry. You just met this woman.*

"Not holding up so well, are you?"

I grind my teeth and look away, wishing she'd quit.

"Hard to be the one left behind."

Bull's-eye. Cue ugly cry.

"Faking happy is tiresome, isn't it?" She bobs her head, encouraging me to share.

I swipe at my streaming snot with the back of my hand.

She places a box of tissues before me.

"I'm a mess . . . a fucking . . . utter . . . mess." I whisper the last few words, only to realize I'm oversharing. I look up at her, eyes wide. "I-I didn't mean . . ."

She clasps her veiny hands in her lap. "Sometimes those are the only words that make sense in circumstances like these. Say them loud, get 'em out."

I sniffle. "I've lived in this city my whole life, now everything feels foreign."

"So leave."

"I can't. Not yet, anyway."

"Do you have family nearby?"

I shake my head.

"Are you in school?"

"I'm interning at an ad agency. They don't know any of this."

"Everyone's got stuff."

"I'm pissed off." I sputter more snot and spit everywhere.

She leans forward, dipping her chin. "You should be, baby girl—their deaths are still fresh. Give this roller coaster of grief some time. There's no universal standard for mourning. Everyone's different."

I swallow the ache in my throat. "When they died, we weren't on the best of terms." They were so angry at me. Cody tried to smooth things over . . . but I couldn't let it drop.

She sighs, smiling. "I'm sure they loved you."

"I really hurt them." My voice is on full wobble now.

"Our kids can break our hearts, yet we still love them."

I glance down and fiddle with the hem of my skirt where I ripped the seam with my She-Hulk strides racing to my interview. Girl clothes can be so restricting. I yank on the loose threads, making it worse.

I suck in a slow breath. "My boyfriend also died that night. Struck by a car outside a music store in Westchester. Hit and run. We planned to travel the world together, make it as singer-songwriters. We talked about getting married one day."

I picture the two of us on the lawn in Sheep Meadow in Central Park. Me in a pale blue peasant blouse, Cody wearing my favorite green button-down of his, looking all vintage Abercrombie with his surfer-blond hair, threading daisies through my hair.

Deb blinks a few times but doesn't say anything.

"I have so many regrets from that night. Like I could have done something." My gaze drifts. "If I had, they'd all be alive right now."

"Do they know what caused your parents' accident? Was it a drunk driver?"

"Um, t-they never found the other car. Only tire marks." I roll my fingers into a fist.

"Now you face each day without your mom and dad . . . and your young man."

"Yeah, can anyone be more cursed?" A fever rises up my neck. I dig my nails into my palms, creating half-moons of blood. I hide my hands and swallow, releasing my balled-up breath. The vacant eyes of the old woman from the elevator float into my head, then Rikki's face contorting in fear when the man threatened to burn them. "It's been a day." I blot my lashes with my finger.

Her expectant eyes stare back.

"I shouldn't bother you—"

"Go ahead, bother me. I've got all the time in the world, baby girl."

"It's funny you call me that. My mom . . ." The words get stuck.

A look of recognition registers on her face. "I may be old, but not a day goes by when I don't miss my parents."

I nod along, not wanting to talk about them anymore. Nothing will bring them back. Ever. "Do you have children?"

"One. He's grown, lives in Nevada. I don't see him much."

"Any grandkids?"

Her eyes light up. "Would you like to see a picture?"

I take a long swig of beer, savoring the break. A warm buzz travels down my legs. Cody liked to tease me for being a lightweight.

"Here she is, Georgina. I call her Gina for short."

"She's precious—all those freckles," I gush. "How old?"

Debra looks up to the sky as if calculating. "She's five."

"Does she visit often?"

"Only once. My son's a pilot for American. You'd think I'd see them more." She snorts. "His wife doesn't care for me much."

"I can't believe that. You're so kind and welcoming."

"She doesn't trust me around Gina. When my son was small, I still partied—did some hard drugs, too. Been clean for the last twenty years though. Guess you can say I've been born again."

I eye her beer.

She turns the label to me. "No alcohol in this one." She frowns a little. "Still, booze was never my issue."

I blink. "It's good that you've stayed clean."

She sighs, breaks eye contact. "A few of my friends weren't so lucky." Her voice drops off. "I was a young mom, alone . . . lonely . . . I needed a break. So I'd leave my son with my folks in Park Slope. Come back two or three days later after a binge. His little face would light up when he saw me. He'd come running. No matter what, that little boy loved me." She shakes her head. "One day I left him with my parents for another few days. But that time the few days became a week, then two . . . a year." Her fingers flex in her lap.

I lean in and think about touching her strong, veiny hand, the same one that wrangled the necks of our beers like a bartender's.

Her face falls. "I regret who I was back then . . . what I put him through."

"Does he know how you feel?"

"We're both hard-nosed." Her chin falls. "At least Gina can see me on television."

"I'd give anything to have another day with my parents," I say wistfully. "Tell them about my internship, get their advice. I find this adulting thing rather overwhelming."

Her eyes settle on mine. "You can tell *me*."

Something skips inside my chest and I'm drawn to the etched lines pushing up her high cheekbones and folding in waves on either side of her mouth, each one earned from her colorful life. Her heart, perhaps, strums a lonesome chord like mine.

"I'd like that." But not today. I take a mouthful of beer and then press my lips into a smile. "Tell me more about the good ole days—especially how you met Mick Jagger."

Chapter 12

MICAH

My game's off this morning. My head spins, thick with fog. I was awake all night, and cried at the pink morning sky.

Sleep deprivation wreaks havoc on someone like me. Val's doctor friend said these new meds would slow the Shadow People from parading around in my life. She thinks she knows what's best for me. But I pretend for her too. She'd be crushed if she knew. Val's been the one constant in my life these past four years. She's also a nut job.

I stand taller passing through the agency's glass doors. Each step measured, concealing the knives digging into my skin.

Eunice halts her phone conversation and throws me a look.

I return it with one that shuts her down.

I count my steps to the long table by the far wall, where I lay my bag on my desk chair and slip out my notebook. I release a long breath, ignoring the shadowy figure leaning against the conference room doorway, and step into the room.

"Morning."

The team glances up from their phones for a nanosecond.

Scott often skips our client updates, knowing I can run them. Makes them less formal. This one should be quick. I settle in the seat next to Brynn, facing the door. Best to see if more Shadow People decide to join us.

No one gives me a second look. I exhale and open my notebook.

"My cousin—you know, the one who's a content producer for that new meditation app . . ." Priya's eyes gleam as she entertains the room with another family story. The girl has more relatives than a polygamist.

"The hot mess?" Josie's eyes pop wide as she grins.

Priya smiles. "The very same. She says they get a phenomenal number of clicks advertising with AA and rehab websites, and even breastfeeding moms groups. Meditation enhances milk production, apparently."

"Bingers and lactators." Donovan throws her a wild grin. "Sounds like a party."

"Dentist offices too." She giggles.

He nods. "Cue the micro-drillers."

My eyes bounce around the table. These two will go at it all day if I let them.

Brynn gives me the side-eye.

Shit.

Without drawing attention, I scan myself. Limbs relaxed. Nothing twitching. What's her deal? Go save somebody else. "You have a thought?"

"Several." She turns away.

Guess she caught me laughing at her clumsiness yesterday. Seems she's not afraid of me. Too bad. More fun when they are. And hey, I'm giving this girl a chance to shadow our creative team and maybe learn something. You think she'd attempt a modicum of civility.

Priya stops talking and her cheesy grin expands, as if she knows our new intern is getting under my skin. Priya may play the ingenue, but she's intuitive as hell. This time, though, she's mistaken.

"Growing a beard, Micah?" She taps her index finger on her lips, supporting her elbow.

"Going for the thug look today." I turn the wattage up on my smile to quell her nosiness and ignore Josie's glower over my choice of words. She's our ambassador for political correctness, or whatever they call it.

Brynn's brows knit together.

"Thought I'd start wearing skirts too." I return her askance look.

Her head whips back, sizing me up like I'm the homophobic subway guy from yesterday.

Eunice hovers near the door, her stooped stance not helping her job security. "Max would like to see you after."

I nod, ignoring the same look she gave me when I walked in. "Let's begin." I clear my throat. "Meredith, update us on Bradley Products and Quotagian, if you will."

Val's texts light up my phone.

Talk to your dad yet?
You're being a wuss
Ignoring me won't make it go away
WTF?

I hate when she does this. In Val's world, everything happens in the now. She loathes procrastination.

I silence my phone and wait for Aunt Max to end her call behind Granddad's mahogany desk, accented with solid brass hardware, gilded scrolls, and a growling lion's head at the center of its base. My aunt, the ever-dutiful minion, never bothered to redecorate. A far cry from the Max I knew growing up, the wild '90s skater girl with intelligent eyes and a shrewd face like my grandmother, who once dressed in ripped jeans and layered shirts and crushed hard on Courtney Love. That girl would have taken an axe to this thing a long time ago.

When we lived at Granddad's penthouse, she'd come home after a night out in Brooklyn with her girlfriend Jenna and make pancakes for the two of us. I think she felt sorry for me. One parent dead, the other MIA. Like her father, though, she skirts around my psychosis, pretending it doesn't exist. Kershaws don't do unpleasantness. I let it slide when it comes to her. Granddad can be a handful, and this agency she carries on her back is far heavier than his Victorian desk.

"You wanted to see me?"

"Close the door, have a seat." She motions to the caramel leather settee and rotates her chair toward me, tucking short, dirty-blond strands behind her ears.

I prop up my head on my hand, resting my elbow. "I have another meeting."

She taps a few keys on her computer, not looking at me.

"What's up?" I rub my forehead; this day has already been a shit-show.

"Tell me the last time you visited Granddad."

"I can't remember—why?"

"You should check in. He gets antsy when he doesn't get updates."

"He can ask you the exact same questions."

"Humor him, please. Also, Scott said your team's been under billing these last few months."

I shrug. "They haven't had much work. Reduction in client budgets and lack of new business. I've never been a fan of billable hours. I think it discredits our work."

"Right now, it's how this agency gets *paid*," she says with a sigh. "Got to keep the doors open . . . for Granddad."

"I'll look into it. What else?"

"The beard?"

"Thought I'd try it."

Her hazel eyes study me, her zipped lips fading to white.

She's probably recalling my self-imposed hiatus from taking showers when we lived together. The Shadow People like to get up in my face in close quarters. They start shouting and my claustrophobia ramps up. A feverish heat rips through my body. My chest locks, I can't breathe. I've learned to leave the shower door open and can handle a quick one now. Moving metal boxes like elevators, not so much.

My headache lowers into my eyes. I apply pressure to my temples. "What else?"

Her bottom lip disappears.

I sigh. "Which Kershaw, your dad or mine?"

"I wish those two would start talking to one another and not using me for a mediator."

"Something to do with me?" I already know she'll shake her head to protect me.

"Scott's looking to eliminate a few heads, Micah." She rises. "Tighten up your team."

"Something else is going on too. Spill."

She pauses, closing her mouth before settling into a frown. "It can wait."

Chapter 13

BRYNN

"Show time." Meredith's eyes twinkle. "Donovan, when you're ready."

He pushes back from the oblong white table where the team, including Scott McKenzie, awaits in black-mesh chairs. Not surprising; a vinyl decal with his name is stuck to the entrance door.

Scott carries himself like the next millennial running for president. Besides his startling blue eyes, curly, textured hair, and pretty-boy goatee, the man can dress. When he enters the room, the molecules shift.

Scott turns over his phone. "Okay, let's see what you came up with."

"With such a *unique* product compared to what's on the market today"—Donovan chews his cheek, gesturing to the samples on the table—"our campaign should reflect its inherent strength and playfulness with an active, sporty-girl vibe. Fitness Girl Makeup." He writes the three words across the whiteboard behind him. "Whatever your sport or however you like to train, this makeup lasts through any workout—with SPF protection, of course. Sweat-resistant, won't run or streak or clog your pores. Perfect for active teens and those needing a little inspiration to become more fit."

He arches a brow at Meredith.

What a dick.

"We could feature female athletes in the ads." Lucius leans forward. "Maybe an Olympian like Simone Biles or Lindsey Vonn."

Meredith wrinkles her nose. "I'd go younger."

He rests his elbows on the table. "Sky Brown, the skateboarder from Great Britain, is like fifteen, I think."

Josie picks up a dumbbell. "They're fun. I can see teens bringing them to school and lining them up in their lockers. Go from after-school sports to getting smoothies with friends."

Donovan nods like he's figured it all out. "Young ladies want to look good working out and for their makeup to last. You agree, Meredith, Brynn?"

Meredith doesn't say anything.

I shake my head. "Not everyone wears makeup to work out or play sports."

"This will *inspire* them to, then." He flips his hair out of his eyes.

Meredith turns to Scott. "*Fitness Girl Makeup* lends itself to a lot of possibilities. I also like *Fit Girl Makeup*. What do you think?"

"I-I also came up with some ideas." I gulp the air. My heart beats in my throat.

Donovan's head twists to me then back to Meredith. "I haven't seen them. I have no idea—"

"I just thought . . ." I look at Micah. "You asked us to brainstorm together, I thought that meant . . ."

"It's fine." Micah nods. A slight smile creeps up on his face.

Lucius and Josie snicker at one another.

Uh-oh. My face grows warm.

"Well? Show us what you got, newbie." Donovan yanks back his chair and sits with his arms crossed.

Oh boy. I shift in my seat, staring at my notes. "Um . . . Priya helped me since you were out, Donovan."

Meredith jerks back in her seat. "Out? When were you out?"

Daggers fly from Donovan's eyes in my direction.

Micah sits up straighter. "Scott, this is Brynn, our new intern. She's shadowing our creative team for a couple of weeks."

Scott flips over his phone. "I've got a few more minutes. Let's hear it."

I take a deep breath and rise. Adrenaline courses through my limbs. Here goes.

"Shopping for cosmetics at a store can be intimidating, especially for young people who are new to it and insecure about the process. They don't know where to start or feel like they belong at a makeup counter at all."

Blank stares travel around the table.

My stomach drops.

Priya nods for me to continue.

"I began thinking about the kids at my high school and what I see on social media and on the street. Gender identity goes beyond masculine or feminine. People also live between or outside the binary. Makeup can be a great vehicle for creative expression and gender fluidity. How young people today want to use makeup to express themselves can vary upon the day. There's a need right now for more gender-neutral products."

Scott checks his phone.

"Since people in general use fitness dumbbells, this makeup line could target not just fit *girls*; it could be makeup that fits *everyone*."

I pick up one of the dry erase markers and start writing where Donovan left off.

"FIT Cosmetics. The FIT part could be an acronym like Face. Inclusion. Transformation. Or we could play on the *I* as in *eye*." I point to mine. "Something like: Face. I(Eyes). Transcend—meaning a product that goes beyond gender lines. To help young people feel more comfortable trying out the products, we could have a beauty influencer demonstrate how to use the makeup online. Advise customers how to cover a beard shadow or accentuate one, for example. A cosmetic line for everyone that offers a safe place to get advice without having to approach some model behind a makeup counter."

"Whoa, who *doesn't* enjoy that?" Donovan shoots his hand up.

Meredith rolls her eyes. "I like the inclusive theme. However, focusing only on the trans community limits its reach. Bradley Products wants this mainstream. We shouldn't lose sight of that."

"I'm not saying we only target those who are transgender," I explain. "Cis young men and women as well. I'd use this line if I knew it benefited a larger community outside my own. Most cosmetic packaging can be rather girly. These dumbbells are not. We could capitalize on that. Promote it as makeup for everyone to play with and explore—find strength in being themselves."

"Sounds like another tagline." Micah taps the table in front of him with his index finger. "How do you envision the campaign for this more inclusive line?"

My thoughts stall. He made that crack the other day about wearing a skirt when Priya asked about his beard scruff. Is he being genuine or wanting to poke holes in my idea?

I clasp my shaky hands and clamp my wet armpits to my side. My blouse feels cold against my skin. "I'm not sure—maybe use diverse, gender-fluid models in the ads?"

Priya smiles. "I think that could be beautiful."

I take a breath, clueless if I'm overselling it. At this point, no one's even looking at me.

"The packaging comes in a rainbow of colors, which adds to the focus on inclusivity." I hold the air in my lungs. "It would gain an even wider appeal if we could advertise it as being cruelty-free and made with nontoxic ingredients."

Donovan contorts his face. "Bradley Products can't afford to change its process and formulas now. Can't ask a company to start from scratch. What happened to promoting the product as is? Doing what they hire us to do?"

"Clients also hire us to make them better." Thank you, *Adweek*. I swallow and face Scott and Meredith. "This *is* marketing to the mainstream, depending on your definition of *mainstream*." I exhale and flex my fingers, releasing them from their death grip.

Josie turns over a few of the dumbbells, examining them.

I wave my hand. "They don't have color labels."

Meredith glances at Scott. "They should have them in time for the launch."

He picks up one of the lipsticks, studying it.

I take a sharp inbreath. "What if *we* come up with the color names, ones that convey strength and individuality? Instead of *bubble gum kiss* or something frilly and demeaning, give them more meaningful names to tell customers, *We see you.*"

"I like that." Josie's eyes consider me like we've just met.

Meredith rotates her chair toward Scott. "Do you think Bradley Products would go for it? It'd broaden their customer base."

Scott angles his head away from her.

Micah clears his throat. "We don't want this campaign to appear self-serving. The messaging needs to be authentic." He sends me a look of encouragement and rests an elbow on the back of his chair.

I nod, feeling the heat rise in my cheeks.

Priya raises her finger. "Maybe Bradley Products would consider donating a percentage of the revenue to support the LGBTQ+ community. Might inspire people to change from their favorite brands."

"Wouldn't the messaging be *demeaning* if it suggested our client created this makeup line 'just for you, transsexual boy'?"

Micah flinches. "Try *transgender*, Donovan."

Okay, Micah's more with it than I thought.

Donovan tosses his head. "Yeah, yeah. Whatever."

I wait for someone else to react. This guy can't get away with talking like this.

Scott peers at his phone.

My head whips back to Donovan and in a tone I'd use with a toddler I say, "It would be a makeup line created for all—him, her, *and* them."

Meredith sighs. "The packaging does come off quirky. Why not pitch both ideas?"

Donovan's face stiffens.

Scott slides his eyes from Micah to Meredith. "I appreciate the out-of-the-box thinking. However, asking our new client to dive into the nongender market—"

"Fluid. Gender fluid." I bite my lip.

Priya's eyes bug out.

Meredith throws me an icy look.

"Excuse me. Gender fluid." His nostrils flare. He pulls his cuff from his suit jacket, his large gold watch gleaming. "Though trendy, it's simply not right for this client. Let's present a few variations of the *Fit Girl* idea, clean and wholesome. Lucius, get me art on these by Friday, first thing. I told Bradley Products we'd have comps by Monday. Micah, Meredith, we good?"

They nod, faces impassive.

My bottom lip trembles. I look down, mash my lips together, and try not to cry.

Chapter 14

MICAH

I hang back by Priya's workspace, waiting for her to return so I can give her Scott's changes on the media budget for Bradley Products.

Brynn, two seats down from her, slumps in her chair, her eyes shooting bullets at her computer screen.

Meredith stands gathering her stuff at the other long table facing us. She throws her red leather Tory Burch bag over her shoulder and eyes Brynn. "Don't take it to heart. You're still learning and every client's different. Sometimes the creative misses the mark."

Brynn pushes back her chair. "He wasn't willing to give it a chance."

Josie stops beside Meredith and rolls her eyes at Brynn. "You weren't even supposed to present. Be grateful they let you speak."

Meredith shakes her head. "You still have the Quotagian campaign. By the way, the team is going to the Playwright Irish Pub for happy hour and a little team bonding." Meredith walks over to her. "You coming?"

Brynn glowers at Josie. "I'll pass." She wheels herself back in.

"You should go." Meredith digs for something in her purse. "Other teams will be there. Interns are expected to show."

Brynn's eyes dart between Josie and Meredith like she's a trapped animal.

"We'll go over together, the place is a couple blocks from here." Meredith nudges her chair. "Gives me a chance to bestow more of my great advertising knowledge on you."

Three days in and the new girl has managed to melt Meredith's igloo? Impressive.

She fared better than I expected presenting her ideas to Scott and the entire team. No intern has ever done that. It took me weeks to summon the courage to speak up in a Scott meeting. She doesn't get intimidated. And now Meredith's acting like she actually wants her around.

I sigh, shaking my head. I guess I have to go to this thing too, dammit. I was looking forward to writing tonight.

The combination of beer and fried food assaults my senses when I duck under the Major League Soccer banner strung across the entrance of Playwright's. Zoe and the other interns are gathered at one of the high-top tables, deep in conversation, their glittery nails wrapped around cocktails.

Zoe elbows the girl next to her. Their eyes swing over to me.

Brynn sits alone at the far end of the bar, flattening her white straw wrapper with her fingertips. She glances up at one of the TVs. She folds her wrapper into tiny squares.

Where's Meredith?

I signal to the bartender. It takes him a minute to respond; his attention is fixed on the match. I slide onto a barstool alongside several patrons wearing the same striped scarf around their necks.

Zoe makes a face, gesturing behind Brynn's back. Her cohorts laugh.

If our newest intern disappears before her two weeks are up, Meredith will never let me live it down.

I count the liquor bottles lined up across the mirrored bar. Twice. My heart gallops like I'm about to deliver a speech in front of the entire bar. I grab my lowball and plant myself next to Brynn, bumping my knee into her. Real smooth.

She jerks back.

I avoid her face. "How did your first week go?"

She acts like she doesn't hear me. She eyes my glass. "Vodka?"

"Evian. Lucky us, the underage ones." I raise my glass to clink hers.

She sips her water instead. "Zoe and the other interns too."

"I'm certain this place will serve you. Want me to get the bartender?"

She shakes her head, squeezing the end of her straw.

A long minute passes.

I watch the TV like I care about soccer, my fingers tapping SOS in Morse Code on my glass. "How do you find working with Meredith?"

"Fine." She shrugs.

"The others on your team?"

"Okay."

"One-word answers, nice. I told you it'd be a lot of grunt work."

She sighs and her brows furrow like I'm bothering her.

"I liked your presentation. You seem to have a knack for it."

"I don't have much time to prove myself. And I'm not sure everyone here wants me to succeed."

I nod. Her ideas took the group by surprise. Especially Donovan.

She straightens her back and gives me the side-eye. "So, what do you have against senior citizens?"

Ah, so you do remember me from the elevator. "Yeah, about that . . . I was running late that morning, jetlagged, and um . . . and a bit distracted." I tap my temple. Not sure why. "Whatever happened to the old lady?"

She pulls a thread off her sleeve and turns her eyes to me. Her plum-colored blouse sets her amber eyes aglow.

I forget my question.

"I helped her to a bench in the lobby and asked the security guard to keep an eye out while I got her some water. She told us she was waiting for her son who worked in the building. I stayed with her but no one showed. A Silver Alert came across the security guard's phone, and he called the number."

"A what?"

"Like an Amber Alert for senior citizens. If they have Alzheimer's or another form of dementia, they can wander off and go missing."

"Never heard of it. Guess I have those notifications blocked." I chuckle.

"We registered my grandmother."

I wince. Of course you did. "Her son must have been worried."

Her face pinches. "He died in one of the towers on 9/11. She searches for him in high-rise offices all over the city. Rides elevators to the top floors to warn him."

Damn. I swirl the liquid in my glass. "She must be exhausted."

Brynn pulls a face like I'm an a-hole. "Her aide arrived frantic. They were outside of Macy's, admiring one of the window displays, when she disappeared."

A thunder of cheers erupts, vibrating our drinks on the bar. The soccer fans pump their fists toward the television. The roar escalates.

Without thinking I wrap my arm around the back of Brynn's stool and cover my ear with my other hand.

She holds hers too, ducking her head and cringing.

The bartender quiets the fans down so he can hear the commentators.

I swivel in my seat, retrieving my arm without her noticing. "I see Meredith and the rest of our team in the back there."

"Yeah, I know."

I swig my water, smiling a little. I order us two more. "I've got to say . . . I wouldn't have stopped to help that old lady. I'd never make it to work with all the people on the street asking for a handout. Cynical, I guess."

She stares into space. "That could be any one of us, someday."

Donovan jumps between us, his eyes all over Brynn. "You two want to go to Walter's in Chelsea?"

She wrinkles her nose.

"The whole team's going. Come on, team player. I'll forgive you this one time for calling me out in front of Scott and Meredith today."

"Unpaid intern, no funds." Brynn rounds her fingers into a zero.

"We'll spot you."

"No thanks."

He throws up his hands and spins back toward Zoe's table.

"You're new." I glance over my shoulder. "He can be a bit of a jerk, but he's acting even more obnoxious than usual around you. He must want you to like him." I look at her, waiting for her to nod or something.

The bar's volume grows muffled.

She turns to me, forehead creased, lips parted.

Did she ask a question?

The air thickens with stale beer and humidity like the air-conditioning's off. My hands grow cold with sweat. A haze falls. Grayish figures rise from the floor, pointing gnarled fingers in my face, their eyes burrowing into mine.

I squint, faking a yawn. A scorching sensation hikes up the back of my neck. I can't get enough air in my lungs. I've got to get out of here.

I place a tip on the bar. "Most of us aren't that bad. I hope you enjoy your time at the agency."

She glances away.

Something falls inside my chest. It touches down to the lowest depth. Pushes off from the bottom of a swimming pool, kicking and flailing to expedite its ascent to the surface. My lungs burn for air.

I spring to my feet and exit the bar before ugly words fly from my mouth. A geyser shoots down the back of my dress shirt; my eyes boil.

Too much adrenaline is pumping through my ears for me to wait on a cab. I dash across the intersection. Horns blast. I switch direction. Herald Square. Nothing looks familiar. All at once, I'm lost.

There. The subway entrance. I pass it. Must get downtown. Recalculating course. Traffic lights swirl in glowing balls of color then snake around in hypnotic spirals. I blink, they reverse direction. Their serpentine coils screw into my forehead, gripping my skull.

I stare down the Shadow People approaching, counting heads. I need to outpace them. Conceal my unhinged state. Not give them the upper hand.

A couple begins to follow me. With every step, they diminish the distance between us. They strut in my blind spot, their soles smacking the pavement. I sense their urgency. I pick up the pace. Let them push me forward.

I glance over my shoulder.

One of them steps out wide. A female my age. She wears a black camisole, cutoff shorts, and a flannel tied at her hips. The Woman in Black.

My chest relaxes. We cross paths often. Early on, before I understood that only I could see her, she'd appear mainly at night. I once thought she worked or lived nearby because I never saw her go inside a building. Now she's a regular participant in my world.

She smiles.

I smile back. I get the feeling she's shy. She doesn't intimidate me like the other Shadow People. I wonder where she goes, whom she sees. What does she think about when she sees me? Do I comfort her in the way she comforts me?

I turn back. Say something. Maybe I'll start with *hello*; how bad could it be?

She's too quick. Escapes my line of sight. Her favorite game.

Her menacing henchman aims for me—narrowing the sidewalk between us, constricting the air in my lungs.

He reaches me first.

How am I going to fight him off alone on the street?

I must shake off the fear. None of this is real; it's only my head, having one of its more colorful field trips.

In my mind, I summon the line of whitecoats, the team of experts assigned to help me. They frown at my sixteen-year-old self.

Only one of them smiles. Dr. Val sits in a different chair than the rest of them. Hers has a motor. I decide right then to forget the others, to focus only on whatever comes out of her mouth. Like how to make the Shadow People fade.

I inhale automobile exhaust mixed with the stench of urine and wet garbage lining the curb for six consecutive one-one-thousands, exhale for another six, and repeat the sequence.

John. Paul. Ringo. George.

Too easy.

Alvin. Simon.

My urgent stride downgrades to a medium stroll.

Theodore. Got it.

Kim. Khloé. Kendall. Kylie.

I blank on the oldest sister's name, the little one with the annoying vocal fry. I run through every K name I can think of. Nothing.

The pulsating blood in my ears slows its tempo; my fever cools, leaving my shirt damp. My broken brain sputters to a dull finality. The sound of the Woman in Black's combat boots gets swallowed up by a passing taxi, then another.

I smile like I always do. I'm good, never better.

Before I can reach the next corner, the Woman in Black floats up beside me and loops her arm through mine.

Chapter 15

BRYNN

I ditch team bonding night soon after Micah leaves. Something about him unsettles me. Not his khaki eyes or the way his sculpted fingers strum the side of his glass. The way he acts. The guy insinuates I hate everyone at the agency, then bolts. *"Most of us aren't that bad. I hope you enjoy your time at the agency."*

I barely pull my thoughts together and he runs out. Why bother if you don't care what I have to say?

I catch the F train downtown while my head stacks with excuses of why I didn't stay at Meredith's table tonight. For one, I don't have the money to keep up with them. Second, having to be *on* with people drains me. Ironic, since my parents never left a party early. They could bend anyone's ear, from the moody Grand Union checkout lady to the taxi driver with the shifty eyes in the rearview mirror. Have them grinning, their faces animated, in minutes. Not me. I piss off people the second I open my mouth, like with Donovan today. I need to prove I can play nice. Be team-player Brynn.

I didn't always act this way. I used to be social, had two best friends. Tess and I met when we auditioned for LaGuardia in eighth grade. Along came Lucy, and we started calling ourselves the BLT.

Then sophomore year happened.

It began in the doorway of Dr. Kendrick's homeroom. My heart airlifted out of my chest at the sight of Cody Waters, a California surfer type with twinkling green eyes and sun-kissed blond hair that swooped to the side and dipped below his chin.

He seemed oblivious to how everyone was staring.

Some snickered at the leather messenger bag slung over his shoulder, which made it look like he'd just stepped off a yacht circling the Greek Isles and not off a subway with a sooty film on his skin, like the rest of us city kids.

Dr. Kendrick passed Cody his new student paperwork and I became enraptured watching the pen thread through his fingers, his strong hand bracing the paper. I daydreamed about those digits tracing the length of me.

We both auditioned that spring for LaGuardia's school musical. By then I'd practiced ignoring him and steering clear of his fluttering flock. In addition to his highly pleasing looks, the boy could stream magic from his lips. His rich, throaty voice and unique tone made him a standout. Next to him, everyone else's talent dimmed.

Our last performance junior year, Cody's finale propelled the audience to its feet. Mr. Prescott, our musical director, declared it the longest ovation in our school's history.

The curtain closed and throngs of our classmates surrounded him, nibbling for a morsel of that magic.

His bottle-green eyes searched over the tops of their heads and found my face.

We fell hard, we fell fast, with an intensity that eclipsed everything in my life before him. I'd never felt more alive and filled with possibility than I did in Cody's orbit. He was rocketing for the stars, and I wanted whatever galactic leftovers fell my way.

Like that, BLT lost their B—so instantaneous it gave Tess and Lucy whiplash. But I was too wrapped up in Cody to care.

I get home to the coffin and kick off my shoes. I strip off my mother's blouse and the black dress pants I wore in all my LaGuardia performances. I pick up the long T-shirt that's still tangled in my sheet on the floor and slip it over my head.

Tess and Lucy would have laughed at this place. Neither of them even speak to me now, especially Tess. What happened senior year cemented that we'd never be friends again.

What was I supposed to do? My parents and Cody were gone.

I open the fridge and pull out a bag of baby carrots and hummus. My daily cuisine these days. I'm going to turn into a carrot. I should have let someone from my team buy me food at the pub tonight. It's the least they can do since I'm working for free.

God, I need this job to work out.

The stained dome light above, filled with dead flies, flickers then turns off—along with the air-conditioning. Great, power's out. Yet again. Walking conversations on Bleecker fill my ears, the sound of a large truck revs in the distance.

I fist up my hands, gritting my teeth.

I yank on the fridge door and return the food to the shelves untouched.

I lie back on my mattress, knowing I'm in for another long night.

This wasn't supposed to be my life.

Cody and I had a chance at making it. We planned to sing all over the country, and one day the world.

Summer before our senior year, we were on a mission, writing new songs together at his family's studio apartment on the Upper West Side. His parents spent the majority of the year in the Cayman Islands for his dad's job. Mine lived at the Flaming Flamingo. In between fooling around, we composed and harmonized as he played guitar.

Cody dazzled me with his stories of performing on the road from Maine down to Florida. His band in Elmsford had gained a following and was headed on tour.

Lounging together in bed, he announced the band's new name for the tour: CB Drunken Waters. I told him how cute it sounded putting our initials together, then I kissed him.

Will you join us, Brynn? he asked. *I need you there.*

We're not going to finish high school? My parents will flip. What about college?

We'll light up the night sky together, Brynn.

Going on the road meant living together. I knew that wouldn't fly with my dad.

It didn't stop us.

Not long after that conversation, I hit my parents with this new plan—including the fact that I wouldn't be applying to schools in the fall, arguing that since they'd spent my college fund bailing out their precious club, I might as well have a go at a musical career first.

They didn't appreciate the guilt trip.

You going on the road feels like losing our first baby girl all over again, Mom said.

Geez, I'm not dead, Mom.

Later after I cooled off, I told myself they'd come around in time.

Then . . . time ran out.

The air in the apartment clunks on, along with the overhead light. Its brightness forces me to shield my eyes.

We'll light up the night sky together, Brynn.

Chapter 16

MICAH

The cold water cramps my gut the more I chug. My mouth's like a cotton ball. I push aside my glass, lean into the kitchen sink, turn on the water, and tilt the kitchen nozzle into my mouth. My phone buzzes behind me on the island, where a much younger version of my dad and Aunt Max used to eat breakfast.

Less than a minute—got to be a new record. I slide the back of my hand across my mouth. "Music Man, thought I missed you."

From photographs, I can piece together the few memories I have of being on the road with my dad and when I began calling him Music Man. Like the time I was hospitalized with a fever in the Philippines and when I met his parents and younger sister, my Aunt Max, in New York for the first time.

The Music Man played Madison Square Garden that night and some woman in a uniform put me to bed in the guest room down the hall from Aunt Max.

I couldn't sleep, missing the lull of my dad's guitar. The next day, I searched for his things but they'd disappeared. I remember crying, thinking he'd died.

He'd only gone on tour.

Looking back, I should have asked more questions when Granddad started calling me *Son*.

"Micah? I can hardly hear you. The guys keep messing with the guitars onstage."

I sit at the island, my limbs heavy. "Move to a quieter space."

"You go, girl! You can put that over there." He slips a smile into his voice, probably for one of his roadies.

I rub my eyes. "*Dad . . .*"

"Okay, okay. Take a chill pill."

A door closes.

"What's crack-a-lackin', my main man?"

"I wanted to hear your voice." My throat tightens.

"Crank up the tunes, fool." He cackles like a smoker with the warmth of smoldering embers. "Been taking your meds?" he asks, his tone suddenly hushed.

"Yes, though . . . some days . . ." I swallow the golf ball rolling up my throat.

"The docs said this could happen, remember? You're still growing, your body's changing." He laughs. "How tall are you now?"

"Six one."

"Well, you passed me. How's it going staying at the old homestead?"

"Quiet." But my ears still ring from last night's soccer fans. I couldn't settle after walking back here—my mind was still at the bar. "Dad, those dreams have returned where I'm somebody else and I feel, I don't know, all peaceful inside. Then I wake up and I'm the same guy who brought this bad shit into everyone's lives. What if this doesn't work?"

"You and your wild imagination. Remember filling up all those notebooks, asking me to send you more? While other kids read stories, you *envisioned* them."

If only I could live someone else's story. "I don't know how much longer—"

"Give it a few more weeks. Then call Dr. Barnes to change your dosage. She warned us it'd be trial and error until we got the right cocktail in you. Hell, if you'd stop growing, maybe these meds would have a chance to work on that thick head of yours." He chuckles.

"Dad—"

"Hey." His voice goes gentle. "Is it too much, Mic? Let me know and I'll fly you back there. Say the word."

Brynn's face flashes in my head. Our lowly intern would laugh hearing her boss whine to his daddy, my carefully crafted façade obliterated.

I squeeze my forehead. Why do I bother?

A group of high school kids passes by the window facing MacDougal.

One walks backward, leading the pack. He wears sunglasses too large for his face and an open Hawaiian shirt. With his chin raised and shoulders back, he shouts something.

His crew doubles over in laughter.

A suitcase filled with rocks rests on my chest. I used to be that kid, a leader among my friends. Now I'm just an empty shell.

My dad speaks to someone off to the side.

My cue. I shouldn't burden him with this. When did I become such a basket case?

"I can wait and see if it gets better." My vision blurs.

"Atta boy, Harmonica."

I sniffle, blinking. "God . . . you haven't called me that in . . . I don't know how long."

"Your mom, so convinced you'd be a girl; she picked out that name and wanted to call you *Monica* for short."

I muster the energy to play along. "I know, and when I came out—hello, baby boy on deck, watch out for that thing! And Monica became Micah."

"Your mom would have approved. Or called you Joe. Whichever one." He cackles. "I'm . . . I have to get back. They're buggin'." He laughs like I'm in on the joke.

"*Dad—*"

My phone goes quiet.

I fling it on the counter and drag myself to the yellow couch in the living room, pulling the cotton blanket over me. The same old dull ache rises inside my chest. Still I pretend. I like to picture him here—slinging an arm over my shoulder, assuring me in the same whispery voice he uses when discussing my psychosis that this monster inside will one day discover a new body to inhabit.

What Dad makes time for I see as distractions. Interruptions from his eager fans and endless handlers, working like dogs to fulfill his needs so everyone gets paid.

Dad thrives on it. Keeps us from sharing anything real. He doesn't like to dwell on the less glamorous part of his life. Doctors, experimental treatments, and a deranged son can be a real buzzkill.

I can count on one hand the number of times I've seen him in the past two years.

In high school, before the Shadow People came around, my close friends were my brothers—their moms and dads my surrogate parents.

I've always been good at rewriting my story. I've had no choice.

Chapter 17

DAHLIA

I flip my Falcon Messenger cap off my head, landing it on the table in front of Teddy where he sits with his feet up outside of Caffé Dante. "Ta-da! Your turn."

His dark, silky curls bob to something playing on his phone, my off-brand earbuds he borrowed a month ago in his ears.

I plop down next to him in one of the cream-colored wicker chairs.

He doesn't acknowledge my presence.

Back in middle school, this place was an Italian coffeeshop. The barista once comped our coffees and slipped us free muffins when the tattered dollars and change in our pockets failed to cover the bill. Teddy and I felt like grownups coming here.

Dante's looks fancier now, serves booze, and has a real menu. They hired us after we graduated high school last spring. Soon Teddy will head to our other job, the one I just came from—delivery person extraordinaire for Falcon Messenger.

I attempt to snatch his phone. A cruel memory from another night I tried to take Teddy's phone floats in my head. I stuff it back down.

"Knock it awff!" He twists his broad shoulders away.

I've always found that thick Yonkers accent of his endearing.

"Lunch slow?" I sigh. The West Village regulars, like the rest of the people in this city, swap the sweltering streets and garbage and human excrement stink for sandy beaches this time of year. Another reason why we also work at Falcon Messenger and take shifts at The Duplex on Christopher Street. "I need that shirt on you for tonight."

Teddy drops his feet and straightens up. "Gawd, bad enough we gotta work these jobs. Now we're sharin' uniforms?"

"Good thing we wear the same size." I smirk. In length, at least. I grew up lanky, with long baby giraffe legs adding to my awkwardness. Dishwater-blond hair. Green eyes. Sometimes called cute. Never pretty.

Teddy, meanwhile, is cut like an athlete, with Sicilian skin and dark, thick lashes.

What's with the heavy breathing? A white puff ball of a dog with beady black-licorice eyes stares at me from the woman's lap at the next table. I stick out my tongue at the offender.

It licks its nose and resumes its serenade of panting.

I longed for a dog growing up. A companion that would give me the unconditional love I craved. I didn't grow up having a mom—not after the police took me away from her as a baby—and I never stayed long enough with any of my foster families to know what that kind of love felt like. I was never good at making friends at school, either. As a child of an alcoholic, it takes me longer to pull my thoughts together. Made me an easy target for bullies when I got to elementary school. I'd hold my breath until I got dizzy, just to not say something stupid. I nearly passed out once.

One day at recess, a skinny towheaded kid in my grade told the meanies if they messed with me, they'd have to go through him first. Everyone liked Cody, the smiley kid with the silly voices who could make everyone laugh. They listened to him.

I stuck by his side after that. And that same year, when Teddy's uncle went to jail for killing someone and he had no other relatives to live with, we invited him to play with us. The three of us became fast friends—in time, a family.

The white puff ball on the woman's lap indulges in a healthy yawn.

I eye the platinum credit card poking out from her napkin as she signs the check. I hate running down the street after customers.

She gives me the stink-eye and slides the card closer to her.

I've served the couple seated at the next table, dressed in workout clothes and sharp kicks, a few times. Newly dating. Polite. Not great tippers, but at least they leave something. I take what I can get to afford my voice and guitar lessons.

One time a customer ordered a spring water and left me a twenty under her glass. A crisp fall day. Nothing like today's icky stickiness. When I lifted the glass, the twenty blew onto the chair. That rascal floated to the sidewalk. Next thing I knew, my tip was lying in the middle of MacDougal Street. I rushed to retrieve it, pausing for passing cars. By the time I made it to where it landed, it was gone. My heart sank in my chest.

"Here, you lost this."

I turned, my eyes glazing over the twenty in his hand and up the muscular arm of the guy in jeans and a T-shirt beside me. His thick brown hair was wet and uncombed, his scent like fresh woodchips in Central Park.

I opened my mouth to thank him.

"Coffee to go," he barked like a drill sergeant, before I could get the words out.

He followed me inside while I prepared his order. He talked to himself the whole time, his dark eyebrows dancing through every thought.

"Are you rehearsing lines or something?" The guy being an actor made perfect sense—those velvet brown eyes, that strong Roman nose.

He pulled a face and continued whispering to himself.

Hmm, maybe a method actor? What a strange dude. I glanced down at his credit card. MICAH KERSHAW.

I saw him the second time while wiping down tables outside. He exited one of the Easter egg–colored row houses across the street, again in deep conversation with himself. He belonged to the lavender one, my favorite color, located just two doors down from where Bob Dylan once lived. I can't even.

I spotted him a few weeks later on a delivery for Falcon Messenger at one of the ad agencies in midtown. He must work there. Duh, Kershaw McKenzie. He didn't see me, but I sure saw him. This time dressed like a member of an '80s pop band, skinny tie and tapered pants showing off his well-defined legs. His eyebrows were still jigging up and down but his lips were pulled tight. To rein in all that self-whispering, I imagined.

A flower delivery van interrupts my daydream while more cars stop and go, waiting to turn onto Houston. At a break, my eyes slide up to the lavender house, longing for a glimpse.

Nope. Just dudes whistling and hollering as they pass. They make life look easy.

Take the ringleader in his square, oversize shades and Hawaiian shirt. He trips over his blinged-out Nikes and the other boys bend over in hysterics. Kids from rich families have no idea how good they have it. A far cry from Teddy's and my childhood.

Teddy yanks out an earbud. "Dahl, you gotta stop posting those videos from freshman year."

"I know, I'm being stupid. I just loved that show. Cody sounded amazing."

"So did you. Even with the dyed hair, *Gabriella*." He winks, his gap-toothed grin stuck on me.

I bat my eyes. "Oh, stop."

His smile fades. "So . . . I called Silas. Wanted to talk, ya know. What the news said and all. He assured me St. Ignatius was handling it."

I whistle through my teeth. "Silas said we shouldn't keep bringing up that night." I keep my voice low.

"I'm not. Just with you. Coffee?" His dark, feathery lashes sweep toward the espresso bar inside.

I shake my head.

"Ya sure?"

A woman laughs walking alongside a man. Maybe in their forties and holding hands, they stroll toward us in black jeans and T-shirts with the sleeves cut off, revealing toned arms and tats from their necks to their fingers. They look like two musicians coming offstage.

I freeze in my seat.

Their bodies touch as they walk. I imagine Katia and Basilio Gallardo to be like that, though I never met them.

"Sup?" Teddy follows my gaze.

"Ghosts." I massage the pain atop my breastbone, squeezing in and out from nipple to nipple with every new breath.

He grimaces. "You wigging out? Not sure I can handle this right now."

"Yeah, well, you didn't kill three people." My voice rises. I wince.

He looks away, shaking his head.

I fish a piece of Nicorette gum out of my bag.

He rolls his eyes. "Not again."

I clench my jaw, chewing. "Ever wonder how much *she* knows about what happened that night?"

"Ya mean Cody's girlfriend? Yeah, I do."

"She didn't even come to the funeral. Who does that?"

"Call it effed up."

My eyes well up picturing Cody, his smile brighter than Rockefeller Center's Christmas tree. He treated me like I was his favorite person on earth. He should be with us now. I blow my nose into a napkin.

White puff ball barks.

"God, I miss him."

"Always will." Teddy stares off, his brows slope downward.

"Sometimes I wake up at night and I hear them. Their screams."

He puts up a hand, stopping me. "We did what we had to do, Dahl. Like Silas said, 'They never believe people like us. That's how it is.'"

"I know." I look away, tasting the tears in my throat. "Thank god for Silas."

"Yeah, thank gawd."

Chapter 18

BRYNN

Meredith's resting her butt on my desk, her Tory Burch bag under her arm, when I arrive Monday morning.

"What's up?" I slip my no-name backpack purse off my shoulders.

She swipes up on her phone. "Give me your number. I'll text you after we meet with Bradley Products."

A phone. Right. "Um, my screen broke. I'm getting it repaired."

"God, you must be dying."

I nod, though I haven't had a phone in months.

"Okay. I'll fill you in when I return. I also need to see your Quotagian ideas. Donovan's not in yet."

"The app for literary romantics, right." I click on said file and stare at the empty page. "It would be easier to write a song." I sigh.

"What's that?" She leans back on my desk.

"How about a jingle?"

"Yeah, no. This client doesn't have the budget." She glances up at Scott walking down the floating stairs. "'Kay. I'll find you after."

Lucius rises, his leather backpack over his shoulder. He gives me a little wave. His dark eyes linger on me for a long moment before he turns away.

Strange Donovan's not going with them to present his *Fit Girl* idea.

Donovan arrives a half hour later, wearing a pressed button-down and khakis with dress shoes.

I look up from my laptop. "They left for Bradley Products already."

"I can see that." He glares, eyes bloodshot, acting like the venti-size coffee in his hand hasn't kicked in yet.

"Meredith wants our ideas for Quotagian. Have you started?"

"I'll get to it." He rubs his temple.

"She sounds like she wants our ideas today," I press. "It'll go faster if we brainstorm together."

Donovan crinkles his Cro-Magnon brow at me. "I call writing love letters to a prospective hookup working too hard."

I pull a face. "Creative intelligence can be sexy. Like composing a love song or creating a painting for someone."

"I don't know one guy who does either of those things to get laid."

"Well, I know a few." I smile at my screen like I have a bevy of artistic admirers tucked away somewhere. Timmy McGillicuddy in kindergarten once conveyed his feelings for me through a crayon rendering of the two of us holding a heart. Big mistake. I liked to brawl back in the day.

Donovan's eyes roll back. "You do it then. I've got more important things to deal with."

"Anything wrong?"

"Nothing I'm going to tell you." His jaw tightens as he reads something on his phone.

"Nice," I mutter. I hate this guy.

I watch him leave through the metal screens toward the lobby. Hope he's dressed for an interview. He sure doesn't work much. Five short days ago he sounded like he enjoyed it here. *Yes, Meredith, I'd be happy to train for Donovan's job. And his paycheck.*

I smile to myself and head over to the *Little Shop of Horrors* plant wall for my free coffee and a bagel or two.

I'm almost there when blue-haired Zoe, wearing a peacock-inspired A-line dress straight out of the '60s, steps into my path.

I blink a few times, adjusting to the sensory overload.

"Oh, hey, Brynn." Her eyes flick over to another intern who's standing by the coffee machine. I've never met her, but I see the two of them palling around a lot. The girl grins at Zoe like she knows what she'll say next and ignores me.

"Hi." I take a step back.

Zoe folds her arms over her fowl dress. "Heard you presented to Scott. I'm curious how that came about."

"Just trying to get hired." I shrug.

"Other interns have been at this agency longer than you."

I squint hard. "Meaning?"

"Not fair they let you present creative in your first week when the rest of us are still getting coffee and cleaning conference rooms."

My head jerks back. "Not *my* problem. Like I said, I'm looking to stay on here. Maybe get a copywriter position."

She scoffs. "Good luck with that."

Echoes of freshman year, when girls like Zoe accused me of taking roles away from them, flood my mind. I grit my teeth, working up a good comeback.

She zips down another row of workstations.

Coward.

I walk back to my printer desk, a coffee with oat milk in one hand and a bagel in the other.

Inside a conference room, Priya leans her shoulder on one of the glass walls, her feet and arms crossed. Donovan stands inches from her face, speaking rapidly. She frowns and nods.

They must be close. She did buzz out of here when I told her he'd left the other day; bet she met up with him.

At least she's nice enough to me—so far, anyway. Between Donovan and Zoe, I've already managed to form a couple of enemies after one week here.

Sounds about right.

Since Donovan's clearly not going to help me, I need to work harder and prove to Micah and Meredith I can do this.

Josie walks by my desk, looking at her phone and fingering the silver hoop in her septum. She pivots to her workstation at the other table, where Meredith and Lucius sit. I detect her gum chewing from the way her scalp moves where her head's shaved. Her cell chimes and she lifts her eyes in my direction.

"Brynn, Meredith just sent a text: '*Great meeting. Asking for a 3rd spec. @Tropical question mark flavor.*'"

"Um, anything nondairy." Hm, that's unexpected but still cool. Wait. "A third spec? I thought they went to present only Donovan's idea."

"'Bout time this agency became more inclusive. Even if the patriarchy doesn't agree." She sighs and disappears behind her monitor, the tips of her hair still bopping.

Meredith breezes in thirty minutes later carrying three large smoothies. "Good news." She passes me the one with an X over an illustrated cow's head.

My stomach bubbles over with glee. I love food surprises, especially free ones.

She puts her drink on her desk. "Let me pull in Micah. Donovan here, Josie?"

Josie's eyes track across the room to the long table next to the exposed brick wall where Micah usually sits. She flips a hand in that direction. "Micah's around. Haven't seen Donovan since this morning."

Meredith types something on her phone. A minute later, Micah exits from one of the far conference rooms and heads our way.

I enjoy a long sip of my kiwi and strawberry concoction, suppressing the urge to gape at how his navy dress pants hug his quads and his white button-down tapers at his waist. And don't even get me started on his dark Harvard-meets-rocker hair. My pulse quickens as he nears.

"We have a direction change on the Bradley Products account." Meredith's face lights up. "They'd like to see a combination of both ideas."

I stare at her. "Wait, you presented my concept?"

She grins. "Micah pushed Scott to let Lucius mock up both, like I'd suggested. Thank goodness we did. *Fit Girl* came off pedestrian, you could see it in their eyes. Marketing it as a gender-fluid line made them uneasy but they definitely found it interesting and said they'd consider it. They requested to see more specs before making a final decision."

My breath catches. Micah's trying to help me?

He reaches out his hand.

For a split second, I imagine him touching me. My cheeks heat up. I drop my eyes.

He fist-bumps Meredith. "Nice work."

His smooth, well-groomed fingers return to his hip. He dips his chin, his soft brown eyes on me. "You have good instincts. Keep going."

"Um, thanks?"

Meredith shoots me frosty eyes like I'm some ungrateful child.

An inconvenient warmth spreads across my neck and chest. Without looking, I know I'm getting blotchy. I open my mouth but words fail me.

He moves his head a fraction. "Appreciate the update." He does a swift about-face.

My gaze follows his erect posture, the way his shoulders swag when he walks. Moths flutter in my belly, lots of them, sending tingles through my legs.

Meredith's fingertips touch my arm.

I jump.

"Micah's got a million things going on." She gives me a knowing look. "If he likes it, that's good. He's intuitive and good with the clients and knows what the partners at Kershaw McKenzie want."

"Donovan called him aloof."

She laughs. "Because he's jealous of the guy. Don't be deceived by his age—Micah's sort of a wunderkind. I find him difficult and pretty snarky most days. But he's got a shrewd eye for design and more so for copy. If he helps us keep our jobs, more power to him."

Chapter 19

MICAH

Long-distance relationships never last. First her Wi-Fi lost connection. Then her mic wouldn't work. Now everything's a go and Dr. Val's putzing around while I wait for our session to start. Telehealth, my ass; more like tele*hell*, being forced to discuss my many defects.

I reposition my laptop on the surfboard-shaped coffee table, a mid-century Scandinavian find of my grandmother's. After Granddad moved uptown, he'd pull me away from video games to go with him to check on this house. I used to play in this living room, running my LEGO space rover along the table's chevron inlay, conjuring up new worlds.

I stare at the pristine birch logs in the fireplace, same ones since my grandparents divorced, and drop a long sigh.

"Pa-tience, Mi-cah." Dr. Val speaks slowly, pronouncing every syllable. She clears her throat and pushes up the bridge of her glasses with her bird hand.

I would never say that to her face. But her frozen hand—straight fingers fused together, bent wrist—really does remind me of a bird's head.

She squints at her screen, smacking her lips.

She's killing me today.

"Things cook-ing swell by you?" She grins, her eyes turned skyward.

I rub my temples, trying to stave off a headache. "I don't appreciate the bullshit about my dad."

"I'm not the one a-fraid to dis-a-ppoint him."

"He likes that I'm better. Keep it at that." I clench my teeth.

"Still the poor lit-tle eight-year-old, left to live at Grand-dad's pent-house. Boo-hoo."

"I don't need this." I slide my fingers on the touchpad.

"Don't run a-way yet. Let's start a-gain. What's shak-ing?" Her bird hand moves her carrot-colored bangs out of her eyes. Those are new. She's still getting used to them.

I sigh again, twisting my lips.

"Con-vin-cing you are not." She juts out her bottom lip.

"Okay . . . um, the stress at work brought on some episodes."

"How do you man-age them?"

"Taking long walks . . . using pop culture to distract myself. Getting strange looks on the street when I tell the Shadow People to back off."

She giggles. "Lots of peo-ple in New York talk to them-selves." Her arm jerks to the side. She pulls it back into her lap with her other hand and leans into her headrest, grinning clear up to her gums.

Behold the happiest person on the planet. I find it annoying.

"I debated telling you . . . I dreamt about killing her again."

"Oh, boy . . . was go-ing to ask a-bout how you're sleep-ing. Let's hear this one." Her eyes dance. I bet she'd rub her palms together if she could.

"We're on a train. She's in her usual black attire, hiding on the floor from me, surrounded by other passengers. I'm crazed, out of my head, wielding a gun. The fear in her face . . . it's so real. Then I'm this Neo-Nazi and she—"

"Has a yel-low star on her jac-ket?" Her left eye stalls on the ceiling, the other one dips right.

"Something like that. I think the dream turned into a school shooting."

"Watch-ing the news again. You have-n't dreamt of your mom in a whi-le. What brought this on?"

I trace the table's chevron pattern with my index finger. "I don't know . . . someone new at work."

"Ooh, do tell."

"I won't pursue it."

"Ah, to give your heart a-way."

"Nowhere close to that." I sit back, crossing my arms. "And not the best circumstances."

"They ne-ver are. Tell me what you like a-bout her."

"I don't." The laughter on MacDougal stops me. Not long ago, I used to hide from those kitchen windows. Thought people tracked me from the street.

Dr. Val caught on after realizing I was sitting in the dark during our sessions.

Now the laughing heads poke at me, telling me I don't belong out there with the happy and content. I'm not sure where I belong.

"Mi-cah, where did you go just now?"

"She's a pit bull once she puts her mind to something." I laugh, recalling her first day. "Hair like the color of the sky when I can't sleep at night, fiery amber eyes, bow lips—"

"The fi-er-y yang to your i-cy yin?"

I shrug. "I sense she's endured a lot."

"Sounds like some-one I know."

"A bit different." I look away.

She leans into her headrest. "Tell me why."

"I'm not right. No one needs this nightmare in their life." I hang my head, squeezing the back of my neck.

"Your psy-cho-sis is all you got?"

"This brain controls everything, if you haven't noticed."

"You don't need to tell me that." Her words come out flat.

"Sorry." I shake my head. "I just know once she finds out . . ."

"She'll run?"

I hover my hands over the keyboard, longing to write, to be free from these incessant thoughts, if only to escape into another world like I did as a kid.

"What if this girl de-cides she likes you e-nough to stay the course?"

"What if." I roll my eyes.

"I see. You don't de-serve a chance at love?"

"I haven't seen it work out for my parents, my family. Doesn't seem realistic."

"Nei-ther is push-ing peo-ple a-way." She turns her wheelchair, repositioning herself.

"You should talk."

"You think *I* push peo-ple a-way, Mi-cah?"

"I've known you for what, four years? Not once have you mentioned going out with friends or if you're dating someone."

"Who's the one in ther-a-py?" Her voice jumps an octave.

I throw up my hands. "How do you go about relationships?"

"What the hell does that mean?" Her grin flatlines.

I groan and drag a hand down my face. "I meant, how do you trust?"

Her lips soften. She exhales. "It's ei-ther that or al-i-en-a-tion . . . lone-li-ness."

I squeeze my eyes shut. The familiar ache compounds in my chest and travels down through my fingers.

"Dr. Val . . ." My voice breaks.

"Let's start there, Mi-cah. You and me. I got you."

Chapter 20

BRYNN

Been doing this commute for two weeks now. You'd think it'd get easier. But the subway hates me this morning. The first train zooms by without stopping. No one exits the next one, which is stuffed to the brim with passengers.

Beyond late, I arrive at my printer desk with my mom's cotton wrap dress sticking to me. I'm about ready to rotate under one of the bathroom hand dryers.

"Brynn." Micah tilts his head, his lips pressed together.

My insides turn to liquid when he says my name. What is wrong with me? I'm about to get chewed out for something—either being late or not getting along with Donovan. It could be my aversion to team bonding nights. I have yet to get anyone coffee or clean a conference room, and my time here is up.

We step into the office where I interviewed. Kind of fitting that I'll get fired here too. I was hoping he'd let our initial arrangement slide.

He faces me in a wide stance, his arms folded over his white dress shirt and charcoal-colored skinny tie. "Close the door."

My stomach drops.

He stares at the floor; his eyebrows pull into the center of his face. "Meredith and I agree that your copy ideas have potential." His head snaps up, his eyes meet mine. "With these new pitches this summer, your fresh-out-of-high-school perspective will be useful. We'd like you to continue working with the team as a paid intern."

In the morning sunlight, his soft, brown suede eyes dissolve me. His lips. Those well-shaped lips. Under his top teeth, wet from his tongue. The color of burgundy, ready to drink.

Wait, did he say *paid intern*? I'm going to get paid? Hallelujah! Without thinking, I take an eager step toward him, my hands ready to grip either side of his arms.

His eyes expand into saucers.

I take a sharp inbreath and hug myself instead. My cheeks burn.

He shuffles his weight between his feet, blinking. "That a yes, then?"

I exhale, my heart thundering. "Y-yes. Thank you."

"Conference room in five."

My body floats over to the communal coffee pot. I can't stop smiling. My hand trembles through the pour. I retrieve my laptop and the used flip phone I got for next to nothing on my way home last night off my desk and head to the meeting.

Priya and Donovan sit bent in conversation when I arrive.

"I'm here if you need me," she says quietly, squeezing his shoulder.

I watch the two of them, hoping to hear more, but they break apart when they see me.

Micah sails through the door and takes a seat at the far end of the table, facing the door. He opens his notebook. "Before we begin: Brynn's been invited to stay on through the summer."

Meredith smiles my way.

I need to thank her later.

She turns in her seat, facing me. "Now that you're staying, you could be in the running for a permanent position in the fall . . . unless you have new college plans you haven't told us about?"

"Nope, I'm here." I grin. *You're not getting rid of me now.* "How many summer interns get an offer?"

"It depends." Her eyebrows lift. "Maybe you should present the Quotagian ideas, since Donovan seems less than enthused about the client."

He glares at me.

"I didn't say a word." I put up my hands.

"Your attitude hasn't gone unnoticed, Donovan." Meredith's saucy smile brims with satisfaction—perhaps payback for the snide comment he made about her needing to work out more? "Besides, we have other accounts requiring your expertise."

He nods, his jaw tense.

Meredith glances at her phone.

Donovan scowls my way again.

Watch it, dude, I'm coming for your job. I look back at Meredith. "Can we contact Quotagian for more information about the app? I have some questions."

"Sure, tell me what you need. I'll call them. Give me your cell so I can add you to our team's group chat. You must have gotten your phone back by now." She brings her Starbucks Venti to her lips.

"What?" I'm only half listening, still pinching myself I'm going to get a paycheck soon. One step closer to getting a permanent position this fall.

"Your cell number?"

My stomach nosedives. "Yeah, um." I don't move. Not about to wave this relic in front of everybody's fancy iPhone. Wait, does Priya have a SpongeBob case?

"Everyone, I'm updating our group text for this project. Brynn, text me so I can add you." Meredith bugs out her eyes at me.

Micah's eyes are on me too, his gaze intense.

Yes, I could share my number like a normal person . . . if I knew it. The muscle in my jaw twitches. *Do not look his way.*

"Text it to my number." She flashes her phone.

Cradling the phone, I fumble through the unfamiliar icons as sweat drips down my back. At last, I hit send.

Meredith presses her thumb to her screen, swipes up, and repeats.

Their phones ping, including Micah's. Their heads drop on cue, like synchronized swimmers.

Priya scrunches her face. "Your number looks so weird. Where's this area code?"

I bite my lip and hold up my phone. "It's, um, a prepaid phone and not an iPhone."

"Is that a burner phone? Girl, you get more interesting by the minute." Donovan rubs his hands together and the corner of his mouth pulls into a sly smile, as if he's uncovered one of my secrets.

Lucius's dark eyebrows shoot up and he studies me, stroking the trimmed hair on his chin.

"Not a burner phone, just a refurbished one." I swallow. "I lost my phone last weekend and needed a quick replacement."

"I thought you only broke your screen." Meredith purses her lips.

"Been a rough couple of weeks. This one doesn't even get Internet."

"Such bad luck." She shrugs. "Okay, update me when you get a new one."

I smile, breathing easier. Maybe my luck's changing. I can dig myself out from my parents' debt and start a new life all on my own.

I gaze over at Micah at the same time he looks at me. I squeeze my thighs together and look away.

Chapter 21

MICAH

Meredith spins her chair away from her workstation and into the aisle, her heels raised. "Brynn, our intern extraordinaire, we have a surprise for you."

I stop walking at the word *surprise* and loiter by Priya's desk like I'm reading something important on my phone.

Brynn looks up from her computer, eyes wide. She gulps. "Okay?"

"In celebration of your new status, the team's going out after work. Dream Downtown reopened its underground cocktail lounge and the agency scored a few passes to its private party tonight."

"The Electric Room?" Lucius claps. "*Eyval!*"

"If you're into cultural appropriation and lounging on national symbols." Josie snorts.

Brynn shakes her head. "Sorry, guys, I don't have the funds right now. Plus, I don't have a fake ID."

"Didn't you use one in high school?" Priya wrinkles her nose.

Brynn shrugs. "We always just drank at friends' houses."

Meredith clicks her front teeth. "Mandatory team bonding, you need to go."

"You always say that." Brynn slouches in her chair, squinting at her screen.

Meredith turns. "Micah, you coming?"

"Other plans." Let them think I have a date. Tight spaces and crowds belong to another time in my life.

I know this routine by heart. Me—trying to outpace the Shadow People down Fifth Avenue as if they possess real legs. The real fun happens when one of them walks backward ahead of me, commentating on my every thought. But routine went out the window when Brynn entered my elevator.

You got that right, the Woman in Black's henchman sneers.

"Stop. I'm going home." No reason for me to be in an underground nightclub with some DJ and his strobe lights.

I wipe the sweat above my lip.

The Woman in Black tilts her head and wraps her hand around my bicep.

"Get off!" I yank my arm away.

A few people stare. Most steer clear.

Someone will probably ply Brynn with drinks and make a move tonight.

The henchman cackles. *Donovan, Lucius . . . take your pick.*

"Shut up!" She's not like that. Doesn't even have an ID. She'll sit by herself again, practicing her straw origami.

I should really go keep her company. Meredith and her inane "team bonding" nights.

I turn west on Bleecker toward the Meatpacking District.

I'm not spying, I'm checking up on my underage team member.

Okay, I'm spying.

I travel down a neon-lit loading ramp covered in graffiti. The further I commit, the walls edge in closer. My scalp perspires. I hold my breath, moving faster, and duck inside what looks like a British movie set—gothic chandeliers, leather couches upholstered with Union Jack flags.

Josie's comment this afternoon makes a lot more sense now.

A wave of cool air with hints of coconut hits my face. My chest thumps to the beat of the Sex Pistols song pumping out of the speakers.

I order a sparkling water at the bar. No fish and chips here. Only vibrant-colored cocktails in the hand of every enthusiastic twentysomething present. I scan the room to find her. Before my brain can register, my lungs seize.

She's dancing with Lucius at the far end of the room, a fancy green drink in her hand. I knew he liked her. He may take part in the ribbing spurred on by Donovan, but his eyes tell a different story. The way he watches her in meetings.

Dammit.

Sipping his drink, he grabs for her hand.

They look awkward together.

Her eyes survey the room; maybe she's bored by him?

Find me, I implore in my head.

Her gaze lands on me, and she offers a small wave.

My chest bursts.

She turns back to Lucius.

Acid climbs up my throat. My eyes burn, staring. She doesn't look again.

Stop stalking and walk away. Better yet, leave.

I zigzag through the crowd. The vibe in here is like a shiny penny. In a few weeks, after the bridge-and-tunnel crowds descend, this place's appeal will dull.

I frequented similar club openings back in high school with my then friends. Even at fifteen, someone always knew a bouncer or manager who could get us through the door.

I operated like a player then, verbally beating down lesser opponents to impress the hardest-to-get girl in the room. I didn't care if feelings got hurt. Once I scored her tongue in my mouth, perhaps more, I lost interest. The hunt far outweighed the catch.

Until now.

I circle the room a couple of times and stop at a neon sign accenting the hallway bathrooms.

Brynn exits one of them. "Found you!" She points to me, her voice volume on high. "Thought you were hiding."

"The lights give me a headache." I smile. "Did you follow me?" *Really, that's your line?*

"What? I can't hear you. The music . . ." She taps her ear to illustrate like a kindergarten teacher.

We move down the narrow hallway toward the emergency exit, escaping the thump-thump of the speakers.

With my back to the wall, I prop my foot against it, hands in pockets, heart exploding. "I saw you dancing."

"Not very well, I imagine." She grimaces and shifts her weight to her other foot. She's wearing my favorite red dress of hers that shows off her curves and exposes her thigh when she walks. Her spicy vanilla scent fills my nostrils. I inhale, wanting more.

She grins wide, not looking at me.

I hear her speak but I'm too busy staring to make out the words. "I'm sorry, what?"

"Thought you had plans tonight," she says louder.

Not going to answer that. "Everyone still here?" Gone home, I hope.

"Dancing, I think." She glances back toward where I first saw her.

Lucius and the others are standing by the bar, getting more drinks. They don't seem to have noticed us back here; good, gives me a chance to be alone with her. Tucked in this hallway, we're hidden from most of the club-goers—apart from the blonde who's sitting at the end of the bar, gawking.

She smiles my way like she knows me. I can't place her. Not from my high school. Too young to be a client.

Then she sees Brynn, her eyes grow large, and she drops the glass in her hand.

People around her stoop to help.

Her eyes remain glued on Brynn.

"Do you know her?" I tilt my head in the blonde's direction.

Brynn looks around me and shakes her head. "Never seen her before."

We both shrug.

"On the subway the other day, who was the guy you helped?"

She stares off for a few seconds. Her amber eyes glow. "Oh, a friend from middle school."

"Is that where you got the idea for the gender fluid makeup line?"

"I guess they were the first person I knew who identified that way. Rikki was always so creative and comfortable being themself. Some people can't deal when others don't fit the mold. I got some of that growing up, people saying I'd be prettier with makeup or if I dressed more feminine. They labeled me a tomboy, called me gay."

She's never spoken more than two words to me before now. My head spins with all this new information.

"It doesn't matter to me if you are." Where the hell am I going with this? "I mean, no one should tell you how to be."

Color flares on her cheeks, she avoids my gaze. Her eyes sparkle from the alcohol, lips wet. I've never seen her like this: hair tousled, that smashing dress slightly askew, baring her shoulder. Her honey skin calling my name.

Voices exit the bathroom behind Brynn. A group in flowy minidresses spills out. One of them, red-faced, leans over to say something in her friend's ear—knocking her into Brynn's back and pushing her into me in the process.

I catch her just as her face skims my chest.

Our eyes lock.

Hints of russet swirl like fire in her amber eyes. I'm transfixed. A thirst rises in my throat.

Her hands graze her arms where I touched her. She parts her lips, her shoulders press into her back. She lifts her face toward mine. Her breath's sweet, like a green apple lollipop.

Not the time or place. Still, I want to . . .

Her gaze breaks from mine. She squints toward the bar.

It's just us, I say silently. *Stay.*

She backs up against the wall, her cheeks colored a deeper shade than before.

I hesitate, then step toward her. I imagine hoisting her hips and sliding her up the wall, pressing my mouth and pelvis to hers.

"Um, I should go," she mutters. "Priya's holding my purse."

My thoughts stammer. The words *I'll go with you* fail to leave my lips before she disappears into the sea of people and the Shadow People descend, smirking.

Chapter 22

DAHLIA

I look like a frumpy church girl ready for Sunday choir in this maxi dress, not an alluring femme fatale. A short skirt would have been a better choice for this swanky speakeasy. Feels like I'm wearing a blanket around my giraffe legs—my best feature, if I were pressed to name one.

I check my phone. Teddy and his friend Sam should arrive soon.

Sam works for a new stylist who's getting a lot of buzz. She scored us the guest passes for tonight. But I got here early and managed to get in without one, acting like I knew the guy at the door. Oldest trick in the book. Surprised it worked.

This place has an *Austin Powers* feel to it and excellent people-watching. I recognize a few guys at the bar from one of the ad agencies. No one recognizes me from Falcon. I wear my hair pulled back under a ball cap, the brim low over my eyes, when I'm doing deliveries. I hate the uniform almost as much as being a delivery person. Can't knock the steady work, though.

Speaking of ad agencies: Micah could be here. Though something tells me this isn't his scene, despite the fact that we've barely said two words to one another.

My breath stops. I do a double take, blinking. He's standing with his back to me; still, I'd know him anywhere. The rescuer of my twenty-dollar tip.

He pivots a little.

I sit up straighter, craning my neck. That distinct profile. Like a Roman warrior.

He's talking to someone. Long, dark hair. He looks away a lot. Maybe he's not interested.

See me. Come on. *See me.*

My eyes grow hot, scoring every cell in his body. Turn. Around.

He looks over.

I grin like a Cheshire cat hoping he recognizes me from that morning at Dante's. The only time we've spoken.

He says something to the girl beside him. All at once, two sets of eyes zero in on me.

I drop my drink. Holy crap. It can't be. This is how you mourn his death?

Shit. I need to stop Teddy from seeing her too. He'll go ballistic, say something he shouldn't. Cody's girlfriend doesn't know who we are and it needs to stay that way.

Still I can't tear my eyes away from her.

Her body language gives her away. How she arches her back, throwing her chest at him. Her eyes wide like he's the best thing on the menu.

Unbelievable. Fresh dirt rests on Cody's grave and she's out and about, batting her eyes at another guy—*my* crush, by the way—like nothing's happened. A red-hot iron drags down the middle of my back. If I don't leave now, I'll wind up doing something stupid.

I'm leaving, Cody. For you. Only for you.

The bullying hit a new level in fifth grade, with me on the receiving end of the popular girls' social agenda: Kill or be killed. I attended school in Westchester, one of the wealthiest counties in the state. My classmates wore designers whose names I couldn't pronounce and paraded around carrying the latest Macs and iPhones.

My clothes came from donation bins and clothing drives. Homework got done on a school tablet. And it didn't help that I towered over my entire class thanks to an early growth spurt.

One day, my teacher announced our upcoming field trip needed parent volunteers.

My hand shot up. I planned to ask Silas, the director at St. Ignatius, a church in Westchester that worked with the Department of Social Services. He was the only adult in my life I trusted.

Seated a row behind me, Stacey Whittaker, with her dip-dyed hair and low-rise jeans, sneered through her braces, "Put your hand back down. You don't *got* parents, trash."

Kids around me began chanting *trash* under their breath, each one cutting the hole in me deeper.

I told Cody about it later, walking home from choir practice, choking back tears.

"Dahl, quit being jealous of jerks like Stacey." He flung his arm around me. "Her family probably sucks. Not like us. You, Teddy, and I got to choose *our* family."

In foster care, you could have more than one placement in any given year. It's hard to get close to people when they're mainly there to help out and not interested in being your parent or sibling.

Cody and Teddy understood this.

"I'm tired of kids and teachers treating me like I'm some poor orphan. Why do we have to keep paying for the bad stuff our parents did? We're not them." I jumped on the little black fencing around one of the trees, flattening it into the dirt.

Cody stopped in the middle of the sidewalk, watching me grunt and wipe the sweat from my forehead as I put the fencing back up.

"Change the line, change your life, Dahl. You're better than all of these losers. One day we'll do great things. No one will care where we came from, and everyone will know our names." Wearing a grin, he created a rainbow with his hand as if onstage, his eyes beaming at the audience seated in the balcony. "We're like soaring stars, bright and bold, lighting up the night sky. Imagine it. Creating our own Hollywood marquee in the stars!"

He always found a way to weave in his dream of stardom with telling me how special I was.

Cruel memories of Cody's last night crash through my head in vivid detail after I see Brynn with Micah. My brother's face. The things he said. The unforgivable thing I did, killing all three of them. The lie I choke on every day.

I scan the street outside the Electric Room, unable to get my feet to move.

Teddy, where are you? I can't do this again.

The night of Cody's death, Silas went into protector mode. He told me to factory reset Cody's phone to erase all data and uninstall his apps before disposing of it so the Elmsford police couldn't trace us back to the accident. *They'll never believe people like you*, he said. *That's how it is.*

But I vowed to myself to never do what Silas asked; I could never erase Cody.

So I kept his phone intact. Pictures, videos, everything. And I've kept it tucked away these past seven months.

His phone could change everything—if only I had the guts, which I don't. In the right hands, it would rewrite the facts about that night and implicate Teddy and me. I could never do that to him. They would separate us. I'd go to jail and lose Teddy forever. People would call me a stupid girl who followed her brother blindly because she didn't possess a backbone. And they'd be right.

They'll never believe people like you. That's how it is.

I stop short, blinking at the sight of our third-floor walk-up in Hell's Kitchen. I couldn't tell you how I walked home; the last thirty minutes feel like a blur.

I pace in a tight circle through wafts of fried chicken—courtesy of Sticky's Finger Joint, which occupies the first floor of our building—my jaw cramped from all the clenching. My legs ache with adrenaline.

What if Micah sleeps with her tonight?

I scrounge through my purse for the Nicorette and settle on a cherry cough drop. Cherries and fried chicken. Yuck. I sigh and head upstairs.

Teddy and I turned our small apartment into a home with thrift-store finds and second-hand instruments: my two acoustic guitars (mine plus Cody's), a crackling old amp, Teddy's drum pad with the one good side, and the keyboard he uses for composing.

What if he and Brynn start hanging out . . . like, a lot?

I change into a tank and shorts and check my phone. Nothing from Teddy. I move his keyboard off the futon that converts into his bed. I sit. I pop back up.

Brynn will go through him like she did Cody. Micah doesn't know her capacity for evil.

They'll never believe people like you. Silas's words gnaw at me like a rock in my shoe. Make me feel more like a pariah than I already do. I know he wants to protect us. But if they'll never believe us, how can we believe in ourselves? I wish I had a fraction of Cody's optimism.

CHANGE THE LINE, CHANGE YOUR LIFE . . . Cody's words, written in red on the side of my amp. I use them for inspiration when I'm writing songs.

Change the line.

Change the line.

Change the *damn line*!

They'll never believe people like us if we don't believe in ourselves.

Isn't that what they teach us, to believe in ourselves? I replay the new phrase in my head. Like a new lyric that excites me, its rhythm beats stronger in my chest with every repetition. I whisper the phrase aloud, letting it settle on my tongue. I cup my mouth like a megaphone and repeat the words, drowning out the street sounds below.

My pulse quickens like it does when I'm onstage, ready to strike that first chord. I want to turn up the volume on my life. *That's how it is* no longer works.

I raise the window and step out onto the fire escape. "They'll never believe people like us if we don't believe in ourselves!"

The rush of cars, sirens, and voices echoing from the street swirl together in agreement. I lift my chin and chest to the night sky, my arms spread like Supergirl.

A shooting star. I gasp.

A sob sticks in my throat. "I miss you so much, Cody." I lay both hands over my strumming heart. "Thank you, brother. Thank you."

Fifth-grade Stacey silenced me by calling me trash.

Silas told us to stay silent, to erase our part in and all evidence from that night. While Brynn slithers up to the next guy . . . ready to spread her venom.

I'm done being silenced.

Chapter 23

Priya nibbles on a cube of roasted sweet potato. Her self-made Buddha bowl from Saladworks lays in a color wheel. Instead of tossing it together, she works it by section, eyeing Lucius's Philly cheesesteak.

"Like I said, something feels off about her." She stabs a tomato, then hovers her fork by her mouth. "When I asked her about her college plans, she threw me a look. The girl couldn't get away from me faster." She scans her teammates' faces around the white conference table. "Anybody else think she's harboring secrets?"

Lucius lifts his index finger. His cheek expands as he chews a large bite. "Well," he says, swallowing, "she could certainly afford to go to college if that's what she wanted."

Priya picks up a pink watermelon radish. "Why do you say that?"

"Last night while we were dancing, she blurted out that her parents are Basilio and Katia Gallardo." He leans over the table. "Yo, she's a descendant of music royalty! Got to be loaded."

Josie's mouth hangs open. "Why didn't she tell us? We wouldn't have treated her any differently. Though I'm sure if Scott knew, he'd find a way to leverage it."

Lucius eyes his phone. "She looks foreign, like her mom in this picture."

"Foreign, really? So racist." Josie pulls a face.

"What?" Lucius laughs. "I'm Persian. People say it about me. I get the side-eye terrorist treatment every day. When they ask if I speak English, I mess with them and start cursing in Farsi. Judgy Josie." He sticks his tongue out at her. "All I'm saying is, she looks exotic like a Kardashian. You're not quite sure where she's from. I think she's hot. Tiny waist, great boobs."

Priya rolls her eyes. "Objectifying, much?"

"Didn't the Gallardos recently croak? Must be nice living off your parents' wealth. Snobby little bitch." Donovan sniffs, crossing his arms.

"She's not rich. Have you seen the way she stuffs bagels in her purse?" Josie snorts.

"The girl does like to eat. *What?*" Donovan shrugs at the faces Priya and Josie make. "I'm not saying she's *fat*."

Meredith descends on the group with a stack of files in her arms, winded. "What are you guys talking about?"

"Our mysterious intern, Brynn." Donovan winks at her.

Meredith plunks down in the nearest seat. "You guys, listen. My brother's ex-girlfriend's best friend's younger brother's friend graduated with her this past spring." She pauses, checking she has their attention. "Brynn's parents were these famous musicians turned club owners who got killed in a car accident a few months ago, same night her boyfriend got hit by a car. All three, dead. Isn't that awful? Explains her antisocial attitude and bitchiness."

Donovan nods. "Snobby little bitch, like I said."

"Didn't the Gallardos own that famous club in the East Village?" Priya wrinkles her forehead. "What was it called?"

"The Flaming Flamingo. Birthplace of punk and new wave." Josie whistles. "What a loss for the antiestablishment."

"The club filed bankruptcy, right? Maybe they owed money and their deaths weren't a coincidence." Priya flourishes the lettuce on her fork.

"My girl's got a nose for a juicy angle." Donovan slurps his protein shake and leans back in his chair.

"*Or* the three of them were murdered and Brynn's a key witness. Sounds more intriguing than simply committing insurance fraud." Lucius shrugs.

"Listen to you guys." Josie narrows her eyes. "I'm not surprised she doesn't want to hang out with us. She's barely out of high school. Her parents and boyfriend are dead. She could probably use a friend. Bet we seem old to her."

"But we're *so* cool." Donovan grins.

"And good-looking." Lucius fist-bumps him.

Priya sighs. "I couldn't wait to get out of high school and away from my parents. I grew up in a traditional Indian home; they were so overprotective of me, compared to how they treated my brothers. I wasn't allowed out past ten."

"Plenty of things can happen before ten, *darling*." Donovan jumps to the seat next to her, grinning and rubbing his hands together.

Josie ignores him. "I get it. My mom got pregnant with my oldest brother, Joe, when my dad was stationed in Okinawa. She kept the reins tight on me so history didn't repeat itself. I would never have been allowed to go out with twenty- and thirty-year-olds at Brynn's age."

"Is there anything about her parents' car accident online?" Meredith motions to Josie to open her laptop. "Search Saw Mill River Parkway crash."

"Here it is!" Josie says almost immediately.

Two Killed in Saw Mill River Parkway Crash

Elmsford, New York (WNBC) – The New York State Highway Patrol came across a single-car crash at 9:11 p.m. Saturday evening in Westchester County. The vehicle was heading north on the Saw Mill River Parkway near Elmsford when it rolled and sparked an explosion. Emergency responders on the

SCENE DISCOVERED TWO PASSENGERS STUCK INSIDE THE OVERTURNED VEHICLE WITH AIRBAGS STILL INFLATED. INVESTIGATORS LATER IDENTIFIED THE VICTIMS AS 43-YEAR-OLD BASILIO GALLARDO AND HIS WIFE, 43-YEAR-OLD KATIA GALLARDO, FORMER OWNERS OF THE FLAMING FLAMINGO IN GREENWICH VILLAGE, NEW YORK. BOTH PASSENGERS WERE WEARING SEATBELTS AND PRONOUNCED DEAD AT THE SCENE. THE CAUSE OF THE CRASH REMAINS UNDER INVESTIGATION. THE POLICE ARE ASKING ANYONE WITH MORE INFORMATION TO CONTACT THEM.

Josie covers her mouth with both hands.

Priya gasps. "Oh my God, they were burned alive."

Brynn appears in the doorway.

Priya elbows Donovan.

"Not now, P." His eyes are glued to the same news article on his phone. "This is so messed up!"

"What are you guys doing?" Brynn takes a couple steps into the conference room. Her eyes blaze into the back of Josie's computer, then over to Donovan.

They jump like errant children.

The color of Josie's cheeks rivals the beets in Priya's salad.

An air of tension snakes around the table. No one utters a word or glances at Brynn.

"What are you looking at?" She folds her arms.

"Checking the sports scores from last night." Donovan coughs like his shake went down the wrong pipe.

"Um . . . doing emails." Josie closes tabs on her computer, sweating.

Tears spring to Brynn's eyes. She storms out.

Chapter 24

MICAH

Brynn blurs past me through the lobby's double glass doors. I follow her down the hallway.

Coming around the turn to the elevators, she collides with a Falcon Messenger delivery person.

The gangly blonde loses her balance and bungles the tower of boxes in her arms.

"Sorry," Brynn mumbles, then stoops and picks up the fallen packages.

"You okay?" I look at Brynn, her eyes black like marbles.

"I'm fine," both girls' voices echo.

The girl gives Brynn a pinched look as she takes the packages back, her face ashen like she could hurl in the hallway. She hurries away without a word.

Brynn waits until the girl's out of earshot before turning to me, her lips tight, fighting back tears. "Some people need to get a life."

Uh-oh. I check the time on my phone. "Did you bring lunch?"

"I need some air." She double-taps the elevator button.

I sigh, thinking of the number of Shadow People that may come along for the ride. Still, I take my chances when it arrives and step in beside her.

Her eyes stare ahead as more people hop on—real ones, I presume—pushing us to the back.

I keep up with her when she exits onto Fifth Avenue. "So, you hungry?"

She musters a half-hearted smile. "Thanks, but I brought my lunch today. I just needed to get out of there." She starts walking away.

"You like Indian?"

She hesitates, then pivots. "You know, that sounds amazing. But I'm not sure I'll be great company. And I don't have my wallet."

"I got this."

She sighs, her face softens a little. "I think my salad can hold another day in the fridge."

I play it casual walking beside her on Thirty-Fourth over Park to Lexington, my hands in my pockets while my heart ricochets inside my chest. I want to mention last night, gauge her reaction. She doesn't act like she loathes me. Did her pulse quicken or her hands perspire like mine did? Does she know how close I came to kissing her—like, full-on kissing her? A part of me feels relieved it didn't happen; she might have pushed me away. The other part dreams of how she might have responded.

I bite my lip, trying to read her face.

She's quiet. Her cheeks still blaze a bright red.

Maybe Zoe and her disciples ganged up on her since she's the only intern being allowed to work on new campaigns. I heard Zoe say something about Brynn in passing. No one pays attention to her. She's never demonstrated an aptitude for advertising the way Brynn has.

We enter the restaurant. Brynn snaps up a menu near the door and walks over to the counter to order.

"Here, we have time." I motion to one of the booths.

The server places a menu in front of me as we sit down.

Brynn glances at me.

I tilt my head. "What?"

"Nothing."

"What set you off back there?"

She looks away. Her shoulders rise and fall with a sigh. "People running their mouths about stuff that's not their business."

"Your business, I assume."

Her eyes harden. "I need this job. I'm not here to make friends."

Including me. My chest deflates; the sting of her words cuts deep. I blink a few times and lower my head into my menu. I guess I imagined last night.

I sense her eyes searching my face.

I rearrange it, pretending to be absorbed in today's specials.

She clears her throat. "I've been forced into adulting sooner than expected."

Haven't we all.

"Can I ask how old you are?"

"Twenty."

She squints at my answer.

"What, you thought I was older? I started as an intern four years ago."

"You? An intern?"

"Same year Scott came on as creative director. He mentored me."

The server pops up next to us.

"I'll have the *chana masala*," Brynn tells him.

The server jots down her order.

I guess we're doing this. "Make it two. And some naan for the table, please."

Brynn's face brightens a bit.

I'm done talking about work. "So, what kind of food did you grow up with? I mean, did your family make any traditional dishes?"

She crosses her arms, her chin in her chest. "Yeah, cooking and sharing meals was a big part of my family's culture. My dad tried to teach me all the time, but I wasn't interested." She shifts in her seat, her face wistful. "He learned to cook authentic Peruvian from *his* mom, who immigrated here in the '70s. Before I became vegan, I used to love coming home to the smell of *seco de cordero*—um, lamb stew—cooking on the stove. I ate a lot of *lomo saltado* too . . . beef stir fry with onions, tomatoes, and, believe it or not, French fries."

"Quite a combination." I fold my arms, mirroring her. "Never heard of it."

"He'd add his own flavor with whatever we had on hand. We'd stop at our favorite . . ." Her eyes narrow.

"What?" I smile a little. "You've got my mouth watering."

"Why are we talking about this?" Her face stiffens.

Because I'd rather not talk about myself. "I find it interesting. You have an accent when you speak Spanish. Are you bilingual?"

"Only when it comes to the food." Her amber eyes dance a little.

I doubt I saw fire in them last night. Just my wishful wanting that she felt something too.

I can't deny being somewhat in awe of this girl. How she puts herself out there helping others: the lady in the elevator, her friend on the subway. At work, meanwhile, she's a font of creativity and laser focused. Hard to believe she's only eighteen.

When our plates arrive, the spicy aroma restores my appetite. The air buoys back inside of me, the wound mended by a giddiness born of being alone with her. Hearing about her family makes me want to meet them, see where she grew up.

"Thanks for this. I haven't eaten out in a while." She lays her fork on her plate.

"You looked like you could use a break."

"I'm not a fan of the gossip." Her gaze drifts from the table. "Especially when people don't know what they're talking about."

"Yeah, the agency can feel like an extension of high school. Now that you're officially one of them, makes you fair game."

"You don't seem to run with them."

"I already know what they think of me. I do my job and don't see them outside of work."

"What *do* you do outside of work?"

Besides fend off the Shadow People? I shrug, pushing the food around on my plate. "I work out; run in Central Park sometimes."

"I have to ask." She snickers. "What's up with the notebook?"

Busted. Guess I'm not as stealthy as I thought.

"I'm sort of a . . . collector. I jot down phrases and words that I like."

"Are you a writer?"

"I wouldn't call myself one. Words calm me."

"Should I even ask?" Her eyes crinkle above her smile.

"No." I grin. "I see you hanging back after everyone goes home, word-crafting away."

"I'm new, it takes me longer to come up with ideas." She holds her opposite shoulder and crosses her other arm underneath. "And other times . . ." She cocks her head like she's trying to decide whether she should continue.

"I won't tell." I hold up my hands.

"Um, I do a little research. The agency has better Wi-Fi than I do at home."

I don't want to know if she's looking for another job, though I wouldn't blame her. "Well, I hope you find what you're looking for."

Her lips disappear into a line.

I stop myself from asking more and sign the receipt. "Back to the grind?"

She nods. "Thanks for lunch. Felt good to clear my head."

"Don't let them get to you. Besides, after this summer, I doubt you'll see this motley crew again." I sigh. "I know what Meredith said—and this is not what you want to hear— but Kershaw McKenzie hasn't given an intern a full-time offer in forever. Our hiring budget's tight these days."

Her head snaps up. "What if Donovan leaves?"

"Why, you heard something?"

"No . . . I thought . . ." Her face falls. "Never mind."

I could appease her, tell her it'll all work out, but I don't want to lie. Not to her. So I say nothing at all.

Chapter 25

DAHLIA

I'm on a Broadway stage, playing the aspiring singer awaiting her big break. She sings while busing tables at The Duplex, a piano bar and drag revue in the West Village.

One day, people will remember me. *See that famous singer standing by the piano? She used to work here, Tetris-fitting the glasses and plates like a boss.*

Using my Captain Marvel muscles, I balance the gray rubber tub on my shoulder and move through the green room with its iconic arched windows. Tonight's crowd: a bunch of pretty boys, one bachelorette party, and a table of swinging baby boomers.

Of our three jobs, this one's my favorite. If the manager likes you during your interview, you get to audition. Some nights, Teddy and I kick off open-mic night and perform between sets. One day, I'm going to headline here and Teddy's going to be a sought-after songwriter and producer. We'll create music full time and move out of our tiny apartment above Sticky's.

The dishwasher called out tonight and Teddy stepped in, taking the extra shift.

"I call it more than a coincidence." I bend my knees, lowering the tub of dirty dishes onto the counter between us.

Teddy cocks a Sicilian brow and raises the metal arm on the dishwasher.

I wipe my hands on the towel tucked into my waistband. "What you said this morning."

"Ah, took ya a minute." He smiles like someone who's put up with me and my slow brain for years. The rising steam glazes his face and dark curls. He pulls his head away from the heat. He turns to retrieve the dirty dishes I've collected, his gap-toothed grin widening.

I grab the side of the tub. "Come on, Cody's girlfriend's rebound guy just happens to live across the street from Dante's and they *both* work for Kershaw McKenzie?"

"That makes sense, being he's a Kershaw." He winks, waiting for me to let it go.

I jut out my hip and fold my arms over my chest. "Okay, smartass. What if Cody's trying to tell us something? Like the shooting star the other night."

"Should have killed her with the boxes you were carrying."

"She rushed out of nowhere like a bull, heading straight for me. Made me look like a complete ass in front of Micah."

"I dunno why ya go for these guys, Dahl. He owns an ad agency. Out of your league, don't ya think?"

"Gee, thanks." I sigh.

"They don't know how extraordinary you are." He frowns, his gaze lingering on my face.

"She's all curvy and sexy, with that café au lait skin, and then there's me, dorking it out in my Falcon Messenger uniform."

Teddy waves me off. He's heard my buffet of insecurities too many times.

I look around. We're alone. I lean over the stainless-steel counter. "I wanted to smack her and say, 'I know what you did to my brother.'"

Teddy stops. His large, dark eyes consider me. "I thought about what ya said, about us accepting the shit they pull on us. Like we're not as good. Why should she get away with turning Cody into a killer?"

My pulse picks up. "Yes! People should know he died a hero."

"Ya know what ya gotta do, Dahl."

I shake my head.

"Your plan to connect her to that night."

"Admit to the cops we're murderers?"

"You're smart. You'll think of something." He smiles, eyes tender. He moves the sweaty strands of hair that have fallen over my eye behind my ear, kisses the inside of his hand, and cradles my face.

My eyes tear up. Best brother a girl could have.

My heart swells as I watch him reload the machine with dirty glasses. His unconditional love for me is unfaltering—even when I'm about to do something that could make us lose everything.

Chapter 26

BRYNN

"What's shaking, copy buddy?" Donovan hovers near my desk. "Going to blow them away with your Quotagian presentation?"

"Yep." I steady my eyes on my blank screen. Historical romance writers are not my jam. I need more information about this app from the client. For some reason, Meredith keeps putting me off.

He places an iced Starbucks coffee in front of me.

"What's this?"

He tilts his head with a shrug. "Some of us are going out after work. You should come."

I look around. Monitors off, chairs pushed in. When did everyone leave? A wave of uneasiness rises in my belly. "I have a lot more to do. Besides, I'm not legal, remember?"

"So what? Mixed in with us, they won't even card you like last time. Why don't you have a fake ID?"

"I'm not a big drinker. Anyway, I should keep brainstorming." I bite the skin on the side of my thumb.

"All these extra hours; you trying to show us up or something?"

"If you haven't noticed, I'm new at this." I try to keep my tone upbeat. "Besides, the agency has better Internet connection than my apartment does."

"Nice place, huh?" He winks. "Got any roommates?"

I shake my head. Need to shut this down; I've shared too much. What's next, is he going to ask about my late parents? I can't even look at him.

His pro-feminist T-shirt today: ANYTHING YOU CAN DO, I CAN DO BLEEDING. Yuck.

He catches me reading his shirt and his smile grows. "We should hang out sometime."

His tone sets off alarms bells in my head.

"Y-you should go," I say, eyes back on my screen. "I'm sure everyone's waiting, including Priya."

"You could be a little friendlier, you know."

I jerk back, my fingers freeze over the keyboard. "I'm as friendly as I want to be."

He edges closer and plays with a strand of my hair, twirling it, his knuckles less than an inch from my breast. "You expressed an interest in staying on in the fall. I could help make that happen . . ."

I retrieve my hair from his grasp, leaning away, my tongue like sandpaper. "I don't need your help; I'll have your job soon enough."

"What did you just say?" He bares his teeth, his cheeks flexed.

Micah steps out of an office. "Everything okay here?"

I gather a notepad and pen off my desk. "Thanks, Donovan. I'll be happy to write that one down—how you'd like to *help* me. I'm sure HR would *love* to hear your suggestion."

"Sorry, no HR here, honey." He pats my back.

I wiggle away from his touch.

His breath heats my ear. "You're a bitch, you know that?"

My cheeks sting like I've been smacked. My eyes and nose fill. I turn away—biting back a scream, denying him the satisfaction.

He hovers a moment longer before finally leaving.

Good riddance. I should be ignoring this creep, not letting him intimidate me. I knock the Starbucks coffee into the garbage.

I squeeze my eyes shut and fist up my hands.

If Cody were here, he'd have me laughing and making fun of that jerk—and helping me devise a plan to replace him. He doesn't deserve the job he has. *I do.*

What Cody must think of me.

He's only been gone seven months—and here I am, nearly kissing Micah at the Electric Room. I almost made a fool of myself the other night. He's my boss. I can't have these confusing feelings for him.

"Brynn?"

I jump in my chair. Shit. "I didn't realize you were still here." And right behind me.

Micah hesitates, looking like a thought's stuck between his lips. But he just turns and walks away.

He's been decent, letting me stay on through the summer as a paid intern. I can't mess this up and become a joke. The team's already gossiping about what they think they know about me. I don't need to give them more to chew on.

I hear him walking out with Eunice. My scalp prickles. It's too quiet here by myself. I gather my things and leave the office.

As I step off the elevator downstairs, I thread my keys through my fingers. Walking with vigilance, I take myself home.

Chapter 27

MICAH

I text Meredith for the address, expletives flying under my breath. I turn toward Thirty-Eighth Street. I ride the Hotel Hendricks's elevator to the twenty-ninth floor, reciting in my head my teachers' names, starting in kindergarten and continuing all the way through online high school.

I pass through a pink and green fog of velvet seating occupied by happy hour attendees, their elbows propped on their tables, libations in hand.

I spot the top of Josie's hair first, then see the rest of the team on Daintree's rooftop terrace under strands of white lights.

I stride toward Donovan, forcing him to step backward.

"What's up, boss man?" He smiles, lips tight.

I invade his personal space the same way he did Brynn's. "Cut the crap. And lay off our interns for once."

"I have no idea what you're talking about." He holds up his hands like a scolded child.

"I bet you do: Maia, Celeste . . . do I need to go on?"

"What did Brynn *tell* you?"

"I didn't have to ask. Her face said it all."

"Just helping her with some copy ideas. She seems a bit confused. I'm not sure how well she's working out. Also, I don't trust her."

"Not your call to make. If I see you harassing her or anyone else again, you're done. Got it?" I glance at his T-shirt and shake my head. "We'll see who bleeds."

He narrows his eyes and opens his mouth.

I don't wait to hear it.

Priya and Lucius move out of my way as I stride off, their jaws scraping the floor.

Out of the corner of my eye, I see Josie grinning.

On the street, I uncurl my hands and consume a deep breath, the veins in my neck pulsating. Looking for a way to distract myself from losing it out here, I attempt to conjure up a pop culture reference, but one escapes me. Instead, I imagine Brynn's face.

I start from the beginning: In the elevator the morning of her interview, when she helped the old lady, and then moments later, when we formally met. How she wouldn't look at me, her knees bouncing all over the place, until she sold me on giving her a try. The way she threw herself in front of her friend on the subway. Always saving people.

I see her pissed-off face when she's dealing with Donovan or pressured into another team bonding night. How her amber eyes catch fire when she smiles. The baby carrots she pulls out every day, snapping them in her teeth at her desk.

The way her bow lips move when she edits copy.

My cantering heart slows to a trot. I breathe deeper; my shoulders relax.

I picture her lying in bed, stressing over whatever Donovan said.

I pore over the rest of the snapshots in my head of her face as I walk downtown toward home. She travels with me and into the night. She's become the last thing on my mind as I drift off to sleep and the person I picture when I wake.

In the morning I shower, dress, hop on the subway, and grab my double espresso from the new guy on the corner. I search for her when I get into the office, scanning the floor and conference rooms.

I find her at last, laughing with Meredith. She doesn't see me and I don't want her to. My face would reveal too much.

I walk away and wait.

Kevin, Joe, and Nick Jonas . . . Brynn, Brynn, Brynn.

Chapter 28

BRYNN

My laptop slips in my hands. I clutch it to my beating chest and dry each palm on my pants before reaching the conference room door.

Donovan sails in ahead of me wearing a smirk above his T-shirt. This one reads, INTERSECTIONAL FEMALE. We haven't spoken since our encounter two days ago. Fine with me. I'm sure he'd enjoy throwing me off my game before my Quotagian presentation.

All at once, my mouth dries up and my stomach goes queasy. Too many bagels this morning. I need to pee again. Except. I'm out of time.

It's already July; this pitch must go well if I want to secure a full-time job this fall. My next few minutes need to be dazzling.

It's just like singing onstage, Brynn—something you've done hundreds of times. Breathe from the abdomen, open your mouth, and the rest will follow.

If only this was an audition.

An eternity ticks by before they look up from their phones. A whole crew sits gathered around the table; my team, including Scott, plus two other associate creative directors. I guess I *am* auditioning. Glad Micah isn't here to distract me.

Meredith's eyes bubble with anticipation. She gives me a nod.

The room stills.

"Quotagian's new singles app . . . um, an app . . . a singles app designed to bring the art of love letter writing back to the dating world. You don't need to be a great writer. The prompts make it easy to express your feelings." My voice sounds strange, my breathing jagged.

I share my screen on the widescreen and take a gulp of air so big it makes me cough.

Love Letters Attract. You've Got the Love, We've Got the Words.

Love Letters Attract. Want Love? We've Got the Words.

Love Letter Singles. Woo Them with Words.

Love Letter Singles. Put Your Love into Words.

"Based on your profile and person you desire, the app generates a customizable love letter. Its filters allow you to select the tone, from 'traditional romantic' to your favorite TV, movie, or book character. You can send the same love letter to multiple people." I resist the urge to roll my eyes, thinking of a few guys who would opt for that.

"What happened to *Couplet Couplings* and twentysomething fans of historical romance like Shakespeare and Austen?" Meredith twists up her nose.

"I thought Quotagian's original concept wouldn't appeal to Gen Zers and Millennials." Not true. I was just clueless. "So I called them."

"You did what?" Her voices rises.

Uh-oh.

"Our team's been so busy this week, I wanted to come up with copy that made sense. Our contact put me through to Jessica, one of the developers at Quotagian, and her boss, Marnie. We started throwing around ideas for what this app could do . . ."

Meredith closes her eyes.

I feel sick; those bagels are sitting like lead in my gut. My mouth waters and not in a good way.

"You billed your time, correct?" one of the ACDs from the other team asks me.

"Yes, of course." I return her nod with enthusiasm. "Turns out the app is still being developed, providing the perfect opportunity to give feedback and discuss ways to widen the audience if they want twentysomethings to use it."

"Sounds like someone did *your* job, Meredith." Donovan snickers.

"N-not at all." My voice cracks. "I just didn't know how else to get more information."

"Who came up with these filters?" Meredith's shoulders slump, her earlier spark snuffed out.

"Um, we did." I bite my lip. "Users can still generate a love letter in the vein of Shakespeare or Austen, but they'll also have all these other options. And as the number of users grows, new filters will be added based on their feedback, keeping the app fresh and interactive. The client really liked that."

The room falls silent. I'm not sure what to do.

"Do you have more?" Scott leans forward.

"After you secure the person of your dreams, the app moves into relationship mode, meaning you can use it to write a love letter for your significant other's birthday, anniversary, Valentine's Day, and so on."

LOVE LETTER COUPLES. KEEP YOUR LOVE LIT.

I smile. "Get it—*Lit*? It's a play on words."

"I thought it was meant to be a dating app." He cocks his head.

"We thought the app could be used in three ways. One, it'll help you attract the person you want; two, celebrate the love you have; and three, help you win them back if things go awry."

"Interesting." He types something on his phone. "Your idea?"

I dart a look over at Meredith. "It was, um, a group effort with Jessica and Marnie." I smile and scan the room, straining to read their squinting faces. Do they think I've made Meredith look bad in front of Scott? Or made their jobs harder by expanding the project?

Meredith continues to glare at me—but what else could I do? She ignored my requests for more information. I couldn't blow my chance to impress the team, in particular Scott.

My antiquated flip phone vibrates across the table next to my computer, the outside screen lighting up.

Standing by the whiteboard, I ignore it.

It stops for a moment as all eyes fasten on it, then flit back to me. The phone changes its mind and lurches off the table again. This time performing semicircles.

"Looks like someone's desperate to get a hold of you." Donovan stretches across the table and grabs it. "Elmsford, New York . . ."

Warm bagel dough rises in my throat. I gag, feigning a cough, and swallow it down. "C-can you end the call? Thanks." What was I saying?

My phone jerks back to life like a vibrating bug.

"Same number."

"Shut it off . . . yeah, shut it off."

"It stopped." He leaves it face up on the table.

Lucius and Josie discuss the campaign rolling out in phases.

I press my hand to my belly, exhaling. I wish I could sit down.

My cell resuscitates once more.

Donovan snaps it up. "El-*lo*?" He leaves off the first letter like a guy answering the phone at a pizzeria.

My eyes bounce between his face and Meredith's.

"Sure, Detective, she's right here." Donovan smiles like a villain and passes me my phone.

I swear under my breath. This cannot be happening.

I could hang up, but then it would look like I'm hiding something, which I'm not. Why would they be calling, and how the hell did they find me? Should have sprung for the burner app.

All eyes focus on me, waiting.

"Um, okay." My voice sounds wimpy after being reduced from Brilliant Brynn, the girl impressing the room, to the intern who can't get her personal life together. Like they'll hire me now.

I hurry out of the conference room with my phone pressed to my stomach, leaving my computer and their mouths agape. I grab my purse from the bottom drawer, beeline through the lobby—zigzagging around Micah, who is standing next to Eunice's desk—and zoom through the double glass doors.

I keep going until I reach an alcove by the maintenance closet near the elevators. I rest my forehead on the wall and shut my eyes. "Um, this is Brynn Gallardo."

"Detective Ana Simone from the Elmsford Village Police Department."

The voice sounds young, like she could be someone from my high school. If only this were a prank.

"We have some questions regarding your parents' car accident. Best if you come in."

Something tells me it's not.

Time stops while I'm tucked away in this short hallway, my backside on the ground, my shoulders against the wall, bagel puke in a rolled-up napkin next to me, my nose running from the floor cleaner fumes. I listen to the elevators gliding between floors. I need to pull myself together.

Few more minutes.

I grip my old cell phone tighter, the one from a life that no longer includes me. I keep it tucked inside the zipped pocket of my purse. My last lifeline to my parents feels cold and sobering against my cheek. I gaze at my mom's smiling expectant face through the cracked screen. I don't need to press play; her last words to me are forever engrained in my memory, starting with her attempt to sound calm so I wouldn't worry.

I shake my head and do it anyway.

> *Honey, it's Mommy. Shit, is this thing recording? Um, Daddy and I had an accident. A small one. Uh, we're fine . . . We really wanted to hear you sing tonight. I'm afraid we may miss it now.*
>
> *Look! Someone's running toward us. That didn't take long. A good sign, my love!*
>
> *The police are here, baby girl. I'll call you later. We love you.*

Even now, my mom's swearing chokes a smile out of me. For such an intelligent woman, most forms of technology tripped her up.

Cody and I met my parents at Roberta's in Bushwick the week before. It was the first time I'd spoken to them since announcing the tour.

My father didn't look at Cody once during dinner.

I told them I wasn't feeling well and went to the bathroom. Held my sweater over my face, muffling sobs in a restroom stall.

Alone, Cody decided to invite them to our first performance in Elmsford.

We'd never discussed it.

He swaggered around his parents' apartment afterward, stoked about what he'd done.

Look! Someone's running toward us. That didn't take long. A good sign, my love!

A warmth mushrooms in my chest hearing my dad's unfailing optimism in the background . . . how he loved my mother to the end. Especially since those last few months I often saw my mom with puffy, bloodshot eyes after a shower and my dad taking off at odd hours to God knows where. I couldn't be in the same room with them without wanting to hit something.

The final part of my mom's message sends a chill through me . . . when her voice fills with relief.

The police are here, baby girl. I'll call you later. We love you.

That night, I watched as the last band stepped offstage. I'd bitten off all my nails waiting for Cody to get back.

Two officers walked through the doors at Pete's.

My heart stopped. I ran over to them. *My parents never arrived. We can't find my boyfriend, Cody.*

One of the officers talked into his radio. He then motioned to his partner, his lips pulled into a tight line.

They turned their backs to me.

My body felt strange. My hands numb. *I want to go see my parents.*

The first officer frowned and shook his head.

His partner uttered words like *faulty airbags never deflated . . . trapped them inside probably . . . then the car ignited*, and asked questions I couldn't answer.

Adrian touched my shoulder. *They're okay, right?*

The second officer closed his notepad. The radio clipped to his belt crackled. They'd found Cody.

I discovered my mom's voicemail sometime in the early morning. With my heart in my throat, I dialed the Elmsford Police. *They're alive! My parents are stranded on the side of the road.*

The night duty officer exhaled into the phone. *The Gallardo couple have been transported to the local hospital. You'll need to bring in their toothbrushes or a hairbrush to help identify the bodies.*

No, no, no! That can't be true . . .

He stayed on the phone as I cried.

The police are here, baby girl.

My mom and dad were supposed to be rescued. If they had been, my life would be whole. I'd be on tour, singing, and not struggling to write some damn ad copy. The universe didn't effing do its job: save the good people. My parents were never safe, never okay, even when they thought they were.

Why didn't I pick up my mom's call?

"Found you." Micah pokes his head in from the hall, breaking my spell. "Have you made an executive decision to work out here for the remainder of the day?" He twists his lips, holding back a grin. "Fine with me."

"Something like that." I clear my throat, my fists push in my temples.

He eyes the cracked screen on my phone. "I can get your bag for you."

"I have all my stuff." I can't look at him. So not cool I'm losing it right now.

"Take off, then. No big deal."

I wipe underneath my eyes. "I'll be fine. Give me a minute."

"Whatever it is, I'm sure it's more important than *this* place."

I sigh. "What will you tell them?"

"That I heard you killed it in there presenting your Quotagian ideas, so I gave you the rest of the day off." He leans his shoulder against the wall.

"No, really."

"You're in a holding pattern until Josie and Lucius come up with some specs anyway. They got your ideas. Now their work begins."

I press my back against the wall and slide up it until I'm on my feet. "I left my laptop in the conference room."

"I'll make sure it gets back to your desk." He lifts his palm. "Wait here, I'll hit the button."

When the elevator dings and the doors open, I book it over, duck inside, and press the button for the lobby.

"Now go straight home," Micah says. "No helping little old ladies today, got it?" He curls his lip for a moment—then his face breaks into a smile.

I grimace as the doors close. Such a smartass—and the only ally I've got.

Chapter 29

BRYNN

The weekday commuter crowd has thinned by the time I step on the Metro-North train at Grand Central Terminal late the next morning. Walking down the narrow aisle of bright blue and green seats, I catch a whiff of something fishy mixed with disinfectant. I choose an empty row and lower my butt into a window seat.

No response from the text I sent Meredith about not coming in today. I can almost hear the whispers around the agency regarding my parents' and Cody's deaths, with Donovan at the helm, telling people I'm in jail. A month on the job and now I'm a convict.

Last night, I flipped around on my mattress, punching my pillow and staring at the cracks in the coffin's ceiling, running through the kinds of questions the detectives could ask—and searching for the answers I still don't have.

The train chugs forward through the tunnel. A baby cries. Passengers in the facing section past the door nod off as if they've just finished a long shift at work.

We climb out of the darkness and into the gray light. Raindrops drag across my window. My foggy head finds a less than comfortable spot where the curved headrest meets the glass and my gaze drifts out to the patchy sky, the buildings and homes rolling by.

For once, my mind stills.

Thirty minutes later, I exit at White Plains and catch the bus at Tarrytown. By the time I get off at East Main the rain has eased, so I walk the rest of the way. Hard to imagine Cody growing up in this upper-crust town—something I didn't dwell on the last time we visited, holding hands in the back seat of Adrian's car, heading to Pete's on Central Avenue, both of us giddy. This Westchester gig was supposed to be the beginning of all our dreams.

If someone had told me Cody would never play that night, I wouldn't have believed it.

Stay, Cody. Don't go.

I've searched the Elmsford Village Police Department for updates from that night so many times, each time holding my breath. Yet every attempt, I've found nothing new. So why am I being summoned now?

I recheck the address. This can't be it.

The building before me sits back from the quiet suburban street with beautiful homes on either side, giving off a country club vibe with its fresh-cut lawn and circular driveway. The police station's brick façade, dormer windows, and white columns that flank the entrance strike me as being a far cry from the city's gritty-looking precincts.

I trudge up the narrow cement steps, my legs like logs moving in water. I hesitate on the top step, staring at the glass doors. My throat constricts. I wish I wasn't doing this alone.

I utter my name through the plexiglass pinholes to the large, barrel-chested officer at the front desk, unable to tear my eyes away from the round swirl of greasy black hair in the center of his bald head.

Another officer ushers me down the hall to a brown-paneled room with a rectangular table and chairs in the center, just like in the movies. She closes the door.

My pulse thuds in my ears. I pace, sidestepping the human-size stain on the cement floor. Do I need a lawyer? How would I pay for that?

Footsteps sound. My body tenses. The door handle turns. I drop into the single chair. A bead of sweat escapes down the back of my T-shirt.

A towering Black woman with unblinking eyes and sharp cheekbones enters, followed by a much younger-looking Asian guy.

The female officer's curls cover her brows and scrape her shoulders. She offers me a polite smile. "We appreciate you taking a trip out here, Miss Gallardo. We spoke on the phone. I'm Detective Simone." She lifts her chin toward her companion. "My partner, Detective Clive Bodie."

Simone looks older in person than she sounded on the phone, but is this Clive guy even old enough to be a detective? He looks like he's my age.

Simone presses her palms to the top of her thighs. "Water, soda?"

"Coffee, please."

"How do you take it?"

"Um, black is fine." I won't ask for almond or oat milk; I don't want to be seen as difficult.

One glance from her and Clive exits the room. When he returns he has my coffee in one hand and a cardboard box with *Gallardo* written on the end in black Sharpie in the other. He places it next to Detective Simone.

My stomach plummets. Am I about to see my parents' personal effects?

I can't.

I won't.

I bite my thumbnail.

He closes the door and sets down the cup of coffee in front of me. An oily film swirls like gasoline on top.

Clive takes a seat next to Simone and across from me, looking like a member of a K-pop band with his tinted hair flow. His dark, close-set eyes give me a start. He studies me, chewing on the end of a pen and clicking the top of it.

"Um, I told the officers at Pete's everything I knew." I take a tentative sip of my coffee. It tastes as bad as I expected.

Simone clears her throat. "The report states your father lost control of the car driving northbound on the Saw Mill. The tire tracks reveal his vehicle skidded and then spun along the road. It flipped and slid several hundred feet, landing in a ravine before it—"

"I already know this."

"We received new evidence." She averts her eyes.

I suck in my breath.

"A jogger in Pocantico Park"—she cocks her head as she reads the report—"found a cell phone near one of the trails containing traces of blood."

She folds her arms over the table; the corners of her mouth sag. "It belonged to Cody Waters."

Clive opens the box between them, fishes out a plastic bag with the phone in it, and slides it onto the table.

Cody's blood. Oh my God.

That video we recorded together that night was the first of many we planned to do, a mini documentary to be streamed by thousands someday. We kissed like crazy . . . we were so damn happy before he . . .

I need to see his face.

I reach for the bag.

Simone snatches it away.

A small cry escapes my lips. I stuff it back down. "Where did you find it?"

"Pocantico Park, as I said." Her lips press into a line.

I swallow. "Which is where?"

"North, off Saw Mill River Road."

"In what town?"

"Elmsford."

I straighten my back. "That makes no sense. They found him outside the music store in Dobbs Ferry."

"Their security tapes don't show him ever entering the store. No purchases were made by anyone fitting his description."

"He never made it inside? I don't understand."

She looks at Clive.

He moves his chair in closer, facing me. "The location-sharing app on his phone shows him leaving Pete's Saloon in Elmsford at 8:24 p.m. He gets on the Saw Mill driving south, then loops around to go north. The car circles around twice." He lifts a piece of paper from the box. "I've printed out an enlarged view of the app's map. See here. Your parents' vehicle went off the road *here*, within that circle. Notice the slight deviation where you can see the second loop." He points out the car's path with his pen. "Looks as if the car Cody rode in passes the accident, then comes back around, arriving in Dobbs Ferry a couple of hours later."

I squint, feel my stomach knotting up. "What was he doing for two hours?"

Clive shrugs sitting back in his chair.

"Did he know your parents' car?" Simone asks.

My ears grow hot. "Maybe, I don't know." Hard to miss the dilapidated Monte Carlo with its patchy exterior and potato-smelling maroon leather seats parked outside our apartment. My parents didn't drive it much.

Clive clicks his pen. "One theory I've been noodling: Your boyfriend sees the accident, may or may not have recognized the car until he comes back around. Either way, he pulls over to help."

I bite the inside of my lip, wrapping my arms around my belly. "Okay . . ."

Simone takes the printout from him. "Or . . . what if . . . first pass, he causes your parents' accident. Second pass, he attempts to rescue them and play the hero."

My throat catches.

"Hero syndrome, interesting." Clive raises his brows at me.

"Causes the accident?" My knees start bouncing. "No way. Apps aren't always accurate. Did you find my mom's phone?"

Simone angles her head. "Why do you ask?"

Clive flips the printout over and jots something down on the back.

"Just wondering." I run my hands under my sweaty thighs, my blotchy skin poking out from my jean shorts. The air in here hangs heavy, like someone's turned off the air-conditioning, making it difficult to breathe.

"Remind us why Cody left Pete's." Simone rests her chin on her hand.

"He snapped his guitar string during warm-up and needed to run to the music store in Dobbs Ferry for a replacement."

"Whose car did he borrow?"

"He didn't tell me but I assume Adrian's, one of his bandmates. He picked us up at the train station in White Plains earlier that evening."

"Did he leave alone?"

I nod, not liking the look on her face.

Her eyes pick me apart. "The officers interviewed Adrian and the rest of the band and tech crew that night. No one reported loaning him a car or seeing him get into one outside the club. Either way, it's hard to explain his body being found down in Dobbs Ferry while his phone turns up north—six miles away, in Pocantico Park—with blood on it. Did Cody have any enemies?"

"N-not that I am aware of." The heat from my ears spreads like a fever to my face. "He said he was going to catch a ride with someone but didn't say who. He rushed out pretty fast so he'd be back in time for our set. That night meant a lot to him. He couldn't wait to play in front of his old buddies. He'd talked about it for months."

Clive coughs. "Miss Gallardo, do you know a Dahlia Schenkel?" *Click*, *click* goes his pen.

I swivel my head a fraction. "No." Who the hell is that?

"Your parents' club closed two months before the accident, correct?" Simone refolds her arms. "Were you aware they took out a second business loan the year before?"

I shake my head. "They didn't discuss their financial issues with me; all I know is from the bits I overheard . . . like how the club wasn't drawing the crowds like it once did. My parents were trying what they could to drum up business."

"What kind of *things*?"

I stare at her, my heated face turned up to broil. "I don't like what you're implying. My parents would never have attempted insurance fraud. What a *vile* thing to suggest. They were good people. Honest . . . to a fault."

"Would you call your relationship close?"

I blow out a hard breath. "Yes. I loved them very much."

"They didn't like the idea of you going on tour."

My head snaps up. "Who told you that?" Been a while since I spoke to anyone from LaGuardia. Tess never mentioned being questioned by the police. She'd be the first to tell me, for the drama alone. Maybe Lucy said something. I clasp my hands in my lap, squeeze them together. "My parents hoped I would go to college."

"They must have been disappointed, you being their only child. Maybe that caused some friction between them and Cody?"

"My mom and dad were coming around." I dig my fingernails into my palms.

Simone plants her fist on the table and pushes herself up from her chair. She leans toward me, her brown eyes burning into mine. "The first night of your tour, your parents somehow flip their car and it explodes. Quite a coincidence, isn't it?"

I lean back, increasing the space between us. "What are you doing?"

"Did you and Cody conspire to kill your parents that night, and unfortunately, it went badly for him too?"

My pulse climbs into my throat. "No! Never! I loved my parents.

They were my world, *my life*. They were good people. More worthy than me!"

Clive's elbows hit the table.

I jump.

He holds the pen next to his face like a spear, his eyes slicing into me. "You're positive your boyfriend never mentioned a Dahlia Schenkel?"

I start coughing, my throat thick and dry. I reach for my coffee, my hand shaking. "I told you . . . I have no idea who that is." I can't get enough air; all at once, I feel woozy.

Breathe—come on, Brynn, breathe.

My gut clenches. Horrific images thump through my brain.

Cody's last words: *The sooner I go . . .*

Mom and Dad's faces engulfed in flames.

No. No. No. These two are not going to turn this into anything more than a shitty accident.

"I-I wish it were *me* who died that night!"

Chapter 30

MICAH

The crammed subway lurches forward, taking me and a group of enthusiastic weekenders with it. Bantering with one another, Cameron, Cooper, and Carter appear Hamptons-ready in their flowy shirts and sandals. Sweat drips down the inside of my dress shirt as I watch them exit ahead of me, taking their frat-boy frivolity to the street.

Every year, I avoid Kershaw McKenzie's Fourth of July party, the last bang before we hit our summer lull thanks to reduced work schedules and client vacations.

However.

After Meredith announced Brynn had called out, I found myself lost at my desk for a good hour, unable to write or work. I took off, then putzed around the house, uninterested in reading or listening to music, my energy level zapped. I couldn't bring myself to do anything outside of getting myself off in the shower to calm my incessant thoughts of her—Shadow People be damned.

Her mad dash after the Quotagian presentation has agency staffers placing bets on what sort of trouble she's in and whether we'll see our fearless intern again. I refuse to entertain such speculation. I continue my way to the party, hoping against hope that she'll show.

I fly up the steps ahead of my entourage, leaving the foulness of the subway behind. My phone lights up.

"Did you get it?" My father's voice brims with pride. He likes to gloat when he does something extra and unexpected.

"Sure did. One question. Why?"

"After you called, I wanted to get you something."

"I'd rather see you," I mumble.

"Whatcha say?" I envision him cupping his ear.

"Nothing. Where am I going to put that thing? Wish it had wheels . . ."

"You'll figure it out, Harmonica. Oops, gotta go—I'm on now."

Yep. Call me when you can't talk. Feels like holding on to a slippery fish—one that can't wait to get back into the water. I don't even know the city or country he's calling from.

I slide my cell back in my pocket, absently rubbing the hollow ache in my chest. Maybe *I'm* the fish. The sound of my dad's voice reels me in, then he cuts the line and throws me back.

The Shadow People join me on either side.

Sucker. The henchman snickers.

The Woman in Black reads my face. *Kid, you need to toughen up.*

Dr. Val says, *We teach people how to treat us*. And that I should put an end to my father's antics. But what if he stops calling?

I distract myself by trying to remember the last ten books I read as I ride the elevator up to Dear Irving, a bi-level rooftop bar and lounge overlooking the Hudson in Midtown. You'd never know we tanked last quarter's billable hours by the way Kershaw McKenzie throws a party, all decked out in patriotic balloons and streamers and complete with a DJ and a notably large buffet.

The celebration's humming by the time Brynn appears beside the James Bond–themed, mirror-tiled bar with its hexagonal leather stools and sputnik chandeliers with reflective gold balls above.

She stuns in a hippie-chic dress that's snug around her hips.

My heart skips at the sight of her.

I'm not her only admirer. One of the servers to my right needs to wipe the drool from his chin.

She bites her lip and hugs her dress around her. Her eyes wander the room—looking for Meredith, I presume.

I want her to find *me*. The curious looks she's seeing only know a detective contacted her yesterday—thanks to Donovan, of course—and that she called out today. She may not be in the market for new friends, but I'm not ready to call her a felon yet.

Her eyes bounce over to the buffet, set near a vertical wood screen with portholes. Her body comes to life; she beelines for it.

I chuckle inside, not listening to whatever it is Lucius is saying to me.

All I see. Is her.

I'm about to excuse myself—in a sudden mood for sustenance myself—when the posse descends. Donovan, Josie, Priya, and Meredith corner me to shoot some whiskey. Their in-my-face proximity and wild eyes confirm their pregaming.

"Right on time, Mic. A toast to another winning campaign. I sense an ADDY this year." Donovan grins like we're friends.

I nod, my jaw tight. The buzz around our team's latest campaigns has everyone pumped—thanks to our new intern. Brynn pushed us all out of our creative slump. I should be over the moon.

And yet.

I accept the shot pressed to my chest, disregarding the chemicals swimming in my body, and throw it back. I roll the empty glass in my hand, biting back the burn. I rescan the crowd to find her.

Donovan pops up by her side, all doe-eyed. How'd he even get over there so fast?

I can't read his lips.

She crosses her arms, frowning.

He tilts his head, grinning. He nudges her like he's trying to garner a smile. He thinks he can charm his way into—what? *Having* her?

More brown liquid arrives in my hand. I slam it back, my gaze glued on the two of them.

Josie goes over and wraps Brynn in her arms like she's a long lost family member.

Her victim cringes.

I'm with you, girl; drunken work folk who gossip behind my back don't make my hang list either. Then again, after all these shots, I'm unsure which list I'm on.

Brynn bestows a polite smile on Josie and waves away the next tray of shooters.

Lucius proceeds to grab one for her and tries to hand it to her.

She shakes her head.

The geometric accents in the room rotate a little. I blink in rapid succession. The music's infectious, igniting the liquor coursing through my body.

Dr. Val's #1 Rule: Never drink when crazy and/or on meds.

Brynn steps away from the group without looking back and refills her plate.

Colleagues from other teams approach her with animated faces and pats on the back. Tonight, she's our young star. Everyone wants a piece.

I stride around the crowd, avoiding engagement.

A few chatty coworkers step in my way.

"Yes, the team did an amazing job; they blew the creative away. An ADDY contender, for sure." I run these phrases on loop, my voice robotic.

Then I hit a roadblock.

"Aunt Max, you look great." I kiss her cheek and catch the top notes of the perfume she keeps in her BMW.

Kudos to my aunt, dressed this evening like a fashion model in her sophisticated halter jumpsuit. Quite the departure from the baggy jeans and Vans she used to sport. She tucks her blond bob behind her ears, revealing the piercings she still has from those days—four in her left ear, three right. Minus her old nose ring, of course.

I smile. "Check out those guns; someone's been hitting the gym."

"Yoga, darling, Ashtanga. You should come sometime. Calms the mind." Her lips tighten. "Since when do you drink?"

"Little team bonding."

She touches my arm.

"Fine. Never better."

She arches her brow, following my gaze to Brynn across the room. "Bet it gets lonely living in the old house by yourself."

"I need to look out for my underage staff. Excuse me."

Her hand circles my wrist. "We should do dinner sometime, Mic."

"We will. Soon. Promise."

I muster my sincerest face. She releases my arm, and I move past her. I love my aunt, I do. But I can tell she still feels responsible for what happened.

She was out of town the day I experienced a psychotic break at work.

That day, I arrived back at my desk and my coffee tasted funny. In my messed up brain, I figured that the guy loitering nearby must have poisoned it. I never liked him. And I couldn't let it drop. Neither could the voice in my ear egging me on . . . *Every last Kershaw will die*. He'd go after my aunt next. I had to ensure that didn't happen. I got violent, started pummeling the guy.

Eunice got between us, her soft, repetitive words calming me, before I did any serious damage.

I threw up and got carted off to the hospital.

The guy ended up quitting.

Aunt Max blamed herself, which I never understood. Besides, how can she help me when . . .

Brynn. That dress.

This girl's the first one to jump up when the fresh bagels arrive and the last one to arrive to a team meeting. She doesn't knee-jerk apologize for things like other girls tend to do. She's tough with a soft spot for strangers, a fighter for her friends . . . and has been infiltrating my heart since the day I hired her.

The DJ kicks on an Ace of Base song.

Chatting coworkers break apart. Some step out on the balcony. My team gathers on the dance floor and begins an impromptu dance-off.

Josie motions for me to join them. "Come on, Micah, let loose for once," she projects over the music.

I shake my head, knowing my limitations.

In the center of the lounge, other execs bend and flail their body parts to the music—some forgetting which box they check for "marital status."

House of Pain's "Jump Around" comes on and people start catching air. The wood flooring vibrates as more join.

The DJ's lights begin to pulse.

I step back into a dark corner and face the other direction.

The interns take the middle of the floor.

Brynn hangs back.

Couches and round end tables get moved to the side.

Eunice and Aunt Max have already snuck out.

I should too, but I'm incapable of leaving her alone. I'll order her an Uber later. See that she gets home. Nothing more.

Donovan pulls Brynn's hand to dance to a Backstreet Boys song.

She rocks back on her heels.

My legs move forward before I can think. I touch her shoulder. "Scott wants to talk to you."

"Now?" Her forehead creases.

Donovan spins back into the crowd, his next unsuspecting conquest within reach.

"Over here." I tilt my head. "Sorry to keep you off the dance floor." I hold back from laughing.

"Yeah, right." She rolls her eyes in Donovan's direction. "What does Scott want to talk about?"

"Nothing." I grin.

"Huh?"

"I just . . . are you okay?"

"Yeah. Did you see all that *food*?" She gestures toward the buffet.

"Blows away our whole budget for Bradley Products."

She giggles.

My chest skips. I lean in so she can hear me over the music . . . and to get closer to her.

Lucius approaches, clearly looking for a dance.

I motion for her to walk with me, and he backs off.

"Thanks for the save." She smiles. "Again."

"They won't leave you alone until you dance at least once. Let's make this quick." My hand floats near the small of her back, leading her away from the circle around Donovan, who's rotating through the same three dance moves on repeat, to the far edge of the floor. My heart pounds as I face her. What now? I raise my arms and sway my hips.

She mirrors me—or maybe she started it.

I make spotty eye contact with her. Throwing back my head, I chime in with the Backstreet Boys—sounding superb, for some reason.

Her head nears my chest. "Did you say something?"

My mind fails to compose some witty reply.

The music grows louder. The room spins. The DJ's lights stream from different directions, bouncing off the walls.

My shirt sticks to my skin.

We sway closer. I bask in her spicy vanilla fragrance, the heat coming off her body, her lips.

Our heads pull away.

Her gaze fastens on mine.

For a moment I'm lost in her amber eyes, longing for that russet fire. Time stops until I sense people staring. "Let's get some air."

"Look who's messing with the intern now," Donovan bellows, sliding up next to us with Lucius close behind him.

Brynn jumps. "Shut up, Donovan." She takes off, weaving through clusters of people toward the exit.

I scout out a route that will allow me to cut her off.

Out of nowhere, the Woman in Black grabs hold of my arm.

I swing her off of me. My feet stumble backward. I thrash about without a soul around me as Lucius and Donovan watch.

Chapter 31

BRYNN

I need to clear my head after the week I've had. Been eyeing this gym's three floors of fit, sweaty bodies from the street and its first-month-free deal in the window on my way home from work for weeks; I've missed working out.

I should know within the month if I'm going to get a full-time offer. I push through the glass doors and fill out the paperwork, excited to disappear for the next couple of hours.

Except.

The last person I expected to see appears to be a fellow member.

Micah's beautiful hands grip the long bar at the lat pulldown machine.

Some guy I don't recognize goes over to talk to him.

I turn and walk the other way.

He insisted we dance last night. I got caught up in his brown-suede eyes and forgot where I was, relishing having his attention to myself. Then Donovan made that comment—aimed at Micah, sure, but it cut me too. The earlier praise and encouragement from coworkers I hadn't met before fell away, degrading me to the intern who messes with her boss. My hard work this past month and a half, erased.

I gawk a little at the eye candy around this place as I decide what to do first. The militant rows of cardio machines facing the TV screens scream of boredom. Maybe I'll take a class and hide somewhere in the back. Working out with others tends to motivate me.

Before I met Cody, I played soccer and ran cross-country. I was a decent endurance runner, could chill in my head for miles. I stopped running spring of junior year, about the same time we started dating. He'd pout his lips until I agreed to go with him to Starbucks or the deli after school. Skipping practice once turned into twice a week. Coach cut me from the team, thought I'd gotten lazy. But I just loved being with Cody and didn't want him to be with anyone else. I knew other girls would be all too willing.

A small crowd gathers outside one of the studios. I shuffle in behind them, trying to act like a regular. The bikini-bod instructor calls the class together, her eyelash extensions focused on me. Am I that out of shape? I shift my weight to either foot, folding my arms, and spot Micah out of the corner of my eye out in the main room.

Geez. Don't look over, of all people, and see me in a sports bra and shorts with my hair piled on top of my head. Damn glass walls.

The music starts. Jumping jacks, squats . . . the warm-up has me winded. I keep messing up, I'm so out of practice with doing this kind of thing.

I walk out of class afterward and see Micah using the TRX. His mouth is moving, though no one's near him. Must be counting reps.

I lay a mat down in the stretching area, lie on my back, and close my eyes.

Moments later, I sense a shadow over me. My eyes pop open.

"I thought that was you." He wipes a towel across his face. "Never seen you here before."

I jerk up to sitting and pull my limbs into a tight ball. "First time." Of all the gyms in this city, I join the same one as this guy. "I took a class." Like you didn't know that already.

"Any good?"

I nod and extend my legs. I didn't plan on talking to him, but I can't ignore him now. Plus, I'm not mad at *him*. Not his fault Donovan says things for attention.

Sweat marks stretch across his T-shirt from his neckline to his abs.

Stop staring, Brynn.

I lower my head and eye my crusty kneecaps. I catch a whiff of my own stink and clamp my armpits to my sides, hoping Micah doesn't notice it.

I glance back up at him and my mind wanders a bit, imagining the view underneath his shirt. I relax a little and let my pits air out.

Funny to see him not in work clothes. He could be someone at my high school. I like his hair without product in it. Free from its edgy style and for my fingers to run through its thickness.

He's staring at me. Shit, did he just say something?

"W-what?" I stammer.

"I said the gym gets crowded after work. Not so bad Saturday mornings though."

I slurp up my drool, pulling my arm across my chest.

Out of nowhere, he joins me on the floor. "Have fun last night?" He bends his knee and twists his body away.

His cut thigh and calf say hello. Focus, Brynn. "Um, how are *you* feeling today?" Let's not forget the Backstreet Boys serenade.

"I had one shot too many." His eyes avoid my face. "But I remember everything. Do you?"

"*I* drank water."

His shoulders slump. "About what Donovan said—"

"He likes to stir up drama."

"That he does." He shakes his head.

I rock forward to stand. "Well, have a good weekend—"

"Want to grab an iced coffee or a smoothie downstairs?"

Uh-oh. I bite my lip, blinking at the wall clock for an excuse that doesn't come. "Uh, sure, I'll get my stuff."

In the locker room, I press a towel to my face and neck and spray some of the gym's fancy deodorant in front of a long row of sinks. Even the revitalizing hand wash and restorative body crème look expensive. Behind me, stacked gray lockers line the perimeter of the changing area, with black-and-white-striped benches in the middle. I sit down on one of them, trying to still the pounding in my chest. Do I have time to take a shower? Should I use the gym's fancy dry shampoo I saw by the showers?

I'm being ridiculous.

I pull my tank top on over my sports bra and inspect my flushed cheeks and damp hairline in the full-length mirror.

It will have to do.

I walk up behind a guy with wet, combed-back hair standing near the counter in the café.

Wait.

"You showered?"

Micah turns and smiles. "Nope, just trying to tame the mane."

"Still wordsmithing, even on the weekend."

"What can I say?" He shrugs, eyes crinkling at the corners. "What would you like?"

We carry our almond iced lattes to the street.

"Thanks for the drink." I lean away from him, dismissing the tug in my chest that urges the opposite. Monday can't come soon enough.

"I'll walk you to your subway. Which way?" He lifts his coffee toward Fifth Avenue, the opposite direction of where I catch the train.

"I live in the Village."

His head pulls back. "So do I."

"Bleecker."

"MacDougal." His mouth flings open.

I mimic him. "I've never seen you in *my* neighborhood."

We turn on Fifth, heading downtown. I guess we're walking.

He lifts his shoulder. "I'm not there a lot. I'm often in California on the weekends."

"Oh, you have a girlfriend." I cringe, digging my teeth into my tongue.

"No." The corner of his mouth twists up slightly.

He's gay then, great.

"Are you seeing someone?" His eyes stare straight ahead.

I suck in a sharp intake of air. Should he be asking me this? Then again, I did start us down this path. "I shouldn't have asked about a girlfriend. Not appropriate."

"Don't worry about it. Let's put work aside. It's Saturday."

"Then, no. Not a great time for me."

He nods a few times. "Yeah. I get that. Sometimes getting through the day feels like enough to manage, let alone adding someone else to the mix."

"Something like that." I steal a side-glance.

"At least you got your workout in—now you can face whatever comes your way, right?"

"It does help. Sort of like therapy."

He doesn't say anything beyond a sly smile.

I eye his muscular arms. He's nicely proportioned and . . . I so wish we didn't work together.

"What?" A wrinkle forms between his brows.

I shake my head. "I'm not used to seeing you out of your work clothes." Really, Brynn? Not okay.

"Yeah, I'm fairly grubby. I probably stink."

"Me too." I laugh and take a sip of my latte.

"These streets stink more. We're perfume compared to them." He gestures to either side of us.

I guffaw and snort, at the same time managing to knock into him. Damn pheromones.

He sighs. "Turned out to be a nice morning."

Nice? Meaning the weather, or because we bumped into each other?

We fall into step with one another, passing shop owners hosing down sidewalks and raising metal cages from storefronts. My skin tingles under the sun's warmth. A summer Saturday in the city. Every cell inside of me is on alert from the endorphins and caffeine—and him.

"Hungry?" He stops underneath the arch in Washington Square Park.

"Um, sure." Like that's ever in question.

"How's Jane on Houston sound?"

My stomach rumbles in agreement, and I nod. "They have great vegan scones." I dismiss the fact that other places are closer.

We arrive ten minutes later to a crowd standing underneath a blue-and-white-pinstriped awning. More cluster inside awaiting a table.

I hesitate. "I'm not sure we're dressed for the weekend brunch scene. Want to go somewhere else?"

He holds open the door. "Let's see how long the wait is."

I excuse myself to make a pit stop in the bathroom. My eyes sparkle back at me in the mirror as I wash my hands. I blot the shine from my face and redo my ponytail. A memory flashes: Fighting with the zipper on my bag at Pete's. Makeup I don't own anymore coloring my eyes, cheeks . . . lips.

I blow out a hard breath. No. This is nothing like that. I swing my hair behind my shoulders and press them back.

On the other side of the bathroom door, a wall of patrons blocks my path. Every table, booth, and square stool in this place is occupied.

I hear my name and spot Micah at the end of a long counter. He gestures for me to stay put, then weaves through the line of people waiting.

A woman with a bright-painted mouth and her friend stand between us.

Micah stops and stretches out his hand.

My breath catches. I'm not . . . I shouldn't. I look away, then back to his hand.

"This may be your only chance." He tilts his head, a gleam in his eyes.

"Chance at what?"

"Freedom."

The lady between us raises her brows.

I hold my breath and look down at my toes as if they're hanging over the edge of a high dive. I don't think; I jump.

His hand feels warm and strong and nice all at the same time. He threads me back through the crowd.

Dazed, I knock into people and step on a few feet, soaking in the tingles riding up my arm. I gape at his bicep and vein-popping forearm. The thought of touching him there spreads a warmth into my cheeks.

We reach the counter and he releases my hand.

My chest tightens.

"They said an hour wait for a table. I ordered us a couple of scones and waters."

Oh my God. I'm such an idiot. He held my hand to drag me through the restaurant. Nothing more.

"Let me get this since you got the coffees," I offer.

"Too late." Grinning, he switches the bag of scones and his water to his other hand and passes me my drink.

"Thanks."

His soft brown eyes find me. He extends his free hand. And suddenly, right there at the pick-up counter, I'm holding Micah's hand. Again.

I stare at my fingers inside of his beautiful, strong hand. If he reads my face, he'll know I've been crushing on him this whole time. Is he blushing too?

He lets go when we walk out onto the street.

I look away to conceal my disappointment. Guess it would be hard to eat and walk with our scones and water *and* hold hands. Still.

Less than a block from Bleecker, he gestures to a light purple row home with a brown door that sits below street level. "This is me."

"You live in MacDougal-Sullivan Gardens?" I step back, taking in the colorful row of historic houses. "You share a private courtyard in the back, right?"

"Want to come in?"

"Um . . ." No. Yes. Not sure I should.

"Maybe you can help me with an obstruction in my décor . . ."

I clench my teeth. He hired me. He leads our team. Nothing good can come from this. All these mixed signals I've been giving him. Now he assumes I'm easy? I blame the handholding.

"Um, I don't decorate." I turn on my heel and hoof it down the street, leaving him holding the bag with my half-eaten scone.

Chapter 32

MICAH

What the hell just happened? How did our nice morning turn into her bolting? *Decorate?* I didn't ask her to decorate.

Shaking my head, I walk through the kitchen to the back of the house and give the six-foot-three statue holding court in the center of the living room a shove. It moves a millimeter, if that.

I blow out a pent-up breath, scratching my head. Then I sniff my T-shirt. Maybe I do reek.

The employee database shuts me out from logging in on my personal laptop. I can't find Meredith's group text. I don't recall deleting it. I scroll through old emails to find Brynn's internship application. Her address: Brooklyn.

Should have escorted her to her place first. She thinks I'm more of a dick now. *Want to come in?* does sound a bit sleazy, considering she works for me. I search *Brynn Gallardo* and find a Basilio Gallardo on Bleecker Street.

I jump in the shower, not waiting for the water to heat up first. Dammit, I wasn't trying to come on to her.

Well. We *did* hold hands for a minute. I'd hoped I could be the exception to her no-new-friends rule.

This girl, this girl. She infuriates me, yet I can't stop thinking about her. I need to fix this. Why the hell did I let her walk away?

I check my phone for a text from her—a bit comical, since she couldn't wait to get rid of me an hour ago.

Chasing after a girl is not my thing, but I need to fix this.

I trek up MacDougal and hang a left on Bleecker, my head whipping around nonstop like I might see her. Crossing over into the afternoon, the Village hums with weekend visitors. I dodge around them and bound up the steps to her brick building.

The directory lists apartment numbers without names. I sigh, shading my eyes, peering through the electronic door, ready to ring all the residences—when a guy pushes the door toward me, on his way out. I slide in behind him before it closes.

The floor runner along the entryway smells like a wet dog. Make that a pack of wet dogs. Holding my nostrils, I wander down a narrow hallway with beige walls and gray Florentine floor tiles to a black metal stairwell that echoes under my ascent.

I walk each floor, some twice, until I finally see *Gallardo* on one of the doors.

My heartbeat slides into my throat. I swallow and knock.

Footsteps sound. They stop.

I sense eyeballs peering through the peephole. I gaze down at my shoes.

The door opens without urgency. Still dressed from the gym, Brynn rubs her face, working through a yawn. Then her forehead creases into a scowl, as if she's only just remembered our last exchange.

Shit. "Hi."

She blinks a few times.

"I was in the neighborhood. Thought I'd come by."

"For decorating advice?" Her voice is tinged with unmistakable snark.

"Nope. Not looking for decorating advice." I grimace. "Not now and not earlier today."

She sighs, crosses her arms over her chest, and shifts her weight to her other foot.

"I'm embarrassed to admit this."

"Try me." She huffs.

"I received a very heavy . . . uh, present . . . a stone sculpture that I can't move by myself."

"So ask a friend."

"I did."

"Oh." She cringes.

"I'll spring for a late lunch or early dinner afterward? No pressure." I hold my breath.

"Um, when?"

"How about now?" I peek around her. She didn't mention having a roommate.

"I don't know. I'm pretty beat. Long walk earlier." She half smiles.

My shoulders relax. I grin like a dork. God, she's irresistible. "Are you hungry?"

She holds her stomach, pausing. "I need to shower first."

"Done."

She hesitates; her eyes consider me for a moment before glancing back over her shoulder. Her lips turn down. She opens the door wider.

I steel my jaw from dropping. Talk about tiny; this place is like an interior cabin on a cruise ship tiny. The mattress on the floor eats up most of the space. The short wall holds up a combo mini fridge, stove, and sink. Sheets lie rumpled in a ball on the floor. I can't help but picture her tangled in them. Stacked boxes occupy the other wall beside a rolling rack of clothes.

"Just move in?"

"Something like that." She lowers her lashes, yanks a towel off the curtain rod, and throws it over her shoulder.

Her apartment could fit inside a walk-in closet on Park Avenue. It's maybe three-hundred square feet, if that. "Is this place legal?"

No response.

I'm not sure where she wants me to wait. I don't see anywhere to sit unless you count the mattress.

She retrieves something blue from one of the open boxes and holds it under her arm. From another box, she grabs smaller items and scrunches them up in her hand. She picks up a plastic container of toiletries and exits.

"Hey . . ." I step into the hallway.

She keeps walking, inserts a key into a door a few down from hers, and disappears inside.

I'm not sure what I'm supposed to do. I stare after her, my mouth sprung open.

She sticks her head out. "If I'm not out in ten minutes, call the police."

I can't tell if she's joking.

I meander around her apartment, looking for traces of the girl I think I know. A couple of framed pictures rest on a low stool next to the mattress. In one, she's with a blond surfer-looking guy, wearing more makeup than I've ever seen on her. Must be from Halloween or something.

The woman in the next picture shares Brynn's raven-colored hair. Her parents, I presume, the pair jamming on low-slung electric guitars with big, toothy grins and starry eyes locked on each other.

I suck in my breath.

Meredith said they both died in a car accident not too long ago. Like a jerk, I kept bringing them up when we went out to lunch.

She goes from living in Brooklyn to this shoebox? You'd think a creative person like her would have colorful posters or art everywhere. Maybe she's on meds too.

Outside, a car horn blares for an obnoxious length of time. More horns join the cacophony; people start yelling. Her open window faces Bleecker Street. I imagine it's hard to hold a conversation or hear yourself think with that constant commotion.

I'm studying one of the boxes against the wall when I feel Brynn behind me. I startle. That was a fast shower. She's already in a different outfit—a sleeveless royal blue sundress. Stunning.

Catching my breath, I gesture at her window. "How do you live with the noise?"

She shrugs. "The street keeps me company."

"Does it wake you up?"

"Yeah, if I leave the window open. On Sunday nights, a pack of motorcycles likes to storm the street at three in the morning. The first time it happened, the roar sent me straight up in bed. But I can sleep through anything now."

I nod a few times. "Bleecker. Always so loud."

"MacDougal. The quiet away." She studies me for a moment before bending over to comb through her hair in front of the window. Water droplets seep into the pale wood floor around her bare feet. She straightens up, glances at her reflection in the upper window pane.

Okay, I have to ask. "Are you a minimalist or something? Why don't you have any furniture?"

She turns around; her eyes slice into me. "Would need serious funds for that."

I drop my head, the schmuck who had her working for free and is still only paying her minimum wage. It's standard industry practice for newbies; everyone wants to be in advertising. I didn't know she lived like this. Explains her bagel thievery every morning.

I motion to the picture of her mom and dad. "Where was your parents' club?"

"Where Bleecker meets Bowery."

"Wait, the Flaming Flamingo? Wow, that place was legendary. What happened to it?"

"Started to hit hard times when I was in high school. It got some negative publicity." She shakes her head. "The building needed repairs and upgrades to adhere to new city codes."

"They look happy here." I pick up the picture again. "Your dad's a badass with his crew cut and tats. You favor your mom."

"Hm." Brynn shrugs. "She's tiny compared to me."

"How do you pronounce their names?"

"Basilio and Katia."

"I like the way they sound."

"I know, musical. Then they give me such a boring name. Too close to *brim*. I'm always having to spell it."

"You won't receive any sympathy from me."

"Is *Micah* biblical?"

I return her shrug. "People always leave off the *h*, like the mineral. Or nickname me after a countertop."

Her lip curls. "Donovan sucks."

I don't want to talk about work right now. "It's cool you're Peruvian. Does *Gallardo* mean anything in Spanish?"

"Means *gallant*." A faint smile graces her lips. "My grandparents almost Americanized it to *Gallagher* after fleeing Peru's dictatorship in the early '70s. I'm glad they didn't."

"I am too; I like Gallardo."

"My mom's maiden name was Baez."

"As in Joan? Music legends run in your veins."

"No relation." She laughs. "But I did grow up onstage. My mom would wear me inside this wrap she tied around herself, put pink headphones on me to protect my ears. She told me I'd fall asleep to her singing. The show must go on, I guess."

"Or she couldn't bear to leave you." My voice falters. If given the chance, would my own mother have worn me watching my dad play? Never crossed my mind before. My throat constricts. I look away.

"I don't know, maybe." The corners of her lips turn down.

I clear my windpipe. "How did you find *this* place?"

"My parents owned it. Rented it to musicians. They bought it after college in the late '90s. With the communal bathroom and this being a pre-war building, the rent seemed reasonable for the West Village." Her cheeks turn pink. "I think they conceived me here."

I stare at the darkening ring by her feet. "I only ever knew my dad. And he wasn't around much."

"So, this thing we're moving . . ."

I shake off the heaviness in my chest. "My father sends these unique gifts every so often, ones I can't possibly use."

"Rich people problems, huh?" She shoots me a wry look.

"He's a musician too, actually. Plays in a different city every night, no forwarding address or working cell." I sniff. "Okay, that last part's untrue."

She chuckles. "Sounds like a country song. Would I know his music?"

"Ever heard of 'Cherry Wine Bride' or 'You Melt My Boots Off'?"

"That's *your* dad?" Her eyes widen. "You hear his songs everywhere. Even in those erectile disfunction commercials."

"Yepper." I sigh and pull her tiny fridge door open, peek inside. What am I doing? I slam the door shut. "Sorry."

She lifts her hair off her neck, and the gesture dissuades me from making my joke about checking on her baby carrot supply. She has no idea how breathtaking she looks. I wet my lips, imagining tasting the delicate area between her head and shoulder, inhaling the scent of her skin.

"I know something about having famous parents." She pivots and reaches into a small box. "Did you feel a lot of pressure growing up?"

I slide my hands into my pockets and grip my thighs, hoping to quell my attraction to her. "Oh, I can't sing. So, no."

"He must be amazing to see live," she says, her back still to me.

"I wouldn't know."

She turns toward me. "I'm ready."

I blink a few times, taking in the full effect—the blue sundress, and sandals, her shimmery-wet hair.

She threads a small gold hoop into her ear. "Too hot today for restrictive clothes."

No complaints here. "You should wear that color more often."

She smiles a little and points to my green T-shirt and tan twill shorts. "I've never seen you dressed so casual, except for at the gym."

"A lot of firsts today."

What an idiotic thing to say.

On the street, I resist the urge to take her hand, not wanting to confuse things again. I like getting to know her outside of work.

"You could loft the bed." I look over at her.

Voices travel to us from the coffee bar across the street.

She side-eyes me.

"Dorm-room style. You already share a bathroom on your floor; it's kinda like a college residence hall. Raising the bed frees up space underneath. You could maybe fit a table in there."

"I don't know how long I'm staying. I call that place *the coffin*."

"That's pleasant. How about *petit palais* instead?"

"Sure you're not a copywriter?" Her eyes smile.

We pass a group of guys on Bleecker. Each grabs an eyeful of her.

She sticks a little tighter to my side on the busy sidewalk.

It starts to drizzle through the sunshine. We hasten our pace, moving around the slow walkers, and arrive at my door a couple of minutes later.

I wipe the rain from my forehead, glancing back. "Let's try this again."

She crosses her arms and twists up her lips.

I give her what I hope resembles a reassuring smile, push the door open, and step back so she can go in first.

She runs her fingertips along the wainscoting that connects the vestibule and foyer, then traces the wandering gray veins in the kitchen's white quartz island. She walks toward the white cabinets, brushing her index finger over the square pewter knobs.

My mouth waters as I watch her every move. Reluctant to pull my eyes away, I lift a couple of towels from the hallway closet and pass her one.

She dries her arms and face, then wraps the towel around her shoulders before strolling into the living room. Her eyes float around the space until they stop on the tall windows that open to the garden. "I love the white walls against the gray hardwood and brick fireplace. So modern with all the black accents . . . lucky you."

"My granddad owns the building." I stop, realizing I'm tapping my foot. I steal a glance at her, then bury my hands deep in my pockets. "The families who live in the MacDougal and Sullivan Street historic district share the big garden. My dad used to run with the Garden Kids. He said they had their own set of rules and liked adventures, whatever that means."

"Do you use all four floors, or did he break them into apartments?"

"I hang out on this floor and sleep on the third. The fourth floor has a terrace and solarium, but I'm not keen on heights."

"Even growing up in Bushwick, I heard about the families who lived on Rainbow Row and their secret garden in between." The corners of her eyes crinkle; her voice grows wistful. "My high school friends and I used to sip lattes across the street at Caffé Dante and fantasize about this mythical place, wondering how rich you needed to be to live here."

I shake my head. "My dad didn't grow up wealthy. Granddad thinks working hard is the only virtue that matters . . . he didn't go easy on him. My dad left home before finishing high school. Then my grandparents divorced. My grandmother passed away a few years ago." God, I'm rambling.

She peers out the white, multipaned terrace door into the garden, the towel around her like a cape. "Who takes care of the area beyond your yard?"

"We've got people. We'll venture out after the rain stops."

She glances back over her shoulder. "You haven't decorated either."

"Like I said, I'm not here a lot."

She turns to the center of the living room. "Who's this guy?"

"A statue of *great* limitations." I snicker. "Alexander the Great. A little joke of my dad's."

She tilts her head, taking in the sculpture. "I did a school project on him once—king of ancient Macedonia, known for his great military mind, right?"

"I don't recall."

"Is this an original?"

"A cheap replica—heavy too." I grimace.

"Must have been a bear getting him in here."

"A neighbor let in the delivery guys. Scared me to death. Thought I had an intruder."

"Why do you think *I* can move it if you can't?" She gestures to the figure draped in a sheet around his waist.

"I've seen you work out." In the class I pretended I didn't know you were in. "And save people in elevators and subways. Pretty tough."

She laughs.

My heart skips a beat.

"Where did his right arm go?"

"Doesn't need it, I guess."

Her forehead creases. "What's he holding in his left, a spear?"

"I think."

"Okay, where do you want Old Righty?"

I scan the living room. "Hadn't thought that far ahead."

"Are you going to use him for anything . . . maybe a coat rack?" She wrinkles her nose.

"Come on, some call it *fine* art."

"*Fine* art? You sound like the kids at my high school."

"Is it true LaGuardia kids dance on cars like in the movie?"

"Oh yeah, all the time." She pulls a face. "Show choir closes its spring concert with the music from *Fame*. The school's gotten a lot of mileage out of it. They even sell *Fame* T-shirts."

"Let me guess, theater major . . . dance?"

"Vocal."

"Right—you sing better than Halsey, but more like St. Vincent."

She frowns, her eyes distant. "I grew up around musicians. Was singing before I could talk."

"Do you still sing?"

"Not anymore." Her tone shifts. "How about next to that yellow-gold couch? He could be a conversation piece. You could decorate him for parties."

I shake my head. "I never have people over."

"Yeah right. I'm sure you invite the ladies in all the time."

"Ahh, no."

"Why? Look at you." She contorts her face like I'm full of it.

"Look at *you*." I ditch my towel on a nearby chair and step in front of her.

Her eyes meet mine, slow and cautious. The sounds of raindrops and my thumping chest fill my ears.

She doesn't move.

I step closer, cementing my arms to my sides, resisting everything in my being that's screaming for me to touch her.

She closes her eyes and sways her hips.

I suck in my breath and watch her, waiting for her to tell me I'm not imagining this pull between us. First that night in the Electric Room, then at the Fourth of July party, and now here. "What's the song in your head?" I ask, my throat thick.

A serene smile crosses her face. She doesn't answer.

I'm ready to surrender to her terms, whatever they may be.

Don't screw this up, Micah.

The floor vibrates underneath our feet for several seconds.

She giggles. "How often does the subway come by?"

"Too many times a day to notice it anymore." My gaze doesn't waver from her face; an earthquake could hit right now and I wouldn't flinch.

She moves closer.

My breathing stops.

She leans her head on my chest.

I draw in a sharp breath. My heart flips, kicking her in the forehead. After a split second of hesitation, I pull the towel around her tighter and then circle my arms over it, holding her like she could run away at any moment.

We don't have to proceed any further. I can stop. We'll have a nice dinner somewhere and be friends. This doesn't have to mean what I want it to mean. She was shivering, after all.

A spicy vanilla scent passes through my nostrils, her fresh soapiness from the shower. I've gotten this dizzy feeling before, when she's been near me at work. This time, I don't have to pretend otherwise.

Every cell in my body crackles with electricity. With one shake of the head, an indication that she thinks this is a mistake, she could topple me over. With one blissful touch to show me she feels it too, she could do the same. Either way, I may never recuperate.

Her towel drops around her feet. Her fingers claw at the front of my damp T-shirt, gathering the fabric in her palms. Her knuckles sink into my abs.

I stop myself from drawing her in closer. "This was not my plan when I invited you over, I swear."

She looks up and almost through me.

"You okay?" I search her eyes. Her exquisite face beckons my lips to trace it.

She bites her lip.

I pull her again into my arms, one layer closer less the towel. "You don't have to help me move the statue if you don't want to." I clear the husky sound in my voice.

She giggles.

I hug her tighter; no doubt she can sense the heat below my hips. For a fleeting moment, I think about carrying her up to my bedroom . . . showing her what's been building up inside of me since the first morning she ventured into my elevator.

Don't even try it, you idiot.

My heart hammers inside my chest. If only I could peek inside her head, see where she stands. I want her to lead the way. My feelings for her have never been more obvious. If I'm overstepping, she'll slap me or something, right?

We stand almost motionless, holding on to one another.

Time stills. The rain grazes the windows.

Her chin tips up toward mine.

I restrain my desire to drag my lips over it and down her neck and throat.

Something new creeps into her eyes. A sadness—she's hurting.

"Tell me." Let me kiss it away. Her parents, the guy in the photo, her face beaming next to his. Maybe he hurt her.

I couldn't care less about them.

I only care about her.

I want to do *everything* to her. For her.

She coughs, looks like she's trying to talk but can't get the words out.

"Want some water?" I motion toward the kitchen.

She nods, but I don't let go. Her eyes expand, drinking me in. She moistens her lips.

My hands shake; any second, I feel, she'll bolt. She's given me this look before, but not to this degree. The same look I fantasize about when I'm in the shower. My water bill and level of cleanliness have never been higher. She's always broken the connection first, though, leaving me guessing.

She pulls my T-shirt toward her.

My lips drop onto hers like a fallen edifice, fated to be hers.

Her mouth pushes back on mine.

I respond, hungry for her. In this moment, she's everything I want, everything I need.

Her hands slide underneath my T-shirt and her fingertips climb the sides of my ribcage to my chest.

Oh. My. God. I moan.

She presses into me harder, swallowing me up.

I'm good with whatever she wants. I want her too, so much.

She knows this, it's like she has been reading me this whole time. I guess my face can't keep a secret—not from her, at least.

And then . . . she jerks her head away.

"What?" I ask, my voice barely audible.

Her head swivels *no*. She releases a long exhale and a strained look rises in her eyes.

"What's wrong?" I whisper. A hollow ache pierces my chest. *Let me back in.* She's going to leave. *Please . . . please don't.*

She shivers.

I rub the sides of her arms. "Show me."

Chapter 33

BRYNN

"Show me."

Show him what? That I hate being a person who says one thing and does another? That I swore I wouldn't catch feelings for him, yet here we are? Why did he have to catapult into my life *now*?

Cody was my first—my only. We were so crazy in love with each other. What if kissing Micah erases every kiss I shared with him? What if one day I won't be able to remember my first love, only the man before me now? I don't want to forget.

My body's sure ready, though. My heart's exploding like a firecracker just went off in my chest. Micah's turned me on so much, I'm already more than halfway there. If I was home alone, I could get him out of my system without crossing that line.

Except.

I've already crossed it.

I stare at his lips and a primal aching overtakes me. My parched body can almost taste the release he'll bring. I gather the side of my dress in my hand, sliding it up my leg. My thong's drenched. I slide the fabric away, let my fingers continue up, and get lost in that delicious face of his.

He breathes through his mouth, watching me, eyes wide.

My eyes roll back; it feels so . . .

Charged currents run up my legs. I grasp his shoulder, crying out. My body quivers, my toes . . . go . . . numb.

He grabs hold of my hips.

I drop like a rag doll into his arms, panting.

He holds me longer.

I sigh a spent breath and tilt my face to his.

His Adam's apple rolls along his throat. "You're incredible."

"I've never . . . no one's ever . . . watched . . ." I feel my cheeks flame. I can't look at him.

His tender hands lift my face, he kisses the tip of my nose. "You better run."

I stall, my mouth flopped open. His words sink in. I take the staircase's wide wooden planks two at a time.

He gives me a lead.

I hear him come after me, both of us laughing. My short legs can't match his long strides.

When I reach the third floor, I follow his familiar woodsy scent into a bedroom painted the color of the sea. Industrial pendant lighting hangs on either side of a gray tufted headboard with rustic wainscoting all around. The unmade king-size bed faces another empty fireplace; the room's gauzy drapes hang drawn.

He comes up behind me. "Great guess."

I laugh a little at the clothes draped over the dresser, spilling out of drawers, and tossed to the ground. Notebooks similar to the one he carries at work lay strewn on the floor alongside empty water bottles, Starbucks cups, and torn pages filled with writing. "You're a mess."

He moves my hair off to the side and caresses my shoulders. "You have no idea." His breath tickles my ear.

My back stiffens. A low buzzing sound fills the room. My hands tense, cold with sweat; my heart sprints inside my chest.

He kisses the back of my head, stroking my arms. "We can stop. Just say when."

When. "Do you . . ."

His muscular arms encircle me. "Yes. In the drawer next to the bed."

"Thought you didn't—"

"I dreamt of one day asking you out." His lips trail down the curve of my neck. "I bought them in case you couldn't resist me."

We burst out laughing.

My body relaxes into his. Closing my eyes, I take a deep breath, slowly exhale. "Undress me, Mr. Irresistible."

"Yessssss, ma'am." He inches my sundress over my head, his fingers like feathers against my skin. Goose bumps rise. He sweeps his lips across my upper back. "What a gorgeous view." He wraps his hands around my stomach.

I gasp and tighten it, flinching a little.

He holds me firmer, sucking the soft spots at the base of my neck and clavicle.

I squirm and giggle at the same time.

He rests his chin on my shoulder. "Let me look at you."

I suck in my belly and turn in his embrace.

Our bodies press up against each other. His pelvis snug to my belly, I can feel his pulse. His khaki eyes burn into mine.

"Your turn." My voice sounds throaty, unfamiliar to my own ears.

He yanks off his T-shirt and slides off his shorts in one sweeping motion. His lips crack into a smile.

About to comment on his *Magic Mike* skills, I get sidetracked by his ripped shoulders . . . abs . . . golden brown skin. My brain sputters to a stop.

He doesn't let me gawk long. His strong fingers cup my shoulders under my bra.

My pulse quickens. With both hands, I haul his face down to mine, arching my back, the curves of our bodies joined as one.

He makes desperate noises, his breathing audible and erratic. "I wish . . . I want—"

"Show me," I whisper.

He cradles the back of my head, lifts me with his other arm, and presses me down onto the bed.

The heated weight of his nakedness sends a renewed throbbing between my legs. I run my fingers through his thick hair, at last.

He devours me inch by inch . . . gently sucking my lips, cheeks, and . . . ooh . . . up my jawline.

I need to see his face; I roll us onto our sides.

His eyes drink in the length of me like I'm a rare treasure.

My heart gives a kick. I climb on top, straddling him, and reach behind me to unhook my bra.

He cups my face, stopping me. "You're beautiful, Brynn."

I half smile. "You make me want to work out more."

He moves strands of hair away from my eyes. "Your body would make a poet cry."

I flash him a playful grin. "Know any?"

"I do." He smiles, his eyes longing. "Come here."

A glaze of sweat covers our faces and tangled limbs. We slide apart, breathless.

I pull the sheet around me.

He leaves his glistening chest exposed.

We lie nose to nose, on our sides. I smile a little and shiver, hesitant to speak and start dissecting everything.

"Cold?" He tugs the sheet higher, covering my shoulder with it.

I trace his face, discovering its nuances. His broad nose bridge (great for singing) thins in the middle before widening again, similar to the one I saw on the Alexander the Great statue downstairs. And the corners of his mouth curl up even when he's not smiling—which he doesn't do a lot, except for today.

He stares past me, transfixed by something.

I turn my head. "What?"

"Nothing." He kisses my nose.

The intensity of being with him washes over me. I don't know how we can reverse this. I'm not sure I want to. I feel different. Lighter. Lifted from the black vortex that's been sucking me down since that night. The knot in my chest has come loose, letting me breathe again.

I nestle under his arm. The sudden silence pokes at me. I need to know what he's thinking.

I peek over and find his eyes closed. Something inside of me deflates a little. I shake off the impulse to wake him and sink into his dreamy bed, his silver gray sheets made with a thread count I could never afford.

Watching the birds flutter in the trees through the blowing gossamer curtains, my eyelids grow heavy. I'll rest for a minute, then go.

A bird squawks in the garden below. My eyes pop open. Micah. His arm and leg slung around me. His bedroom dark.

Oh, shit.

I inch and slide, inch and slide, traveling to the edge of the bed. I pick up the nearest piece of clothing and tiptoe into the bathroom, which is a mausoleum of white marble walls and vessel sinks with fancy black handles. I find my face in the frameless backlit mirror. The windows to my soulless soul stare back. I collapse in half, hands on my knees like I've been sucker punched.

How can you let them down like this? Sleeping with your boss when Cody's been ripped from this world so cruelly? You're the only one left—what is wrong with you?

A bigger knot reties in my belly. My nose runs. What *is* wrong with me? I'm not ready to hook up. What happened to *no new friends*?

I need to find my clothes and slip out of here.

The floor creaks on the other side of the door. Shoot.

I splash cool water on my face and feel around for the plush hand towel I spotted when I walked in. I blot my face and do a sloppy job of refolding it. Gathering my breath, I hover my hand over the knob, swing open the door, and step forward.

Right into Micah's smooth chest.

I cup my nose.

His short shorts hang from his hips, revealing a V-shaped crease below his chiseled abs. I lift my jaw off the floor. My head is spinning. I need to sit down.

He folds me into his strong arms.

The heat from his bare chest melts my insides. My legs become jelly. I sigh, relishing being this close to someone again. Whatever this is between us, it feels grown up, not like some high school crush. Micah's different. I'm different. I can't explain this pull toward him or why I'm tearing up again.

He lifts my chin. "Can I take you to dinner?"

"I didn't exactly move the statue." I smile, sniffling.

He runs a gentle thumb under my wet lashes. "You okay?"

Cody's face flashes in my head. He and my parents died eight short months ago, and I'm acting like their lives meant nothing. I swallow the tightness in my throat.

"Dinner, um . . . sounds nice." I rise on my tiptoes and miss his lips, land one on his neck instead.

We never make it outside.

Chapter 34

MICAH

We rise early, starving, and go out in search of an establishment willing to feed us before 9:00 a.m.

Brynn sees the SoHo bistro, with its green-striped awning and cluster of potted plants outside, first. "Ooh, they're open!" She tugs me toward it.

Inside, rows of white globes hang from the ceiling like an airport runway. The simple tables and curved-back chairs cluster in front, with a small bar in the back.

The servers, dressed in non-matching striped shirts, yawn at us as they buff glasses and set out silverware. The stench of stale beer from last night and freshly brewed coffee battle it out for dominance.

I can't stop touching her. A magnetic force keeps drawing me back to wherever she is—beginning with our knees, which keep meeting under this ridiculously small table.

She doesn't move her legs away.

I end up hugging hers with mine like a love-struck puppy who can't stop wagging his tail.

The trajectory of last night—from my anxious worrying that she'd take off again to then watching her pleasure herself in my living room to at last having her in my bed—has my mind exploding. This girl, this girl. I haven't wiped the smile from my face since last night's unexpected sleepover, outside of the moment the Shadow People decided to join us in my bedroom. I worked so hard to tune them out, I fell sleep.

I find the way she orders her tofu frittata and avocado toast mesmerizing.

When the server leaves, she catches me staring and does a double take. "What?"

"Nothing." I tone down my giddiness and strike a serious face. "So, how long have you been a virgin? Vegan. I meant vegan." Shit.

She smirks and makes a show of perusing the drink menu, seemingly confident we won't get carded. "In answer to your *second* question . . . My class went to a farm in elementary school. I got bored and wandered off—and ended up watching an axe come down on a pig's neck. Its little legs kept moving as they dismembered it." Her body recoils from the memory.

She casts a spell on another passing server with her radiant smile and orders a Bloody Mary, extra spicy. Like her.

He forgets the part about seeing her ID. I can't say I blame him.

"My mom and dad called it a phase. I didn't know anyone who cared about animal cruelty. When people started researching where their food came from, that it doesn't magically appear on a supermarket shelf, veganism became trendy. Then my parents got on board and posed naked for PETA. The headline read something like, *Ink, Not Mink*."

"Nice, they wanted to support you."

She rolls her eyes. "More like get publicity for their club."

"Was your boyfriend vegan?"

Her lips twitch. "No."

"He's the surfer-looking guy in the photo next to your bed, right?" I work to keep my tone neutral like I'm asking about the weather. "You're prettier without all that makeup. No offense."

"Cody liked it. Um, let's talk about something else."

I'm not ready to drop it. "Sounds like he had his claws in you."

Her eyes flash. "You know nothing about him."

"So, what happened?"

She winces a little. "Can we drop it?"

I raise my palms. "I just want to get to know you."

She gives me a blank stare. After a long beat, she exhales. "We met in high school; both of us were impatient to get our music careers going. Cody's band put together a tour the fall of our senior year and invited me to join them."

"So, less than a year ago."

"The first night of the tour, a car hit him."

I take a sharp breath. "You saw it happen?"

She shakes her head, looking away.

I dated a few girls in high school. Never once did I plan to run off with any of them. I can't even imagine it now, at twenty. She's so young; what was the rush with this guy?

The server arrives with our food. "The plates are hot," he cautions.

I wait for him to leave before asking, "If you studied voice, why aren't you singing now?"

"Just no desire to." She shrugs and takes a bite of her frittata.

"You could still tour with his band. Could be cathartic."

"You don't get it." She lowers her fork.

I reach for her other hand. It disappears into her lap.

"That same night, my dad lost control of his car driving to Westchester to see our first show. Both my parents died." Her voice drops.

"Wait, he hit your boyfriend?"

She narrows her eyes. "Why would you say that?"

I tilt my head. I need more coffee and a better timeline. "Sorry, I misunderstood."

She rubs the side of her face. "Someone else hit him outside a music store."

"Two car accidents on the same night?" I shake my head. "Weirdly random. Do you have other family?"

She clenches her jaw. "It's just me now."

"How about your friends?"

"I haven't seen them since graduation. Both of them headed off to college, anyway."

"I get that. I don't talk to my high school friends either."

She swirls her celery in her glass. She bites the end like it's my head.

"How's everything tasting?"

We nod in silence, waiting for him to leave again.

She brings her Bloody Mary to her lips. "Are you in college?"

"I took a few classes in San Diego." I glance away, unable to look at her. "I hoped to see my dad more if I went to school in Cali. I didn't. Our relationship's kind of complicated."

She pushes the food around on her plate. "What about your mom? You said she wasn't really around?"

"My mom . . . well . . ."

The morning sun shifts behind her, filtering through the glass entry door and windows and creating a tunnel effect. My ears clog, muffling the sounds around me. Brynn's head becomes backlit like a halo, her facial features concealed in shadow. She could be anyone right now.

Someone asks me to repeat what I just said. Problem is, I haven't a clue.

Does she think about Cody when I kiss her?

Do I even want to know?

Am I merely the rebound guy?

When I touch her, does she think about his hands on her?

Am I a casual fling, something to fill time?

Am I attracted by the fact that her heart seems unattainable? Some macho notion she'll become more obsessed with me than she was with him?

Did the last twenty-four hours mean anything to her?

I'm afraid to see the answer in her eyes.

I'm sort of grateful her circumstances led her to me. Pretty sick, I admit. Selfish too. We wouldn't have met. Does she think I'm the one silver lining?

"Micah? *Micah*."

My eyes refocus. "Yeah," I say, my tone confident, like I've been with her the whole time.

She cocks her head. "I asked about your mom."

"Ah, I never knew her."

She blinks. "You look angry."

"I'm not." I smile wide, rewriting the moment.

We walk outside afterward. Holding my breath, I intertwine my fingers with hers.

She sidles closer to me and I'm wagging all over again.

"Down for a little adventure?"

She glances up at me, shielding her eyes from the ball of fire high in the sky. "I think so?"

"We could trek uptown for some music in the park."

"It's already boiling out here."

"We'll get some floppy hats and sunscreen along the way."

Her skeptical look softens. "What time does it start?"

"We have time." I grin.

We come up empty at the first couple of thrift stores so we walk west to catch the subway. After transferring a few times, we arrive at Seventy-Second and Broadway.

I gesture up the street. "Isn't there a thrift store up here?"

She squints ahead. "A few blocks up, I think."

Inside, we skip past the store's rounders of clothes organized by decade to the hats and accessories displayed in the back. My nose twitches from the mix of floral air freshener and that musty thrift store smell.

"I like this top hat." The corners of her eyes crease as she picks it up. "Bet it's full of stories. Can you imagine wearing this for a night out on the town?"

I slap on a hat and turn to her. "How about this?"

"Nice, amigo. It suits you." She laughs at the pile of straw on my head and puts a wide-brimmed number on. "Ooh, how does this one look?"

"Like Janis Joplin headlining at Woodstock. Perfect."

She steps up beside me at the register. "So, where's the concert?"

"In the big shell."

Her eyes expand. "Naumburg Bandshell, on a Sunday?"

"Ever perform there?"

She shakes her head.

"Let's take an Uber." I clasp her hand. "We don't want to be late."

Chapter 35

BRYNN

My thoughts drift out the car's window as we take Sixty-Fifth through the park. Our driver pulls off on the Fifth Avenue side. I hear Cody calling me a traitor.

We used to spend hours in Central Park when the weather was nice, much like today. Cody didn't talk about his parents much. I got the feeling he didn't get along with his either. They stayed away a lot. But unlike me, he seemed good with that. He enjoyed his freedom, was too busy chasing his dream—to light up the night sky like a Hollywood marquee. Something like that.

Micah extends a hand, helping me out of our ride. We walk the rest of the way through the park.

I feel a tug inside my chest. Not too long ago I held Cody's hand and walked on these same hexagonal pavers under this same canopy of trees. I shake off my déjà vu and try to focus on this carefree day, one where everyone's outside.

My parents took me to a free concert at the Naumburg Bandshell once. The music bored me to bits. Who knew Micah had a thing for classical music? He would have liked my parents. Everyone did.

The top curve of the iconic amphitheater's white limestone shell comes into view through the trees. We get closer; a scattering of leaves covers its stage. In front, not a chair or patron can be seen.

"There's no concert here." I side-eye him.

"Soon." He suppresses a smile.

"Uh-huh. When does it start?"

"Any minute now."

"Wait." He's not thinking . . . "Micah, I'm not going to sing for you."

"Nope. I am."

"*You're* going to sing? Are you sure that's a good idea? I heard your Backstreet Boys rendition at the company party, and, well, you shouldn't quit your day job."

"Encouraging, you are not." Micah leaps onstage and begins swaying to some bizarre beat in his head. He snaps his fingers, opens his mouth. A sound comes out. Not a good one.

I squint like it hurts, fists over my ears. "Please, stop. I can't unsee or unhear this. The birds are dropping from the trees."

He rolls his hips like he's hula-hooping. "I'll stop. If *you* sing."

"You play dirty." I cross my arms.

"I play to win." He reaches for my hand.

I decline it and climb onto the stage.

He moves stage right and sits down in the shade. He leans back, resting on his hands behind him, grinning.

I cough a few times, thinking back to the last time I sang.

"You okay?"

I shake my head, chewing my tongue, glaring. A whispery sound trickles from my mouth.

He slides closer.

I expand my lungs and dive deeper into my next note. Closing my eyes, I envision the rehearsal space at my high school. My freshman and sophomore years flood back in sweet, wistful fragments. How I loved the showcases we did, being onstage, the high it gave me. I never wanted those nights to end.

A familiar energy rises from my diaphragm. A power. My power. I visualize my musical director, Mr. Prescott, beaming offstage. A surreal sensation comes through and out of me, an unexplainable joy longing to surface. Tears spring to my eyes as I remember my dad's trick to quiet my nerves. *Like singing in the kitchen, imagine only us in the audience.* Oh, Daddy, how could I forget?

Then spring of junior year, before we were even together, I caught Cody watching me perform my solo during rehearsals. I peeked back at him, expecting the same rapt expression I saw on the faces in the front row.

His features were like stone—eyes dead.

My mouth became dry, my tongue stuck to my palate. I bobbled the note and asked Mr. Prescott if I could start again.

Cody didn't wait around for take two.

My heart sank and I wondered, *Am I not as good as I think I am?*

I no longer went out for solos after that. Mr. Prescott kept encouraging me to audition but I told him, *I'm okay being in the chorus. Really.*

Under the Naumburg Bandshell, I sustain the last note, my voice big and full. I practiced this song a hundred times for our end-of-year showcase sophomore year; it was my favorite performance at LaGuardia. I sang the hell out of it that night.

My eyes flutter open to see Micah sitting before me.

He sits up straighter, eyes like saucers. "You gave me goose bumps. I can't believe how good you are."

A heaviness falls on me like a cloak, knowing it's the last time I'll ever sing that song. Those sweet days, working so hard at something I loved, are gone. My vision blurs over trembling lips.

Micah jumps to his feet and picks me up. "I got you." He twirls me around in a slow circle, kissing my tears.

I float in his arms, never wanting to come down.

Chapter 36

MICAH

I want us to hang out. Build on this moment. But the Shadow People—the Woman in Black, her henchman, and others—all at once crowd the stage. The Woman in Black isn't acting mean, just cranky. The rest of them, however, start shouting at me, mocking all my secret thoughts.

Leave her, her henchman sneers, dark eyes blazing.

I grit my teeth, steady my face, and grip Brynn's shoulders. I lean in, using my body to shield her from their onslaught, and wheel her around them.

She shoots me a funny look.

We walk west through the park and find a rare patch of shade in Sheep Meadow surrounded by round, lush green trees. Buildings poke up like fingers behind the treetops. Our spot is far enough away from the flying Frisbees and wireless speakers that litter the lawn to give us some privacy. We lie perpendicular in the grass, her head on my chest, our knees bent to the sky.

"Why would you ever stop singing? Your voice is incredible." I rest my head on my hand and use my free one to slide her hair off her face.

She sighs like I'm not the first to tell her that. "Not like Cody's. Everyone knew he had a real chance at making it. I felt lucky to go on tour—thought maybe, singing with him, I could get a recording contract too."

"Did your parents support your dream? They had to, right? Being in the music industry."

"They liked that I got accepted into LaGuardia. Junior year, they encouraged me to apply for college scholarships and study music so I could teach one day. My 'safety net,' my mom called it. I don't think she believed I could make a living at it." She shakes her head. "Then the club started to lose money and everything went on hold—including my future."

"So, the tour."

"Exactly."

"Were your parents cool with that?"

"They didn't like Cody much—and definitely didn't like the idea of me blowing off college. But the club ate up most of their time. They were never home anymore." Hints of a deep sadness creep into her voice. "When I was younger, we used to share stories, laughing with our mouths full, around the kitchen table. I loved spending time with them. My dad's cooking brought us together every night. He could whip up anything, from twelve-alarm chili to curry surprise." Her voice wobbles. "Coming home to a busy, warm kitchen with cumin and coriander in the air . . . I miss it. Our Brooklyn apartment wasn't big, but in comparison to the coffin, it was ten times the size. The large living room . . . all that natural light."

I squeeze her arm, encouraging her to go on.

"One day, he just stopped cooking," she says flatly. "I ate a lot of cereal for dinner. My parents would come home after I was in bed, arguing or too beat to talk. At breakfast, I'd see another new bill piled up with all the others on the table. Even my college fund couldn't save their beloved club."

"I'm sure they didn't choose the Flaming Flamingo over you."

Her body stiffens.

"Brynn . . ." I raise myself up on my elbows so I can get a better view of her face.

"They put our apartment on the market fall of my senior year. That club was like an oil spill, polluting everything that was good. My parents let our family drown in it. We couldn't talk anymore outside of fighting. Kids at school envied me for having famous parents, like I had a perfect life." She releases a hollow laugh. "What a joke. My mom and dad left me in the undertow. Cody was the one to pull me ashore. Refill my lungs with air." She stares off, hugging herself.

I tilt her chin toward me. "You didn't need him."

"The most gifted singer at LaGuardia? Yeah right."

"The most gifted singer . . . Are you sure about that?" I gape at her. "The hair on my arms stood up when you sang. Didn't any of your friends or teachers tell you how talented you are?"

She sits up and swings her legs around. "You're being sweet, but you don't understand. It takes more than talent."

I shield my eyes, watching her face. "I know about blind drive, Brynn. My father went from sleeping in his car to women throwing their thongs at him onstage. He told me that as a teen, he strapped on a guitar in some music shop in SoHo, not knowing how to play. He caught his reflection in the store's window and it was the first time he'd liked the person he saw. Connecting with people through his music brings him his only happiness. He can't live without the adoration, even if it means sacrificing his own family . . ." I blink and turn my head away.

A Frisbee flies over us. A girl in a bikini top and cutoffs runs over and fetches it. She smiles at me, sun flashing off her aviators. "Sor-ry," she singsongs.

Brynn scowls at her.

Frisbee girl hurries off.

"I don't possess that blind drive anymore." Brynn claws the ground to either side of her, staring down at her legs. "I'm not even sure I deserve to be here." Her chest rises and falls.

"Why do you say that?"

"Listen to me—I sound awful." She twists up her face in disgust. "What kind of daughter talks about her late parents like this?

Anyway, what do I have to sing about anymore? The people I love are gone."

I sigh, wishing she'd look at me. "Use your heartache and create art. Plenty of people do. My dad . . . Taylor Swift."

She rips out blades of grass and shreds them. "I don't hear the beats in my head like I used to. I try, but it's like I've grown deaf to the rhythm. When they died, the music died with them." She shivers. "Time for me to grow up."

I cup her face. "Not ever."

Chapter 37

BRYNN

I don't know what I'm supposed to feel. I'm having a sexy weekend with a guy who steals my breath away and holds doors open for me. I keep squashing the pestering thoughts whether any of this is real—and if so, what does it mean?

Then Micah looks at me like no one before him ever has—not even Cody—and I feel like I'm being called out. As if he knows my secrets. When his khaki eyes seek me out, a tingling sensation runs through my breasts and into my belly, clear down to the warmth between my thighs. I can't get enough of him.

I pray he doesn't tell anyone about this. I don't think he will; it would look bad for him too. He seems to operate outside the fray and agency gossip . . . unless *we* become the gossip. What then?

He laces his fingers through mine and leans into me on the crowded train as we head back downtown. His chest muscles are like armor against my cheek—my Alexander the Great, ready to protect me.

I'm no longer alone out here.

We exit at West Fourth to a boisterous crowd taking in the basketball game on the corner. A White guy with leathery skin sits on the sidewalk, his legs outstretched on a flattened cardboard box, a plastic bucket by his side. I've passed him a million times on my evening commute.

I draw back and look up at Micah. "Some days, I feel like I'm one step away from living on the street like Subway Saul."

"Who?" He gives me a quizzical look.

I nod in the homeless guy's direction. "I heard someone call him that once."

"Huh. I've seen him before, haven't ever really thought of him as having a name." Micah sniffs. "Anyway, that wouldn't happen," he adds, his tone nonchalant.

"Micah, I'm by myself." I hear the edge in my voice.

"Not now." He squeezes my hand.

I smile, letting his words wash over me. Today's been an unexpected, good day. Because of him. Hanging out this weekend has made me feel almost normal again. Maybe we're meant to happen.

I steal a sidelong glance at him in his T-shirt and shorts. He's sexier dressed like this than he is in his skinny tie ensembles. Acts more his age, too. My belly twinges at the thought of sitting in our Monday morning meeting together. We can't act weird or the team will sense this new vibe between us. Especially Priya.

"What do you want to do?" He looks at me, his soft-suede eyes dancing.

Go back to bed, I say in my head.

He kisses my hand.

I guess my face gave me away.

Chapter 38

DAHLIA

I see them on the subway together with their crazy hats and sun-kissed faces like they've been out all day. They lean on one another, threading their fingers together, becoming one.

His eyes follow her every move.

She revels in the attention.

I look away from their shiny brightness; my eyes sting from not blinking. I'm so stupid. Of course he's falling for her. The same way Cody did.

I'm drawn back in seconds later, feeding the ache of my broken heart. My hands clench underneath my thighs. Buffered by the other passengers, I trail behind them out of the subway and onto the street toward MacDougal.

Brynn strolls into Micah's house like a VIP, tossing her long hair back at something he said, his hand contouring her hip.

My shredded heart rips a little more.

I've watched girls like her get the guy my whole life while plain, gawky freaks like me have faded into the background without a second look.

Maybe personality means more to some people. But I can count how many times a guy's looked at me the way Micah looks at her.

Zero.

⸻

Teddy's brows rise when I enter Dante's. We need no words. I'm sure my face conveys it all.

I take the open seat by the door.

He hustles about, taking food orders and delivering drinks. He places a coffee before me. His kindness draws out a muffled sob from my throat. He bends down and kisses the side of my forehead, holding his lips there to transfer some of his strength to me. He knows me so well. I'll tell him everything later, after this rush quiets down.

For now, I sit in the window, waiting for that bitch to come out.

Chapter 39

BRYNN

All weekend at Micah's, I've fallen into a deep and dreamless sleep after indulging in pleasure I never knew my body could handle. He awakened urges I never knew I possessed. His lovemaking is so deeply satisfying; he makes me braver in bed—powerful, even—without me needing to have a flat stomach or be perfect.

As we lie next to each other in our hazy after-sex glow, his hand clasps mine like I could run away. An NYC boutique hotel could not compete with this posh bed. His bedding must be woven from that expensive Egyptian cotton; his sheets feel like velvet against my skin. If I lived here, I would never own pajamas again. His pillows are like clouds. He must take it for granted, seeing how he lives like a disheveled slob with garbage and clothes scattered about his bedroom.

"Good late afternoon." He kisses my nose and rolls onto his side. "Where were we?"

He smells so good, like a forest in autumn.

I wrap his free arm around me. "I like you better out of your work clothes."

"Me too." He smiles, moistening his lips.

"I meant—"

"I know what you meant." He gathers me in his arms and I'm floating again. He makes me feel . . . cared for.

"Micah."

"Say it again."

"Micaahh." Like how Eunice calls him over at work.

He laughs. "I feel high when you say my name."

Oh shit.

"Now I've scared you. Don't overthink it. Just be, Brynn."

"Be Brynn?" I make a face. "Except that tomorrow—"

"I will continue to admire you from afar."

He's pretty damn charming.

"I wasn't expecting this to happen. I'm glad it did." He stretches himself long in the bed. His hand finds another part of me to caress. His legs, fingers, and lips stay in continual contact with my skin.

He cups my face. I like it more and more when he does that.

Our eyes meet.

"Want to make out again?" His lips twist into a lopsided smile.

"I think I need a shower."

"Now you're talking!"

Chapter 40

MICAH

She colors my black-and-white existence. Distracts my mind from all the ugliness, including the cast of characters in this bathroom with us. I'm getting better at refusing them my attention. Her presence eclipses them all.

I don't want to let this weekend go—this unfamiliar lightness in my chest, the sparks radiating through my limbs. This girl, this girl. She keeps me on my toes in a vigilant way. I can't afford to mess this up. Feels like I'm running with a snow globe: One trip-up from my Shadow People world and the glistening flakes could settle into a new pattern—one that excludes me.

I can't let that happen.

We play in my grandparents' cast iron clawfoot tub. Sudsy water splashes onto the floor's ivory tiles, dampening the charcoal-colored runner next to us. The smallest things make us laugh. Until one of us gives the other the look. The one that keeps getting us into trouble.

I like the kind of trouble she brings to my flat, clinical world.

Under the bathroom's unfiltered lighting and without the hindrance of covers, I invest in finding every freckle and birthmark on her. We're like new lovers on an intimate expedition, afloat in the middle of the ocean. An ocean I continue to refill with hot water to keep her in here longer.

"When did you know... about *this*?" She flutters her lashes, gesturing between us, our necks resting on opposite ends of the tub.

I sprinkle water droplets from my fingers onto hers. They seep into her skin like they belong there. What if all of me liquefied and melted into her—would I finally feel whole?

I hold my thoughts and turn over her hand, voyaging up her wrist to the dewy underside of her arm.

She squirms at my touch and lets me do more.

I clench my eyes shut. "When you helped the old lady in the elevator."

"No!" Her mouth falls open. "You acted so mean to me!"

I blink, unable to recall my actions, only hers. "I saw you doing something decent for a stranger . . . putting yourself out there. I wanted that level of kindness in my life. So pure, I guess."

"Like a virgin?" She rolls her eyes.

"No, like a human. A better human."

"What? You're not a *good* human . . . should I be worried?" She laughs.

I break eye contact. "I'm not like you. One of those people who do the right thing when no one's watching."

"You make me sound like a meme. Do you think I'm a goody two-shoes or something?"

"No. I don't know . . . I've just wanted to be somebody else for some time now, I guess."

Her forehead creases. "What's so bad about being you?"

"Everything." I splash water in her face like she's the prettiest girl at summer camp and I'm trying to flirt with her in the pool. I wish I'd known her then. Before the morning I woke up, unpleasant visitors invaded my life, and everything turned sideways. My chest tightens as I eye those intruders, currently standing to either side of her.

Brynn retaliates. More water cascades over the side of the tub.

She stops suddenly and stares off.

I do my best not to gawk at her breasts.

Her lips press together. "About tomorrow—"

"Don't rush it." I cup her breasts, too weak to ignore them.

She giggles and lets my hands continue what they're doing. "I think that ship sailed." She glances down and arches her brow.

"I meant, don't rush our time together."

She nods like she understands.

"I'm not looking to strip you of your memories, Brynn. I'm here for when you want to make new ones."

"Like this weekend?"

"Like every weekend."

She spreads her pruned fingers in front of my face, simulating a flower's petals opening to the sun.

I kiss her head and step out of the tub, leaving runny footprints across the tiles.

Her eyes follow me.

I pull out two towels. After securing one around my hips, I gesture for her to stand. I wrap her in the other one, patting her dry.

She laughs, but I can tell she likes it.

I like caring for her. It feels good to attend to someone else for once and not be the one fussed over.

I enjoy having you near me, I want to say, but instead I just fold her into my arms.

Until our rumbling stomachs send us in search of our clothes.

Scrounging around for my shorts on the floor, I spot the notebook I kicked under the bed when I carried her in here earlier. Maybe if she knew this part of me . . .

I open it to a recent entry—a tame one—and pass it to her. "Here."

She gasps. "Your notebook!" She glances down, her eyes and lips moving in serious concentration. "Are they lyrics?"

"No." I go to grab it out of her hands before she stumbles upon previous passages.

She turns her back and continues to read, then spins back to me. "Who's the girl?"

I shake my head, unable to say.

She sizes me up like she's recalculating something. "Huh, I didn't know you could write like this."

"What, better than you?" I laugh.

"Better than the whole agency."

Dressed, she leads the way downstairs, her fingers trailing the iron balusters.

My head's halfway in the fridge when I hear drawers opening behind me and something about a pen. My throat closes up. "Wait!" I whirl around.

This is why we don't have people over. The Woman in Black chomps on a fingernail.

"Micah, what's all this?" Brynn raises one of the pill bottles. "I can't even pronounce this. Are you taking all of these? There's got to be twenty containers in here."

I lay a hand on my chest to hold in my frantic heart. "Some for allergies, a couple for migraines."

"So many," she says, blinking rapidly.

"I fill six months' worth in California. Cheaper that way." I take her hand and lead her away from the incriminating drawer.

She stops. "You know, I think I'm going to head out."

Her words cut me off at the knees.

"I thought we were getting something to eat."

"It's kind of late."

"Late for what?"

She doesn't clarify.

I trudge behind her to the door.

We stand facing one another in the foyer, the ceiling hovering near my head. She looks small.

Her eyes flick past my shoulder to the staircase, then back to me.

I have a million things I want to tell her. If she'd give me a damn minute.

The tight space crowds with the voices and shapes of the Shadow People.

One fills my head. *Let her go*, the Woman in Black repeats, growing louder, surprising me.

I glare at her, my lips shushing the air.

Brynn follows my eyes, unable to see what I see. Her gaze returns to me, and she searches my face.

My neck and head perspire. I'm too weak to ignore the rest of them when they join the Woman in Black's chant. *Let her go*, they command in unison.

I shift my weight and roll my eyes, acting bored. It comes off cocky—and cold. A memory resurfaces. My actions in the elevator the morning Brynn met me, the actions of a schizophrenic who's scared shitless and incapable of holding it together.

Brynn's eyes search mine. Her parted lips clamp down. She backs away from me, slips through the door, and dissolves into the passing crowd on the street.

Chapter 41

BRYNN

Debra waves when she sees me lumbering down the hall. She gathers her floral caftan to the side and stoops to pick up a large box outside her apartment door. "Did you get away this weekend?" she asks, her voice bright.

"I-I stayed with a friend." I shove my key in the door without looking at her. My limbs hang heavy like I've been away for a week. Why does this hallway look smaller than it did yesterday?

"That's some friend." She eyeballs my crumpled blue dress I've worn all weekend and the floppy Woodstock hat on my head.

I flash her a weak smile and duck through my door. A sadness fills my chest—that feeling of disappointment I always get the day after Christmas. I collapse onto my mattress. Hard as a rock. Wonderful. The mildew smell has returned. Thanks, rain.

I roll on my side, envisioning Micah next to me. I gather my hair and pull it over my nose and mouth, breathing him in, eyes closed.

Uh-oh.

I've got to shake him off. Be by myself, refocus, not let myself be swept away by those soft suede eyes that follow me everywhere.

It got weird after I found those pill bottles. He sure pulled a mood when I wanted to leave. His tone came off almost nasty. I guess he gets mean when things don't go his way. Good to know.

Another reason I should end this before it goes further. He's charming, sure, and I won't pretend it wasn't fun, but who am I kidding? It won't last *or* end well. For me, not him. Bet the agency executives compete over who can sleep with a summer intern first.

My phone vibrates on the floor. UNKNOWN CALLER.

I forgot Micah sent himself a text from my phone.

"Can we talk?" He sounds rushed. "I know I acted badly back there."

"Um . . . yeah." I exhale, all breathy, unaware I'd held it.

"You hungry yet?"

I swivel my head toward the sink filled with dishes. "About to boil some pasta, you?"

"I picked up some Chinese. Too much to eat by myself."

"Mmm, what kind?"

"Buzz me in and I'll show you."

"Micah . . ." I sigh.

"Say my name again and I'll kiss you in the morning meeting."

"I'll kick your ass."

"Yeah, you could. I'll take that chance."

The staccato drips from the kitchen sink distract my ability to form a solid excuse. My mouth waters at the prospect of Chinese food awaiting below my window. My stomach and I hit the buzzer.

I spot him at the top of the stairs with a large to-go bag and a huge smile. I leave my door ajar and scurry to the communal bathroom to brush my teeth, hair, and whatever else needs attention. When I return, a tablecloth covers the floor along with a couple of those religious candles they sell at the bodegas. "What's all this?"

"Excuse the mood lighting. The selection at the corner store was kind of slim."

I flop down cross-legged on the floor facing him. My stomach leaps at the sight of a small carton of vegetable spring rolls. I snatch one and bite off the end.

Micah grins at me.

I grin back as I chew, savoring the sweet and spicy flavor, the aromas of garlic and ginger, and the breath-stealing delivery guy before me.

His intense, unguarded eyes watch me.

My brain starts to poke holes in this carefully crafted sweet moment. The pieces of cabbage in my mouth lose flavor. They travel down the wrong pipe. I cough, choking.

His eyes widen. "You alright?"

I take a sip of water. "Um . . . this weekend together . . . I know you said to not overthink it. But I've never done anything like this . . . and this is my first real job. I can't afford to lose it. I don't know how things will go—"

"I don't know either." His body sags. "Wish we'd met at a college bar like most people our age."

"What if someone from work saw us walking around the Village or in the park holding hands?"

He blinks a few times, his lips pressed into a line.

I bend my knees to my chest. "I don't want to be a joke tomorrow."

His eyes flinch. "People could easily say I took advantage of *you*, the high school intern."

"Doesn't matter. *You're* not going anywhere; *your* name is on the door."

His face clouds over.

"I didn't mean—"

"Yeah, you did." He scowls.

"I didn't mean to ruin our last night together."

Micah's face drains of color.

Shit. I'm better at eating than speaking. Always have been. I want to thank him for one of the best weekends of my life. His attentive affection, and most of all his kindness, lifted me out of my funk. Beyond the earthshaking sex, I had fun hanging out with Micah. Walking around the city with our fingers interlaced. I'm sure to onlookers we appeared to be a real couple and not some shady office hookup.

I'm torn. I think I really like him. Our unforeseen weekend together put a pin in the crushing sadness and stress I've been carrying since losing everyone I love and finding myself alone in this adult world.

I watch his face through the awkward silence. I don't know how to retrieve my words or fix my habit of dishing out brutal honesty. If I could chase off the raincloud hanging over us, I would. Truth? I wanted to feel him on top of me one last time.

But come on, he must have known it wouldn't last. These things never do. I'm not rich like him, living rent-free in a historically registered house in New York City. I need my job.

My palm starts to itch. I shift around; suddenly, the floor feels unbearably hard.

I wish he'd just go and leave the food.

Chapter 42

BRYNN

For once, I'm early on a Monday. The subway car jolts forward. I regrasp one of the middle poles. My ragged nails make me look like I spent the weekend rock climbing, not romping around in bed with an attractive, sexually talented guy.

I peruse my arms for other evidence of my weekend with Micah. This morning, I practiced my poker face in the communal bathroom mirror. *You got this*, I tell myself, leaning my shoulder into the pole and running my thumb along the uneven edges of my nails.

Rikki stands at the far end of the car. They must live somewhere in the Village or SoHo. Looks like we both left Brooklyn.

I wave and they turn the other way. Maybe they didn't see me. They're talking to a blonde in a black ball cap with her back to me.

The lights flicker. We speed through the tunnel in darkness.

I hold my breath and my purse a little tighter.

The car slows, the lights resume full brightness.

Rikki and the girl are gone.

The subway doors open.

I think of Micah and my heart takes off in a sprint. I imagine the scene when we see each other. Will he even look at me? Will we pull off acting normal in front of everybody? What if they already know?

I don't see him when I arrive. More importantly, I detect no secret smiles or loaded looks between my coworkers. I even get a wave out of Donovan.

I release a long exhale and tap my keyboard awake. Feeling like a grownup, I bring my Starbucks coffee to my lips and peruse my emails.

MICAH KERSHAW OUT OF OFFICE – SAN DIEGO OFFICE.

I gasp.

He didn't mention he'd be traveling this week. Maybe he scheduled it to help things settle a bit. So then he agrees with ending this thing between us. Good.

My eyes fill. I pull a tissue off Priya's desk.

He respected my wishes. I got what I asked for.

My lips start twitching.

"You okay?" Priya stands on the other side of her chair, laptop in hand like she's just come from a meeting.

"Yeah, sure." I flash her a quick smile and sit up straighter.

I bury myself in copy revisions.

I've been working heads-down for a couple of hours when my computer pings. An email, subject, 90 DAY PRE-FORECLOSURE.

Oh shit.

I meant to call my parents' accountant to have her ask the bank for an extension. I'm sure Rhonda would help me. I'll need every cent of next week's paycheck to make last month's mortgage. I eye this morning's Starbucks splurge.

This intern needs a serious raise. Better yet, I need Donovan's salary.

I trudge over to the plant wall to pillage today's bagel selection—only to discover the breakfast bar's been wiped clean. My shoulders deflate.

I take the floating stairs for the first time and walk the perimeter of the second floor, admiring the bird's-eye view of the agency. It's quiet up here.

I walk toward a sitting area with red leather couches and stacks of industry magazines displayed on an oversize glass coffee table. I hear a hushed whisper behind one of the office doors. Scott's voice, swearing at somebody.

I follow a faint floral scent leading to an open office door. My jaw drops at what looks like a Broadway set with dark Victorian oak furniture and dusty Tiffany lamps. Behind the grand desk, on prominent display, is a picture of Micah with his aunt and an older gentleman in a suit with thick gray hair and a piercing gaze. Micah looks nothing like his aunt; with her sharp, long nose and twitchy hazel eyes, she reminds me of a scarecrow. Her clothes hang off of her like those anorexic models from the '90s.

"What are you doing in here?"

I jump.

Scott narrows his eyes at me from the doorway.

"Um, guess I got a little lost." Think. Think. "I was looking for Mic—I-I mean his aunt. She around?"

His wiry black brows draw down over his eyes. "You shouldn't be snooping."

"I-I wanted to talk to her about open copywriter positions." Remember me, how you liked my ideas? I stand straighter, smiling wide. "I think I've shown I can be more creative—"

"What, than Donovan?" He crosses his arms over his turquoise dress shirt and striped tie, his gold watch catching the light. "Tell me. Have you worked on large-scale brand initiatives, collaborated with cross-functional teams, earned the number of awards he has?"

My stomach drops. "No, but . . ."

He swings his arm like a theater usher with a mini flashlight. *Exit this way*.

The door closes behind me. I lower my head, biting my lip, and bolt downstairs, where I beeline it to the bathroom.

Blowing my nose on the toilet, I hear coworkers come and go. I just want to curl up in a ball on my mattress. But I can't stay here all day.

I exit the bathroom and drag myself back to my desk.

Donovan and Meredith enter one of the conference rooms with takeout bags.

Time to pivot.

I hesitate in the doorway, my plastic lunch container from home in hand. "You guys mind if I join you?"

Seated, Meredith eyes me standing there, then turns back to her food. "Sure."

I know. First time ever. I need to make amends with Meredith. She's been a bit frosty since my Quotagian presentation.

Donovan locks eyes with her.

She gives him a faint nod.

He shovels a forkful of chimichanga into his mouth. "Just discussing the Quotagian account."

"What about it?"

He chews. "We're wondering who'll take it over."

My mouth goes dry. "Why, where's it going?" Did Scott or the client request that I be taken off the account? Could explain him ripping me a new one.

"Well, with Micah gone . . ." He throws up a hand.

"His out-of-office message said he's working at the San Diego office this week."

Donovan and Meredith share a look.

I hold my breath like I'm a balloon about to burst. "What am I missing?"

He steeples his fingers, looks over them at me like I'm a child. "If Micah's not here, it means he's back there."

"So? He goes to college in San Diego, I thought." I act like I heard it in passing.

"He doesn't go to college." His head snaps toward Meredith. "Does he?"

She bugs out her eyes at him.

"But . . ." I stop myself. How can I tell them they have it all wrong without tipping them off to the fact that we've been hanging out?

"Micah's spent the last two years in a nut house." Donovan twirls a finger next to his head for emphasis.

I jerk back. "What?"

"He comes to New York every summer, spends time with his ailing grandfather, and works at the agency while keeping him apprised of things. Sort of like a spy. Guess his family thinks he'll get his act together and run things one day."

I turn to Meredith. "Wait, I don't understand. He's so smart and good with the clients. After the Bradley Products pitch, you called him a *wunderkind*."

"Doesn't mean he's not twisted in the head." Donovan grins, leaning back in his chair.

"Um, what he's trying to say"—Meredith pulls in her lips—"is that Micah battles some sort of mental illness. An incident occurred here one summer when he was in high school."

Donovan pitches forward, back into my line of sight. "Yeah, he went off—screaming, beating on another employee for no reason. Only Eunice could settle him down. The EMTs carted him away, then they sent him back to some treatment center in San Diego."

Blood rushes from my face and flashes of light spot my vision. I swallow the warm acid in the back of my throat. "Micah's . . . mental?"

"Hey, good one! Mind if I use it?" Donovan laughs, clapping.

"Please don't. I shouldn't have said that." I cover my mouth.

Meredith's brow furrows. "Hey, you okay?"

"I told you, the guy's weird." Donovan smirks, oblivious to my freak out. "He's only here because of his legacy. Promoted to associate creative director at twenty? Please. He should be in a nut house full time."

I shudder. "What a cruel and ignorant thing to say."

"What, now you *like* the guy?"

"Yeah, he's a good guy." I tune out their voices as scenes piece together: Micah not engaging with the team outside of team meetings . . . how he never invites people to his place . . . the piles of garbage on his bedroom floor . . . oh my God, all those pill bottles.

"He knows a lot about shrink stuff," Meredith volunteers, interrupting my thoughts. "Once, a guy I was dating kept throwing me all these mixed signals and Micah helped me understand some of the underlying causes of his behavior. Felt like I was talking to a therapist."

"No way he's relapsed." I shake my head.

Their eyebrows shoot up. Both stifle a smile.

Micah was acting normal last night . . . until I opened my big mouth. What did I do? Wait, I'm overthinking this. He left to cool things off between us. Nothing's wrong with his brain. We slept together, more than once. *I'd know* if he wasn't right.

They start talking about the weekend. Their mouths move without sound.

I bite off one of my ragged nails, then another, retrieving the half-moons from the tip of my tongue and flicking them onto the wood floor. I move on to my cuticles.

I'd know.

Wouldn't I?

Chapter 43

MICAH

I booked my ticket the second I left Brynn's apartment, deserting the city of Chinese takeout boxes before her. Not entirely sure what I did after that. I must have also scheduled a car to the airport, because here I am now, on a plane.

Good thing. The last few hours and how I scored this aisle seat in the back of first class remain a mystery to me.

The plane keeps taxiing like we've decided to *drive* to California.

Delay.

Delay.

I shift in my seat, unable to settle. Someone's cranked up the heat.

The plane heaves forward, heavy with people. Planes with too many passengers tend to crash, don't they?

Sweat drips down my face.

The flight attendants glance my way, their lips pressed into frowns, perhaps conferring over the potential trouble I might cause.

I pity the poor guy snoring next to me, clueless that I'm about to pull the lever on the cabin door and deploy the evacuation slide to escape like a badass.

"More water?" The flight attendant with the violet-silver hair and brown sun-spotted skin waggles an Evian bottle in my face.

I take the bottle, throw one of my pills to the back of my mouth, and chug the water. Next time I wake, I'll be in Cali. Except these green ones never affect me the same way twice, and I'll have no security net if things go sideways up there. Whenever I feel like this . . .

Dr. Val says, *You shouldn't be flying.*

My dad tells me, *Sleep it off.*

Aunt Max suggests, *Meditate more, try yoga.*

And Eunice gives me a wrapped spearmint candy off her desk.

Rewrite your story, I tell myself. *Forget her scent on your skin right now, the scratches she left across your back. Get over her by hooking up with someone in California.*

Because meaningless dalliances have worked so well for me in the past.

I left her apartment tonight before I did something regretful. Something I couldn't take back. I arrived at her door with candles and sustenance, prepared to spin my sudden odd behavior into a charming narrative. Because spending forty-eight hours with someone doesn't merit a schizophrenia reveal.

But I screwed it up. By the time I left, it was like our weekend had never happened. Like *we'd* never happened.

I'm done. Not coming back to this city. Screw Granddad's plan. His lack of acknowledgment of this . . . thing . . . in me.

Christ, go to sleep already.

"Harmonica?"

"Music Man. Surprised to hear from you." I switch my phone to the other ear and grab my bag off the conveyor belt. Time to find the poor schmuck holding the iPad with my name.

"I called you a thousand times last night."

I have two missed calls from him. "I'm in Cali."

"Dr. Val called. What the hell happened?"

I slide a smile into my voice. "I felt myself slipping. Came back for a tune-up."

"You're doing so well, why—"

My neck grows cold. "Chill!" I spit in a low voice. "No one knows Beck Kershaw's son is going back into the looney bin."

"Micah, it's not *like* that."

"Really, Dad? How is it? Staying in New York and working at Granddad's agency means I'm *fixed*?"

"So damn dramatic." He blows air into the phone like I'm an irksome toddler.

"*This* is not real to you. Never has been."

"*You* need to chillax—"

I hang up on the a-hole.

"Nice to see you in the flesh. I'd say you are look-ing good, but if I did I'd be ly-ing." Dr. Val screws up her lips; small folds of skin appear at the outer corners of her eyes under her carrot-colored bangs.

"Good to see you too." I mirror her expression.

I spread myself across her blue pleather couch and rest my head and feet on the rectangular foam armrests. My paper hospital slippers sit on the floor next to me, ready for a quick getaway. The toes in front of me wiggle, unconnected to my legs. Damn. What did she prescribe me?

She bounces her brows. "Oh, come on. Us cra-zies need to stick to-ge-ther."

"Stop. Be my doctor for once." I cross my hands behind my head, cringing at my snowflake hospital pajamas.

"Don't wor-ry. I won't try to jump your bones to-day. Been get-ting an-y ac-tion in New York?"

"Nope. Saving myself for your withering—"

"Stop. Stop right there." She holds up her ruddy palm. "O-kay, let's be ser i-ous. What the hell hap-pened in New York?"

"I'm not . . ." I sigh; it's useless to pretend with her. "One minute I'm with this girl in her apartment, getting dumped, and the next I'm on the floor in my kitchen. It got bad fast."

"You ex-per-i-enced an ep-i-sode in front of her?"

I shake my head. "We spent an incredible weekend together. I can't remember the last time I felt so normal. Like the old me." I throw up my hands. "But she flaked out. Doesn't feel the same. I get it. No one wants to take a chance with me. I sure as hell wouldn't."

"You told her a-bout your psy-cho-sis?"

I look away.

"Then how do you know it played a role? May-be some-thing else is go-ing on. Blam-ing your-self turns into a self-ful-fill-ing proph-e-cy."

I bare my teeth. "Kind of hard to hide, you know. People sense something's off about me."

"You mean when you don't let an-y-one see the real you?" She leans back on her headrest, her eyes focused skyward.

"I know what I am, and shit yeah, I'm a handful."

She clucks her tongue. "Mi-cah the vic-tim."

"I knew you'd say that. Anyway, I can't compete with a dead guy."

"Dead guy?"

"Her boyfriend—he be dead." I laugh.

She studies me. After a long beat, she angles the pointer attached to her wrist toward her screen. "I'll ad-just your dose."

"Why? Feels like I'm flying. Now, let's talk about your love life, Dr. Val."

"We'll pick this up la-ter."

"I don't regret being with Brynn. So I got dumped. Whatever. She's not what I need right now."

"Oh?"

"What's playing?" I lift my chin in the direction of the stereo behind her.

"You like it? Franz Schu-bert's Ninth Symph-o-ny; quite a ro-man-tic comp-o-si-tion, if you ask me. Makes me want to dance all night long." She smiles, waving her bird hand at me. "Come on, once a-round the of-fice. You can sit on my lap like they do in that Jo-jo Moyes mo-vie." She cracks herself up.

I roll my eyes, seeing through her twisted sense of humor. She uses it to get me to lighten up when I'm feeling like this . . . like I've just been *passing* as normal this whole time. I'm never going to get better. Destined to be alone.

Her eyes turn gentle. "Why are you here, Mi-cah?"

I sit up fast, throwing my feet to the floor.

Dr. Val shrinks back and her elbow slips from the armrest. She lists to the side, unable to right herself up.

I bounce up. "Sorry, I—"

"I got this." She rocks her body back into place in increments. "No harm done."

I close my eyes, digging my fingers into my scalp.

Dr. Val gives me one of her gummy smiles. "Sit. Tell me why you're here."

Out the window behind her, a little girl in a red dress walks beside a man in a pale yellow suit with salt-and-pepper hair. Holding his hand, she stops to pick up something from the sidewalk. She passes it to him, her toothless grin lighting up her face.

He raises it toward the sun and flips it over in his fingers, talking to her. He gives it back and pulls her along.

She digs her heels into the ground and leans away from him, her legs rod straight.

I look back at Dr. Val. "I want you to reset my brain so I can forget her."

Chapter 44

BRYNN

I knock on Debra's door as soon as I get home.

No answer—then she comes whipping out of the communal bathroom with a psychedelic-colored toiletry bag tucked under her arm, her blue-gray hair combed through, the dripping ends darkening the shoulders of her orange-and-pink-flowered caftan. "What happened?" Her eyes widen. "You look like death, baby girl."

I wince.

"Sorry, poor choice of words."

"I think I screwed up."

She unlocks her door and waves me inside.

I pass through, inhaling the aroma of soup, and flop down on her pink sofa like I've been here a thousand times. I hug one of her decorative pillows. "I had a fling at work with a guy who's sort of my boss." I close my eyes, cringing. "Sounds so cliché when I say it aloud."

"Tell me about him." She folds a leg under herself, sitting beside me. Her head rests on her hand.

"He's a couple of years older and the grandson of an advertising icon, Gabriel Kershaw."

"A mighty Kershaw, huh?" Her face brightens.

"You know the family? Who don't you know in this town?"

"Never met his grandfather." She shakes her head, then nods. "I've seen *Beck* Kershaw at The Bitter End a few times. He finger-picks his guitar like Lindsey Buckingham. Then add that distinctive, husky voice of his . . . Hard not to swoon."

"His son writes poetry. They could be lyrics. He wouldn't show me much, but I could tell he's talented."

"You like him." She nudges me. "Maybe a little more than like?"

"I like him a lot," I admit. "Just that . . . I need this job. I'm hoping they'll keep me on through the fall, not an easy feat for an intern." I play with the fringe on the pillow. "It hasn't even been a year since I lost my parents . . . my boyfriend. I can't be with someone this soon."

"Probably right." She sighs.

"Then you agree with ending it before it got serious?"

"I buy that." Her brows raise. "But seeing those pitiful big eyes of yours, I'm not sure *you* do."

"It was the right thing to do." I pick the skin on the side of my fingernail. Micah's face pops in my head, his lips kissing my fingers. I squeeze my eyes shut.

"But a part of you is not so sure."

"My last relationship with Cody, my late boyfriend, was intense." I open my eyes and look at Debra.

"In a good way?" Her pupils magnify like I'm about to spill something juicy.

"I started keeping things from my parents . . . stopped hanging out with my friends and doing the things I loved."

"Because he'd swept you off your feet and nothing or anyone else mattered?"

"Yes . . . and because it led to less fighting." I shrug.

Debra stares at me hard. "What does *this* one demand of you?"

I smile. "Micah? Nothing. He said I should go back to doing the things I love. He even got me singing in Central Park. I haven't sung in forever."

She angles her head, smiles at me. "Your eyes light up when you talk about singing . . . and Micah."

"He goes to a treatment facility in California for some sort of mental illness."

"Sounds like a deal breaker. You did the right thing." Fiddling with the gold cross around her neck, she rises to her feet and walks away with one of her teacups.

I recoil from her words. "Kind of harsh." I cross my arms. "Lots of people live with mental disorders."

She spins around with a knowing look; her wicked grin gives me pause.

I narrow my eyes at her. "You knew I'd react that way, didn't you?"

"Yep. I think you like him. A lot." She makes a popping sound with her lips.

"I'm so confused, Deb!" I drape myself over the arm of the sofa.

She sits back down and rests her strong, veiny hand on my back. "What would your parents want you to do?"

I straighten up and gaze down at my lap. "Find a way to go to college. Return to the strong, independent person I used to be before I met Cody."

With a gentle hand, she tilts up my chin and smiles. "There she is. Welcome back, baby girl."

Chapter 45

MICAH

I lie like a corpse on my second bed of the morning. My hands and feet lie cold with sweat, my stomach raw from not having eaten or drunk anything since last night. I debate ripping up the waiver I signed exonerating the doctors from whatever happens to me after they zap my brain with one hundred joules of electricity.

It could all go south from here. I turn into a vegetable and they hang my mug in the museum of medical mistakes.

Where the hell did Dr. Val motor off to? We agreed electroconvulsive therapy (ECT for short) would be the next step in my treatment after my body's resistance to the last few medications. She said she'd observe my first round.

I called my dad, not wanting our last conversation to be a fight. He knows I'm apprehensive about going down this road. It went to voicemail.

This part of the La Jolla facility harks back to the 1950s with its low ceilings, frosted windows, and sickish light spilling over the bed and equipment.

My nose twitches from the stench of bodily fluids and antiseptic.

A handful of whitecoats putters around me, attaching electrodes to my head and cardiac pads to my chest.

The Woman in Black leans against the wall in the corner, biting her nails.

They harness my ankles and wrists, though the docs say most patients' bodies don't convulse like you see in the movies. Nor should I feel the currents when I'm asleep.

I need to pee.

A woman in pink scrubs leans over my chest. Electric blue liner circles her eyes; fleshy, rosy skin pokes out around her mask. "We're going to start your anesthesia, Micah. I'm going to put this in your mouth so you don't bite your tongue. Count back from twenty for me?"

I inhale a quick breath. My vision blurs, and I squint to find her again. Dr. Val said after these next few weeks of ECT treatments, all the Shadow People could be gone. At last, I locate the Woman in Black, expecting her emotions to mirror mine.

She looks away and spits out a nail.

"Out loud." The woman's eyes pierce mine like blades above her mask.

"Twenty, nineteen . . ." Tears roll down my cheeks and into my ears. I mouth *goodbye* to the Woman in Black, wishing she'd come closer and hold my hand one last time.

Chapter 46

BRYNN

"Brynn?"

I turn back and stop just short of slamming into her.

Tess aims one of her shopping bags into my leg.

"Ouch."

She laughs, swinging her honey-brown, stick-straight hair—once naturally curly and jet black—behind her shoulders. Achieving her sleek new style looks like a lot of effort in this humidity.

Something else has changed since the last time I saw her walking across the stage at graduation: She looks collegiate in her cute rugby dress and white Adidas, while I hardly recognize myself in my mother's ill-fitting hand-me-downs.

"Tess. Hey."

"I didn't realize that was you at first, all dressed up with your hair down and not in one of your messy buns." She gives me her best Miss America smile, in case I'd forgotten it.

"I have an internship in midtown." I shrug. "*Your* hair's gotten long. I like it blown out."

"And all mine." She shakes it behind her shoulders. "I'm leaving Saturday for Stanford. Wanda and Mike want to ship my stuff before I get there. You wouldn't believe how much I'm bringing. And get this—they *insist* on flying with me." Her face drops. "Sorry . . . I didn't mean . . . I'm an idiot."

"I'm happy for you." I keep my voice even. "I'm sure they're busting with pride."

"How are *you*?" She leans her head to the side. "When we spoke at graduation—"

"We did? Was I nice?" I cringe.

She laughs. "Of course not. I expected nothing different. You acted mad at me, Lucy, the whole world."

"I know, I'm—"

"Hey, do you want to grab a latte?"

No, not really. "Sure." I keep up with her long legs down MacDougal Street like I've done countless times before, coming here after school with her and Lucy.

She stops at Caffé Dante and tugs open the door.

The purple house across the street floods my head with bittersweet memories. I glance up at the darkened windows, letting the twinge in my chest settle, forgetting for a split second that I'm following someone. If Micah were in town, I'd skip across the street for one of his amazing hugs. I drag my gaze away and walk behind Tess through the door.

The café's familiar creamy brick walls, checkered floors, and strong espresso aroma rouse me. In middle school, this place was an iconic neighborhood hangout, gritty yet historic, with its round white tables and the celebrity photos and faded murals of Italy on its walls. The new owners gussied it up, making it more upscale. I miss the former place.

Tess chooses a table across from the bar. She slides into the upholstered booth against the wall and spreads her bags well into the next empty seat.

"How *are* Wanda and Mike?" Her Ghanaian father and African American mother own an Afro-fusion restaurant on Carmine Street. Lucy and I used to eat there for free all the time. Tess is an only child like me. Having to share our parents with a more needy sibling—the family business—bonded us early on.

"The restaurant appears to be booming, they're adding two more locations. So, they're good." She sends me a knowing look.

A server comes up behind me. "What can I get you to start with?"

The pale girl lifts her blue-green eyes to us—and, without warning, fumbles the pen and pad in her hands.

I flash back to her doing the same thing with a stack of boxes. "Do you work for a delivery service?"

She flinches and tucks a strand of caramel-blond hair behind her ear. "Yeah, part time." Her wide-set eyes pull into the center of her face like I'm going to charge toward her again.

I almost feel bad.

"What will you have?" She doesn't look up from her pad.

"A latte with almond milk."

"Make that two." Tess smiles.

I watch the girl walk away.

Her head turns back at the last second before she disappears.

Tess poses her chin on her hands, batting her eyes. "Wanda and Mike put together a going-away party for me this Friday. I know it's been, like, forever, but I'd love for you to be there." Oh, here she goes. This girl employs more mannerisms than anyone I've ever met—like her George Clooney head tilt right now. She can never just chill.

"I don't know." I sigh. It would be nice to see everyone, but I'm not up for the barrage of concerned faces ready to gossip once I leave. I mirror her head tilt. "Been a while since we've all hung out. I wouldn't want your last night to be awkward."

"It would mean a lot to me and Lucy . . . and my parents . . . if you came. Like old times."

I force a smile, crossing my arms over the sudden, gassy pain in my belly. I squirm in my seat, wishing I could lie down.

She stretches across the table, opening her palms to me. "Lucy and I really missed you. End of junior year, you really changed."

I rest my hands in hers. "I let Cody come between us . . ."

Someone gasps behind me.

I turn at the same time our lattes crash to the floor.

Our server rushes back into the kitchen.

"Okay, strange." Tess pouts her lips. "Poor girl."

An Italian-looking guy appears with a mop and broom. His dark gaze locks on mine.

Fine hairs rise on my arms.

"Earth to Brynn." She follows my eyes.

"He looks familiar too. Haven't we seen him—"

"Perform?" She nods. "He was one of the leads in the show we saw at that other performing arts high school that shall not be named. It was one of the few nights I managed to pull you away from Cody." She snickers. "Teddy Jenkins. Those yummy, broad shoulders. Handsome."

It all comes rushing back. "I remember him. He was good."

"They both were. Butterfingers went there too. She played that indie tune on the guitar. Maybe she's working here to pay for a vocal coach."

"Like you used to do."

"Long time ago. Now I can shop." She grins.

"Must be nice to get a full ride." I can't keep the edge out of my voice.

"Yeah, almost didn't happen." Her eyes tighten.

I gulp and look away. No point going there.

She opens her mouth, looking ready to pounce.

I hold my breath. Coming here with her was a mistake.

Teddy places two napkins in front of us and then sets our steaming cups on the table, staring at me. He knows we were talking about him.

"Wouldya like to see our menu?" The short black curls framing his face move when he speaks.

I shake my head and wait until he leaves. "Um, who else is going to your party?"

"Like everyone," she cuts me off. "First, let's discuss how you let a guy come between our friendship."

I exhale. Thank god she dropped that other thing. Not my finest moment.

"You fell hard. Who wouldn't? Cody *was* easy on the eyes—and that voice. Plus, he was obsessed with you. But that doesn't explain how you acted. Lucy and I would see you at school, you'd walk the other way. Always ready with another excuse not to hang out. Then the makeup—his idea, right?"

I swallow back the sudden tightness in my throat.

"I knew it! Never saw you as a girlie girl. You became his arm candy."

"Not true." I bunch up my napkin and throw it at her.

"I cried when Lucy told me your plan to leave school and go on tour, thought I'd never see you again. God, then the accident." She holds the sides of her face like her head weighs a ton.

"Wait, did the Elmsford police reach out to you about that night?"

"No, why?" She licks some foam from her latte, her eyes focused on her cup.

I squint, watching her. "Just . . . wondering."

"Lucy and I organized a candlelight vigil for Cody, hoping you'd show."

"I didn't know. So sweet of you guys." *Hate him in life, cry for him in death. Always creating drama when it serves you, right, Tess?*

"And oh. My. God. Katia and Basilio! How? Why? They were the *best.*"

"Everyone loved my parents. All anyone ever talked about." I clench my jaw.

"Remember when they got invited to judge LaGuardia's talent night and they broke out into that amazing duet in front of everyone? Gave me chills."

"Yep. Another night to showcase themselves." I let out a strangled laugh.

Her face drops, her eyes stare off.

I take a hasty sip of my latte.

She wrinkles her nose. "Did Cody's family have a funeral? I kept waiting for someone from school to post something."

I blank at her question. "Um . . . I was so out of my head, I don't know. I never met them."

"You'd think they'd want to meet you." She looks away. "Let you spread his remains somewhere alongside them or something. You *were* his girlfriend."

I nod. "I should try to contact them. Those first few months after, like I said, I was just . . ."

Out of my peripheral, I see that Teddy guy watching us.

She grabs my hands again. "Oh my God, Brynn. When Lucy saw that your parents' place in Brooklyn sold, we texted you and each got the same *no longer in service* message. We thought you left the country."

"I wanted to disappear." Still do. I sniffle.

Her lower lip wobbles as she embraces my hands, her watery eyes on the brink of flowing.

My chest squeezes. "You still care"—I look down at the table—"even after what I did?"

The café becomes quiet. Several seconds pass.

She must not have heard me.

But then her beautiful face rearranges itself into something ugly and unrecognizable.

An iciness runs through me. I close my eyes. Why did I even go there?

She rests her chin on her hands, her pupils like slits. "I couldn't understand why Stanford stopped responding to my emails . . . or all those phone calls I made . . . but *you* knew why."

I rub my face, squeezing my forehead.

"What was it? Jealousy?"

My throat constricts. "No . . . I-I . . . You kept forgetting your lines . . . then the numbness in your hands, and your foot kept turning in when you walked . . . I was worried for you."

"You planted that seed in your buddy Mr. Prescott's head . . . telling him I had developed some neurological disorder, knowing he'd written my recommendation and was a Stanford alumni . . . You wanted them to rescind my acceptance into their theater school."

"I swear, I only confided in him because I was afraid of the stress the senior musical was having on you. I never imagined he'd contact someone there."

Her lips disappear. "You knew how scared I was . . . I *cried* to you . . . And then you tried to take all my dreams from me."

"No! Never!" I search frantically for the right words. "Your doctor figured out what it was, right? You're fine now. I never meant for it to get out like that."

"You didn't stop it, either."

True, but . . . *I did it to score points with Mr. Prescott so he'd help me. With Cody and my parents gone, he was my last hope. LaGuardia was a dog-eat-dog world. My last-ditch attempts at getting a college scholarship somewhere had dried up. Mr. Prescott appreciated that I was saving him from the embarrassment. They'd never take one of his recommendations again if I hadn't said something. Besides, who knew you only had some temporary inflammatory thing going on from an infection? I'm not a doctor.*

She takes in a long, cleansing breath, emphasized by lifting and lowering her palms like a yogi. "Let's talk about something else." Her eyes dart over to Teddy and Butterfingers, talking behind the counter. "So . . . when do you leave for school?"

"Not happening."

"What? That's—"

"Like I told you, I'm interning this summer. Hoping they keep me on full time. I need to make some serious cash. I've been staying at my parents' place on Bleecker that they used to rent out. Praying to not get evicted."

"You mean you've been living around the corner from my mom and dad's restaurant *this whole time*? Wait, what's the number?"

"Uh, 193 Bleecker." I swivel my cup around on my saucer. "I thought about reaching out. But I didn't know what to say or if you still wanted to talk to me. Maybe when you come back on winter break or something, we can spend some time together . . . like old times."

"Will you come to my party Friday?" Her brows lift.

My mind slips back to being fourteen again. We met that first day of auditions. Miss Drama Queen knew she'd nailed her acting tryout and pushed me to ace my vocal audition so we could be best friends. Her confidence in me without ever having heard me sing propelled me to give it everything I had. We were so naive. And yet it all happened like she said it would. She's the real reason I got into LaGuardia.

I force a feeble smile. "Of course I'll be there."

"Good! Don't let me down or I won't be able to forgive you . . . this time." She smiles, exposing her teeth like a she-wolf. "Anyhoo, I need your advice on this pair of boots I want to buy . . ."

I roll my eyes, smiling for real this time. "One store, Tess, not eight. Got it?"

"Lucy's going to be so excited to see you!" She throws back the last of her latte.

I swirl the milky liquid at the bottom of my cup, now cold. I don't need to see Lucy. Or Tess. I haven't thought about either of them in forever. They can't do anything for me now.

Tess clears her throat, watching me.

I grin, grinding my teeth.

"One store. Got it. Brynnie, Lucy, and Tess—BLT, back together again. We've missed our *bacon*, even if she is vegan." She winks.

"I've missed us too."

No way I'm going to her party.

Chapter 47

MICAH

"Micah, are you there?

"Micah?"

"Granddad, I'm here. What's up?" I sit up in bed, rubbing my eyes with the bottom of my palm, my phone pressed to my ear. Been over a week since my last ECT procedure and five since I left New York. I must have answered the phone in my sleep.

"I'm calling it." He sighs.

"What do you need? I'm not in the city—should I call for an ambulance?" I blink hard a few times, adjusting to the dark room. Beside this narrow bed floats a lone nightstand attached to the wall, a plastic-upholstered armchair, and my notebooks piled on the carpeted floor, along with my slippers near the bed. My mind's foggy with fragments of Brynn from my dream; my damp T-shirt sags against my skin. Another momentous day in the psych ward.

"She had a good ride, Sally. Shame what happened to those astronauts in '86."

Granddad should have been an astronaut. The guy loves all things space. From NASA to SpaceX, he can rattle off past missions, launch dates, and many of the crew members' names faster than Wikipedia. He used to let me admire, never touch, his collectable astronaut figures and trading cards dating back to 1963.

"Granddad, you're mixing up your *Challenger* missions. What's going on, you alone?"

"Eeeeyah, look at her go!"

I hear a pop, followed by a crash. "Are you launching one of your rockets? You still there? Granddad!"

"I'm fine. Stop shouting!"

"You almost gave me a heart attack."

"Micah, I need to tell you something. Can you listen for a moment, son? Your Aunt Max got an offer this morning. We're selling the agency to those snotnosed bastards at Day & Foster."

"What? But—"

"Time to let this thing go."

I fall back onto my pillow, exhaling into the phone. Brynn's face, then Eunice's, emerges in my head.

"I need you home, son."

"Granddad—I don't know how to tell you . . . I need to stay here."

"Dang it to high heaven, she's back."

"Who are you yelling at, Mr. Kershaw?" another voice says. "I swear, these damn rockets. It better not be the police again. Hand me the phone. Hand. Me. The. Phone! You are going to put me into an early grave. Who's this, now?" she says into the phone.

"I'm his grandson, Micah. And you are?"

"Deidre, his nurse. Sorry Gabriel called you. He's having one of his episodes and refuses to take his meds. Like I've told him a million times. I swear."

Episodes? What sort of meds? Not sure she can tell me anything due to medical privacy, something I know plenty about. "Anything I can do to help, Deidre?" *Besides charm you to death with my smooth demeanor.*

"Actually, yeah. Are you in contact with his daughter?"

"Yes, I talk to my Aunt Maxine every day about my granddad. We're all worried about him. She keeps me updated on his condition."

"Oh. So you know about the lithium he's taking."

"Of course." It helps I'm an expert on the drug. "He's at twelve hundred milligrams a day? Do we need to adjust to eighteen?"

"I think that's a fine idea."

Whoa. Lucky guess.

"Have Miss Maxine contact me, okay? Or, better yet, ask her to set up a doctor's appointment for him. Once they see what he's doing, they'll up the dosage for sure. I don't want him endangering himself—or anybody else, if you know what I mean."

"I understand. It won't be a problem, Deidre. I'll place a call now. Thanks for taking such good care of him."

"Thank you. I appreciate that. You have a good day."

What the hell—Granddad's on lithium? Since when?

I toss in bed, my mind racing along with my pulse. I help myself to a cup of decaf from the nurses' lounge and stroll through the halls a while. Hearing Granddad's voice and knowing he's not right has put a dent in my self-imposed exile. I can't lose him too.

I book the next flight to New York.

I step out of Granddad's private elevator and into the foyer.

Deidre, a stocky, muscular Black woman in her thirties dressed in a white polo and matching cargo pants and sneakers, jumps up from the navy velvet settee in the living room, sending her book toppling to the floor.

I drop my bag and catch my reflection in the oversize arched entry mirror, unshaven and bleary-eyed from the meds and long flight.

Her light blue eyes stall on my face. "Oh my goodness, I love all your music."

"Wrong Kershaw." I drag a hand across my chin. "You mean my dad."

She rearranges her slack-jawed mouth into a frown. "Your grandfather's out here."

Paying Granddad a visit outside one of our obligatory familial functions, where most of the extended Kershaw family members remain oblivious to my psychosis, doesn't happen often. I prefer not to be watched like an animal in a zoo or asked questions I can't answer. Yeah, I could be a better grandson.

He moved from the MacDougal house and bought this swanky five-bedroom, six-and-a-half-bath penthouse on Sutton Place South to spite my grandmother after they separated. Grandmother preferred the uptown socialites to the bohemian West Village hippies and had wanted to make the move for years.

I met Granddad and Aunt Max the year my grandparents divorced and lived with Granddad in the penthouse until I hit eighteen, two years after my diagnosis. Dr. Val suggested I live on my own to get me out more and perhaps make some friends. I may live in the MacDougal house, but I don't call it home.

With its glossy wood floors and snow-white walls peppered with oversize pop art, a few from the agency's iconic campaigns, Granddad's penthouse reminds me of the Whitney Museum.

As a kid, I skated around these floors in my socks, ignoring the maid's warnings and scuffing up the walls with my frequent misjudgments in speed. It wasn't bad living here, aside from being the only small person around. My mind liked to wander and I often found trouble—like the time I built a campfire in the living room.

When Granddad got home, he stood over me and said, *Draw it next time.*

Notebooks from my father began arriving shortly after, and ideas spilled out of me. At first I came up with short, illustrated stories sprinkled with crayon captions. In time, I drew less and wrote more, filling up every notebook he sent. Once, Granddad asked me to draw an ad for an opening of a new children's museum. It still hangs in the dining room today.

I walk through the sparse rooms and stop in front of our space wall, a floor-to-ceiling display of the NASA replicas we built together, all pointing left and mounted at a 45-degree angle on a clear plexiglass stand. If you unfocus your eyes, they appear to be flying.

I continue on from the wall and find Granddad reclining on one of the balconies, rocket debris on the ground next to him. He once towered over clients with his athletic shoulders, thick onyx-colored comb-over, and perpetual suntan. Today he's a scarecrow version of his former self—thirty pounds lighter, skin translucent, hair Einstein-wild—napping under a blanket in emerald paisley pajamas.

"There you are."

His obsidian eyes pop open, big like craters. "Oh, Micah. You came back. Eunice told me you would."

Impossible, but okay. I veer away from the long drop off the side of the balcony and slide onto the other chaise. "How are you feeling?"

"Tired. They drugged me up good this time."

"I don't like you being out here by yourself. I'll talk with Deidre."

He waves me off. "Can't move anyway. She has my walker. Sly devil, that one."

"Do you want a new nurse? I can let Aunt Max know."

"Forget it. I finally broke this one in."

I prop my hands behind my head. "What's going on?"

He cocks his head. "Nothing. What do you think is going on?"

"You sounded funny on the phone."

"How would you know? You didn't call me."

I stare at him for a beat. "Do you want to talk about the agency?"

His black brows fly up to his hairline, then dip low. "Ole Sally's sinking. Sad, really. My father's life's work." He snaps this fingers.

Bingo. Losing the agency prompted this temporary breakdown. Nothing more than that. I get it. The man devoted every ounce of himself to that place. It was his baby. He's crushed.

My eyes tear up without warning. "Ugh, these allergies." I pinch the bridge of my nose. "Bad this summer. If it's any consolation, you've always been more than Kershaw McKenzie to me."

"Shut up, Beck. You never appreciated a goddamn thing."

I catch myself before falling off the chaise. "I'm Micah, Granddad."

He blinks a few times. "Am I dying? Why are you here, blubbering?" His large pupils harden like black ice.

"I'm not." I pat his arm, looking away. "Just wanted to spend time with you." I close my eyes, containing the dam, indulging in long breaths under the crackling afternoon sun.

A moment or two passes.

A light snore floats through the breeze.

I peek over at his strong warrior nose, which he passed on to me. I bet he could still reel in the ladies today, if he wasn't so out of it.

He honks louder.

Silent tears spill down my face and neck.

The thing about Granddad, he's incapable of expressing his emotions and doesn't tolerate anyone else's.

Dr. Val calls it *cold parent syndrome.*

When I was a kid, he'd make me chase him in parks and across busy streets, laughing when I fell. If I reached out to be comforted, he'd push me away.

She said it most likely triggered a traumatic memory for him.

The guy can be an a-hole. Yet he's the only father who stuck around. Who read to me when I got mono from kissing Sydney Oliver, the prettiest girl in elementary school. He was the first one out of his seat when I received the creative writing award in sixth grade and the same guy who came home with a new bat when I made all-star baseball. He couldn't look at me in the eye when I tried to explain the Shadow People. Yet he spent all those afternoons with me, building rockets.

A sob rips from my chest. I can't lose him too. I just can't.

Chapter 48

BRYNN

"Eunice, hi. This package needs to go to Quotagian. Where should I leave it?"

"Over there." She points her elbow behind her to the table under the phallic rocket painting.

"Thanks. Um . . . so how's Micah doing?"

"How the hell should I know?" Her gaze doesn't veer from her computer screen.

Old grump. Not the welcoming face you want at an ad agency—or any company. I press on a smile. "Thought you two were close." I circle behind her desk.

The good-looking guy from Caffé Dante—Teddy, that's his name—strides through the glass doors in a black Falcon Messenger polo and holds out a hand. "I'll take that."

His voice is smooth like a baritone, his accent almost charming. I remember him performing; he moved rather fluidly for a guy.

He relieves me of the package before I can tear my attention away from his dark, feathery lashes.

"You and that blonde girl both work at Falcon *and* Caffé Dante?" I blurt out.

He narrows his eyes. "Ya mean Dahlia?"

Dahlia, Dahlia. Sounds familiar . . . "Wait, Dahlia *Schenkel*?"

His eyes widen, his lips clamp shut.

Tiny hairs rise up the back of my neck. That young detective, Clive Bodie, kept insinuating that I knew her. Has she been watching me this whole time? "Uh, never mind." I back away, my legs swaying underneath me. I brace myself on the side of Eunice's desk.

Eunice jumps to her feet. "We're done here." She shoos Teddy back through the double glass doors.

I turn to her, shaking like a bobblehead.

"You're welcome." Her rat eyes narrow.

I flounder back to my desk and collapse in my chair. The workstations around me sit empty. Everyone must be in meetings. I open my browser and click on the search bar. My hands hover over the keyboard, my chest thundering. I shake my head, blow out a breath, and stand up, my legs itching to sprint somewhere.

I lap the first floor a couple of times, eyeing the uneaten bagels from this morning. I run my hands under hot water in the bathroom and camp out in one of the stalls until my thighs go numb. I rewash my hands and return to my desk. I doodle a few flowers on a notepad I stole from Priya's desk.

Times moves like two slugs racing.

At five o'clock, I close my laptop and jump to my feet. At the double glass doors, I spin around to Eunice at her desk. "I don't know if you've heard some things about me . . . Anyway. I wanted to thank you for earlier."

Her eyes stay on her book.

I sigh, swing my bag over my arm, and push on one of the glass doors.

"I lost my parents too . . . in Saigon." Her voice vibrates so low, I almost didn't hear her. "The Viet Cong detonated a car bomb under our hotel on Christmas Eve."

I inch back toward her desk. "Geez."

She fills the skin under her bottom lip with her tongue. "A week before my ninth birthday." She pulls her elbows into her body, shrinking.

I stare, open-mouthed. "Mind if I ask, how did *you* survive? How did you . . . move on?"

Her pointy shoulders rise off her hunched back, her lips disappear.

I've overstepped once again. Of course I have.

"How did I move on?" Her beady eyes grow twice in size, her face childlike. "I'm still there."

I freeze, waiting for an explanation.

She shakes her head like I'm too thick to understand. She stares off as if searching for the words. "A soldier pulled me from the rubble. I screamed, wanting to stay with my parents. What was left of them." She shudders. "I couldn't understand, why did that bomb take them and not me? I wasn't strong like them, I was just a little girl. What could I do?" Her voice locks up. "Anger ate at me. I thought my hate made me strong. Resilient. I'd show them. Then one day, the truth became clear: Biting into the bitter apple let those terrorists win. Don't you see? They've still got me there, buried under the rubble. Don't you do it . . . don't let evil win."

A chill runs down my spine. "What if I don't know who the evil is?"

She sends me a blank look. "Then you're screwed."

I skip the subway after work and walk the eighteen blocks up Fifth Avenue, passing the main library at Fortieth to the Fifty-Third Street branch like I've done countless times since my parents died. After seeing Teddy today, I need answers.

Don't let evil win. I'm trying, Eunice, I'm trying.

I feel it in my bones that Dahlia had something to do with what happened that night. It took everything inside of me not to search her name at work. My teammates enjoy being all up in my business too much as it is; I'd rather not feed the gossip-whores like Donovan or give anyone else a reason to think I'm lying about knowing Dahlia or her connection to that night.

The air-conditioning blasts the sweat beads on my skin as I walk through the sun-drenched lobby and around the sunken amphitheater. I pass the backs of people hanging out on the light oak bleachers, some wearing headphones and watching a sporting event on the main screen. I continue to the computer area. A memory floats by of coming here before the big renovation with my parents to get the latest Percy Jackson book.

I'll find out who did this to you, Mom and Dad. I swear.

I join the short line waiting to use a computer.

A librarian I've never seen before grants me access to one on the end.

I lower myself into the chair, my legs burning after my speedwalk up here. I scan my library card and enter the pin. I type in my parents' names. The same old article appears. No updates. I've read this one so many times, I could recite it from memory.

I hesitate before scrolling down to their picture, identical to the one next to my bed of them performing during a headliner's encore—a tradition at the Flaming Flamingo that would send the crowd roaring.

A familiar ache edges into my chest.

The trouble with traditions is, they fail to evolve . . . No matter how many times I asked, I was never good enough for that stage.

I type in Cody's name and click on the link.

Man Killed Outside Music Store in Dobbs Ferry

Dobbs Ferry, New York (WNBC) – 19-year-old Cody Waters, a resident of Elmsford, New York, was struck by a car outside of the Muzic Store on Cedar Street in Dobbs

Ferry and pronounced dead at the scene at approximately 11:18 Saturday evening. An investigation is underway. Anyone with any information is requested to contact the Elmsford Village Police Department.

Your death remains a mystery, my sweet Cody. I release a long sigh. *What happened to you? If only I could reverse that night and never let you leave Pete's.*

My nose begins to run at the same time the new librarian walks behind my chair. I straighten my back and watch her exit my peripheral.

I open YouTube and search "Cody Waters LaGuardia High School." Several clips of his school performances pop up, posted by fellow classmates. One caption reads: Gone too soon but never forgotten.

Someone named Gabriella posted one of him singing a solo onstage. His face appears rounder, less angular, his body thicker—looks like it was taken before his growth spurt. It's gotten more than ten thousand views. I don't recognize the stage. Must be at his first high school. Who the hell is Gabriella? President of his fan club?

I search all the Dahlia Schenkels out there and find one in North Carolina, another in Indiana. Neither resembles the blonde I've met. She's not on social media, either. Odd.

My forty-five-minute session expires. I grab a couple of the library's blank checkout cards, once glued inside of books to record borrower's name and due dates, to use as scrap paper, and exit into a hanging curtain of heat waiting for me outside.

Traveling home on a near-empty subway car, my legs grow restless. I recross them, trying to shake off the creepy-crawly sensations running through them. Two young girls sitting across the aisle from me laugh, their outfits, like their feet, intertwined. A man leans near one of the doors, holding a brown bag with grease spots.

My stomach rumbles.

The express train's high-pitched roar rattles my teeth and thoughts, like how Dahlia works at Caffé Dante, right across the street from Micah's house, *and* at the same messenger company employed by Kershaw McKenzie. I would love to know when she took those jobs.

According to Tess, Dahlia and Teddy went to another performing arts high school in the city. Still doesn't explain their connection to Cody. Maybe his parents will know. Someone at LaGuardia's admissions office should have their number. After all this time, they need to know that I—the love of his life—exist. Maybe we can spread his ashes together, like Tess said, if they haven't already.

My knees start bouncing. Three more stops.

Cody often asked when we could hang out with my parents. I think deep down it was because he missed his. They didn't call him much. He also knew how much I'd enjoyed spending time with mine before they went AWOL. He could be sweet like that, wanting me to be happy.

I push that memory aside and pick up the pace once I'm out on the street at West Fourth. I pass the entrance to the coffin on Bleecker and turn down MacDougal.

I meander past Caffé Dante a couple of times before pausing and loitering in front, one eye on my phone, the other stealing glances at the servers inside. I don't see Dahlia, only Teddy with a smile between his ears, talking with someone.

He refills the long-haired girl's glass . . . oh my god . . . it's Tess.

She must have gone back to flirt with him after we met for coffee. Wait. Wasn't her going-away party, the one I ditched, weeks ago? She said she was leaving for Stanford the next day. What's she still doing in the city?

My stomach tightens. I hurry away from the windows. Hell if I'm going to go in there now.

I peek back at Micah's, wrap my arms around my waist, and squeeze, wishing he was here to bury me in his arms. I know I pushed him away, but he's what I need right now. Those eyes. His lips. A distraction from all this stressing. I hate being that girl who needs a guy, but I could use a friend.

If the detectives think Dahlia and I are somehow connected to what happened the night my parents and Cody died, I need to find out why.

I'll track you down soon, Miss Butterfingers. Count on it.

Chapter 49

MICAH

"Micah, what's up? What time is it?"

"Sorry to call so late. I couldn't sleep. I took the first flight this morning to see Granddad. I met his nurse. When were you going to tell me he's taking lithium?"

Aunt Max exhales into the phone. "Where are my glasses? Hold on." She speaks in a hushed tone. "Let me take this in the other room. I don't want to wake—"

I hear her wife groan like an Olympic weight lifter.

I'm glad I'm not there. Aunt Jenna's not fun to be around when she's cranky.

A door closes. My aunt sighs. "Okay, tell me again."

"The doctors asked you and Dad about our family's medical history, including a genetic disposition to schizophrenia, and no one said, 'Hmm, his granddad suffers from the same thing.'"

"When you were sixteen, we weren't so concerned about Granddad's behavior," Aunt Max says patiently. "Mood swings aren't uncommon for a perfectionist. Sure, he was erratic and overzealous about his work, but he was also a creative genius. When his highs and lows got more severe, we kept it quiet for the sake of the agency. He managed million-dollar accounts; we couldn't risk our clients and other agencies discovering that the man in charge had gone mad."

"*Mad?* Really, Aunt Max? Do you think I'm mad as well?"

"Of course not—"

"Well, I understand now why Dad and Granddad don't get along: Dad resents me for having the same thing his dad has, doesn't he? It explains a lot."

"Micah, you're spiraling—"

"More like freaking out *for good reason*, Aunt Max." I grit my teeth. "I just uncovered our family's biggest secret."

"And now you need to forget it." She exhales into the phone.

"Is this why Grandmother left him?"

Several seconds tick by. In my mind, I see her rubbing her eyes under her frames like she does when she's stressed. "Yes."

"That happened when I was a kid. You've always said we're so alike."

"Creative. Passionate. Brilliant. I should never have used the word *mad*. That was insensitive."

"My dad's story about the fever I caught in the Philippines when I was little causing my psychosis . . ."

"Speculation. Perhaps a genetic predisposition is more accurate."

"Why leave me in the dark?"

"It's what we Kershaws do best. I'm sorry, Micah. I wanted to tell you that day in my office . . ." She clicks her teeth. "I need to tell you something else. He's developed Alzheimer's."

I suck in my breath. The old lady in the elevator . . . Brynn's warning. *That could be any one of us someday.*

"Hard for me to talk about, even with you," Aunt Max continues. "He's the only parent I have left." Her voice shakes. "I've been trying to manage his care by myself. Beck's useless."

"I'm here."

"I know . . . but I didn't want to pile more on you."

"My schizophrenia is never going away. You can talk to me."

She's quiet for a moment. I imagine her thinking of me as the same little kid her brother dropped into her life. "Um . . ." I hear the catch in her throat. "I miss my dad." She sniffles. "The man he was. His sharp mind. I could ask him anything. He always knew the answer. I miss talking with him every day. He's fading away . . . and I can't stop it."

I blink a few times at the shadowy figure coming through my bedroom door.

The Woman in Black props her combat boot against the wall and gives me a hard eyeroll.

My chest fills. Strange to have missed her, but I did.

"Micah?"

"Yeah, I'm still here. Let's do brunch tomorrow, okay? I'll come up to your side of town."

"I'd like that."

The next morning, I text Dr. Val: *Need to see you.*

She makes room in her schedule an hour later and shows up late to our video call. I can see her fussing with the wheels on her motorized chair even after she logs on.

Anytime now would be great, I think to myself.

"I'm read-y." She looks back at me, her eyes dancing. "Caught me oil-ing up the old girl." Her lips curl into a smile. "How's New York?"

"Did you know about my granddad?"

"That he's tall, rich, and a grump-y sort of fel-low?"

"That he's schizophrenic too," I spit.

"He's not," she says matter-of-factly. "He's bi-po-lar—which, as you know, is dif-fer-ent."

Oh. "Did my father tell you that?"

"No, your aunt did. Your dad and I ne-ver dis-cuss his fa-ther. Your grand-dad sees the e-steemed Dr. Pen-der-gast there in New York. Beck's fun-ny about fam-i-ly. I could tell from the few in-ter-ac-tions with your fa-ther that dis-cuss-ing your grand-dad re-mained off lim-its."

"I think my dad hates the two of us for the same reason."

"I would-n't call it hate." She sighs and waits for me to look at her one eye that's focused on me. "Fear, may-be. He does-n't un-der-stand, so he pulls a-way."

"He's a fair-weather father *and* son."

She moves her head in a jerky fashion. "Can't change what he's a-ble to give you. You need to find the love and un-der-stand-ing in your-self. O-pen your heart, Mi-cah. I've said this be-fore, don't let your di-ag-no-sis de-fine you."

"You sound like Oprah."

"What-e-ver works. Hey, I like the beard stub-ble. Look ver-y de-bon-air."

"Weirdo." I sigh and shake my head.

"Time's come to stop play-ing the vic-tim and take re-spon-si-bil-i-ty for your life."

"Like you, Dr. Val?"

"Damn straight." Her grin sits crooked. "You don't see me wal-low-ing about liv-ing my life from this damn wheel-chair." She looks down at her lap for several seconds, her bottom lip juts outs. "O-kay, I lie. I al-low my-self a good wal-low at times. Helps me keep go-ing."

"You do manage to power through no matter what, though." I nod a few times. "It's part of the reason I picked you to be my doctor. That and your stupid jokes, of course."

She clucks her tongue. "Not my sex-y bod-y? How dis-ap-point-ing."

I roll my eyes and get serious again. "My aunt told me about Granddad's Alzheimer's. Does this mean I'm at a greater risk for that too?" I grip my elbows, pulling them into my body.

"Mill-ion dol-lar ques-tion. May-be. May-be not."

I rock forward and stare down at the knots in the hardwood. In the past, when my heart's started racing and it's become difficult to breathe, I've counted these planks to avoid passing out on the floor. And now this. How much shittier can things get?

Dr. Val leans back against her headrest. "Stop think-ing the worst. We know so much more now, how di-et and a heal-thy life-sty-le can help."

"Granddad couldn't even look at me when I told him about the Shadow People." My voice goes reed thin, remembering that day. "He got so disgusted, he pulled me out of school. Shut down my world."

"What if the shame was-n't a-bout you but him?" Dr. Val purses her lips. "What if he feels a-shamed for pass-ing the same de-mons he strug-gles with a-long to you?"

I squeeze my eyes shut.

"Stop. Stop what you're do-ing. Look at me, Mic-ah. Look. At. Me."

I lift my eyes from the ground and huff at the screen.

Her gummy smile folds into a deep frown. Her chin trembles.

"Shoot, you okay?" Dammit.

She blinks in slo-mo, like the way she speaks. "You're twen-ty, Mi-cah, with four gor-geous, work-ing limbs. Go live while you're a-live."

Chapter 50

BRYNN

Mid-morning, the agency's big room sits quiet, accompanied by a noticeable lull in walking conversations. I lift my face out of my laptop. The long rectangular tables around me lie empty. Meredith and Lucius left for some off-site client meeting and Josie and Priya went to grab coffee somewhere. I'm not sure Donovan even came in today.

Perfect.

I type in my high school on my computer, pull out my phone, and dial the number on the screen. "Hi, I'm hoping you can help me. I need to contact the family of a former student."

"Requests must be made in writing to release personal information unless you're listed in the student's records." The woman's voice sounds like car tires driving over gravel. I don't recognize it. "Name of student?"

"Cody Waters. I was his girlfriend."

A long silence follows.

"Brynn Gallardo. I graduated this past spring."

"I'll put you through to Principal Gibson, honey."

I wait for what feels like forever. Scanning the floor, I see Donovan—ick, guess he *is* here—talking to Zoe, who's grinning like the devil and dressed as one of the B-52s.

"Hi, Brynn. How are you doing?" Ms. Gibson's voice overflows with maternal tenderness. Her face would light up whenever she'd see me in the hallway at school. Her kindness toward me always felt steadfast and genuine.

I blink away the warm liquid pooling in my eyes.

"You still there, dear?"

"Yes," I manage, my voice raspy.

"Things are never easy after such terrible loss. What can we do for you?"

"I'd like to contact Mr. and Mrs. Waters. I wasn't prepared to before now."

"I understand. Let me pull Cody's file."

Donovan strolls back to his desk. No bag. He must have arrived before me. His eyes zero in on mine. "Ready?"

I swing the bottom of the phone away from my mouth. "For what?"

He shrugs.

"One second."

He rounds his brows and keeps watching me.

Ugh. Stay out of my business for once. I turn my back to him.

"Cody listed only one name on his paperwork."

His new student paperwork. I can still see his long, tapered fingers filling it out on his first day in Dr. Kendrick's homeroom.

"Um, here it is. Silas Walker."

"Must be a typo. You mean *Waters*." I clear my throat.

"Nope. Walker. Westchester area code. Do you want the number?"

"Yes, please."

She reads it out and I jot it down.

"I'll try it. Thanks."

"Hey, Brynn, do something with that voice of yours. Your gift is truly special."

"Thank you, I appreciate it. Take care, Ms. Gibson." I swivel my chair back around, scoping out the sea of workstations and glass conference rooms. No Donovan. I mash my lips together and dial the number. It rings forever. What am I going to say?

Hi there, this is Cody's—um, your late son's—girlfriend? We never met, but . . .

"St. Ignatius."

She gave me the wrong number. "I was looking for Silas Walker."

"Speaking."

"I-I'm, was a friend of Cody Waters—um, his girlfriend."

Like magic, Donovan reappears next to my desk.

I lift my index finger up to his face.

He stays put.

"We wondered when you'd call . . . Brynn."

Uh-oh. My stomach reels inside. "Is this Cody's dad?"

"Nope. That guy's been fish food for some time now. Nasty mob hit."

Huh? This doesn't make sense. "Are you a relative?"

"I'm not doing this over the phone."

"Hello? *Hello?*" I glance at my phone; he ended the call. Shit. What was *that* about? Cody's dad is dead? Did he die in the Caymans? When did this happen? And what's the deal with this guy's attitude?

Foot-tapping commences next to me.

I swing around, eyes blazing. "*What*, Donovan? What's so important?"

"Zoe's been given the copy revisions for Bradley Products and Quotagian."

Zoe writes copy? Since when? My jaw drops. "But I'm on those accounts. She's not even on our team."

"We think she'll be better at following direction." He cocks a brow.

Translation: Do not call the client behind Meredith's back and show her up in a Scott meeting. "So what do I do now if I'm off those projects?"

He tilts his head like I'm slow to understand. "We're swapping interns. You now report to Benji, the other account supervisor."

"Meredith's agreed to this?"

"She's all in." He walks away, whistling some bastardized version of "Happy Birthday."

Shit. I'm being kicked to the curb.

Chapter 51

MICAH

I make it home from the gym with plenty of time to spare before I need to head out for my late breakfast with Aunt Max.

Dr. Val says a regular fitness routine will help get me out of my head and deal with stress better. I have to admit, it did feel good to sweat again. It was my first time back since seeing Brynn there, but I knew no one from the agency would show up during a workday, her included. That didn't stop me from thinking every raven-haired girl on the fitness floor was her, of course.

Switching my coffee to my left hand, I fish out my key and unlock my door. Some Shania Twain tune streams from inside. I drop my keys in the canoe-shaped wood bowl in the foyer and walk toward the living room.

A breeze hits my face from the open terrace doors leading to the garden. My dad's hard to miss, standing there straight out of a movie—the one where the country singer stares up at the city's tall buildings for the first time. Except *this* cowboy grew up here.

A familiar pang rises in my chest. My mouth goes dry. I set my coffee on the counter, no longer wanting it. The house smells like his aftershave and I'm a kid again, catching drips from his razor in my palm with him above me, stooped over the tour bus's bathroom sink. "Dad . . ."

"There he is!" He rushes over.

I stretch my arms out wide.

He claps me on the shoulder and steps back, frowning.

I wince; the ache inside my chest doubles in size.

He makes his way to the Alexander the Great statue, still draped in the towels from my weekend with Brynn.

"About what I said on the phone . . ." My throat constricts.

He waves me off. "He fits this place, don't you think?" He smiles, looking around the room. "Surprise."

I'm unsure if he's referring to the statue or himself.

He smacks his lips. "I loved growing up here." He steps back onto the patio.

I don't join him.

"A piece of heaven." He sighs. "I learned to do a flip off the bars over there." He checks that I'm watching him and points to the nearby swing set, his eyes eager.

I don't say a thing.

His smile fades. He comes back inside.

I shake my head. "You used to say this place felt like a prison camp."

"All true. Time and distance give one new eyes. I know I had a charmed upbringing, Harmonica. The old man *was* tough, though. One moment he'd be playing with me and the next he'd be yelling, expecting me to know fun time was over, even though I was just a kid."

"Maybe because he's bipolar." I cross my arms over my chest.

He motions in disagreement. "Well, that wasn't a thing back then."

"Right. *Then* they called it manic depression. Same thing, though."

"I suppose. Me and Aunt Maxi didn't know those things. Mother didn't either. We could have been closer."

"What's your excuse now?" I scoff.

"Cut it out," he snaps. "I'm still your father."

"Who shows up at his convenience. I don't get it." I blink, fighting back tears. "I worshipped you—you were my Music Man. I never got tired of seeing you out there under the lights, pulling in the crowd with every song. Then you cut me out . . . took the music with you." I exhale, clasping my hands behind my neck.

"I never told you this, but your granddad was the one who convinced me the road was no place for you. He called me selfish." He shrugs. "I just wanted you with me. Then you caught that bad fever and I realized he was right—saw what I was putting you through."

"I wanted to stay with *you*, not him."

"I had to grow up and make the hardest decision of my life. I knew he'd provide you the stability I couldn't. Give you all the check marks a growing kid's supposed to have."

"When did you ever follow a checklist?" I puff out a hard breath. "Guess it was easier than having to deal with your mentally deranged kid."

"Shut your mouth. My son's amazing."

I clench my teeth. "Stop it. Open your eyes and see *me* for once."

He stares at his black-heeled boots. "Should have taken better care of you. Maybe you wouldn't have gotten sick, and this thing inside of you wouldn't have taken a hold of you."

"You think I'm possessed or something?"

"No—no! I just don't have the right words." He turns away from me, gripping his head in his hands. "I hate arguing with you."

"You help so many people with your lyrics, and yet when it comes to your own son, you don't have the words?"

"Oh, I write them. I just can't sing them. It cuts me deep, reliving that time." He buzzes his lips like a motorboat, shoulders drop. "Got me thinking the other day . . . after your mom recovered from the initial shock of being pregnant." He laughs. "She stopped eating those soft cheeses she loved. Quit drinking and smoking pot. She wore her Walkman headphones around her belly, playing classical music so you'd come out smart. Sure worked." He pauses, his eyes far away. "Micah, what happened to her . . . it was nothing short of the devil's hand."

He strides past me and picks up the small, framed photo of the Woman in Black from the side table, her long, sable-colored hair creating a cloak around her shoulders. Dressed in a black camisole and cutoff shorts with a long-sleeve flannel shirt tied around her hips, she stands with her hands in her back pockets, her sea-colored eyes challenging the camera like a badass. Grunge mom. The photo was taken the weekend they met.

"God, I miss her. Every song I sing is for her."

My eyes sting. This guy has nothing in his heart for me and I hate him for it.

His eyes widen like he's reading my thoughts. "Kiddo, that doesn't mean . . . I don't mean that. It came out wrong. Micah, you're the song . . . the one I don't know how to sing."

He clamps a forceful hand on my shoulder, so hard it almost hurts.

We stand silent for what feels like several minutes.

I don't dare meet his eyes or move.

He backs off his grip and pats my shoulder before walking back into the garden.

Chapter 52

BRYNN

Zoe is getting my accounts? Meredith and Donovan clearly have it out for me. I've never even met Benji, the other account supervisor. Will I still be writing copy or demoted to fetching coffee and dry cleaning like Zoe's been doing?

I don't understand; both the Bradley Products and Quotagian campaigns were *my* ideas. I've got to stop this from happening. Discredit Zoe somehow. She can't just waltz in and reap the benefits of my hard work. And Donovan can't get rid of me for being a threat. I wish Micah were here.

Leaving work, my brain spins with ways to fix this. I step off the subway stairs and nearly collide with a skyscraper of a human who's sashaying down Sixth Avenue with their cell pressed to their ear, wearing impossible stilettos and a bodycon skirt.

"Rikki? Wait up!"

They turn, side-eye me, and keep walking.

What is their problem? Lack of gratitude, much?

"Why are you running from me?" I shout after them.

They end their call and swivel around. "What's your problem?" They look me up and down.

"Why are you acting like this?" I come closer. "Ignoring me?"

Their head jerks back; they squint at me from under their sparkly rose eyeshadow. "That stunt on the train, Brynn—you *humiliated* me."

"I was protecting you from that creep." I puff up my chest, leaning in. "He was going to burn you with his cigarette!"

"I could have handled that backassward prick. What you pulled, treating me like some weak-ass Barbie—"

"I was only trying to help."

"Intentions don't count." Rikki juts out a hip, their upright pointer finger holding the space to speak. "I'm inches from a smackdown on the daily cuz of my swagger and charisma, not to mention"—they gesture up and down their body—"all this. You and your do-gooder act is no help to me. If someone was harassing you on the subway and I tackled you, how would that play? Don't act like my WWE Brown Jesus. Be my ally."

"I-I couldn't stand by and do nothing . . ." I stomp my foot, hands on hips.

"Holla atcho queen! 'Hey Rikki, been a minute. What's good?'"

"You're right." I deflate. "I'm the one who's ignored *you*. I feel bad for not returning your texts."

Rikki sucks their teeth. "LaGuardia twisted you."

"It defined me. I've never been happier than I was there." Until everything fell apart. "But I should have been a better friend to you."

Their eyes roll from my face to my feet, followed by a wrinkling of the nose like I smell bad. "What's with the costume and crusty hair?"

"I'm a mess. Whatever." I throw up my hands.

"I'm still vexed, but . . . I legit ugly cried when I heard about your folks." Their voice softens. "Be straight—you and your boo have something to do with it?" They arch an eyebrow, waiting.

My stomach sinks. "Cody? Why would you *think* that?"

"When you were still *Wizards of Waverly Place* fangirling Selena Gomez, you never learned enough is enough. Someone's in your way, *too bad for you*. Shut down the eyeroll, Bull Shark Brynn, you know your ways—aggressive and territorial like the predators of the sea. What, your folks saw through your Kevin Federline?"

"No, nothing like that!" I bite my cheek. "I decided against college to go on the road with Cody's band. The accident happened the first night of our tour. They found him later." I choke on my words. "But it was too late."

Rikki's eyes lose their edge. "I didn't know . . ."

I look away, my head starts to throb.

After a long beat, they shove my shoulder. "Never did see 1D live."

I shove them back harder. "Can't let anything drop, can you?"

Seeing One Direction at the Beacon Theatre was all we talked about that year in middle school. Between our mutual lack of funds and lack of a parent willing to chaperone, that dream got shut down right out of the gate. But we didn't let that derail us. We knew we'd find a way to score some tickets and convince our parents we were studying at the other person's house that night. Things improved when we learned about One Direction's fan contest that called for video submissions using the band's lyrics. Winners received two tickets and got invited onstage to sing with Harry Styles and the crew. We both sent a video to double our chances.

Rikki grimaces, lips crimped tight. "You bugged when I won the tickets. Like I wasn't going to take *you*. You know my old man locked me in my room that night after my brother blabbed to him? And don't act like it wasn't you who told my brother in the first place." They give me another stink-eye.

"I didn't get to go *either*." And my video was way better. "I saw online that when you didn't claim the tickets, they awarded the prize to the runner-up. I'll never forget her name: Marla from Long Island."

"Best move out of the way when Brynnie-girl wants something. Got me fearing for poor Marla—for real."

"I would never!" The words slip from my lips, and I see my parents' faces behind the windshield of the Monte Carlo. *Best move out of the way, Mom and Dad, Zoe. Donovan.* No! I shake off the prickling feeling down my spine. "Guess I need to fix a few things about myself."

"I never met Cody. But your folks were for real nice people." Rikki holds a hand to their heart. "They always welcomed and accepted me even when this queen didn't know who they were. Wish they'd adopted *me*."

I cringe, remembering the stories about Rikki's Malaysian dad and brothers. In a picture hanging in their living room, sandwiched between a quartet of muscle-shirt-and-jeans–wearing he-men, there sat Rikki in a fringe scarf, cold-shoulder top, and red capris. "How *is* your family?"

"No clue." They sniff.

"I think I've been on a mission to redeem myself." I wince, looking down. "The day I saw you on the subway, I helped a lost woman with dementia. But . . . I couldn't save the three people I loved the most." My eyes fill.

"Come on." They wrap their arms around me. "Brynnie, there's doing good. Then there's ego."

"I get it." I nod as we pull apart.

Rikki looks deep into my eyes. "Best watch your back. I heard Cody's family is questioning your old LaGuardia friends about what led up to the night he died."

I swallow. "How do you know?"

"My friend Sam freelances with a stylist who knows his brother. He lives with his sister in Hell's Kitchen. The girl stopped me one morning when I was going to work after she found out I knew you."

Maybe she's the one I saw Rikki speaking with on the subway before the lights went out. I shake my head. "Cody was an only child."

Rikki blows a scarlet lock out of their eyes. "You just cooled all the tea I had for you, then." They point their head up the street. "I'm this way."

"I'm up for taking the long way home. Hey, maybe 1D will have a reunion tour . . ." I lengthen my stride to keep up with them.

"Heard Marla *scored* backstage." Rikki makes a duck face.

I punch their upper arm.

"Ouch!" They scowl, holding the inflicted area. "You still hit nasty."

Chapter 53

MICAH

"What brought on the sale? I thought we weren't entertaining any offers." I prop my elbows on the table. In the booth behind Aunt Max, the Woman in Black rests her back against the wall, her Dr. Martens crossed at the end of the bench.

"With the impending lawsuit, Danny agreed it would be best." Aunt Max reads my face. "Daniel Ash from legal. You met him a couple of times. Damn Scott. Wish I'd delved deeper into his track record before we hired him as creative director and made him partner."

A server places two coffees on our table.

Aunt Max stirs a Splenda into hers. "My fault for not reviewing the billing sooner, could have turned around the overcharging before anyone got wind. Scott got desperate wanting to make the balance sheets look more successful than they were. Selling the client information to a third party and violating the nondisclosure agreement sealed our fate. The agency's lucky Day & Foster is still on board."

I hold my coffee midair. "So wait—*who* discovered the overcharging?"

"After we spoke in my office, I did some digging." She takes a quick sip, glancing away.

"So . . . *you* brought it to light."

Her jaw stiffens.

I hold back a smile. "I never did review my team's billing like you asked."

"I knew you wouldn't." She twists her lips.

"Oh my . . . such balls you have, Auntie."

Her chin dimples under her frown, her eyes brim with new emotion. "It was expected that I'd join Kershaw McKenzie after Beck bailed. Gave me a chance to be a part of my father's world. Didn't know it'd be a twenty-year life sentence."

"You found your out and took it." I shrug. "I'd do the same in your shoes."

Her narrow face contorts and tears slide down her cheeks.

I cover her hand with mine.

She releases a shaky laugh.

We both turn as a tray of food goes by.

She exhales, squeezing my hand. "I think I'm hungry." She blots her cheeks with her napkin.

I grin and signal to one of the servers. "Took you long enough."

Glimmers of my aunt's younger self light up her face. "With no agency to run, Jenna and I can finally travel, take that second honeymoon." She sighs. "What about you, Micah?"

"Still in shock, I guess." I glance down at my coffee. "And worried about Eunice."

Aunt Max nods. "Yeah, I'm not sure of her financial situation. I don't think she has any family here."

"I can maybe help her." I regard my aunt. "But let me be the one to tell her the news. It's the least I can do after everything she's done for me."

She frowns, pushing out her bottom lip. "She always looked out for you. I'm so sorry I didn't do more."

"Having an eight-year-old thrust upon you when you were twenty-eight and putting up with Granddad's periodic inquisition about why you hadn't found a nice young man yet had to be loads of fun."

"You were so cute." She pinches the air as if it were my cheeks. "More like a little brother than a nephew."

The server returns to take our orders and top off our coffees.

"Pancakes." Aunt Max winks at me. "For both of us. Yes?"

"Sounds perfect." I wait for the server to leave, then lean toward my aunt. "Want to know a secret? I used to sometimes pretend you were my mother."

She presses both hands to her heart and tilts her head. "Really?"

I nod. "What do you remember about her?"

Her eyes darken with emotion. "We were all there when Mia went into labor. We went from happy tears to denial . . . to unimaginable pain. For Beck and especially for you. No baby should be without his mother. All my life I longed to have a sister. I finally get one, and like that she's snatched away. And at just twenty, same age you are now."

"Talking about my dad with Dr. Val, I find myself needing to know her."

"She was guarded around our family at first. I wasn't sure I liked her. Back then, no one was good enough for *my* brother. We didn't see much of them. They were on the road a lot. But their last couple of trips to the city, she sort of warmed up to me." She smiles wistfully. "Your mom was spontaneous, with a wicked sense of humor. I try to focus on happier times when I think of her."

"What about her family? Two decades and I've never heard from them." A familiar ache resurfaces in my chest. "They can't pretend I don't exist."

Aunt Max dips her chin, trying to catch my eye. "You have their information. Hasn't changed since the last time you asked me about them."

"I think I'm ready." I feel the wobble in my smile. "Question is, are *they*?"

"If you're here, it can't be good." Eunice opens her apartment door wider.

I step inside. "Why? I love visiting the Upper East Side."

"Liar."

"Whoa, smells like a Vietnamese restaurant in here." I take a long inhale. "Incredible."

"You smell the anise. I made pho. Want some?"

"Perfect timing on my part." I rub my hands together, already moving toward the kitchen.

"Not so fast." Her gruff voice rises. "Wash hands."

"Yes, Mom." I salute.

She calls out while I'm in her bathroom, "I think that intern you like got herself into some trouble. Lots of drama, that one."

I return to the kitchen and pull out a stool from the island. My mouth waters as she places two steaming bowls on the counter in front of me. "First off—"

"Don't lie." She waggles her finger at me, then passes me a set of red chopsticks and a lotus spoon.

I grin, giving up the pretense. "What kind of trouble?"

"They took away her accounts. Cutbacks, I guess."

"Worse. Max sold the agency."

She blinks. "You're relieved."

"It feels like betrayal to admit it." Years of friendship release me from having to say more. We dive into our bowls in silence—except for Eunice, who's never quiet when she eats, in particular when it's pho.

She clears her throat. "You know, I only stuck around that place because of you."

"Same." I nod.

She stabs the air with her chopsticks. "Why you so quiet, don't you like my cooking?"

"I'm slurping!" I exaggerate my next intake of vermicelli noodles.

"Better." A brief smile flashes across her face before she scowls back into her bowl.

Eunice cooks better than anyone I know. Liquid pricks my eyes when I think about not seeing her every week. Maybe when whatever forces are at work in this universe—maybe God, who knows—took away my birth mother, they gave me other mothers in my life: Aunt Max, Dr. Val . . . and most of all, this woman next to me.

"Hey, Eunice?"

"Yeah."

"Thanks for sticking around for me."

She stops chewing, eyebrows raised. "You're my boy."

My nose fills with stingers. I can't stay seated. I start to stand.

She places a hand on my shoulder, anchoring me.

I sigh, letting the moment sink in. "Aah, I didn't expect that." I sniffle and grin at the same time. "Think you and I can move forward from our sudden unemployment?"

"Of course, I'm rich." She snorts.

My head jerks up, my jaw somewhere on the floor.

She exhales like she's counting to ten and rests her chopsticks across her bowl. "I told you about what happened to my family, but not everything." Her eyes dart around the kitchen, her body shifts in her seat. "My father worked for the Republic of Vietnam. During the ceasefire, the Chairman was scheduled to stay at this fancy hotel that also housed American officers." She swallows, her eyes lost in the past. "The Chairman offered his grand suite to my family as a gift."

I suck in my breath. "Then the bombing . . ."

"The government set me up for life." She studies the contents in her bowl, her lips twitch like she's pressing thoughts away. "I lived with my late aunt until I was eighteen; she managed the trust until then."

"Then you immigrated here . . ."

"And I got a job, because why not? I couldn't just sit around doing nothing." She looks at me, her eyes soft. "And one day, a little boy walked into my office . . ."

Chapter 54

BRYNN

The timer sounds and the water cuts off. I haven't finished rinsing off; soap burns my eyes. Damn communal bathroom. I swear one day I'll have my own private bath, linger in a hot, steamy shower for however long I want.

I twist the ends of my hair, releasing the excess water, and throw my towel around my shoulders.

A faint knock sounds. Shit.

"Just a minute!" My robe. Shoot! I left it hanging on the back of my door. I've never forgotten it before.

I blow out a hard exhale. My brain's been off since seeing Rikki yesterday. Glad the agency gives us half-days on Fridays; I don't think I would have made it through a full eight hours there today.

For a moment yesterday, it felt like Rikki and I had slipped back to seventh grade, when my dad would entertain us after school with one of his Flaming Flamingo stories—like the time some lead singer stripped onstage and relieved himself in the middle of a set. Or when Dad showed Rikki how to cut up peppers, telling them to wear gloves when slicing jalapeños, because once he'd forgotten to protect his hands and used the bathroom afterward. Dad said he couldn't stand up straight for an hour.

We laughed so hard, tears streamed down our faces.

Even during the early years of high school, I'd arrive home after show choir and find Mom and Dad in the kitchen discussing their day over a glass of wine before dinner, ready to hear about mine.

Then, one day, a major headliner pulled out of their contract. A *Rolling Stone* article soon followed: FLAMING FLAMINGO FADES. It claimed the once famed venue no longer held its cult-like status among musicians and audiences—its heyday was over. A couple of bad weeks turned into more bad months, making it near impossible for my parents to book bands. Longer hours at the club began to erode our family time, replaced by broken promises that things would return to normal. *We just need a few more weeks, Brynn. Be patient.*

A week could pass where we had no interactions outside of scribbled sticky notes stuck to the microwave.

B, PLEASE TAKE TRASH OUT BEFORE BED
MOM, WE NEED MORE CEREAL
B, FOOD MONEY
MOM, WE HAVE TO PAY FOR MY SCHOOL COSTUME
MOM, COSTUME
MOM?

The stress led to Dad's stomach ulcer. I'd tease him about his chalky lips from all the antacids he consumed. He went to a couple of doctors, cut out fatty and spicy foods, and said he felt better.

Thinking about them makes me miss Micah. Is he ever coming back—and what then?

Someone knocks again.

"One second!" I wrap my towel under my arms like a dress. It comes up short around my thick body. I spread my hand over my exposed hip, the other holding the towel across my breasts. My hand hovers over the knob. *Please be gone, whoever you are.* I count backward from three, and on two dash down the hallway, my wet flip-flops slapping the floor.

One of the corridor lights appears to be out. I didn't notice that earlier.

A tall, broad figure stands at the far end of the hall.

I jam my key in my door and yank it open. In one seamless motion, I slam it shut and secure the deadbolt behind me. Safe inside, I grab my robe at last and shrug myself into it.

My stomach rumbles from the smell of sautéed garlic and onions seeping through the wall. Doesn't anyone eat out anymore?

My phone rings on my mattress. I don't recognize the number; I let it ring until it stops.

I'm looking out the window to gauge the weather when the same number lights up my phone again. Fine, I'll bite.

"Hello?" I clear the unexpected cobwebs from my throat.

I hear muted street sounds from the other end, but no one's speaking.

"Excuse me? Is anyone there? Who are you trying to reach?"

"Brynn Gallardo." This girl sounds young.

I freeze. "And you are?"

Long pause. "A friend of Cody's."

I inhale a sharp breath.

"You should get your story straight before you go back to the cops."

The room spins. "Who *is* this?"

Silence.

I glance down at the phone. "Hello?" I squeeze my forehead.

"You moved on rather quickly, don't you think?"

Blood rushes to my face like a fever. "Do I know you? How did you get this number?"

Through the phone I hear a trash truck going by.

"From the FedEx package you gave Teddy."

I sigh, clenching my jaw. "What do you want from me . . . Dahlia, that's your name, right? Tell me, were you with my boyfriend that night?" I dig my teeth into my bottom lip and pace. "I have to know, please."

I swear, this girl better not hang up. I'll track her skinny ass down.

She coughs, then no sound. She coughs again. "Cody texted me for a ride to the music store. On the way, we saw a car flip on the other side of the highway. We stopped to help." Her voice falters.

My vision blurs. I blow out a hard breath.

"He tried to save them."

My fingertips fly to my lips. He did it for me.

"I'll never forget their screams."

My stomach lurches. I cup my hand over my mouth. "No . . . at the hospital, when I identified their . . . um, the officer said it's likely the explosion killed my parents, that they didn't s-suffer. One of the officers told me that . . . *someone* told me that!"

She clears her throat. "The explosion threw Cody. He was still conscious."

"Wait, what?"

"We got him into the car, and then on the way—"

I spin halfway around. "Who's *we*?"

"Teddy and me. We carried him back to the car . . ."

"I have a couple of friends in town coming to see us," he'd said. "Did you . . . help my parents?" I punch the side of my leg so her answers come faster. It doesn't work.

"I called 911," she adds like an afterthought.

"Wait . . . something's off." I back up, feeling for the mattress by my heels; my Jell-O legs give way and I collapse onto it. "They found Cody in Dobbs Ferry outside the music store. The police reported it as a hit and run."

My phone goes quiet. Not again.

Wait.

I gasp. "You staged it? I don't understand. Why move his body and take his phone?"

"Didn't want people jumping to conclusions, not understanding what happened."

I pop up from the mattress and resume pacing. "*You're* the 'jogger' who found his phone in the park . . . The detectives kept asking if I knew you. Why turn in his phone *now*?"

"People should know he died a hero, trying to save your parents."

I stop in my tracks. "How would his phone do that?"

"Um." She hesitates. "It just would."

The location-sharing app. Clive pointed out how their car made a second loop. Dahlia knows he used the app that night.

"Why didn't you tell the police what happened? Unless . . . he used his phone to track their car and it would incriminate him."

"I-I didn't say that—"

"Who drove? Did *you* cause the accident?"

"No!"

"Why would you help him do this? You're as much of a murderer as he is."

"We didn't cause it," she shoots back. "We just *saw* it."

"You turn his phone into the police, acting like you found it, when in fact you had it this whole time." I connect the pieces in real time. "They discover Cody *was* at the accident. I'm called in for questioning because they think *we* planned this. Is this your way to get *back* at me?"

She doesn't respond.

I rub my temples. "I'm guessing the police don't know any of this. Do his parents, or were they kept in the dark like me?"

She releases a hollow laugh. "What parents? Cody was a ward of the state."

I swivel back around. "Are we talking about the same person? I stayed at their Upper West Side apartment."

"Uh . . . Silas has access to a place up there; it belongs to the church where he works."

Silas . . . Silas Walker? The name Cody put on his new student paperwork.

I shake my head. "Wait—his parents have a house in the Caymans; he went on trips with them to Europe."

She scoffs. "He'd never been outside of the Tri-State area."

I pull hard on my scalp. No, no, no! "His band toured the States!"

"I loved him, but Cody was a showman. Probably thought you'd think less of him if you knew he was a foster kid. Most people do."

"I don't believe any of this!" I shout, making my head hurt. "You read about my parents' accident. You're making this up. You're obsessed with him. Trying to hurt me!"

She sighs into the phone. "Cody was a good person. And it got him killed. Your parents treated him like he'd never be good enough for you. He needed to show them what he could do."

"My parents loved me." Their miracle baby. "They didn't deserve—"

"You don't know what Cody went through, growing up in foster care. Not all people foster kids out of kindness." Her voice drops. "The tour gave him a way out. A chance to take control of his life for once and make a name for himself."

"You mean for *us*. CB Drunken Waters stood for Cody and Brynn."

She squeals like a pinched harmonic on a guitar. "Guess you didn't know his middle name. It was *his* band; you were just his backup singer."

"Duet partner." I grit my teeth.

"People came to see *him* perform, the handsome guy with the soulful voice—"

"Stop. Just stop!" I stomp my feet, clenching my fist. "We *loved* each other. We were going to climb the charts together. No one could touch us."

"Cody never let anyone outshine him." I hear the smirk in her delivery. "You were never going to steal *his* spotlight."

Chapter 55

MICAH

There couldn't be a worse name for a support group.

While most twentysomethings in this city head out to Friday happy hour, I get to attend my first Hearing Voices Support Group in this basement room with 1970s brown laminate wood paneling. Talk about walls closing in on you. The National Alliance on Mental Illness (NAMI for short) seems to think our special type of crazy warrants its own meet-up in a cavernous space that harks back to my dad's childhood.

I exhale like a dragon, scraping the metal legs of my orange plastic elementary school chair across the parquet floor to complete the obligatory circle. Going by the initial introductions, no one here gives their real name. I find it highly improbable that people with the names Dicie, Alf, Emory, and Beryl (or was it Meryl?) would all be in attendance to discuss the inconvenience of auditory hallucinations at the same time.

Bet they assume mine's fake as well.

Our facilitator, Elijah, who looks like Vin Diesel and has the same buff body, makes long, exaggerated eye contact with each of us. "Welcome. I see a couple new faces. I'm glad we have a small group; that means we'll be able to get to everyone who wishes to share this afternoon."

Yeah, I'm not contributing. Not sure I'm even staying.

Dicie, a Black woman with graying hair, and Alf, a Latino kid who looks younger than me, insist on conversing across my chest.

I scoot my chair back.

Their hand gestures continue to invade my line of sight.

"One in ten people hear voices." Elijah clasps his elbows, leaning on his thighs. "Like you, I struggle with intrusive voices. For the new people, this is a safe and respectful forum for you to share those experiences and exchange coping strategies with your peers."

He had me at coping strategies.

"I experience visions along with the voices." My words spew out at lightning speed. Guess I'm sharing after all. Was I supposed to raise my hand?

Alf and Beryl-Meryl both nod.

"Micah, right? That's fun." Elijah stretches back in his chair.

I like him more already. "I see my dead mother. It's almost like she's haunting me."

I look around at my fellow hallucinators. Not a hint of a smile. I exhale—and spill my story, beginning with the day four years ago when I awoke to the Shadow People trapping me in my bed and continuing all the way up to my effed-up existence today.

"My family doesn't know what to do with me. My old friends ditched me, new ones don't stick around. I can't move forward. My life stopped at sixteen. I'm . . ." My throat tightens, reining in my word vomit.

Dicie and Alf each take one of my hands.

Nope. I try to pull away.

They hold on tighter.

The fluorescent light strip overhead buzzes like a swarm of flies.

I eye the door. Elijah's talking, but his words come out muffled. *Thanks for the chat, people, afraid I need to extricate myself.* In my ear, I hear Dr. Val telling me to breathe. I refocus on Elijah. A minute passes, maybe two. My chest releases, my breaths come easier. Taking it slow, I free my hands. The room stays upright. I slump down low in my chair.

Going around the circle, they share their stories. I learn that Emory and Elijah also have schizophrenia. And that Emory, who reminds me of Josie, once lived on the street until someone from NAMI discovered her sleeping under the steps next to the St. Marks Hotel.

My spine stiffens. Never have I passed by the homeless on the street and thought that could be me—unmedicated. My weekend with Brynn, she referred to the man begging for money as Subway Saul and I made that remark about not thinking of him as having a name, like he wasn't a human. I look away, my knuckles over my mouth.

Elijah's eyes slide to me. "You okay there, Micah?"

I nod, my face warm.

We each swap treatment debacles and snicker over the plethora of pharmaceuticals we consume. I learn that being resistant to antipsychotic drugs like I am is common. And though we may have been prescribed similar meds, our reactions differ wildly.

"Anyone else care to share?" Elijah makes eye contact with the only other person who has yet to speak: Beryl-Meryl. A newcomer like me, but with freckles. Lots of them.

Beryl-Meryl's corkscrew strawberry-blond hair trembles like the rest of her as she raises a tentative pink hand.

Elijah nods at her, and she starts talking: She began hearing voices at the age of five and went untreated until her thirteenth birthday, this year, when the voices in her head encouraged her to step in front of a taxi.

Christ. She's only a kid. Same as Alf.

I sniffle back the sudden tickle in my nose. Warm tears heat my eyelids. I pinch the bridge of my nose. I refold my arms and switch the position of my legs. Refold. Switch. Repeat. I don't even like people. What is happening?

I look across and to either side and see it in their faces too. In this wheel of normal-looking people—each with another heartbreaking backstory—I'm one more spoke.

My freak-o-meter shifts.

We talk about our support system. Dicie and Emory don't have anybody, but I do. Aunt Max. Dr. Val. Eunice. Granddad, on a good day. Even my dad, though I never give him credit for it.

Something—or someone—inspired me to come here today. Planted a seed of desire to start the work. My first group session, and it didn't suck. A new beginning, perhaps. Toward a happy future? Maybe. No guarantee. Only this extra space I'm feeling in my already crowded brain.

Hope.

I haven't moved from my chair when Elijah comes over afterward with two Styrofoam cups full of coffee.

He passes me one. "I hope you got something out of our meeting, maybe found some solace this afternoon."

So much I need to process; I don't know how to respond. I shake my head. "I had no idea."

"What, that you're not so unique?" He sends me a wry smile.

"Yeah. Something like that."

He reaches out and squeezes my shoulder. "You're also not alone."

For some reason, I don't shake his hand off.

Chapter 56

BRYNN

In my dream, I'm drifting on my mattress in icy waters and pitch darkness. No floating bodies nearby. No whistle to steal. I scream without sound. The rescue boat can't hear me. My parents and Cody wave from aboard a big ship, smiling at me as it pulls farther away. Sirens sound from its deck.

I wake to an ambulance racing down Bleecker—my throat swollen and dry, my face wet, the sky outside my window dark like in my dream.

I crashed hard after my call with Dahlia, still in the clothes I slipped on after my shower. My empty stomach aches along with my head.

I rub my gritty eyes, grab my keys, and shuffle out of the coffin—only to stop in my tracks. The lights in the hallway glow bright. Was that one light ever broken, or did someone turn the bulb? A chill creeps up my spine. I double-check the corridor, threading my keys between my fingers. Holding my breath, I walk through the building at a brisk clip.

I was planning to go to the grocery store, but then I wouldn't eat for another hour. I'll get cheap takeout this one time and shop in the morning, before I head out to Westchester to meet this Silas person. After tonight, I'll start cutting back. Rhonda said she'd try to get me that extension by reminding the bank of my parents' recent passing. No one wants their financial institution in the press for kicking out the famed Basilio and Katia Gallardo's grieving daughter. I hope.

I head toward the ramen restaurant on Sullivan, dodging the smiling couples out on this sticky Friday evening. My brain still fuzzy from my late-afternoon nap, I about run into a guy playing "Only the Good Die Young" on his sax near the corner. My parents loved Billy Joel. I growl at the universe's timing.

Waiting to cross over MacDougal, I taste exhaust fumes. An EDM remix of some Dua Lipa song blasts from an open car window; another streams Spanish talk radio into the muggy air. I feel a tug in my chest, wanting Micah beside me, holding my hand. The way he'd cup my face, drinking me in, pops into my head. Why did I open my big mouth and run him off?

Someone walks into me.

I jerk back.

Hot, garlicky breath skims my face. "Smile, gorgeous. Don't look so serious."

I don't turn my head. My eyes burn.

The jerk and his friends laugh.

I grit my teeth, step off the curb, and move with the crowd. I look to either side and behind me. I exhale. The back of my neck tingles as I walk like someone's watching me. Not those same jerks. Someone new. I shake it off.

As I near Sullivan, the tingles buzz again. Am I being followed? I look over my shoulder, and Dahlia and Teddy slide into view. I blink, look again. Not them. Just my imagination playing tricks on me.

I dart around the group I'm trailing and duck through the restaurant's brown wooden door. Inside, I press my back against the wall, my heart punching my ribs.

A skinny, tattooed, straggly-haired guy in a fitted I LIKE DOGS AND WEED tank elbows the brunette with the high ponytail and purple tube top next to him. They're wearing matching pearls and silver padlock chain necklaces.

Her violet, deep-set eyes pull away from her screen and take me in. "Picking up, or what?" Her accent straight out of Jersey.

I glance at the takeout orders lined up behind the register, then back at her. "Menu?"

I find large boxes standing in the hallway outside my door when I return, breathless from my sprint-walk. I look for Debra's name and see mine. Sender: St. Ignatius. Why would some church send me stuff?

I drag them inside and leave them by the door. Food first, boxes after.

As I shovel ramen down my throat, I lean back against the wall, stretching my legs in front of me. The idea that Cody lied about having parents—wealthy ones, at that—hurts. Did I come off so shallow that he thought he needed to keep lying to me? And why did I find it easy to believe him when I never even met them? What else did he lie about?

Silas Walker. The name he put down on his new student paperwork. Who is this guy, and why would he give Cody access to some church's apartment?

Wait, St. Ignatius.

Silas answered his phone with the same name.

I gasp. How did he know where I lived?

Holding on to the wall, I rise to stand and leave the empty ramen container next to the kitchen sink and splash cool water on my cheeks. I dry my face with my T-shirt, take a deep breath, and stab my key into the packing tape on one of the boxes. Sawing off the last bit, I open the flap—and the scent of Cody's coconut body wash hits my face like he's just entered the room.

I stumble backward. Our last kiss flashes behind my eyes—his forehead resting on mine before he turned to leave, never to return.

I-I can't do this. I can't. *Dammit, get a grip.*

I blow out a long breath.

I lift out some T-shirts and jeans, and my favorite, his green button-down. I let the soft memory of him threading daisies into my hair in Central Park hang a little longer before shoving the box aside, slashing the tape on the second one, and dumping out its contents. Worn copies of *The Scarlet Pimpernel*, *To Kill a Mockingbird*, and some guitar books fall by my feet, along with his Alexander Hamilton High School ID. His round freshman face stares at me from the floor.

Cody Bennett Waters.

Holy crap. He did name CB Drunken Waters after himself. Cody Bennett, not Cody and Brynn. He never corrected me. He could have told me the truth.

A scream travels up my throat. I bite my cheek, swallowing it down. *Who the hell were you, Cody?*

I slump down onto the floor and flip through his ninth-grade yearbook, past the class photos and sport teams to the clubs. My stomach plummets and I about rip the page when I see a photo of him with his arm draped around a dark-haired girl holding a guitar, both of them wearing jerseys with "Wildcats" printed across their chest like in the Disney movie *High School Musical*.

Something in her eyes bothers me. I chew my thumbnail. I've seen her before.

The same girl appears on the next page. And here's another one of Cody singing in front of more Wildcats. He must have played the part of Troy. A freshman getting the lead role? He never once mentioned that, and he discouraged me from auditioning for any of the LaGuardia musicals.

I study the girl's face. The Falcon Messenger chick and server at Caffé Dante morph into one. Dahlia Schenkel. She darkened her hair to play Gabriella. Same pen name she uses when she posts videos of Cody on YouTube.

I scour the entire yearbook, finishing with the signature pages in the back filled with notes from his many female followers. The boy didn't waste time. One written in red catches my eye, a heart turned 90 degrees replacing the "D" in her name. *Code, Thanks for always being my hero! Love, Dahl.*

This girl's so extra.

I start putting his stuff back in the box. When I pick up one of the guitar books, a couple of folded pieces of paper fall out—online news stories.

The first one is less than a year old. I reread it, remembering the incident. The media covered it for weeks. They called the boys heroes. Why would he save this?

Cody's a showman . . . Your parents treated him like he was never good enough for you. He needed to show them what he could do.

I stare at the headline.

BRONX TEENS SAVE MOM AND DAUGHTER
FROM BURNING CAR

Oh, shit.

Chapter 57

MICAH

Back in NYC. We need to talk.

My thumb presses the back arrow key. My unsent text disappears. I'm not ready to see Brynn, though this pulsing thing inside my chest tells me otherwise. She worried she'd be the joke at work if the team found out about us. She must know by now I hold that title. My glorious mental breakdowns reside in Kershaw McKenzie infamy. But I don't care what they think of me. Like my fellow NAMI-ites, I didn't choose this. Schizophrenia chose me.

I do care, though, what Brynn thinks. She makes me want to work on myself. Get better. Group therapy left me feeling raw, yet anxious to reveal my secret to her. Learning that others living with my psychosis have lovers and spouses turned the story I've been carrying on its ear. I could have someone in my life. Maybe even someone like Brynn.

My feet turn up Bleecker Street before my mind follows. The charged air of a Friday night in the Village surges with shiny, happy people. Headlights stream at me, passing open-air restaurants and bars with couples dining inside and at sidewalk tables. A guy on the corner plays his sax next to a karaoke speaker, some catchy Billy Joel song.

I dash up her steps, my hand outstretched. She could have someone with her. I yank it back like I've been stung. Finding out another guy's up there with her would kill me. I step onto the street and gaze up at her window. No lights.

I wait near the curb. Seconds tick by, my resolve shrinking.

I wimp out and head back toward my house.

On cue, the crowd thickens around me.

Every cell in my body snaps to attention. My gut clenches like I'll be jumped from behind before I can get to my door. The random shouting and raucous laughter, combined with the sweaty bodies on either side of me, escalate the pulsing in my throat.

Navigating Bleecker on a Friday night: huge mistake.

I walk in the street to create a buffer for myself. I gulp pockets of air, unable to take a full breath. I hold the oxygen in my lungs, gnashing my teeth. I plow through the crowd, entering the crosswalk, and clip some slow-walking tourist's shoulder.

The guy flinches and stops in his tracks.

"Sorry." I lift my hand.

"Asshole."

Right back at you.

I call Dr. Val once I'm safe inside the house.

She takes a moment to turn on her video.

The pink and orange California sky behind her relaxes me, soothes my racing heart. My breathing begins to return back to normal. I help it along with a few audible exhales.

"Were you out run-ning?" She peers over her glasses.

"Something like that."

"Oh?"

"You're looking at a proud participant in NAMI's Hearing Voices Support Group."

"Oh, Mi-cah. I'm so glad you went!" She beams her gummy smile and adds a flexed hand clap—not an easy feat for her.

"Better than I expected," I admit. "I may go back."

"Look who's learn-ing to trust. Shar-ing your stor-y with o-thers. The old Mi-cah would have re-sist-ed. I'm proud of you."

The Woman in Black rests her backside on the arm of the yellow couch. She switches her combat boot to the other knee as she listens in, her arms crossed, head down.

Dr. Val leans back on her headrest. "Post E-C-T and start-ing the new med-i-ca-tions, I need you to log your symp-toms so we can track your pro-gress, in-clud-ing how oft-en you're see-ing your moth-er and other hal-lu-cin-a-tions. . . and an-y ep-i-sodes of pa-ra-noi-a you're ex-per-i-enc-ing . . . like this last one."

"How'd you know?" I give her a weak smile.

"I have a con-fess-ion, Mi-cah."

"You're surveilling me?" I tilt my head, smiling.

She clears her throat. It tumbles into a cough that won't stop. Her body starts rocking in fits. Her face draws tight. She releases a faint, high-pitched cry.

"Are you okay?" Shit.

Her bird hand flies all over the place.

I run my hands along the couch and floor for my phone. "I'll get help."

"A mo-ment of hon-es-ty," she wheezes. "And look what happens." She pulls her bird hand firmly into her lap. Seconds drag. Her coughing takes time to teeter off. Her stillness resumes.

"You alright?" The boulder in my throat remains lodged in place.

"When you asked a-bout my re-la-tion-ships and trust-ing peo-ple . . . it pissed me off."

I hang my head. Tonight's been a lot.

"I'm not say-ing this to make you feel bad. I know you were look-ing out for me. I'll let you in on a se-cret . . . I talk a big game . . . but I have-n't been in a re-la-tion-ship in a long time. Something I need to work on."

"You, Dr. Val?"

"Yep. Like you, I'm hu-man."

"So, no sex tips?"

Laughter ripples from her chest. She presses her head back into her headrest, beaming.

I sigh, smiling at her jovial return and the fact that she trusted me with a secret.

"I got you, Dr. Val. I got you."

After our call, I pull out my notebook and review the letter I've been working on since I got back into the city. I lose interest in most things pretty quickly, except writing. I could write all day and night. My dad calls them stories. The truth is, I've been composing love letters to my mom since I was eight.

Back then, I imagined her to be a badass superhero, one who needs to be away from home to make the world a safer place. My embarrassing teenage rants filled up later notebooks, until my psychosis reared its ugly head and my writing came to a halt.

It wasn't until I met Dr. Val that I started again. She helped me get back to my word-collecting and prose-streaming ways, restoring the temporary peace they bring me. I've never shown anyone my writing outside of Brynn that weekend. A big step for me. Words come out better on paper for me than they do from my lips. I'd hoped showing her would bring us closer. I think she needs to know my story to fully understand.

I start my letter: *Dear Mom, It's rude to eavesdrop on my life.* The Woman in Black smiles and lays her head on my shoulder.

I fill up the pages with my anger and love for her. It's confusing, for sure. I hate her for leaving me and effing everything up. Still, I can't help loving her for giving up her life for mine. If she had lived, maybe my dad would have stuck around to raise me. Then again, they could have fallen out of love and divorced like my grandparents. Perhaps my fantasies of her don't come close to reality. I'll never know.

I fall asleep as soon as I close my eyes.

I don't know what time it is when I wake up, but I know I just slept better than I have in a long time.

The Woman in Black is gone.

She'll be back, I'm sure—after she fights some crime.

Chapter 58

BRYNN

"Mr. Walker?"

A bald, pasty-white, fortyish-looking man lifts his head from behind his desk. His face of concentration appears menacing until he sees me and cracks a smile from the side of his mouth, his lips blood red. "Are you Brynn? Welcome to St. Ignatius on this fine Saturday morning. Not your first trip to Westchester, is it?" He guffaws.

My back stiffens. Does he think this is funny? "I'm surprised you knew it was me."

"I guessed." He motions to one of the chairs in front of him.

My gaze stops on the crucifix above his head, travels down it to the worn leather messenger bag on the credenza behind him.

I stare at the bag. "That's Cody's. He carried it everywhere his first week at LaGuardia. He thought he was some hot shot."

Silas blinks. "He needed something to carry a change of clothes in."

"Oh . . ." I swallow. "Um, Dahlia called me."

He pinches his bottom lip while his eyes bounce to the corners of the office. "She and Teddy are still grappling with Cody being gone."

"I miss him too." I clear my throat. "Dahlia seems pretty hung up on him."

His furry brows meet in the middle of his forehead. "They grew up in foster care together. They were essentially siblings."

Huh. "I didn't know. Teddy as well?"

He nods. "They met in elementary school. The kids used to pick on Dahlia. She was a tall, scrawny kid with low self-esteem. Cody protected her. He taught her how to play guitar—gave her confidence. When they sang together, it was really something."

"Were you the one who sent me his things?"

"Couple of the kids took care of it. Thought you should have them. Though now that she's told me how quickly you moved on, I regret being so benevolent." He shrugs. "What can I say, it was a moment of weakness. Just know I did it for Cody. Not you."

This guy's a delight. "So you don't know what's in those boxes?"

"I'm sure not a hell of a lot. The kid schlepped everything he owned in a black trash bag between foster homes. When I learned he had his heart set on that *Fame* school, I offered him one of the parish's apartments if he pulled off the audition." He smacks his lips together. "I heard they hadn't seen such talent since Jason Derulo went there."

I roll my eyes without thinking. "He didn't go there."

His dark gaze shuts me up. Then he looks away, shuffling papers. "What brings you here?"

"Can you tell me about Cody before LaGuardia?"

"What can I say? Kid was a Boy Scout. Biggest heart. Always sticking his neck out for others. His music helped him get through some troubling events, ones no small person should ever endure." A shadow passes over his face, a low whistle escapes his teeth. "Ah, Cody. My boy. No one loved being up onstage more than he did."

"I'm learning he may have had something to do with my parents' accident, and that Dahlia and Teddy helped him. I haven't told the police yet—"

"*Watch it*," he snaps with a force that sends a shiver through me. "These are *good* kids. They face challenges you can't begin to imagine—addicts for parents, guardians serving time. People will take the word of someone like you over a foster kid every time. That's how it is. These kids have to work harder to prove their worth. They get nothing handed to them. All they have is each other. You'll never see a stronger bond. And it's one you *don't* want to cross."

"Cody wasn't exactly a saint." I recross my legs, holding the edges of the chair. "He told me his parents lived in the Caymans."

After a beat, his mouth breaks into a wicked grin. "He didn't trust you. Interesting."

I shake my head. "He loved and trusted me enough to ask me to partner with him on tour."

"People do things for a number of reasons. Your parents were well-known in the music world, probably had a lot of connections, correct?"

The ceiling rises as the room and framed degrees on the wall stretch vertically and the floor drops from underneath me. I close my eyes. I'm falling, falling . . . my stomach plunges in freefall.

He clears his throat; it sounds like a truck's engine turning over.

I open my eyes. I'm still sitting in the chair.

He gives me a hard look, waiting for my reply.

"Yes, but . . ." My voice sounds small and strange.

Silas leans back in his chair. His smug, blood-red smile swells from ear to ear.

Chapter 59

MICAH

I yawn inside my hand, gazing out at the large garden in the courtyard. The sun still hangs low in the sky, but when I went out with my coffee moments ago, the air temp had already reached broiling. Typical for August.

The swing set in the middle of the courtyard sits void of its pint-size citizens. Another hour and its swashbuckling Saturday morning subjects will be overthrowing the nobility out there with the sprinklers running.

"Can you hear us, Micah? Nivaan, where did you go? How do I turn on my video? Nivaan!"

I return my attention to my computer screen. "Lower corner." I steady my voice. Inside my heart thumps, my palms perspire. I'm taken aback by the pair's vivid attire as I tuck in my plain gray T-shirt.

"Oh!" My mom's mother pushes up her glasses. "You look so much like Mia, similar shaped eyes . . . though not the same color."

"Hair too." My mom's father, composed like a deity in his royal blue collarless dress shirt, nods.

"For so long, you've only been a picture, a little baby in Beck's arms. Now you're real." She bounces in her chair.

"Doctors Dhaliwal—"

"Please, Kavya and Nivaan." She readjusts her purple and gold sari over her shoulder.

"I apologize for not contacting you sooner."

They look at me with expectant faces.

My mind blanks. "Sorry . . ."

"Tell us about yourself," Kavya starts, her voice gentle. "You're twenty, right? You go to university?"

"No . . . I work at my granddad Gabriel's advertising agency."

"What?" She frowns. "Education is most important. You must go to university. Study several degrees. We told Mia. She didn't listen. So very smart, that girl. Full scholarship to Barnard, then she forgot who she was." She flicks her hand, her face heavy with distant thoughts.

Nivaan stares straight ahead.

"We were too strict, perhaps." Kavya pulls in her lips. "Mia being our only child, we envisioned many great things for her."

Nivaan touches her hand.

Her shoulders drop some.

"Meeting my dad and following him on the road wasn't what you had in mind for her." I nod a few times.

"You fall in love. Okay, so . . . you fall in love." Kavya's eyes expand. She throws up her hands, releasing a strained laugh. She points at her screen. "But get your education. So important, Micah, we must insist."

Nivaan blinks a couple of times. Guess he agrees.

The stirring of warmth in my chest catches me by surprise. "Thank you for insisting." I smile. "Nice to hear it coming from you."

"You're one-half Dhaliwal family, don't forget it." Kavya's face softens into a warm, lipless grin that reaches her eyes. I imagine my mother's smile in hers. "We're sorry you didn't know our Mia. She was . . ." She stops, brings her curled fingers to her lips.

"Our life," Nivaan says in a low whisper. The whites of his eyes redden.

Her bottom lip contorts. "Yes, our life." She clasps his upper arm. "Our sweet beti."

The back of my throat aches. Their love for my mother makes her real.

"After Mia died, your father asked if we'd raise you, said you'd be in better hands since we both work in medicine." She shifts in her seat.

I cover my mouth. He tried to get rid of me even earlier than I thought. "I never knew that."

Her eyes fall to her lap. "We were heartbroken, angry . . . and a bit stubborn."

My chest tightens. They didn't want me. My father. My grand-parents.

She looks back at the screen, her face pinches. "Understand, Micah, we were afraid of ourselves—afraid to live with the memory of her and not have our daughter. How could we celebrate your birthday and mourn our only child at the same time? But to not know you meant giving up the only piece of our daughter that was left."

My eyes smart. I look away. "I'm sure it was confusing."

"Your father's sister called when you got the bad fever in the Philippines," she continues. "We asked Beck if he would let you live with us. But your father said he couldn't bear to give you up."

I clench my jaw. "He did it anyway when he sent me to live with my granddad in New York."

"Beck blamed himself for Mia's death and again when you got sick." Kavya shakes her head. "He was afraid to lose both of you. Respecting his wishes, we didn't contact you until you were ready to meet us. Your email made us very happy."

If only I'd done this sooner. "Tell me more about my mom."

"When you come for a proper visit to see your nani and nana." She grins. "You'll meet more family then, hear all the stories. We'll put you in a traditional kurta. So handsome, don't you think, Nivaan?"

He doesn't blink this time.

"Where in India are you?" I sit up straighter.

"We came over from New Delhi before Mia was born," Kavya says. "We live in Frankfort, outside of Utica, New York."

Guess we didn't need to chat this early. Good to know.

"Between our families," she adds, "you have fifty-five cousins."

"What? No way."

"Diwali is soon, our festival of lights. You come for that." Her tone leaves no room for contradiction.

I nod. "I'd like that."

"Introduce you to a fine Indian girl."

"Whatever you say, Kayva." I chuckle. College, marriage. My mom's mom doesn't waste time.

"Please, Nani. And you call him Nana." She directs her thumb toward Nivaan like a hitchhiker.

"I like your spunk." I smile. "Especially Nana's."

My grandfather's shoulders shake a little. His toothy grin is goofier than I expected.

I bust out laughing, enjoying the moment, sensing it's just the first of many to come.

I take a deep breath and release it. Might as well put everything on the table.

"I didn't plan to tell you this yet . . . but . . . four years ago I was diagnosed with schizophrenia. Not sure how familiar you are with it . . ."

The call ends before I want it to. The sides of my head pulse like I've just sprinted through Central Park. All these strange, jumbled emotions course through me; it's like a big, lumbering weight's been lifted from my shoulders. My grandparents, so warm and open to having a relationship with me, listened without judgment and then promised to study up on my condition and consult additional specialists. Looks like I have a couple more doctors in my corner.

Alongside all this goodness and positivity, I can't ignore my stupidity that I didn't reach out sooner. I'd convinced myself that they didn't want me, but the story I'd fabricated in my head was nothing but bullshit. All this time, my mom's family was out there, waiting. Loving me from afar.

Fifty-five cousins.

A jittery laugh escapes my lips at the prospect of meeting them. I'm terrible with names. I'm never going to be able to keep them straight. Tears blur my eyes.

I look over at my mom's picture. "Thank you, Mia . . . Mom. Thank you for giving me life. I'm only sorry you couldn't stick around."

My heavy head drops into my hands and I bawl like a baby.

Chapter 60

BRYNN

I feel beaten up after seeing Silas. The guy hates me for existing; I'm a thorn in his precious foster kid world. His insinuation that Cody used me to get to my parents hits me hard. I'm still seeing stars. I left his office with a sour taste in my mouth and more questions than answers, food the last thing on my mind.

I arrive at the police station over an hour before I'm supposed to meet the detectives, but someone shows me straight into the same interrogation room. The sweat trapped under my white capris and striped top sends a chill through me as I watch the minutes tick by.

It doesn't make sense, Cody harming my parents to leverage them. He wasn't like that. He had trouble forming a sentence around them just like everyone else my entire life had.

My stomach starts knocking. *Forget your hunger*, I tell myself. I need to stay sharp. Relay what I know. Find out if Dahlia and Teddy helped to carry out Cody's plan, which was clearly inspired by those news articles. Learn the truth of what happened that night and make them pay.

Simone and Clive shuffle into the room.

"You're early, Miss Gallardo." She folds her arms on the table.

My knees start bouncing. "Dahlia Schenkel called me. She and another guy were in the car with Cody that night. She said she called 911."

"Slow down." She motions with her hand. "We have no record of any 911 calls."

Clive places the evidence box on the table between them.

"Th-that's impossible. My mom's voicemail said the police *had arrived*—that they were being rescued."

They look at one another with blank expressions.

She turns back to me. "What voicemail?"

Wait, what? "I told the officer working the desk that night. I argued it was proof they were still alive. All he said was that I needed to bring in their toothbrush or hairbrush to identify the bodies. He had no interest in anything I had to say."

Simone frowns.

Clive purses his lips.

They watch me pull out my old phone from my bag—the one from a former life, when my world was still whole. I place it on the table and press *play*.

Honey, it's Mommy. Shit, is this thing recording? Um, Daddy and I had an accident. A small one. Uh, we're fine . . . We really wanted to hear you sing tonight. I'm afraid we may miss it now.

Look! Someone's running toward us. That didn't take long. A good sign, my love!

The police are here, baby girl. I'll call you later. We love you.

I gesture to my phone. "If that wasn't a cop, who was it?"

"Not one of ours," Simone says. "Your mother may have assumed it was the police. Who knows the state she was in after the car rolled." She glances at Clive. "Could have hit her head."

"Well, she sounds normal to me. If someone else was there, why didn't this person try to help them?" My voice cracks.

Clive looks up from his notes. "Maybe they did."

"Then why didn't they come forward?" I mash my quivering lips together.

His eyes soften. "Mind if I take a look at your phone?" He points. "I won't delete a thing, I promise."

I hesitate, then slide it toward him.

Simone lifts her palm to me. "You've been carrying around this piece of evidence all these months and only decided to share it with us now?"

"I thought . . ." My ears grow hot.

"This would help take our eyes off of *you*?"

My breath catches. "I was at Pete's, waiting for Cody to come back. And like I said, I *did* tell an officer that night. I had nothing to do with this!"

Clive stops chewing the end of his pen. "The last time you came, we analyzed the location-sharing app on Cody's phone—specifically, the route he took that night—and you asked if we found your mom's phone. I found that interesting."

I close my eyes, rubbing my temple. "I don't remember."

"Did your mom have the same app on *her* phone?" His voice rises. "Was Cody tracking their car that night?"

"Come on, Brynn, level with us." The skin around Simone's eyes creases. "All these performing arts students come together on one night and you're telling us you're not somehow connected?"

"I swear, I never heard of Dahlia and Teddy before now." I grip the edge of my seat.

"Detective Bodie, invite Miss Schenkel to join us. You can dismiss the others."

"Which one is that again?"

"The tall blonde."

I swallow. "Others?"

"Teddy, who was also in the car with Cody that night. A couple members of Cody's band. Oh, and some of your former classmates. We went way back, Bull Shark Brynn."

Oh, shit.

Dahlia takes a step back before entering the small room wearing a green maxi dress that hugs her slight build. She pretends not to see me as she sits down in the chair adjacent to mine. She smooths her dress underneath her and then leans forward in her seat, waiting for the detectives to begin.

A lifetime passes.

She keeps recrossing her legs, keeping her back ramrod straight. This is the first time I've seen her not dressed in one of her uniforms. She's better-looking with her hair down—I'll give her that.

Simone glances up from her phone at last. "Okay, Dahlia, let's start from when you picked up Cody at Pete's Saloon. Whose car were you in?"

"Silas's," she says, her voice soft.

Simone nods. "Detective Bodie tried tracing Mr. Walker's car. St. Ignatius reported it stolen a week after the Gallardos' accident."

Dahlia holds the front of her neck. "Um, when we got there, Cody and I changed seats. He liked to drive. Didn't get much of a chance living in the city." She clears her windpipe. "We headed onto the Saw Mill; we were talking about his band's set that night when, out of nowhere, he saw a car flip in his mirror."

Simone squints. "His rearview mirror? I thought you saw the Gallardos' car from the other direction."

She clears her throat again. "I meant from the southbound side. Sorry, I'm nervous. Anyway, Cody insisted that we try to help whoever it was. He circled back around and pulled off on the shoulder. He ran over to help."

Simone cocks her head. "No one else got out of the car to help?"

Dahlia shrugs one shoulder. "He said he'd be right back. He wasn't gone long before we heard Silas's trunk pop open."

"Hm." Simone taps her finger on the police report before her. "Your friend Teddy says Cody was looking for a tire iron."

Dahlia rewets and bites her lips. "I-I didn't know what he was after. Cody headed to their car again—and then the ground, everything, shook. Teddy started screaming about the other car being on fire. The explosion knocked Cody into the ravine. We both jumped out of the car and started running. Teddy got to him first. He was still alive. We didn't see any burns . . . only blood." She drops her head, hugging her waist.

Her cat-like eyes flit over to mine, then to the detectives.

The back of my neck tingles. She's lying.

My heart begins to pound. That bald guy's car conveniently gets stolen a week after the accident. Dahlia admits they moved Cody's body. It's obvious she and Teddy played a part in Cody's plan. Why else protect him?

Dahlia's lips curl around her teeth as she cries. "I know we should have stayed and not tried to take Cody to the hospital ourselves. When he died, we didn't know what to do."

I shove her shoulder. "So, you and Teddy dump him on the street in Dobbs Ferry to make it look like a hit and run? Like he's nothing to you?"

She recoils, holding her arm. "I'm truly sorry we did that." She turns to the detectives. "We made a mistake." Her voice cuts out.

Simone turns to me. "What about the call Cody made to you that night *after* he left Pete's, Miss Gallardo?"

Chapter 61

BRYNN

"Y-you don't understand," I stammer. "The night of the accident, I ignored my phone when it vibrated in my pocket. I thought my mom was calling to say they weren't coming. I wish I'd answered, told them I loved them . . . one last time," I croak.

Clive leans back, folding his arms. "That was the first call. I asked for your phone to confirm the second call, from Cody's cell. According to your phone's records, it went through and the call lasted about a minute."

Dahlia's head swings in my direction, her hair concealing her half-smile from the detectives.

My stomach lurches. "I-I thought it was a pocket dial. He never spoke."

"Um . . ." Dahlia stuffs her hands under her legs, her head bowed. "Cody was in bad shape when we got him to the car, but he was able to tell us it was your parents in the other car—he then asked to call you. I held his phone to his ear." She gives me the stink-eye. "You yelled at him for taking too long."

I can feel Simone watching me.

"I-I was upset. But then he didn't say anything, so I hung up." I glare at Dahlia. "You could have told me he was in trouble."

Her icy green eyes stab back. "Cody was crying. He closed his eyes and nudged the phone away. I ended the call. He didn't deserve you ripping into him."

"I DIDN'T KNOW WHAT HAD HAPPENED!" I press my hand to my chest, holding in the rising pain. "I was making sure Cody had everything he needed for our set—running around like I always did, double-checking the equipment, ensuring the guitars were tuned. Cody never trusted the roadies to do it right. It was up to me to make sure everything went like it should. Like our teachers at LaGuardia instilled in us: Leave nothing to chance and make it your best. Always." I catch my breath, my heart races. "When his guitar string snapped, I blamed myself for not having an extra pack on hand. He liked a particular brand of strings. He insisted on running to the music store in Dobbs Ferry. The sooner he left, the sooner he'd be back. That was the plan."

"Plan?" Simone's eyebrows fly high.

I slump in my seat, spent. After a moment, I stare off like I do when I'm alone in the coffin, confessing to the walls and the drips in the kitchen sink. "He said, 'The sooner I go . . .' and I replied, 'The sooner you'll be back.' It's just a game we played. He planned to get back in time. That night meant everything to us."

"You initiated this plan?" Simone leans closer.

"No, I-I . . . Cody did." Wait, what am I saying?

"So, you two talked about it. He'd be the one to carry out your wishes. Did he *cause* the accident, then attempted to save them?"

I return their stares.

"Holy . . . shit." Clive's head slips off the hand propping it up. His chewed pen falls from his mouth onto the cement floor.

"*No*, I would never tell him to do that! I loved my parents. Dahlia said they saw the car *after* it rolled, remember? I'm not surprised Cody tried to save them."

Simone presses her lips together. "So you think he knew it was them?"

"I'm not sure." I shake my head slowly. "I do know that Cody needed people to *like* him. My parents still weren't speaking to him. And their car was super recognizable. It may have been the reason he tried to help that night—he wanted to gain their respect."

Dahlia's chin drops to her chest. Her shoulders shake.

I face her. "You said it yourself, Cody liked being a showman. Maybe he needed to show my parents what he could do."

Simone pages through the police report.

Clive returns to his chewing.

A horn sounds. Dahlia blows her nose into a tissue.

I take a breath and reopen my bag. "I loved him. I didn't know if I should give these to you and I'm still not sure they prove anything, but I found them in a box of Cody's things." My hands tremble, sliding the news articles toward Simone. "One talks about those Bronx teens who rescued a mother and daughter last year from a burning car. The other one is about a passerby who awoke a family one night when he saw smoke billowing from their home. Turned out, he'd once dated their son . . . and was the one who had set the fire to begin with."

Dahlia covers her mouth and eyes the detectives' faces.

"Hm, interesting." Simone scans the articles. "For now, we don't have any further questions. We'll be in touch."

Chapter 62

MICAH

"Your keys." I scoop them out of the canoe-shaped bowl in the foyer and hand them to my dad. "Thanks for dinner. I didn't realize the time. You should stay over. I can make up the bed in the other room."

My father pivots, checking his pockets. He follows me through the kitchen into the living room.

"Here." I pass him his cell off the arm of the yellow couch.

"I'm going to bounce, Harmonica. Got an early flight."

A dull pang hits my chest; the slippery fish is getting away.

You teach people how to treat you. Okay, Dr. Val. Here goes nothing. "It'd be nice to spend more time together. Maybe grab breakfast before you go."

"Good dinner." He smiles. "The restaurant was Freemans, right? Like the Alley."

Way to change the subject, Dad. "Yeah, I like that place."

"Your mom and I once stayed with my buddy who lived above it. They called it something else back in the '90s, and it was not a safe place to be at night. Bunch of junkies shootin' up."

I cross my arms, holding my shoulders. "Tell me more about her. What was she like?"

"I've told you—"

"Sure, about being pregnant with me. But what about the rest? I spoke with Mom's parents the other day . . ."

He lifts his head, gaze sharp.

"Aunt Max gave me their email."

"She would." His lips pull tight. "I don't know why you'd bother."

"I want to know her."

"Are you trying to hurt me or something with all these questions?"

"Me hurt *you*? She's my *mother*." I throw my hand in the air.

"You can't know her, Micah. Don't you get that? You never will."

"Why keep her a secret?"

He winces, waving me off. "They probably gave you an earful about me."

"Not really. We mostly talked about Mom . . . her favorite things growing up, her personality."

"A hellion." He snorts.

"They called her assertive."

He snickers, gazing down at his pointed leather boots, then strolls over to the yellow couch and sits opposite the fireplace.

"Did you know I have fifty-five cousins? I'm thinking about visiting them upstate."

Dad's quiet. He looks uncomfortable. Without a guitar, he doesn't know what to do with his hands.

"Want a drink?" I gesture to the bar. Anything to make him stay a little longer.

He sighs. "I never met your mom's extended family. Mia didn't exactly bring me around. Ah . . . yeah, I'll take a small one to send me off. Scotch, if you have it. Are you having one?"

I shake my head. "Not with the pills I'm taking." I walk over to Granddad's bar table, still stocked with dusty liquor bottles that must date back to when he and my grandmother were still married. A tasteful bamboo sign hangs above it: BIANCA'S TIKI BAR. I run the 7UP bar towel through one of the lowballs—cerulean blue, my grandmother's signature color.

He wrinkles his forehead. "Your granddad can't drink either?"

"Definitely not."

"Wish that was the case when I lived here. See that unevenness on the wall over there?"

I follow his eyes and see the indentation for the first time.

"This scar above my eye"—he points to his forehead—"is from when my head went right through it. I was around eleven, I think."

I suck in my breath. Not sure I can handle a bad story about my granddad right now.

"He had terrible aim after a couple martinis. Overthrew the football. I dove and my face met the plaster. Not allowed to cry, of course. He did pull out a bag of frozen peas. One of my fondest memories of him, believe it or not. We moved the old grandfather clock to cover the hole left by my head. Our little secret we tried to keep from your grandmother. She found out, of course." He chuckles, rubbing the side of his face. "The guy had his moments."

"Must have been cool being a kid around here."

"The Garden People ran a tight community, our own little paradise to roam and conquer." He parries with an imaginary sword. "Mom would often disappear, so one of the other parents would watch us. I think they gave ole Bianca some slack given who she married. They knew dealing with Gabriel, both his creative genius and his darker side, was like walking a tightrope."

"Darker side . . . do you mean Granddad's bipolar disorder?" I pull back, my voice rising. "Did you ever think what kind of hell *he* was in? Not knowing he was experiencing manic episodes that were likely treatable? He probably hated himself."

My father's open-mouth stare holds for several seconds. "I wish I knew all this then." He drops his head. "Thought *I* was the reason he got mean and despondent."

"Maybe only half the time." Smirking, I pass him his drink, then step back to the gray couch facing the terrace windows and crack open a sparkling water.

"Do you . . . hate yourself?" His eyes expand.

My dad's frankness startles me into almost spilling my water.

"I hate having something wrong with me." I blow out a long breath, my eyes steady on his face. "And that it keeps people away."

"Like when I ran away from your granddad." He frowns, swirling the golden-brown liquid in his glass.

"And me." I gulp.

He doesn't respond.

"Dad . . ."

"I heard you." He slides himself to the edge of his seat and downs an inch of his drink, readying himself to leave.

I shift forward. "Um, so . . . when did your relationship with him change?"

"When I told him I didn't want to join Kershaw & Son." A muscle flexes in his jaw. "I knew I'd let him down. I couldn't see myself there, consumed with building an empire I didn't want."

"At least you stood up for yourself. Then you met Mom."

He sighs. "The same day she dropped out of Barnard, unbeknownst to her parents. She was downtown with her friends, celebrating her newfound independence. They walked by a club in the East Village—almost didn't go inside, it was a true dive, but they heard live music and decided to give it a go. And there I was on a rickety stage, an unknown country western singer performing the only three songs he knew to a crowd of maybe ten locals." He stares off, returning to that night. "I spotted this tall South Asian beauty in the crowd with gray-green eyes that rivaled the sea, and I never saw another face that night. Sang every song to her. I'll never forget it. My first show at the Flaming Flamingo . . ."

"Wait, what? You knew the Gallardos? No way."

"Oh sure. Basilio and Katia were da bomb—especially her." He blushes. "Damn shame about Basilio. Heard he was battling cancer and they couldn't afford to keep the club . . ."

I shake my head. "They died in a car accident last fall. I hired their daughter as an intern this summer."

"Small world."

"We kind of got close." I feel my own blush coming on.

He grins. "If she looks anything like her fly mother, I understand."

"I'm dreading tomorrow." Except to see Brynn, even if she ignores me. "It won't be fun letting people go. Well . . . I'll enjoy firing a few of them."

"End of an era. Where do you go next, another agency gig?" He sits back, draining the last of his scotch.

"I'm thinking about college again."

"Oh?"

"You don't like that idea?"

"I don't think you need it." He smacks his lips.

"I'd like to go. I think I can manage sitting through a class this time." I roll my eyes, half smiling. "I'll get you a refill."

"Small one. Then I should go." He yawns.

I smile to myself. Having him here is kind of fun. I pick up the bottle of scotch from the bar table. I grip the cap, my back to him. "How about next time you're in the Tri-State area, you stay with me?"

He doesn't respond. I close my eyes. A beat later, I pass him his drink.

"Maybe you could see one of my shows when I'm in town."

I exhale, letting the moment wash over me. "I'll be there." My voice cracks.

Dad smiles a little. His eyes well up. He looks at me for several seconds, the corners of his mouth bow. "Your eyes are hers, and the color of your hair . . ." He whistles through his teeth. "She was really something."

I laugh. "People see you when they see me—same features, but with Mom's olive skin. They don't realize I'm half Indian."

"I'm sorry I couldn't save your mother," he blurts out. "The doctor and nurses tried for over an hour to bring her back. I stood helpless, holding you, whispering prayers into your fuzzy little head . . ." His lips bend funny. He swats the air in front of his face. "Sorry."

"Dad, you don't have to hide with me."

His red-rimmed eyes search my face, then fly upward. "Mia, I'm sorry."

I look over at the Woman in Black, sitting beside him on the yellow couch. Her eyes light up when he says her name.

"Mom knows, Dad. She knows."

"I should have been in California with you this last time. I convinced myself that I couldn't see you tied down with all those electrodes attached to you like Frankenstein or something. Was it awful?"

"It wasn't bad." I avert my eyes, still getting used to this new openness between us. "Definitely not Frankenstein. Anyway, Mom was with me."

He gives me a blank look. "I don't understand."

"She's one of my hallucinations."

His brows shoot up. "What? You never told me. Wait, what if you're really clairvoyant—like, able to see dead people—and not schizophrenic?"

"Really, Dad?" I cock my head, pulling a face. "You'd have an easier time believing that?"

"Sadly, I would." He rubs the sides of his arms. "Are you going to be okay, Micah?"

The floor vibrates under my bare feet, the subway's rhythmic clacking massaging my soles. "I think I'm ready for whatever comes my way."

He gives me a wistful smile. "It's good you're meeting your mom's family."

"Sure are a lot of them compared to yours."

Dad stares into his drink, looking lost in a memory.

I tilt my head again, trying to catch his eye. "Sucks about Granddad."

"Yeah . . . sure does. I messed up blaming him for not being the father I needed, and now I'm too late. I swear to you, Micah, I won't squander the time I have left with you."

"He's not completely unaware," I venture. "You should go see him."

"I'm waiting for him to forget he hates me." He laughs a little. "Nah, you're right. Will you go with me?"

I lay a cotton blanket over my dad on the couch as he snores away. Once I got him to talk about my mother, the guy wouldn't shut up. Even the Woman in Black grew bored and left. What a strange and wonderful evening. For the first time ever, this place feels like home.

I pick up my phone to set an early alarm so we can get a coffee at Dante's before he leaves tomorrow.

Hmm, a missed call from Elmsford, New York. Who could that be from?

Chapter 63

BRYNN

The agency's vibe feels off when I arrive Monday morning. Eunice's perch looms vacant, her multi-line phone and computer gone. Landlines and personal cells ring all over the place. Josie huddles with Lucius by the employee coffee machine, both with a Starbucks in their hands. No one greets me when I pass.

I drop my purse in its usual drawer in the filing cabinet next to my workspace and head down the hall to find Meredith or that Benji guy I still haven't met. I hear crying and pivot around. Priya's in the conference room; Donovan's by her side, his hand on her back. They must have had a fight.

He gives me a wicked smile and mouths, *You're next.*

Uh-oh.

"Kershaw McKenzie is being absorbed by Day & Foster," Zoe announces, a gleam in her eye as she zips by in her white go-go boots.

Is this a joke?

A large, towering man with long, shaggy hair in a gray suit waits in the doorway of the office where Micah interviewed me. He clears his throat, giving off a loud, wet gurgling sound.

Heads from across the room swing toward him.

"Brynn Gallardo?"

"Yes?"

"Come in, have a seat." He ushers me in, closes the door behind me. "Daniel Ash, General Counsel."

"What's going on?" I chew the side of my thumb.

"Kershaw McKenzie has been sold and what's left is the Human Resources part. Guess that's me today. Let me see . . . you're one of the summer interns, correct?"

He doesn't wait for my response.

"Unfortunately, today will be your last day." He speaks like he's on autopilot and not firing a real person. "You'll be paid for the day. Leave your laptop at your desk. Your account supervisor, Benji, can provide references."

"Are any of the interns being kept on?"

He peers over the rim of his glasses. "Only one."

"Zoe Adler."

He considers me for a beat, then nods. "Her clients requested she stay on for continuity."

I jerk back. "*Her* clients?" My lungs constrict; I feel the edge of a blade pierce my back. Was it Donovan, Scott? Who doesn't have it out for me here? I suck in air.

The guy types away on his computer like his sword isn't covered in my blood too. This can't be happening. I have to stop this.

"Um." My voice sounds raspy and strange. "Can I interview with Day & Foster, then?" I'll show up Zoe in a millisecond.

"If they wanted you, we would have been told. Only a handful of the creatives will be moving over after the merger."

"Can I ask who?"

He lowers his chin, sending his glasses sliding down his nose. "No. That will be all."

"B-but . . ."

A gush of cool air hits the back of my head. The skin on my neck tingles.

Ash looks to the doorway. "Just finished. I'm going to get another coffee, want anything?" He waits a beat; when no response comes, he gets up to leave.

The door shuts. My pulse drums in my ears. I grasp the edge of my seat.

"You okay?"

My arms break out in goose bumps. I clench my jaw, my head swimming. Is he here to gloat?

No. Stop that. He's out of a job too. His family's reign is over.

My knees start bouncing. I hold them still. "Did you know?" I bow my head and close my eyes.

"I learned a couple of days ago."

"I'm sorry for your family." A gasp-sob slips out of my throat. "What am I going to do? It could be months before I find another job. I'm going to lose my parents' apartment . . . where am I going to go?"

His long silence turns me around. I'm dazed for a few seconds by the healthy glow on his face; he looks like he's just returned from the Bahamas. What the hell?

"Wait here." His gentle voice triggers a memory of us lying in bed together. "I'll get your bag so you don't have to see anyone. Filing cabinet, bottom drawer, right?"

Two minutes later, Micah and I breeze past clusters of coworkers standing about. Some are red-eyed and teary; a few just look dazed. I see Zoe hooting and hollering across the room, but no one else from my team.

"Where are *you two* running off to?" Donovan's voice rises from out of nowhere.

Conversations drop, heads swivel.

My face grows hot. I clutch my purse in front of me. So much for sneaking out.

Micah holds open one of the glass doors in the lobby. The same one I smacked my face into on my first day here. He frowns and gazes at Eunice's empty curved desk, his eyes pinched.

I glance back at the agency one final time—those funny lightbulbs hanging from pipes in the center, the melting rocket on the wall behind reception, its cone-shaped head and fiery dog bone base never ceasing my mind from going there. Still. Something pulls inside my chest. My summer at Kershaw McKenzie. My first real job. Meeting Micah.

"You weren't going to say goodbye?" Donovan snickers as he catches up with us.

I clench my fists, glaring.

Micah steps beside me. "Sorry about your mom, Donovan." His voice is kind.

I do a double take.

"Now you can spend some time with her before you start at Day & Foster."

Donovan's mouth falls open. "Yeah . . . okay. Thanks."

I walk past Micah through the narrow hallway, my neck buzzing like Donovan's watching what we'll do next. I glance back and exhale.

Micah presses the button for the elevator and registers the look on my face. "Another stroke, Priya said. His mom was forced to step down from her position at the National Organization for Women. Explains why he's been out so much and so moody lately. She's all he has."

Explains his choice in T-shirts too. "He's just mean." I punch the lit button.

Micah shrugs. "More like scared."

"So empathetic. Have we switched bodies?"

"Yeah, trying something new." His smile grows taut. His soft khaki eyes widen, lingering on my face.

The middle elevator opens. I step inside, grateful to have it to myself. I turn toward him. "Thanks for walking me out. Maybe we can talk sometime." *So I can tell you how I missed you. And to not take my silence these past six weeks as proof of my lack of feelings for you.*

If anything, they've magnified.

He just looks at me.

I hang my head; I know I'm the one to blame for not giving us a chance, for believing the worst—that dating Micah would cost me my job. And look, they fired me anyway. I stab the lobby button with my thumb.

We stare at one another; the doors begin to close.

My breath snags. I may never see him again.

He takes a step, then another—he rushes toward me, cupping my face, tilting my mouth up to his.

The elevator doors seal us in together. Where it all began.

Our lips part, hungry for one another. Our tongues fall in step like no time has passed. I moan, relishing the sparks running from the tip of my nose, through my belly, and down between my thighs.

Micah slides me to the back of the elevator, rocking his hips forward and pinning my wrists over my head.

I arch my back, pressing my chest into him, greedy for more.

The floor drops.

My knees buckle.

We fall faster. Clinging to one another.

I crack open my eyes, watching him devour me.

His hands release me and squeeze my hips.

I breathe in his warm scent, like fresh-cut wood. My fingers slip into his hair.

His tongue draws a wet line down my neck.

A bell sounds and the elevator clunks to a halt.

I look past his shoulder at the three-person-deep crowd in the lobby—some with mouths agape, some looking pissed, one couple very clearly amused.

Micah picks me up by my waist like he's twirling me on the dance floor and carries me over the threshold.

The crowd parts as my feet touch the ground.

Chapter 64

MICAH

"When I woke up today, I didn't think we'd ever be here again." I kiss the honey-sweet skin curving around her shoulder. I lift her fingers one by one, dragging my tongue down the inside of her arm, my breath warming the wet trail it leaves behind. My dreams of her from inside the psych ward failed to replicate this intense adrenaline rush of having her back in my bed.

"That tickles." Brynn writhes, giggling. She inches closer to my tufted headboard. Her head sinks into the pillow.

"I thought that last dinner ended us for good."

She rolls onto her side, scrunching up her nose. "You were so sweet that weekend, then I got all weird about the team finding out about us."

"I think they've figured it out." I prop up my head, facing her.

She shivers a little.

I pull the sheet over her shoulder.

She runs her thumb along my hand. "After I found out you'd left for California and didn't know when or if you'd be back, I realized how much better you made that place. Gave me something to look forward to every day."

"I'm sure my sudden exodus provided great gossip for everybody."

"No one talked about it much. I wanted to text but thought you could use some privacy."

Tell her.

"What is it?" A vertical line appears between her brows.

"I'm scared to let you see my bad parts."

"You have a bad part?" She grins, her eyes flashing.

I flip onto my back and rest a hand behind my head. She hasn't a clue where I'm going with this.

Her fingertips graze my shoulder. "We've all got stuff we're not proud of. I've said and done things I wish I could take back. Could've been kinder to my parents, more understanding."

Oh yeah, about that. "Hey, was your father ill?"

Her eyes quiz me. "No, why?"

"Nothing."

"He did develop an ulcer from all the stress when the club was going under. Popped so many antacids, his lips turned white. 'Not a good look,' I told him. He got on medicine and changed his diet."

Guess Beck heard wrong.

She moves her hair off her neck. "Yeah, my dad worried a lot. Both my parents did. I get that from them."

I stroke the curve of her hip. "Sounds like they really cared."

She sits up, pulling her knees to her chest under the sheet.

Shit. "What is it?"

"While you were away, I found out Cody lied to me." She stares straight ahead. "Said his folks lived in the Caymans when in reality . . . get this . . . he grew up in foster care."

"The Caymans?" I suppress a smile.

"What? I had no reason *not* to believe him. Why would he make up such a story?"

"To impress you."

"Am I that much of a bitch?"

Yeah, I'm not going to touch that one.

She rolls her eyes. "Well, he did a good job keeping his garbage clean."

"Wait, hold up. You calling him white trash? Not the amazing Cody."

"No!" Her voice rises. "I mean he was sneaky about his past and what he was up to. Don't judge me." She gives my arm a light slap. "I found out he may have played a role in my parents' accident. They'd still be around if I hadn't let him into our lives."

"Seriously? Holy shit." I sit beside her, combing back the wisps around her face, wishing she'd chill and lie back down. "Tell me what happened."

"That girl, Dahlia, the tall blonde I told you about who works at Caffé Dante? Freaking stalker." She blows out a frustrated breath. "She and Cody apparently grew up together. She was in the car with him that night and claims they saw my parents' car flip and stopped to help. But the police found this location-sharing app on Cody's phone that shows a different story. What if he used it to track them and he *caused* the accident?"

"Why would he do that?"

"To show my parents what he could do."

"I'm lost."

"So he could rescue them and play the hero."

"That feels like a stretch. Besides, wouldn't they know he caused their car to roll?"

"Maybe not, if it happened fast on a dark highway. How could they identify the car? It would be easy to do to my parents, of all people. My dad hated driving. Made him anxious. He rarely drove living in Brooklyn. And my mom never got her license."

My throat tenses. "Sounds like you really thought this out."

Her eyes stare off to the side. "Except. Cody wasn't supposed to die."

Tiny hairs rise on the back of my neck. "What did you say?"

"I-I meant *no one* was supposed to die." She slams her fists on the bed and looks away.

Oh shit. My heart jackhammers inside my chest. My shaky hand cups her face.

She leans into my palm, closing her eyes.

I inch my mouth toward hers. "Did you know his plan when he left the club that night?"

Her body goes rigid. "No . . . I-I . . . he never told me . . . how."

I release her face like I've touched a hot burner. The floor rises when I climb out of bed. I pause, getting my bearings. I step into my shorts, the room swaying like I'm on a boat. I take a few more seconds to steady myself. I rub the new ache in my chest.

Her unblinking eyes watch me retrieve my cell off the floor.

I open my voicemails and press play.

Mr. Kershaw, this is Detective Ana Simone from the Elmsford Village Police Department. One of your employees, Brynn Gallardo, is currently the main suspect in the wrongful death of her parents, Basilio and Katia Gallardo. Please contact us at your earliest convenience.

"I stopped myself from texting you last night. I needed to see your face—wasn't positive you were even speaking to me—but then I found you in Ash's office . . . and then this happened, which I never expected, I swear."

"Me too—"

I hold up my hand. "I thought you'd say the detectives had it all wrong . . . that you had zero involvement in what happened that night. I would have believed you. I wanted to . . . was desperate to, in fact." I pull at my scalp with both hands. The fiery high of being with her cools, along with the sweat on my skin. My body shudders.

Three, two, one.

"Brynn . . . I see shadows shaped like people. I can't escape them. No matter how hard I try. Twenty-four hours a day, they come for me, and no amount of meds or electricity can fix me. I'm never. Ever. Alone. Not in my bed. Not brushing my teeth. Not even with you." I open my palms toward her. "I thought you were my light. The good that could rescue me."

Her mouth hangs open.

"I was falling for you, the person I thought you were . . . a better human than me. So kindhearted, so pure, that I thought someone like me didn't deserve you. A person who stands up for others when they can't for themselves. Who does the right thing when no one's watching."

She closes her eyes tight.

"That day when you wanted to leave here, those shadows chanted, *Let her go*. I thought they meant I wasn't good enough for you. I think now they were trying to protect me. Imagine that. My effed up brain knew before I did. We may have shared a bed . . . and our bodies . . . but I don't know you at all."

I edge away from her like she's kryptonite sucking the energy out of me.

"Micah, wait—"

"I've wrestled with survivor's guilt all my life because of what happened to my mom. All this time, I thought you did too." I blow out a hard breath. "Not true, is it? You battle something far worse. A *guilty conscience*."

I wipe the spit flying from my mouth.

She clutches a pillow in front of her. "I didn't know Cody's plan. I swear."

"You said, 'Cody wasn't supposed to die.' Losing him kills you more than losing your parents does. What the fuck?"

"That's not true! I miss them. Every day." Her face contorts like she's about to cry.

"You miss them? You really miss them? Why, because their deaths forced you to be an adult? You're angrier about your situation than you are sad that they're gone. Should have thought of that before you sent your boyfriend to run them off the road."

"That was Cody's idea. Not mine!" She slaps the bed.

"I can't believe you would do something like this. I'd give *anything* to have had my father around growing up . . . to have known my mother, even if only for a day."

"What?" She shakes her head. "You never told me this."

"You never asked."

"I did!" She scowls, bunching up the sheet in each hand.

"You know what I find ironic?" My eyes fly up to the ceiling, then back to her. "You told me once you live in a coffin. Yet *you're* the murderer."

Chapter 65

BRYNN

I storm out of Micah's house and dash across the street toward Houston. A taxi driver blasts me with his horn. I stumble over the metal curb and face-plant in front of Caffé Dante's black awning. I push myself back up to standing, ball up my scraped hands, and speed walk away, beating the sides of my legs as I go. The passing faces blur through my tears.

Main suspect, my ass. I can't believe Detective Simone called the agency—called *Micah*. Not cool. Somehow, she still thinks I orchestrated what went down that night. I don't get it. Don't those news articles prove Cody's motivation? I could not have spelled it out any clearer for her.

I need to fix things with Micah. He wouldn't look at me when I left. He just needs time to cool off. I'll explain it in a way he can understand. I'd be an idiot to let him disappear again. We're so good together. It felt like coming home being back in his bed. I'm done making up for my sins these past nine months. I deserve to be happy and have someone like him. I love how much he wants me.

This too will pass. I know it.

Maybe I'll suggest that we move in together; I can live in his stylish house and save money while finding another job. Or not.

My phone rings. I grin. Got to be him. 914 area code. Shoot.

"Miss Gallardo? Detective Clive Bodie."

My stomach drops.

"You guys called my job—what the hell? Listen, this isn't a great time—"

"One of the articles you said you found among Cody's possessions? We researched the source, and, well, the reported incident took place *after* his death. Nice try, though."

Heat crawls up my neck, burning my ears. "U-um, there's got to be some kind of mix up. I found them in boxes of Cody's things, dropped off at my apartment by someone from St. Ignatius." My mind races. Oh shit. I bet Silas—or, more likely, Dahlia—put those in there.

"Our tech guy also restored a video on Cody's phone, recorded that night with you saying, 'Tonight, they won't know what hit them.' I'd call that premeditative."

What is he talking about? Oh! "I meant the audience at Pete's . . . stop twisting my words!"

"Brynn." Simone clears her throat, surprising me she's on the call. "Some questions have also arisen regarding the items the highway patrol found at the accident site."

I stop walking.

A guy wearing a large headset grunts and steps around me.

I cup my other ear and move away from the Sixth Avenue traffic. The aroma of spicy red sauce fills my nose. A waiter comes out with a menu gesturing to a table with a red-and-white-checkered tablecloth.

I turn my back to him. "What now?"

"The officers uncovered a small metal box. It got charred, but its contents survived."

I sniffle, pinching my nostrils together. "They kept a cash box in the glove compartment for tolls and parking meters."

"Inside, we found a photo of a baby with pink headphones." Simone clicks her teeth. "Guitar picks, safety pins, floss."

"Okay, so what?"

"And pill bottles prescribed to your father."

I sigh. "For his ulcer."

"No, these are cancer medications."

The air rushes from my lungs, taking my legs out. I hear a crack.

"You still there, Brynn?"

"Um . . . I don't understand. My dad had *cancer*? That can't be right . . ."

Did Rhonda know? She handled all the outstanding bills and the selling of properties after the accident. Did some of that debt include medical bills? If so, she never let on.

No. My dad changed his diet. He was getting better. "If my dad had cancer, why didn't my parents tell me?"

The waiter towers over me, his hands on his hips. "Miss, you can't rest here." He flicks his hand in a sweeping motion. "Move along."

I wander around the Village, my tailbone sore, my heart split in two. The sides of my head feel squeezed in a vise, my eyes cloud with questions I'll never get answered.

My dad had cancer? They didn't think I needed to know?

My life could have been so different if they hadn't treated me like a child. Maybe I still am one, though. Look how I've botched everything up. Even though they didn't like Cody, or the idea of me going on tour, they still warmed up that potato-smelling, crusty old Monte Carlo and drove north. White-knuckling it all the way, I'm sure. Why couldn't I see their effort?

I head up Sullivan Street, not ready to go home. The giddy screams and laughter of children in Washington Square Park draw me closer. A sweltering August day and the large, circular fountain at its center sits dry. The neighborhood kids play in it anyway like I used to, crisscrossing through it, using its center as base.

Under a tree nearby, a keyboardist wearing a wide-brimmed hat plays that Jewel song about saving souls. She smiles, singing to me.

I tie up my long hair and lower myself onto the fountain's concrete steps. The last time I was here, Micah and I stopped under the arch after the gym, then cut through the park. Years back, Rikki and I used to practice our 1D dance moves right where I'm sitting.

Why couldn't I appreciate my parents the way Rikki and Tess did? I got caught up with everything—Cody, the tour. I didn't even notice my own father's suffering. Oh, Daddy.

Wait . . . why did Micah ask if he was sick? How did he know about that?

I text him.

We need to talk
I can explain

I clench my toes in my sandals, trying not to make a sound, as I walk down the hallway to my door. I'm in no mood for Debra's girl talk. I need to look amazing when I meet Micah. Prepare what I'm going to tell him. He's got to believe that I'm innocent, had nothing to do with what happened to my parents. I wasn't even there.

"Oh good!" Debra leans outside her door, her smokey blue eyes dancing as she licks her index finger. "I hoped you'd be home soon. Come meet my granddaughter, Gina. It's her first time baking chocolate chip cookies from scratch."

"I'm kind of in a rush." I dig for my key. "Can I stop by later?"

"She's only here for another hour. I'd love for you to meet her—"

"I can't . . ." Why isn't my key working? Dammit. "I'm sorry, Debra, but I'm bugging out. I just learned something about my parents, and—"

"Is it about your father?"

My neck stiffens. "You knew? Why didn't you say something?"

"That night we met, you looked so raw. I didn't want to aggravate your pain more. We cried so many times about your dad's cancer. The terrible timing of it." She grimaces.

"*We?*"

She leans her shoulder into the wall near me, crossing her arms. "Remember, I knew your parents when they lived here. After they began renting the apartment out, Katia would come by to check on it now and then. When she did, we'd catch up over cups of tea."

"Why would they keep this from me?"

"Your mom saw you doing so well at LaGuardia, and they hoped they could turn the club around in time so you could go to college and study music. When your dad's ulcer worsened, your mom pushed him to see a doctor. He didn't tell her for three weeks about his diagnosis. During that time, he kept leaving home at odd hours. She thought he was sleeping with someone"—she shakes her head—"but then he confessed. He was seeing a homeopath because he knew their insurance would not be enough to cover his medication and treatment."

A sharp hook sticks in my throat. "I gave them hell for blowing my college fund."

Her skinny arched brows draw together. "Your mom told me the Flaming Flamingo *was* your college fund. They worked hard, bled everything they had into that place, so you could fulfill your dream. That club was for *you*."

"What?" Oh my god, oh my god. "I-I hurt them, Deb—"

Her fingers curl around my shoulder. "Like I told you, baby girl, our kids can break our hearts, yet we continue to love them. Your parents never stopped loving you. Haven't stopped even now."

Light bounces off the gold cross around her neck.

"I wish I shared some of your faith." I try my key again. The lock turns with ease.

She frowns. "You need time to process." She steps toward her apartment.

"Deb?" Her big, soulful eyes turn back to me. "I'm glad you're getting a chance to be with your granddaughter. She's one lucky girl."

I close the door behind me and sink to the floor, wincing. I crawl to my mattress. Short, sharp outbreaths pull out of my chest, robbing me of air. I gasp between ragged inhalations, my diaphragm seizing like a train I can't stop. I press my fists to my chest, pushing harder. It won't quit. I punch and punch.

The Flaming Flamingo. My college fund. My future. My dream. The club was for me. They sold their souls to that place . . . *for me.*

I look to the peeling paint overhead. "Mom, Dad, I didn't know!"

My eyes strain in the darkness to see their faces. Hear their voices. Can they ever forgive their daughter who ate jealousy for breakfast, lunch, and dinner—when they'd built the Flaming Flamingo for the baby in the pink headphones wrapped against her mother's chest?

I lower my head between my knees, choking for air.

Exhale.

Inhale.

Exhale.

The staccato drips in the kitchen sink wake me. I rub the sides of my face and drag myself up to sitting. My head's woozy, waterlogged. My sternum's left bruised from all my punching. The afternoon sun tracks through the blinds, illuminating the temperamental half fridge . . . the broken burners beside it . . . the orange countertop the size of printer paper. I fold my knees into my chest and cover my mouth, unable to cry. I'm dried out. I'm going to lose this place, my last connection to my parents. So in love when they found it, they made me here.

And I crapped all over it.

Where am I going to go now, a shelter?

My phone pings.

Corner of Bleecker and MacDougal, one hour

Chapter 66

MICAH

She takes off after my murderer comment. Real smooth, Micah.

I click the deadbolt. The sound reverberates off the foyer's narrow walls and low ceiling. I lean my forehead on the door. What if I'm wrong? I inhale sharply, unlock it, and yank it open. Yet my feet don't move.

I blow out a long breath and text Dr. Val.

Brynn's pleading eyes, her swearing that she wasn't involved in Cody's plan to off her parents, cat at me. Have I been sleeping with a conspirator to murder or the victim of a deranged boyfriend?

I pace around the kitchen and living room; the walls inch closer, the air thickens. I escape out the French doors to the back patio, check my phone. No response. Dr. Val must be in a session.

I walk through the English-style courtyard between rows of square hedges, grateful that it's midday on a weekday and I have the garden to myself. I get to the end and turn around. My limbs feel like lead.

I can't go back in there, in particular my bedroom.

I recline on the grass, my hands behind my head, staring up at the sunless clouds. A memory floats by of lying with her in Sheep Meadow. Her words: *I'm not sure I deserve to be here.*

She made a mistake. I've made plenty. This one cost her everything.

My phone chimes.

Not Dr. Val.

With wet hair and different clothes, I fly down the stairs to the kitchen, trying to remember where I last threw my keys. The greenish sky looms menacingly through the window; the awning across the street flaps around, matching its anger.

A tall blonde dressed in black hurries underneath it.

I hustle outside, dart across the street, and follow her into the café—and inexplicably lose sight of her. I wipe the light rain from my face. The place looks empty. Maybe she's a new hallucination. I go to leave.

She reappears, tying an apron around her waist, walking toward me. Her eyes widen at the sight of me.

"Dahlia."

She swallows her lips when I say her name.

I want to reassure her that I'm not here to be confrontational. If anything, I need answers. I introduce myself.

Her forehead wrinkles. "You live in the lavender building across the street."

Her comment stops me. She doesn't ask if I'm *that* singer. And how does she know where I live?

"Next to where the great Bob Dylan once lived." Her blue-green eyes twinkle.

I smile. "My father performed with him once."

She points toward the espresso machine. "Are you ordering anything?"

"Coffee works."

"Coffee to go, again?" She smiles a little.

Her meaning escapes me.

She motions to one of the tables and heads behind the counter.

Rising from the ground and without warning, the Woman in Black's massive henchman emerges, blocking my path. I thought I'd gotten rid of him after weeks of ECT. He's come alone. Grumbling for me to leave, he takes a swipe at me.

I draw back, my reflexes slow. I need the Woman in Black here to temper him. I shield my face and back up toward the exit.

"Here. Take my hand."

I grasp Dahlia's fingers and step through. My face warms; I look away from her.

She walks back behind the counter.

I glance at the exit. It wouldn't take much to slip out of here and never see this girl again.

But she did just save me.

A moment later, she returns with two steaming cups and sits across from me. She rests her forearms on the table, her callused fingertips tapping her mug.

Shifting in my seat, I blank on better words to say to her. "How did you know?"

"That you see ghosts?" She tilts her head.

"Something like that."

"You just looked like you needed help. So . . . you still with Brynn?"

My eyes snap to hers.

She shrugs. "I see you two around."

Huh. "I'm supposed to meet her. I don't know why I came here first."

She nods and sips her coffee.

"Brynn said you rode in the car with Cody the night of the accident."

Her eyes drop. "Yeah."

"And she mentioned that the police discovered he used a location-sharing app on his phone. Was he tracking them?"

She clears her throat. "Cody saw the car flip and stopped to help."

"What Brynn said to me made it sound like she and Cody planned it."

Her eyes blaze into mine. "Cody didn't cause the accident. He would never harm a soul. He was the kindest person I've ever known. Always putting himself out there for people."

"Including you?"

"Especially me. He was my brother."

I blink rapidly. "What?"

"We grew up together in foster care. When you grow up without a family, you create one. Cody and our other best friend, Teddy, became mine."

"Brynn didn't mention that."

Her eyes tighten. "I'm not surprised he latched on to her. He craved stability and assumed the Gallardos could give him that. In foster care, you get attached to people, and what sucks is, you never know how long you have together."

"How did you end up there?"

Her face twitches. She looks down at her cup. She moves her long legs to the side and crosses her ankles.

"My bio mom blacked out at a party in high school. Months later, she found herself pregnant. No one believed her that it was rape. Her family and the girl she loved wanted nothing to do with her . . . Mom coped with handles of Smirnoff. After I got taken away from her, I was shipped around to different foster homes for years. If it wasn't for Silas, I don't know where I'd be."

"Silas?"

"Director at St. Ignatius, the church that works with the Department of Social Services to run foster care in Westchester. He steered me toward a good high school. Got me my first guitar—used, but I didn't care. The rest has been up to me. I work three jobs now; I'm trying to make it as a singer."

"Brynn thinks you're stalking her."

She smiles a little and takes another sip. "She's not exactly my favorite person. She sure was quick to blame Cody for everything to save herself."

"The detectives said she's the main suspect in the wrongful death of her parents."

Her mouth falls open. "I hadn't heard that they'd narrowed it down to her. I wonder if Teddy knows." She exhales, and tears form in the corner of her eyes. She picks up a napkin from the table and blows her nose, sounding like a trumpet. "I hope this means Cody's name will be cleared." She sniffles.

"Well if it wasn't him, *who* caused the accident?"

"Another car. Not Cody."

"Come on," I scoff. "You'll swear to that if called to testify?"

She lifts her chin, presses her shoulders back. "He was my brother."

I let out a sharp exhale. "Your loyalty is admirable." The guy's dead. Why not bury him with the truth. Whatever that may be.

She folds her arms. "So, what's *your* story, Micah?"

I don't need to tell this girl anything. Apart from working in my neighborhood, it's not like I'll ever see her again. But there's something about her.

"Well . . . I never knew my mother. She died of an amniotic fluid embolism giving birth to me."

She watches my face, her eyes rapt.

"I don't think I've uttered those words aloud to anyone except for my therapist," I admit. "It feels kind of freeing."

She doesn't cringe. Cool.

"My dad's a musician. You listen to country?"

"Not a fan," she says with a snicker.

"Same. He wasn't around growing up. My granddad became my guardian, and the other day I discovered he suffers from a psychosis similar to . . . well, similar to what you saw a few minutes ago."

I wait for the worried look, the backing away.

"Call me insane. Looney Tunes." I stare at her. "Nothing?"

She crinkles her nose. "I'm listening."

"I don't know why I'm telling you this. You're easy to talk to."

The rain blankets the café windows. The dimly lit restaurant suddenly feels cozier.

She looks up from her coffee. "You know, in all of this, Micah, you're not the one who's crazy."

I crack a smile. "Best thing I've heard in a long while." Out of nowhere, a hearty laugh rises from my belly. My ribs contract. I make a wheezing sound, my eyes tearing, reminding me of how I used to laugh with my friends. It's been far too long. I hold the sides of the table, trying to regain composure.

She looks at me; the skin between her brows puckers and her uneasy smile loosens as trickles of her laughter join mine.

I'm not the one who's crazy.

I sigh—and my laughter bubbles up again.

She chuckles at that too.

I feel like I could talk to this girl all day. But I've got somewhere to be.

I catch my breath and push myself back from the table, reluctant to leave. I stand and shake her hand. "Thanks for taking the time."

She holds on for a moment. Her brows rise. "Got a date?"

"Yeah, uptown with a singing cowboy and an aging astronaut."

"Better get to it." Her lips press together like she wants to say something else.

"What?"

"We've met before, you know." She lowers her eyes.

I squint, trying to remember.

"You rescued my twenty-dollar tip that blew off one of the outdoor tables." She motions toward the window. "In the middle of MacDougal."

"When? I'm not exactly the helpful kind." Or is that just the story I tell myself?

"You ordered a coffee, then proceeded to have a whole conversation with yourself."

"As I do." I grin.

She grins back. Hmm. The corners of her mouth turn up like mine.

The bells above the entry door jingle.

"Dahl, you forgot to flip the *We're Closed* sign around." A broad-shouldered, Sicilian-looking guy with dark, curly hair steps inside, wringing out the bottom of his T-shirt and shaking the rain from his arms. His face looks familiar. He's accompanied by a girl in a pink minidress.

His eyes move from Dahlia and then to me like I'm a predator in his territory.

She smiles at him.

He visibly relaxes.

"I got distracted." Dahlia gestures toward the pair. "Micah, meet Tess and Teddy. I told you about him. He works here and for Falcon Messenger."

"Ah . . ." I nod.

"Yo, I'm da muscle of dis operation." He offers up a fist-bump.

Both girls chuckle. Must be an inside joke.

"Guess I'm the insider, the one closest to the target." Tess, a dark-skinned girl with large, expressive eyes, winks at me. She shakes out her matching umbrella and leans it next to the door.

"Don't forget address getter and party planner." Dahlia smiles at her.

"Yeah, that last one was not so great. She never showed up." Teddy snorts.

"Oh yeah? Who almost got caught dropping off the boxes?" Tess flutters her lashes at him, swings one of her shopping bags into the front booth, and slides to the middle facing her back to the window. "I'll take my usual, Dahl."

"And you?" I look at Dahlia.

"I'm the mastermind, of course." She winks at Teddy. "Strange to admit after years of underestimating myself. But—change the line, change your life. It's my new motto."

I laugh. "I have no idea what you guys are talking about. How do you all know each other?"

Tess looks to the other two. "They went to high school together. We met through a recent acquaintance . . . our buddy, Clive. We learned we shared a mutual dissatisfaction with someone . . . that there was an injustice that needed to be righted." She swings her hair behind her shoulders before balancing her chin on her hands. "I flew back into town to see it through. I love a good drama."

"Nice to meet you." I glance at my phone. "I got to go." I frown toward Dahlia. Our eyes stall on one another's. I make my way to the door. I glance back and snag her gaze one final time before stepping outside.

Buckets of rain wash the sidewalk to either side of me. I duck into a cab and give the driver Granddad's address.

He swings a left onto Houston, heading in the opposite direction from where I was supposed to meet Brynn over half an hour ago. The cab straightens out of the turn.

A levity in my chest overcomes me. It travels down my arms and through my fingers. I hold on to my seat and my breath.

A few seconds pass. No change. Then a full minute.

I exhale. My grin widens.

Besides the driver, I'm alone in this cab. Blissfully, utterly alone.

Chapter 67

BRYNN

I'm living up to Rikki's pet name for me, pacing on the corner of Bleecker and MacDougal like a trapped sea predator, my gaze darting from Café Figaro's striped awning to the Cuban place to the vegan restaurant and back again as people scurry around me. The earth-scented drizzle fails to cool my hot steaming cheeks. Damn that Clive Bodie. Why did I bother with those articles? I already had Detective Simone convinced that I'd only played a minor role in that night, the one of the dutiful girlfriend.

I thought it was a good performance.

Come on, Micah, you asked and I'm here.

I look down at my phone. Ten minutes late. I reread his text. I shake my head, looking down MacDougal for him. Those detectives need someone to take the fall; who knows how much time I have left.

We'll step inside the café behind me and I'll explain how things escalated the night Cody and I met my parents for dinner at Roberta's. How he bragged afterward about how he'd downloaded the location-sharing app on my mom's phone and added her to his circle so he could look out for them.

He knew about my dad's anxiety when it came to driving outside the city but not the story playing in my head.

The one where the famed Basilio and Katia Gallardo rob us of our moment like countless times before, like at my LaGuardia performances—people pointing and fangirling over them, pushing me aside. Pete's showcase was *our* night to shine.

I flipped out on him. Threatened to quit the tour—and us. He wanted my parents to like him. I didn't understand it then. He offered to call them, tell them they'd canceled our first show. It should have ended there. But my worrying reared up, I began overthinking everything, afraid that my parents would somehow know the owners of Pete's and contact them or check its website for new dates.

The predicament Cody created set off an avalanche of scalding rage I couldn't contain. I told him, *I hope they never make it to the show.*

His eyes lit up. *I have a couple of friends in town coming to see us. They can get a car. Dark highway. Your dad's a nervous driver, he'll keep to the right lane. Should be easy to do.*

Dammit, Cody. Did you have to pick such complete dumbasses to help you, including one who gets cold feet and turns in your phone with your blood on it? They never suspected me until that app on your phone placed you at the accident.

When he messed with his guitar string that night, I thought, *Here he goes.*

I knew then what he was going to do, and I didn't stop him.

The sooner I go . . .

He wanted to please me. That turned me on.

I could have reversed everything. Told him, *I'm done freaking out. Restring your guitar with the new pack in your case. Stay, Cody. Don't leave.*

And he would never have gone through with our plan.

Eunice's warning resurfaces in my head about not letting evil win. What if *I'm* the evil? I didn't mean to be. I loved my parents. I just needed something of my own.

Starting with an amazing opening night . . . with no *distractions.*

For the record, Cody didn't die because I put him on that

highway that night. He died playing the hero. The one who saves the day before being the show-stopping sensation on his hometown stage and singing the movie's closing credits.

He could be spiteful. The way he discredited my talent at LaGuardia, the faces he made offstage as if I lacked the chops. I didn't comprehend the scope of his jealousy until Dahlia called me his backup singer. He *was* using me, as Silas alluded to. Using my talent onstage, using my parents for whatever connections they could give him. If only I'd realized what his game was sooner—like Mom and Dad did.

Twenty minutes.

Micah, please believe in me again like the day you had me sing in Central Park under the big shell. You wanted to help me heal and use my singing as a way to get over Cody.

A beautiful story, yes, but you didn't have all of the facts. I let you believe Cody controlled me, like with the makeup. The truth—he did anything I asked.

You wanted to swoop in and save me. My king of ancient Macedonia. Micah the Great. If only I hadn't wrecked everything the night you brought me dinner.

The cool rain gains strength, mixing with my hot tears and darkening the sidewalk and street. Cars splash across puddles. I step back from the curb, shivering.

Twenty-five minutes.

You're not coming.

I'm a pain in the ass and not worth the drama. I swear, next time, I'll be a better human. I'll be the story you wanted me to be.

A sigh leaves my lips. Okay, I get it. It's over. We're over. I head back to the coffin, cowering in the pelting rain. Halfway down the block, a prickly sensation crawls up the back of my neck.

The soles of someone's shoes scrape the concrete behind me. I hear my name. Then again.

My heart catches in my throat. I break into a smile, turning around. "I knew you'd come—"

Except . . . no one's there.

I glare up and down the street. Oh, no you don't, universe. I bolt down MacDougal toward Houston, the rain blinding me. The royal blue sundress Micah liked so much sticks to me like a wet rag. Strands of hair plaster themselves to my face. My mascara stings my eyes. My careful primping for this magical movie moment, wiped.

I slam my hand on his buzzer, leaning my weight on it. I pause and listen for movement. I slap the doorbell again. I sense eyes on me. I look about. No one's out in this absurd deluge.

The little hairs on the back of my neck snap to attention. I whip my head around and see Dahlia staring at me from inside Caffé Dante across the street. I suck in my breath.

She's talking to someone. That guy Teddy; he's standing beside her now, folding his arms over his chest. They watch me from the window, smug and dry.

I glance again at Micah's door, my spread fingers freeze over the buzzer. I step back. Turning on my heel, I steal one last look over my shoulder.

I swear Teddy's lips form the word *bitch* just before Dahlia's curl into a smile.

Chapter 68

DAHLIA

Elmsford, New York

Nine Months Earlier

"Teddy, look at all these people waiting in line."

"He get us VIP passes or something? Not freezing my balls off out here."

Cody pops out of the front door just as we drive up.

I unlock his door and he pulls it open.

"Got your text, what's up?"

He slides into the passenger side and fist-bumps Teddy in the back seat. "I've just got to do this one thing before the show. It won't take long."

I huff. "Good to see you too. I see you've missed us."

"Yeah, when we gonna meet the *bitchin'* missus?" Teddy quips.

Cody looks back at the entrance as we pull away. "Soon, family. Things have been rough with Brynn's parents, like I told you, but after tonight, all will be good. I'll get in with the famous Gallardos and then I'll be able to help you guys too. No more working all these extra jobs. Dahl, take the Saw Mill."

I side-eye him. "Why do you keep looking at your phone?"

"Watching an app so we time it right. Pull a U-turn at the break in the median."

"Ahh, I'm pretty sure that's reserved for cops." I make no attempt to hide my sarcasm.

"Just do it, Dahl."

I do, but I don't like it. "Are you going to tell us what this is about, Code?"

"Hijinks and intrigue. Like old times!" Teddy stretches his arms overhead, pressing himself back into his seat.

"Where did they go?" Cody leans closer to the windshield.

"Who? Teddy, any idea what's going on?" I glance in my rearview.

"Not the slightest, babe."

Cody shifts in his seat. "There they are! Speed up. See the car ahead? Come up next to it where the highway straightens . . . get ready to gun it . . . now!"

Out of the corner of my eye, I see Cody pulling up his hoodie and covering his face. Our car edges up beside the other vehicle. Cody reaches over and jerks the steering wheel from my hands. We swerve into their lane.

The two people in the other car jump and turn their heads, mouths splayed open. I can see the whites of the man's bulging eyes behind the wheel.

I push Cody away and veer back into our lane. "Stop! What are you doing?"

He stares into his side mirror.

I look over my shoulder. "Where did they go?"

A loud wailing noise fills the car.

I flinch.

"Oh . . . holy fucking god . . . No! Fuck, fuck. Their car flipped. Holy shit!"

I grip the steering wheel harder. "What the hell was that? Do you *know* them?"

He slaps the dashboard. "Exit here, exit here!"

My eyes fill. "Stop yelling at me! I'm freaking out, Cody!"

"Brynn's parents . . ." His voice lowers. "Loop around. I need to make sure they're okay."

"This is how you 'get in' with them, by running them off the road? What's gotten into you?" I glare.

Cody clasps the back of his neck, swearing under his breath.

Teddy gapes, speechless.

A couple minutes later, I pull off to the side in the spot where we last saw their car and cut the lights. Hands trembling, I take my last cigarette out of the pack in the center console and light it.

Cody slams his body against the seat and headrest. He keeps doing it.

"Code, man, stop!" Teddy takes a hold of his shoulders. "Dahl, do something!"

I draw a sharp breath. "Cody, chill. You're going to hurt yourself . . . Here." I shove my cigarette in his face.

He stops flailing, grabs the cigarette, and takes a drag. Then another.

I sigh. "So what's going on?"

He exhales the smoke toward his window. "I'll tell you, I promise. But first I have to go check on them." He throws open the car door and jumps out.

"Hey, my cigarette!" I call out. "Great. Teddy, you got any on you?"

"What the hell was that?" He taps his open pack of Marlboros on my shoulder.

I grab a smoke, sink the tip into the blue flame of my lighter, and inhale. Leaning back, I blow a smokestack over my head. "He hasn't acted like this since he lived with those sadists."

Teddy hisses through his teeth. He rubs his hands together. "They got food there tonight?"

I check my phone. "I think so. Come on, Code, let's go already."

The trunk pops open. I hear Cody mumbling to himself and moving things around. He runs back to their car.

I shake my head.

A loud noise rattles the car.

"Whoa! What the hell was that?"

Teddy jumps. "Their car's on fire, it's on fire!"

"Where's Cody?" I scream. "Do you see him? Where the hell is he?"

"Lemme find him. Wait here and call for help." He slams the door and I lose sight of him.

I hear him shouting Cody's name. Call for help? And tell them what, we just killed two people? I slip my phone into my pocket and suck down my cigarette. Seconds tick by. My heart thumps out of my chest. I watch the burning car, mesmerized by the flames shooting into the sky. I blink a few times, squinting at what I'm seeing. Are those shadows or real people climbing out of that car? Maybe they did make it.

"Dahlia!"

My body starts working again; I swing open my door.

"I found him! The blast knocked him down. He's awake. Come help me carry him to the car."

I fly over to them.

"Ah'rite, buddy, we got ya," Teddy croons. "The ambulance coming?"

I don't answer.

We lay him across the back seat under the car's dome light, his body like a rag doll. The blood vessels in his eyes look ruptured, the skin around them is swelling.

I rub his arms and legs. "Come on, Code!"

He turns his face toward me; his eyes drift somewhere past my shoulder.

I repeat his name.

He searches for me again. His lips move without sound.

I lean in. "I'm here, Code. I'm here."

He chokes. "Brynn . . . I need to call her." He drapes a limp hand on the front of his jeans.

I slide it out. My hand shakes as I type in my birthday. The screen unlocks. I find her name in recent calls and steady the phone next to his ear.

"Where the hell are you?" Her voice comes through in a sharp whisper. "Hello? They bumped us to play after the next break. Is everything taken care of? Did your friend do it?"

I drop the phone like I've been stung.

Her ranting continues.

Venom pours from my eyes onto Cody's face. A scream threatens to escape. I bite my knuckles. His backstabbing knife twists some more inside of me.

I reach down and end the call. "Does she mean *me*?" I burst out crying.

"I would never have asked you . . . I did this for us . . . our family." His voice drops out. Trails of tears stream down his face.

"She told you to *kill* her parents?"

He swallows, wincing. "To . . . stop them."

Teddy reappears with a tire iron in his hand. He throws it in the trunk and slams it shut before climbing into the car. "Hello? Earth to Dahlia. Did you call 911?"

"No, I-I . . ."

"This is not the time to wig out." He pulls out his phone.

"Wait!"

"Cody needs our help!"

"Did her parents make it?"

He stares at me for a long beat, then shakes his head.

"I was the one driving. People will think I caused the accident."

"What are you talking about?" he cries, his eyes wild.

"They'll think I ran their car off the road."

"Didn't you?"

"Cody did! He pulled the steering wheel from me. You saw him!"

"I was on my phone. I looked up when the car jerked sideways. You guys were screaming at each other . . . thought he was giving you grief again about your driving."

"Shit! What am I going to do? I didn't cause this and now her parents are—oh my god—the cigarette. I passed Cody my cigarette to calm him down. He left the car with it hanging out of his mouth. When he opened the trunk he was talking. Remember? What if he ditched it near their car and caused the explosion? Her parents died because of me!"

"Shhh . . . breathe, Dahl. We'll figure something out. Hey buddy, you still with us? Come on, Cody, talk. Say something."

I pull the front of Teddy's jacket toward me. "You have blood on you."

He looks down at his hands then Cody. "The side of his head . . . it was wet."

I gag, squeezing my lips between my thumb and forefinger. "His b-blood." Tears cloud my vision. I go for Teddy's phone again.

He shoves my hand away, wiping underneath his nose. He turns his back and dials. "Silas, it's me. Hold up, hold up. We got a problem."

Epilogue

DAHLIA

New York City

December, Present Day

"Thanks, everyone, for coming out tonight. I'd like to dedicate this last song to a special couple who I never got the chance to meet." My throat goes tight. "Basilio and Katia Baez Gallardo opened the Flaming Flamingo more than two decades ago. It became the city's heart and soul for new music. It later turned into a coffee shop, then a clothing store, and tonight it returns to its roots. A place to hear emerging artists, thanks to the generosity of country music superstar Beck Kershaw."

I wait out the cheers and stray whistles bouncing off the club's black-painted walls, still pinching myself over the fact that I'm on this iconic stage. Fan graffiti, album covers, and random poetry decorate every nook and crevice in this tiny magical place. Before the crowd arrived, I swear I could hear the haunting riffs of the musical legends who've played here before me humming through its walls.

"The Gallardos helped a long list of young artists follow their dreams on this very stage. I never once imagined I'd be invited to join them." My voice falters.

Teddy sits at the bar, which is so covered in band stickers you can barely see the wood. He beams his gap-toothed smile. His lips kiss the air between us, sending me his strength.

"I also dedicate tonight to my St. Ignatius family and foster kids everywhere—especially our brother Cody." I take a breath. "I hear you singing, bro, lighting up the night sky, getting your own Hollywood marquee at last."

I lift my shaking hand to the top edge of my guitar. An infectious laugh rises from the back of the intimate room. I shield my eyes, looking through the standing crowd. My heart starts to pound.

I see him. After all this time. I'd hoped but wasn't sure he'd read the flyer I slipped through the mail slot of his lavender house.

He winks at me with that mischievous smile. Turned up corners, like mine. Like a scoundrel, but sexier. He tilts his head to one side, and the light near the side door reveals the Fordham University logo across his chest.

He got in. He did it.

It takes everything I have not to go to him. I think of all those late nights at Dante's confiding in one another about our ridiculous past relationships. Him telling me how meeting Brynn, though it ended badly, turned out to be the catalyst he needed to work on himself, to get better. Gave him the confidence to reach out to his mom's family and try again with his dad—to write the future he's always wanted.

We bonded over our shared ache for our mothers—how a chunk of us will forever be missing. We got fired up over the stigmas associated with mental health and foster youths—how he doesn't want to be called crazy, the same way I don't want to be called white trash.

He once told me two-thirds of the homeless in this city have mental health issues and that he wanted to do something about it.

We connected. We dreamt out loud.

Until one day, he stopped coming by. I thought he would after the Elmsford Police charged Brynn with conspiracy to commit a reckless act and involuntary manslaughter of her parents and Cody. I bet she looks bad in orange.

She underestimated me and the bond foster kids share. One you *don't* want to cross. How we'll do anything for one another—sometimes blindly—like sit behind the wheel of a vehicle while your hero runs two innocent people off the road, never dreaming it would lead to their deaths.

I haven't touched a cigarette since that night.

Cody, I forgive you. Please forgive me too.

I let my gaze wander through the audience, soaking in the moment. A moment made possible when I quit silencing myself and thinking I was nothing more than a dumb foster kid born from rape or the forgotten child of an alcoholic teen mom.

What do I know? Apparently, a lot. *I'm the mastermind, of course.* I knew Brynn's ego was far bigger than her love for my brother. That she would claim finding those news articles among Cody's things to prove to the detectives that he acted alone in order to play the hero.

And if I hadn't spoken up to right that injustice, I would never have met Micah. Or his generous father. I certainly wouldn't be performing tonight on this legendary stage.

Maybe I *can* get the guy in the end. I grin at that guy now, my lips forming a slow *wow*.

His smile broadens, reaching those velvet brown eyes of his, and for one solid, marvelous moment—no one stands in our way.

I made sure of it.

"I'm Dahlia Schenkel. This last one is called 'Escaping Shadows.'"

Acknowledgments

The idea of the Shadow People came from a childhood dream where I awoke to see a shadowy figure standing next to my bed. I remember my whole body stiffening from the back of my neck down through my legs. Gripped by fear, I managed to roll over, praying it would go away. Lucky for me in the morning it did. But what if it didn't?

Though the character of Micah was created from my imagination and not based on anyone in my life, elements of his psychosis were carefully researched. I did take a great deal of creative license with his hallucinations.

I couldn't have written this novel without my wonderful readers and your beautiful reviews, posts, and thoughtful messages sharing how much you're enjoying my books. Thank you for keeping me on this incredible journey with your kind words of encouragement to just *keep writing*. I'm forever grateful.

Inspiration can be found every day and in people who don't realize the lasting impact they score on your heart. My Athletes Serving Athletes family continue to teach me the greatest lessons in resilience and courage. They make me laugh until I cry, and help me to see the world with love and gratitude. In the book, the character of Dr. Val Barnes is a love letter to my ASA family who I proudly call my friends. Check them out at ASA.run.

Having grown up on Long Island, New York City has always been a special place for me, especially the Village, where my husband and I fell in love. I wrote this book during Covid out of homesickness. Because we weren't traveling, I needed boots on the ground who could be my eyes. My longtime friend, West Village native, and LaGuardia HS alum Jennifer Vandestienne Gillow was my person. She kindly introduced me to the mother and daughter team, Allison Astor-Vargas and Jessica Vargas, who provided valuable insight on attending there today. However, my characters' experiences at the school were fictionalized to fit the story.

When I asked Jennifer if she knew anyone who lived in the MacDougal-Sullivan Gardens Historic District, she immediately recommended her friend's memoir: *Little Panic: Dispatches from an Anxious Life* by Amanda Stern. The beautifully written book provided a firsthand account of what it's like to grow up on "Rainbow Row," and it bravely shared fears and experiences similar to Micah's character. Thanks, Amanda! I hope to meet you one day.

A high-five to my niece Claire Spasojevic for answering all my questions about today's NYC ad agencies.

I'm grateful to my dear friend and former ad agency colleague Deb Printup for allowing me to borrow pieces of her own story for the character of Debra.

Special shoutouts to my nieces Jamie Alfonsi for giving me a great line that I took the liberty to alter for Dahlia's motto and Cathryn Pulaski for explaining things to me. She knows what I mean.

A big thanks to my very patient and insightful beta readers, Kristen McManus, Caitlin McCarthy, Allison Sneller, Kristen Burnham, Danielle DuPuis, Tom Hardin, and Kelly Skovron, for helping me shape the novel in its early stages.

I'm grateful for the sage advice from Lieutenant Eric Kruhm, who helped me keep things authentic. He's also a pretty great guy whose wife Michelle I adore. I hope I got it right, Eric.

Much love goes out to my Wit, Wine & Wisdom sisters who get as excited over books as I do. Thank you for your friendship and unwavering support.

I owe so much to Brooke Warner, my amazing publisher at She Writes Press, an imprint of the Stable Book Group, who has guided me along this roller coaster of a publishing journey since my very first book. She continues to inspire me and my fellow SWP sisters, to remind us that our words matter, and to share our stories.

Thank you to my project managers, Lauren Wise and Shannon Green, who manage to keep me sane and on track.

To my fabulous editor Krissa Lagos, who's taken this journey with me three times, thank you for shaping this book into something special.

Cheers to Crystal Patriarche, Hanna Lindsley, and Rylee Warner, my publicity team at BookSparks, who helped catapult this book out into the world so beautifully.

Thank you Julie Metz at She Writes Press for the lovely cover design and my talented niece Beth Pulaski for the wonderful profile picture, once again. Check her out at bethpulaskiphotography.com.

I grew up with three brothers and delivered three incredible sons. You'd think I'd have this boy thing down. But when those pieces of your heart suddenly make their way into the world, no one prepares you for them leaving the nest for good. Mac, Finn, and Fletcher, I love you guys. Stay close or I'm moving in.

Finally, many sloppy kisses go out to Mark, my biggest supporter, favorite person on the planet, and the one who holds my hand on airplanes and just because. This twisted Manhattan love story is for us.

About the Author

Heather Cumiskey is the award-winning author of the popular YA crossover titles *I Like You Like This* and *I Love You Like That*. She writes about messy characters and social issues in the hopes that her books will spark compassion and conversation. Raised in Garden City, New York, she was working in fashion in New York City when she rediscovered her first love of writing. Heather now lives outside of Baltimore, Maryland, with her family and a spunky cockapoo named Waffles. Catch up with her at www.HeatherCumiskey.com.

Author photo © Beth Pulaski Photography

Looking for your next great read?

We can help!

Visit www.shewritespress.com/next-read
or scan the QR code below for a list
of our recommended titles.